Conflict In Blue

Behind The Badge
A Novel

D0467517

Richard B. Whitaker

Conflict in Blue
Behind the Badge

PROLOGUE

It's dark. The streets appear deserted, and there is an air of mystery that shrouds the night in the City of the Angels. The intermittent patches of light thrown by storefronts and iridescent streetlights seem only to aggravate the eeriness beyond. The mask of darkness that consumes the city works dramatic changes on the human spirit. Darkness obscures and it hides. It conceals-and in concealing, it frees the mind to actions inhibited by day-light.

For the man who gravitates to crime, there is a cloak of invisibility in the shadows-an added encouragement, an assurance of anonymity, a dimension of omnipotence.

Crimes of violence occur, by overwhelming majority, during the hours of darkness. So policemen work, by the overwhelming majority, at night.

There are added pressures upon the policeman who works at night. He knows that the darkness is a one-way mirror working against him. He must concentrate his faculties to see. For those working patrol assignments, they know that in the dark, their radio car and uniform present distinctive silhouettes. For a patrol officer, he must go where he is sent. He knows that the criminal he seeks is expecting him — and can see him coming.

The policeman knows that he must concede the first move to the man he seeks. He must wait for the criminal to identify himself — by a sound, a rustle of movement, a pistol shot from behind the shield of night. The street cop knows that he must live with these realities and with the expectation of them — it's part of the job.

There is another darkness in police work more ominous than the blackness of night. It is the darkness of not knowing. The great mystery of the night. A policeman can never know what may be waiting for him on his next radio call, or in the mind of the next person he meets.

When he comes to work, he can't know what his tour of duty will hold for him. He cannot be certain whether he will work for eight hours or ten or twelve—-or longer. He cannot even be sure that he will return to his family in the same condition in which he left—or that he will return at all.

The policeman learns to work in both darknesses. He learns to see by scanty light, to know by meager glimmerings of information. He learns or fails at his job and is called to make the ultimate sacrifice.

Los Angeles Police Department
Yearly Report
1969

Although writers spend hours in seclusion, and most would admit that the craft is a solitary venture, they would also concede that many others enhance the final manuscript. To those many others, I say thank you.

First, to the men of the Los Angeles Police Department who, over forty years ago, made the experience most memorable. This includes the Wilshire Division Morning Watch of 1966-1967, who will always be remembered as some of the toughest streets cops to have worn a badge. And to the University Division Morning Watch and Special Operations Squad of 1968-1970, the Concrete Crusaders who always had my back, an eternal thanks.

Thank you to Judith Naegle, a wonderful editor, critic, and dear friend who was instrumental in the completion of this book, and above all, to my wife Cheryle and our seven children, who endured the pains and joy's of having a loved one who was dedicated to the motto: "To Protect and To Serve."

PART ONE

ONE

McLean felt restless. Never before had he seen anything like the events unfolding on the television that hot, smoggy, August evening. Turning from the old set, he glanced out the apartment window and watched as the sun set on a city choked by stagnant layers of brown pollutants. But while the city was strangled by the toxic fumes, the setting sun in the west cast brilliant hues of reddish orange across the horizon, silhouetting the Santa Monica Mountains in a majestic rainbow of colors. As serenity drifted unhindered across the western landscape, tempers in South Central Los Angeles flared.

"Darlene, come here," he called while staring at the television. "You won't believe it! They're burning down the city!"

His petite young wife entered the room and walked over to the large threadbare chair where her husband was seated. She stood transfixed as she watched the pictures roll into a panorama she never dreamed could happen in Los Angeles. Slowly, she sat on the large arm of the overstuffed chair, mesmerized by the violent scenes.

Frightened, she leaned against her young, handsome husband, placed her head next to his, and slipped her arm around his neck pulling closer to him. "What's happening, Nick?" she whispered. "I don't understand it."

"Neither do I," he answered somberly.

As the sun continued its slow retreat, many felt that nightfall would bring with it some release from the suffocating heat and increased violence.

They were wrong.

Sitting in the old chair, McLean let his lithe body sink deep into the cushions. Slowly, his hands moved back and forth on the frayed arms, stopping periodically nervously to pick at a thread spiraling out from a worn spot.

Watching the old black-and-white television that sat on an apple crate placed against the wall in the small, one bedroom apartment, he barely noticed the flickering picture laced with white lines running across the screen.

Across the small room an old window-mounted air conditioner rattled and shook violently in a futile attempt to cool the apartment while the outside evening temperature remained in triple digits. Hypnotized by the ongoing events, he never noticed the thin streaks of sweat as they trickled down his brow and into his eyes until the salt began burning and blurring his vision.

Transfixed by the shadows and silhouetted images, he watched as the city named for angelic ministrants erupted into fiery scenes straight from Dante's Inferno.

It was Wednesday evening, August 11, 1965. The Watt's riots had begun and a violent new era had exploded onto the scene. Rioting brought anarchy to South Central Los Angeles, and domestic terrorism reared its ugly head.

While violence flickered across the tiny screen, McLean's memory faded to the innocent times in which he was raised.

He fondly remembered mowing neighbor's lawns even while heat and smog stung his eyes and burned his lungs. He earned .25 cents for each job, and when paid, thought he was rich. Just enough money for more baseball cards, he thought.

When summer ended, he had the complete set of the 1952 Yankees World Series trading cards. He was elated. Life was great.

Baseball cards, late night games of Hide and Seek, and daily games of football and baseball played in the middle of the wide asphalt street: this was Nick's life in the simpler days of his youth where the boys were the participants, coaches, rule makers, and referees.

All too soon these wonderful, carefree days would end, fading into

priceless memories of times gone by when life was abundant with the
simple naive joys of boyhood.

As he continued to watch, he witnessed chaos and mob violence encircle the city like an octopus wrapping its prey tightly before delivering the final, suffocating death squeeze.

Deeply saddened by an overwhelming feeling of loss, he stared silently, hardly comprehending what he was seeing. The intensity of his emotions surprised him. Incomprehension turned to a growing anger which leaped to agitation that spiraled into a fury he had never before experienced.

Los Angeles was changing, and so was he.

Jumping from the chair, he startled Darlene, who also was lost in the events that were being described in great detail by KTLA television.

"Kill them all!" McLean muttered.

Suddenly the television went black and Darlene stood blocking the screen.

"Whaddya do that for?" he demanded.

"Getting mad and yelling at the television won't change anything, Nick," she whispered.

Stepping forward, she tried to give him a gentle hug, but he brushed her to the side.

McLean stood. Suddenly, he felt not only anger, but also hatred. A red flush erupted on his pale cheeks.

For the next one hundred and forty-four hours, the McLeans watched scenarios of terror and violence rip at the heart of the city. Until now, he never had considered that there was a difference between people based solely on skin color and he was comfortable following the philosophy that all men were created equal.

But that philosophical mindset was about to change.

TWO

August 11, 1965, ten forty-five P.M. Christian Patterson arrived at Seventy-Seventh Street station, grabbed a cup of coffee from the marred tan coffee machine, and started upstairs to his locker.

"Patterson," called out Mike Fry, one of the Morning Watch sergeants. "Hurry up and get changed, we've got problems."

"What problems?" Patterson grumbled, not wanting to be bothered.

"The Highway Patrol got themselves into some trouble over on 116th and Avalon, and it looks like it's heading our way."

"Damn Chippies," Patterson muttered. "Misdemeanor cops in a felony world."

Patterson headed for his locker where he changed and grabbed his gear. Walking into the roll call room, he dropped his black leather jacket and helmet bag against the rear wall and took his customary seat on the back row. Quietly, the room filled. For five minutes, no one spoke. The mud thick coffee hadn't kicked in.

Then the silence was broken.

"Looks like we might be in for some excitement," quipped Billy Grudt, one of the younger cops.

"Ya," Patterson said, his eyes bloodshot from too little sleep and too many boilermakers.

With that comment, the side door opened and Lieutenant Don Gillespie entered, followed by two sergeants.

"We're going to pass on the announcements and training," Gillespie said anxiously. "We've got some problems moving into the division, so we're going to make car assignments and hit the street."

"Patterson and Grudt, 12Adam65."

Patterson agilely slid his massive body from its seat, his steel gray eyes reflecting an anxiousness to do what he loved most: fight. Throwing back the last drops of coffee from the stained paper cup, his pale face was expressionless while the jagged scar that ran the length of his right cheek shown bright red.

Snatching their gear off the floor, he and Grudt headed for the rear door. Once downstairs, Grudt checked out car keys, an Ithaca .12 gauge riot shotgun, and was issued four rounds of ammunition.

"Come on Bowen?" he growled. "What happens if we need more rounds?"

"Call a supervisor," said the old station officer sarcastically.

Grudt grabbed the shells and stormed out the rear station doors, where he found Patterson standing next to their black and white. Grudt tossed Patterson his set of keys.

"Well, how was Bowen tonight?" Patterson asked.

"He's worthless," Grudt muttered angrily. "Just like tits on a boar hog."

"You've noticed," replied Patterson as he slid into the front seat and cranked over the engine.

Grudt picked up the mike.

"12Adam65, clear."

"Shit, it's hot," he grumbled as he wiped the sweat off his forehead with the closed inside fingers of his right hand. Patterson said nothing, but turned the steering wheel with his large hands shrouded in the sap gloves he wore no matter what the temperature.

"Aren't you hot in that leather jacket?" Grudt asked.

"No," lied Patterson ignoring the beads of perspiration that formed on his forehead just below a thin wisp of blond hair. After five minutes of silence, he again spoke.

"The jacket saved my life when some asshole tried to drive a shiv into my back."

"So you wear it rain or shine?"

"Rain or shine."

"How's the family," asked Grudt, wanting to get away from any conversation about the heat.

"Why?"

"Just asking."

"Shitty," Patterson answered. "The old lady found a letter from the girlfriend and a picture of our new kid. She went nuts. Grabbed the boys and left."

"Your new kid?"

"My new kid."

"She want a divorce?"

"Who knows," Patterson said agitated. "She only left yesterday."

"I'm sorry I asked," Grudt said as he stared at his massive partner.

"Why should you be sorry? It isn't your problem."

"Yeah, but I know how much the kids mean to you."

"Must not mean as much as a piece of ass ...cause that's all I'm left with."

"And the baby?"

"That's the girlfriend's problem."

Suddenly, the brief lull in radio traffic was broken.

"All Seventy-Seventh units and 12Adam65. Officers need help, shots fired, 81st and Central. 12Adam65 handle the call Code Three. Be advised that you have no backup."

Grudt snatched the mike from its small metal holder, pushed in the side button and acknowledged the call. Before he finished, Patterson had flipped on the reds, activated the siren button on the floorboard with his left foot and slammed the accelerator to the floorboard with his right. Grudt knew that it was going to be one bitch of a night.

With a throaty growl, the four-barrel carburetor sucked in air and the black and white jumped forward. Patterson's adrenaline began to surge, while his right gloved-hand methodically slid back and forth on the top of his right leg.

As they approached the call, they saw smoke in the distance. As the car slowed, rocks and bottles began to career off the hood, and then a Molotov cocktail flew past and exploded on the asphalt.

"Patterson!" Grudt screamed as he threw his hands forward, sinking his fingers deep into the cracked plastic dash. "Look out!"

Patterson shot a look to his right. Standing in the street was a man with a gun in his hand. Patterson snapped the steering wheel. The man tried to jump out of the way, but was too slow. The right fender struck him in his midsection and sent him flying backwards like a rag doll. Both men watched as the gunman flew into the curb where his head exploded like a watermelon that was dropped from a ten story building.

"Is he dead?" Grudt asked in a strained voice.

"What do you think?" Patterson asked, exasperated at what he thought to be a dumb-ass question.

"Shit, when I saw him on my side of the car with that gun, I thought I was dead."

"You're not."

A block away sat a black and white parked against the far curb. Patterson locked the brakes. The Plymouth shuddered and slid to a stop just behind the bullet-riddled car. Patterson saw four legs protruding from under the car.

"Get that shotgun out the window," he screamed to Grudt, "and shoot anything that moves. I'll get those two cops."

Grudt thrust the Ithaca out the passenger window, snapped back the receiver and slammed a round into the chamber. Peering above the door jam, he saw a man run across the street with a rifle in his hands. Suddenly, the man stopped in the middle of the street and aimed the barrel at Grudt.

The soft flesh of the young cop's right index finger gently squeezed the trigger. As the shotgun jumped, smoke bellowed from the barrel. The echo inside the car was deafening and the pain in his ears excruciating. He squinted through the smoke and tried to find his target. Glancing to the left, he saw a prone figure on the ground. The blast had struck the man in the chest, shredding his clothing. Scattered in the street were small, jagged pieces of what was once the wooden stock of a high-powered hunting rifle.

Grudt glanced out the windshield and saw Patterson leaning against the rear door of the bullet-riddled police car.

"We're out of ammo," screamed one officer as he slid from beneath the car. Patterson reached into his jacket pocket and pulled out four shotgun shells.

"Give me your shotgun," he yelled to the second cop, who was still prone on the ground. In seconds, the weapon was loaded.

"I'll cover you while you get back to our car."

Patterson slid his large frame to the back quarter panel, eased the shotgun over the trunk lid and fired in the direction of an old building located directly across the street. As nine .32 caliber pellets belched into the night, two cops streaked across the open space.

Patterson slammed another round into the shotgun and fired. Running, he fired two more rounds as he dove behind his car.

"*Keep shooting!*" he screamed to Grudt as he threw open the back door and shoved the two shaken cops into the rear seat.

"Keep your heads down," Patterson yelled.

There was no argument.

As Patterson slid into the driver's seat, Grudt fired his last round. Slipping the empty shotgun into the rack, he unsnapped his service revolver and stuck it out the window. He snapped off six rapid-fire shots and then slid deep into the seat. Sniper fire ripped at the trunk and hood, yet the front and rear windshields went unscathed.

Patterson grabbed the gearshift in his massive right hand, slammed the selector into Reverse and punched the gas pedal. The once idling car lunged backward midst billows of smoke from burning rear tires, and fishtailed erratically as he kept his foot on the gas. Then he snapped the steering wheel, spun the black and white around, and before the smoke cleared, again slammed the pedal to the floorboard sending the bullet-riddled police car into the night like a copper-jacketed bullet from a Colt Python.

"You happy now?" he yelled to Grudt, his voice far calmer than it should have been.

"If he isn't, we are," screamed one of the officers from the back seat.

Grudt looked closely at his partner with the long, ugly scar running the length of his right cheek.

"You're one cold son-of-a-bitch," Grudt yelled, smiling, "but I'm not complaining."

"Neither are we," yelled the other officer from the back seat, trying to be heard above the growl of the engine and the hot August air swirling throughout the car.

"Where are you guys from?" screamed Grudt turning sideways in the seat.

"University Division," the two cops shouted in unison as they brushed glass fragments from their uniforms.

Grudt put 12Adam65 out to University station.

"Thanks," the older of the two officers said as Patterson pulled into the parking lot.

"All part of twenty," Grudt answered.

Patterson remained silent. He'd said enough.

Getting out of the car, he followed the two cops into the station, walked up to the small Property room window and slammed his palm down on the counter.

Then he waited.

When no one responded, he walked through the Watch Commander's office, behind the front desk, and into the small room. As he reached for a box of shotgun shells, a frazzled desk officer appeared.

"Who the hell are you?" he grumbled.

Patterson ignored the question and began to stuff shotgun shells into his pockets.

"You can't have those!"

His words were choked off mid-sentence as Patterson spun around, grabbed him by his shirt collar, snapped it tight around his throat, and pulled the confused man closer.

"Look, *friend*," Patterson said softly, his eyes penetrating the man's gaze,"in case you haven't heard, the natives are restless."

A bitter edge laced his words.

With each word, Patterson's face reddened, his neck distended, and he tightened his grip. As the shirt knotted more snuggly around his neck, it forced the old officer's Adam's apple to shoot forward like a pimple on the face of a teenager. Terror flashed behind his eyes as they widened. As he choked, his body trembled and he danced on toes that barely reached the floor. His face turned purple and spittle ran from between his lips and onto his gravy stained tie. He tried to speak, but Patterson's grip was too tight. All he was able to accomplish was a slight nod of the head.

"I thought you'd understand."

Slowly, Patterson loosened his grip and let the man's feet firmly touch the floor. Frozen with fear, the old cop tried to catch his breath and regain his composure.

Patterson turned and filled his coat pockets with shells. When his pockets were full, he shot the terrified station officer a quick smile and walked calmly out the door.

"Here," he said to Grudt, as he handed him the shells, "reload and put some in your pockets."

Patterson cranked the Plymouth over. Once comfortable, his right hand threw the low-slung black Alfonso holster across his right leg and then his hand began to slowly rub the right thigh while the gloved left hand squeezed the steering wheel in a vise-like grip. He was ready to return to combat.

"Don't break the damned wheel, partner."

Patterson was silent, but he did loosen his grip.

Grudt turned up the volume on the radio and both listened as the hot calls bombarded the airwaves like an Allied bombing run over Berlin.

"All Seventy-Seventh units in the vicinity and 12Adam65,

snipers shooting at firemen, 61st and Slauson. 12Adam65, handle the call Code Three ..."

"This is crazy," Grudt commented to no one in particular.

Patterson's gloved fingers began to gently stroke the top of the wooden grips of his Colt, stopping briefly at the four notches cut deep into the dark wood. His index finger moved slowly to the trigger while his thumb slid to the hammer. Deliberately, he pushed the holster deeper between his legs nearer his manhood. To him, both had similar purposes. One weapon spewed forth life, the other death, and each were used with the same reckless abandon.

His large, unpolished black shoe found the gas pedal. Tires spun and smoke billowed into the stagnant air. The black and white flew into the night towards the freeway the cops called the "Coal Chute."

After fishtailing up the on-ramp, the car hit the incline on all eight cylinders. Grudt, thrown violently against the side-panel, reached out, grabbed the dashboard with both hands and braced himself. Struggling, he shot a quick look at his partner and watched in silent awe as Patterson snapped the wheel back and forth, eventually bringing the wildly careening car under control.

"That's a distance!" Grudt shouted.

There was no response.

A state of anarchy gripped the city. Civil servants were both victims and combatants. Citizens became criminals. Seventy-Seventh Division was now a war zone.

Snipers standing on the overpasses of the Harbor Freeway turned it into a shooting gallery. Nothing was safe; not a fire truck, not a police car, and not an ambulance. The role of the rescuer had changed. They were now the ones needing to be rescued.

The chain link fence on the Harbor Freeway blurred as the Plymouth screamed past. The muscles in Patterson's face were taut, and his lips were pursed. He was home, and he was happy. He again had found something to be angry about.

"I love this shit," he mumbled as the warm air blew unabated through the open driver's window, sending his wispy yellow hair pirouetting around his head.

Accelerating down the Slauson off-ramp, the black and white blew past the stop sign at the bottom of the hill and slid sideways onto the street. In the distance, he saw two fire trucks. As his eyes narrowed and he stared into the darkness, his hands tightened on the steering wheel. Drawing closer to the scene, the sound of sniper shots increased. Locking the brakes, he slid into the foray and stopped just shy of destroying the front-end of a Hook-and-Ladder.

Firemen, while dodging bullets, still tried to put out a massive blaze that was burning out of control through a White Front department store.

When 12Adam65 arrived, it became the focus of attention. Staying low, Patterson and Grudt slid out of the car and hurried over to the fire trucks. Crouched over, Patterson shuffled up to the Fire Captain.

"Why the hell don't you blast those assholes off the roofs?" he shouted. "Eliminate them, and then worry about the fire!"

"Hadn't thought of that," the captain yelled, trying to be heard above the cracking of rifle shots and the roaring flames. Grabbing a red megaphone, he shouted, "Turn the hoses on the roof-tops." As the final word was uttered, a grin crossed his face. "Never seen this before," he said. "I guess the rules of engagement have changed."

"No shit," Patterson responded sarcastically.

Deliberate sweeps of water immediately crisscrossed the buildings. Screams became interlaced with gunfire as bodies flew into the night, swallowed up by the darkness.

In minutes, the sniping stopped.

Next came the looters.

Stepping out from behind the truck, Patterson and Grudt opened fire. The Ithaca in Patterson's hands was deadly. His first round caught one man in the midsection as he scurried out the front of the store. The impact picked the man up and threw him back into the burning debris, his screams piercing the night. As he disappeared, a second figure ran from the building. Both Patterson and Grudt opened fire. Each scored hits.

Looters with television sets, food, booze, guns and anything else they could dump into shopping carts tried to escape, however, it was too late. They had angered their saviors. Panic gripped the doomed.

Repeatedly, they tried to escape, only to be thwarted by high-pressure blasts from fire hoses and precisely aimed bullets. Soon, the fire that had shot up the rear wall engulfed the ceiling. Suddenly, an explosion ripped through the store that sent large sections of the burning roof onto those who were trapped in the rear. The screams of the trapped intensified.

The faces of those outside were expressionless. Then the remaining section of roof collapsed, and the blood-curdling screams were silenced. Each man stood silently and watched. Water hoses were cranked off and guns holstered. Only the diminished crackling of the fire could be heard. Dazed, the Fire Captain walked over to Patterson and Grudt.

"Needless to say, this incident never happened."

"What incident?" Patterson answered coldly.

After the riots, Patterson was transferred to University Division, and Grudt went to Newton Street.

THREE

McLean drove his old Volkswagen off the Ventura Freeway and serpentined through Elysian Park. After passing Dodger Stadium, he guided the car under the overgrown ivy-covered arches that led into the Los Angeles Police Academy. Downshifting into first, the VW coughed as it struggled up the slight incline. Dodging the potholes, he carefully drove up the narrow road toward the parking area.

Looking to his left and then his right, he marveled at the giant eucalyptus and majestic pines that surrounded the grounds and made the facility nearly impossible to see from the main road. This dense foliage provided not only a degree of privacy, but also a sense of mystery.

At the top of the road, he saw a poster board sign that read: "Recruit Parking." Pulling into an empty space, he parked and walked to the basketball courts where he was met by others who had been accepted into the Los Angeles Police Academy class of October 25, 1965.

As the recruits milled around, three Academy instructors entered the area. Each wore a pair of blue gym shorts, a yellow LAPD t-shirt and faces that were frozen in stone.

"Form up! Two platoons, ten squads," barked one.

Walking through the rows, the instructors conducted their first inspection and did all they could to tear down and humiliate. Some broke. McLean just became angry.

As time passed, a slow hatred began to build in him toward the instructors. It was an important hatred. In the end, it was that banked rage directed toward a visible enemy that would see him through the more trying times as a recruit.

Daily, he endured the subtle and not-so-subtle pressures, always keeping in mind the advice of an old family friend, a homicide detective, who told him: "Nick, you're brighter than ninety-percent of those guys on the job. You stand out because of your intensity and drive. They'll resent you like hell, but a few'll learn to respect you. I've got a word of advice for ya, though kid. While you're in the Academy, keep your mouth shut and your ears and eyes open.

"Don't be first and don't be last. Stay in the middle.

"On the job, you'll have many acquaintances, but very few trusted partners. You'll figure out who they are. Don't just trust a guy because he wears a badge and carries a gun. Prove him first. Then make your decision."

McLean never forgot that sage advice.

The grueling weeks passed slowly, and he kept to himself. He watched the instructors, observing, as one entered the rear door of the upper classroom after lunch and in a loud voice called out the name of a recruit, ordering him to bring his hat and books. When that man left, he was never seen again, and another seat in the upper classroom was left vacant.

FOUR

Sunday, October 31, 1965, Halloween. A cold stiff wind forced the chill factor down to forty degrees. Small tree trunks bowed their tips as the branches of the older trees swayed back and forth like musical directors conducting a symphony. Dimly lit street lights connected by old wiring snapped with each new gust.

Occasionally, a spark from an exposed wire would crackle, sparks would fly and the darkened night sky would light up. While wires snapped, gusts of wind blew down the streets and through the alleys sending bleak clouds of dirt, dust and paper swirling.

As midnight approached, even the most hearty of trick-or-treaters finally gave up and headed home. The cold, combined with the day of week, meant that it would be an unusually quiet night. For few would leave their homes; leaving the streets of Wilshire Division deserted.

When Morning Watch roll call hit the streets, unit 7Adam1, manned by Simpson and Moody, was the first black and white to pull from the parking lot and onto a quiet Pico Boulevard. Simpson, as senior officer, was behind the wheel. With four years on the Department, he was marking his time in patrol and was eager to take the next Sergeant's written, because Simpson was a climber.

In the police academy, he excelled academically, graduating number one in his class. Physically, though, it was a different story, for daily he fought with another man not to finish dead last.

Following graduation, he was assigned to direct traffic in

downtown Los Angeles. After six months in traffic control, he was transferred to Wilshire Division. His first assignment was on Day Watch where he immediately alienated the older cops. With only nine months wearing a badge, he purported to know more than those who had thirty years on the job. Whether right or wrong, he always had an opinion. As time passed, more and more of the old-timers refused to work with him, and he soon found himself assigned a one man unit whose primary responsibility was to take crime reports. He did this for about six weeks then requested a transfer to Morning Watch. His request was granted and within a week, he found himself working from eleven-fifteen P.M. to eight A.M. and partnered with a young cop named Moody.

Mike Moody was a jock. He was of average intelligence, friendly and easy to get along with. He knew his limitations and realized that Simpson was smarter than he was, so Moody had little problem keeping his mouth shut even when Simpson made a dumb decision that was based on emotion, not common sense. This crack in the granite would prove to have dire consequences.

Moody liked the "professor" as he called him, and was just thrilled to be permanently assigned as the second man on a car. But unlike Simpson, he loved physical contact.

Moody wrestled in high school, played football and competed in the Golden Gloves boxing competition before he married Janet, his high school sweetheart. Nine months later his first son, "Little" Mike was born. Moody was elated with his new little namesake. Now he would have someone to hunt and fish with, someone with whom he could share his police stories, because Janet refused to listen to anything that was in any way related to police work.

Where Mike loved his job, Janet Moody hated it. She had not wanted him to become a policeman and every time he tried to share with her what was happening, she would immediately change the subject. In time, any reference to the job ceased.

As 7Adam1 drove slowly into the night, Simpson glanced

over at his partner and thought that he was unusually quiet. Slowly the black and white cruised through the intersection of Wilshire and Crenshaw.

Moody finished making the last of his preliminary notations in the log, then switched off the small light attached to the steel Hot Sheet clipboard mounted to the dash. He then took a deep breath and exhaled slowly in an effort to relax.

As the street lights reflected off the glass windows of the closed businesses, Moody appeared to be in another world. Staring out into the night, he took another deep breath and then exhaled slowly.

"Problems at home?" asked Simpson.

"Ya, but nothing I can't handle. The old lady wants me to quit and go to work at Lockheed where it's safe."

"Thinking about it?"

"Nope. I'm happy here."

Like a ghost, the black and white cut through the night, while each man continued lost in his own thoughts.

One wondering if the problems at home would affect his work as a cop, while the other wondered if he really had what it took to confront a real bad guy one on one and come out of the experience the victor.

While each stared out the windows, their thoughts struggling in different worlds, the radio crackled calls from adjoining divisions.

"Newton's busy tonight," said Simpson.

"So is University," Moody added. "And here we are idling down back streets with the windows down, freezing our butts off and not seeing a soul. We need to make something happen. It's too quiet."

Suddenly the silence was broken.

"All units in the vicinity and 7Adam1. Four-five-nine silent at Rene's Liquor, 3765 Olympic Boulevard. 7Adam1, handle the call Code Two."

Moody acknowledged the call.

"Well partner, it looks like you just got your wish."

"Come on, Simpson, nine out of ten of these burglary calls are a waste of time, shorts in the system or the wind."

Simpson smiled as he pushed the gas pedal down. Making a quick right on Olympic, the black and white raced down the street.

"Clear right," yelled Moody. With that assurance, Simpson glanced quickly to his left and pushed the accelerator to the floorboard. This they did one red light after another until they came to within three blocks of the call.

Simpson cut the headlights. Idling softly, the huge engine backed down as though it knew exactly what was happening. Quietly the Plymouth approached the front of the business.

"You cover the front, I'll take the back," directed Simpson.

Moody eased himself out of the car and positioned himself in the shadows at the corner of the building where he could not only see the front of the liquor store, but also had a diagonal view of the back alley. Standing in the darkness with his .38 held close behind his right leg, he strained to hear anything that would indicate that maybe this call was the one that would yield a suspect.

As Moody stood in the front, Simpson drove around back and cut the engine, sending the Plymouth silently down a small rear alley located just behind the liquor store.

Rolling to within thirty feet of the rear door, he reached down and pushed the small button under the dash that cut the brake lights. Then he slowly pressed down on the brake pedal applying even pressure, which quietly stopped the police car and left it in darkness. Slowly, he opened the driver's door and unholstered his gun.

Glancing back into the front seat he saw that the shotgun was still locked securely in the rack. Hesitating, he thought about taking it with him, but before he could reach for it, he heard a crash come from inside the liquor store and saw a shadow dance across the sliver of light made by what appeared to be an open rear door. Instantly, he forgot about the shotgun and knelt quietly behind the opened police car door, waiting. Examining his position, he saw that the end of the alley was walled up; leaving only one way in and one way out, and he controlled that.

Moody also heard the crashing of glass from inside the store. Cautiously he peered through the front plate glass window. The interior was dark.

Nothing moved.

He pulled himself back into the darkness and decided to wait a little longer to see what Simpson came up with.

In the alley, Simpson was still crouched behind the car door listening.

He stepped out into the dark, cold alley. All that moved was the wind, and all that loitered were the fleeting, ghost-like shadows. Quickly, he moved to the brick wall that made up the back of the old building. Again, he stopped and looked around to identify what obstacles lay between him and the rear door. He eyed a few wooden crates and cardboard boxes; there was nothing to conceal his approach. Fortunately, the single bulb light that was dancing in the breeze above the door was dim.

He took a deep breath, stepped over the first box and then froze. His eyes were riveted on the back door. The sliver of light he had originally seen was still cutting its way into the darkened alley.

Another step followed by another. Slowly and deliberately, he inched his way toward the door. He held his .38 in his right hand with his elbow pressed snuggly against his right hip. Easing up to the left side of the old weathered back door, he realized that it wouldn't have taken much to slip the lock and force the door open. A small pocket knife would have done the trick. Moving closer, he watched as the dim light dangling above the door illuminated pry marks on the door jamb.

"Gotcha," he whispered.

In the front, Moody continued to stand vigilantly in the shadows waiting for some indication from his partner. As time passed, he began to worry.

While it had been only minutes since they had received the radio call, it felt like hours. As Simpson stood next to the side of the door, he heard more movement from inside. Pushing his back against the wall, he watched as the sliver of light slowly increased until the door was open wide enough for a darkly clad figure to slip out of the store and step into the alley.

The figure shot a furtive glance first to his left, away from Simpson and toward the bricked up wall at the end of the alley. Turning, he took a step to his right, then froze when he saw the darkened silhouette of the black and white with its identifiable two circular lights and siren on the roof. The man never saw Simpson, who still stood hugging the wall. Before the burglar could bolt out of the alley, Simpson knew he must act. As the man stepped further away from the door, Simpson stepped out.

"Freeze, asshole!" he shouted.

The man stopped. He made no movement to run or fight, he just stood silently in the dim light.

"Put your hands on the wall, lean backwards and spread your legs."

The man hesitated, and then the rubber soles of his tennis shoes began to inch their way backwards.

Simpson did everything he could to keep his voice from cracking or showing the fear that began to cause his throat to tighten and heart beat faster. He struggled for breath, coughed up bile, but managed to force the stinging liquid back down. With his .38 still trained on the suspect, he yelled, "Partner, I've got one in custody."

Simpson holstered his revolver, and without waiting for Moody, began a felony wall search. With the suspect's body leaning against the building, he wrapped his right leg around the suspect's extended right leg. He then grabbed the suspect by the collar with his left hand, reached up to the man's right hand and began to slide his hand down the suspects extended right arm.

When he reached the elbow, the suspect bolted to the right, slamming Simpson backwards. In less than a second both men were rolling on the ground, locked in a vicious struggle. Repeatedly, the man grabbed for Simpson's holstered weapon.

Simpson was in trouble.

Instinctively, his right hand snapped down to the holster.

"*Moody, I need help!*" he screamed.

Both the physical reaction and vocal plea came too late, something Simpson realized when he felt his gun jerked from the holster.

Jumping to his feet, the suspect fumbled with the revolver. Simpson, lying on his back, kicked upward, catching the suspect in the thigh. The kick caused the man to loosen his grip on the weapon.

Moody, hearing the shouting, grabbed a metal newspaper stand and threw it through the front glass door. As the glass shards fell, he bolted through the opening and ran directly to the rear door that now stood open. Running into the alley, he saw the suspect standing over his partner, taking aim.

"*Freeze, asshole!*" Moody screamed as he charged forward.

The man spun and fired.

Moody's arms flew over his head, his revolver tumbling into the darkness. Clutching his chest he staggered back, and looked down at the blood as it began to seep from two small holes. Then, without a word, he twisted slightly, looked for his partner, and then fell onto his back.

Two blocks from the liquor store, Officer Brad Wallace drove slowly down Olympic Boulevard. He said little to Leon Abrams who occupied the passenger seat.

Wallace was a large man who had played college football at Oregon State before joining LAPD. His eyes were a bright blue and looked like razor slits cut into a piece of cloth. But they didn't miss much and were set in a weathered face that had known life on the beach. His face bore a strong, aristocratic look; his mouth was hard with thin lips. He had a chiseled jaw and his head sat squarely on an over muscular neck. His reputation went with his size. He didn't take shit from anyone.

"You think that Simpson and Moody found anything?" asked Abrams.

"Who knows? Make a log entry showing us backing them up."

As Moody charged, Simpson stumbled to his feet and staggered to the black and white. Lunging through the open driver's door, he proned himself on the front seat and snatched the mike from its holder. "7Adam1, officers need help, rear of 3765 Olympic. Shots fired!"

As Simpson squirmed back out the open door, he heard two more shots.

He ducked behind the door and hid.

As the third beep ended, Wallace slammed his foot to the floorboard. Abrams was immediately pinned against the front seat.

In mere moments, Wallace turned the corner and slid into the rear alley, his bright headlights illuminating the black and white with its driver's door still open. It was then he saw Simpson hiding behind the door and saw a figure in dark clothing standing over the body of a cop, a gun in his hand.

The cold attacked Wallace's face as he bolted from the car. The figure straightened. Looking into the bright headlights, he saw the silhouetted form of a giant standing silent with his left hand at his side and his right hand extended holding a weapon. A second man stood next to the passenger door.

Wallace stood silent as he watched his own breath plume whitely from his lips while his eyes drew down and stared at the killer. The man held the gun extended, the barrel pointed toward the ground.

Wallace cocked his revolver.

The man took a step.

"Drop the gun!"

The figure hesitated. His eyes squinted as he stared into the high beams of the police car. Abrams slid his revolver from its holster and remained behind his door, breathing heavily.

Wallace's eyes narrowed and his stare intensified. His mouth tightened and he looked through the killer and gave no indication that he even saw him.

The killer threw back his shoulders, tightened his grip and straightened to his full height.

He stood frozen, knowing that his only path of escape was through the silhouetted giant.

The barrel of Simpson's gun began a slow ascent.

The killer hesitated.

"*USE IT!*" Wallace shouted in a tumultuous cry of fury.

The wind had stopped, and the radio traffic had suddenly died. The only sounds that entered the alley came from two combatants. The shadows of death now permeated the narrow alley, and had any non-participants been watching, they would have sworn that they were watching an old West gunfight. The killer stepped back until his back struck the rear wall.

Suddenly, he snapped the gun forward. As he did so, Wallace fired. The .38 bucked in his hand as he watched a bright orange flame shot through with crimson streaks explode into the darkness. The thunderous explosion bore witness that his ammunition was far more powerful than that carried by Simpson.

The eyes of a killer stared forward as the muscles in his body knotted. Then his back began a slow descent to the ground, leaving a massive trail of blood on the weathered bricks. As his legs slid forward, he stopped in a sitting position, his eyes still wide open, staring blankly at Wallace.

The killer never heard the sound of the shot that caught him in the middle of the face.

Wearing an expression chiseled in stone, Wallace waited, and then he lowered his gun and rushed to Moody's side.

He saw that the young cop had taken four shots to the chest. His blue wool uniform shirt was saturated with blood and a small trickle of crimson seeped from between his lips. Wallace listened and heard the familiar death gurgle men make as their lungs fill with blood and life drains from their body. As the blood dribbled down the side of his face, Moody's breathing became more labored.

"Did I get him?" he asked in a raspy whisper.

"Ya kid, you got him."

With those words, Moody curled his lips in a labored smile, exhaled slowly and his body went limp. Wallace had seen many men die, but each time a cop went end-of-watch, it became more difficult. He was not one for emotion, but as he held Moody's head in his lap, small warm tears slowly formed in the corners of his eyes. Then, in a blink, they disappeared.

Reverently, he put Moody's head down on the concrete, removed his own black leather jacket and covered the dead hero's upper torso. When he turned, Simpson was standing at his side, his holster empty.

Wallace's look spoke a thousand words.

Simpson remained silent, his hands trembling and his face an ashen white.

Wallace stood and walked to Simpson's police car. Reaching into the front, he grabbed the mike.

His voice was calm, his words clear and almost emotionless. "7Adam42, show us at the rear of 3675 West Olympic. We have an officer down, victim of multiple gunshot wounds. We also have one deceased suspect. We need an ambulance, a supervisor, the shooting team from Robbery Homicide and the Coroner."

As Wallace broadcast his message, he could hear Abrams retching violently against a far wall.

FIVE

*It was December and McLean's class had thinned from ninety-*eight to seventy-two. Over the Christmas Holidays, the class would be assigned either to direct traffic, or man one of the many divisional jail units. McLean learned of his fate when his name was placed on a bulletin board. He was assigned to direct traffic in the San Fernando Valley.

The day before leaving for his two week assignment, he withstood another of the many inspections that had become routine. Stoically, he stood at attention as instructors strutted in and out of the two platoons, stopping in front of each man, making a note on a small pad, then moving on to the next man in line.

"McLean," barked Officer Peoples, "Why in the hell are you wearing those little white streamers on that beautiful black tie?"

McLean's eyes shot down to his chest. There they were. Two thin pieces of white lint.

"Sir!" shouted McLean. "I'll remove the streamers as soon as the inspection is over, sir!"

"That's not soon enough, Recruit Officer McLean!" screeched Peoples at the top of his lungs as he stood toe-to-toe with the unnerved recruit. "I want it done now!"

Behind McLean's eyes, fleeting only momentarily was the shadow of rebellion.

Peoples didn't move.

McLean glanced down, found the streamers and quickly picked them off his tie.

"Sir, the streamers are gone, sir!" shouted McLean, a touch of anger in his voice.

"Recruit Officer McLean," whispered Peoples. "Are you angry with me, boy?"

"Sir, no sir."

"I can't hear you."

"Sir, no sir!"

"That's good, Recruit Officer McLean, because if I thought that you weren't happy with me, that would hurt my feelings. And you don't want to do that, do you?"

"Sir, no sir!"

Peoples moved to the next man.

McCourt then spoke.

"Even though you have a badge and a gun, gentlemen, you're not Los Angeles Policemen. You're recruits! Is that understood?"

"Sir, yes sir!" the two platoons shouted.

"So don't get out there in those intersections and do anything that resembles police work. You're there to direct traffic. If you decide to play Wyatt Earp, you'll be fired. Do you understand?"

"Sir, yes sir!"

"All right, ladies," he shouted with a heavy overtone of sarcasm, "You're dismissed!"

❦

McLean's first day of directing traffic slowly was becoming becoming a bad memory. As the sun slid into the west, he wondered if this was really what he wanted. He was ready to call it quits.

That evening, he seethed over what he'd been relegated to: a damn traffic signal. By the next morning, all he could do was complain about what he'd done the previous day. Fortunately, a calmer mind prevailed—not his, but Darlene's.

"Be patient," she said softly. "It's only two weeks."

"But I didn't join the police department to stand like an

idiot in the middle of an intersection," he argued. "I joined this department because I wanted to be a street cop."

"You'll get your chance," she said as she put her arms around his neck and placed a gentle kiss on his forehead.

As he looked past his beautiful, petite wife, he could not see the look of anxiety that filled her eyes.

"I hope you're right," he muttered as he finished his breakfast.

After three days on Day Watch, McLean was assigned to nights to direct traffic at a mall in one of the tougher areas in the San Fernando Valley. This mall's clientele were different than in the upscale area of Sherman Oaks, where he had worked days. Unlike Sherman Oaks, in Panorama City, gangs roamed the streets hunting for unwary prey, which included young cops.

Arriving at his intersection, he was met by an old sergeant from Van Nuys Division who drove up to check him in.

"You McLean?"

"Yeah, I'm McLean."

"You know what you're supposed to do?"

"No. But I'm sure I'll figure it out."

"Good."

With that, the old sergeant threw the young recruit a look of disdain, then drove off.

So much for supervision, he thought.

For hours McLean stood in the middle of the intersection trying to ignore the catcalls and lowered cars that veered in his direction. As the night wore on, a car drove by several times and swerved in his direction. One pass came within inches of his toes. As the car swooped by, an arm reached out and a hand snatched at his tie. Gauging the car's trajectory, he jumped out of reach taking the blast of their obscenities. His face flushed and his hand slid to the flap that covered his gun. He realized it was time to take a break.

Walking from the intersection, he smiled when he saw that traffic flowed better without him in the middle of the street. Seeing he was expendable, he headed across the street to a darkened gas station. Locating the men's room, he found the door ajar. Flicking the light switch, he found it didn't work.

"Great," he muttered aloud, believing he was alone.

Pushing into the darkness, he headed for the urinals. Suddenly, he stumbled. "What the hell?" he exclaimed, shocked to find two bodies sprawled across the bathroom floor.

As McLean threw an arm against the wall to keep from falling, moonlight seeping through the cracked open door silhouetted his person.

"It's a policeman," yelled one.

"Lordy, lordy, lordy," cried the other.

"Oh, dear me!" the first whimpered as he struggled to get his pants from around his ankles to his waist.

"We were just talking, officer," the other said in a sweet, high-pitched voice as he wiggled to a standing position and stuffed what little manhood he had back into his pants.

Comically, both scrambled toward the door while shoving violently at each other.

"Me first..."

"No, me!"

McLean stood motionless. No police work, he reminded himself.

After a brief struggle at the door, the two men disappeared into the darkness. McLean walked to the open door and looked into the night. He was alone.

"And that's another assignment I don't want—vice!"

Leaving the bathroom, he felt the coldness pierce through his thin wool Melton jacket. Shivering, he walked towards the rear of the mall.

Moving deliberately down the rear sidewalk, he wove a path in and out of the crowd, while his eyes darted back and forth like an eagle in search of prey. In the midst of the crowds, he kept his hands out of his pockets, his left hand near his baton, and his right resting on the holster flap covering his gun.

As he stood in the center of a moving mass of humanity, his eyes were drawn to two men in the distance. They walked purposefully toward him. Approaching, they stopped directly in front of him, blocking his way.

"Now whada' we have here?" sneered the larger of the two.

"Looks like an asshole cop to me," said the smaller man, laughing.

McLean inched his right foot back and shifted his weight. His hand gripped the wooden baton. Grasping the wood just below the leather thong, he readied himself for the first thrust. Suddenly, he felt a presence to his left and a non-threatening hand was placed softly on his shoulder. Glancing to the side, he saw an older and much larger man.

"Need some help, officer?" asked the tall stranger, never taking his eyes from the two men.

"Sure could use some backup, sir."

"You've got it, son. I'm Sergeant Ken Robinson, Hollywood Detectives," the stranger said as he threw open his coat exposing a badge and revolver. Robinson stepped forward and stood nose-to-nose with the larger man. His arms hung at his sides and his large hands formed fists. He was prepared to kick some ass.

"Why don't we all step out into the parking lot and we'll see how bad you two really are?" Robinson said, his voice quiet and controlled.

"You game, officer?" asked Robinson.

"Nothin' I'd like better, Sarge."

McLean and Robinson waited. Then, it was over before it began. The larger of the two men grabbed his buddy, pulled him to the side and pushed him into the crowd.

"You assholes'll get yours," the smaller man yelled.

McLean watched closely as they disappeared into the crowd. Confident that the threat was gone, he turned to thank Robinson, but he had vanished.

SIX

Four darkly clad figures walked single file into the darkness while their warm breath wafted slowly upward into the cold night air forming a thin vaporous cloud. Then, just as the warm breath froze still, a sudden brisk wisp of wind would appear from nowhere and blow it away. Soon the four men were at the corner of Santa Barbara and Brighton where they could see the liquor store and watch the traffic both up and down Santa Barbara Avenue.

The iron gates of the store were still wide open and the lights from inside shown brightly. Stepping around the corner, they remained concealed and away from the dim glow of the old street lights.

Intent on the business at hand, no one saw the old wino who was huddled deep in the shadows just two blocks away. Seeing the four men, he knew what was going to happen. Wrapping his dirty wool coat tightly around his body, he stood in the doorway and stared. Then he swayed, feigned he was going to pass out, slid back into the darkness, and continued to watch.

Bubba Washington, Willie Gunn, Terrance Potts and Eddie Woods snapped their heads in unison when they heard the movement behind them.

"It's a drunk," Washington whispered. "He ain't no problem."

Each man then refocused on the liquor store.

Gunn pulled the World War II M-1 carbine out from under his trench coat, quietly slid back the dull drab gray slide, then shoved a greenish colored thirty caliber round into the chamber.

He stroked the rifle softly, and then place it back under his coat next to his right leg.

Up the street, the wino waited and watched. When he felt it was safe, he hurried across Santa Barbara Avenue and began to walk in the direction of the University police station hoping to see just one black and white.

Potts and Woods slid their small revolvers out from under their jackets. Throwing open the cylinders, they nervously checked them. Satisfied, they placed them back under their coats.

The four men walked to the side of the large, front plate glass window and stopped. Washington cautiously peered around the corner into the brightly lit store. It was empty except for the owner, Yung Lee, who was behind the counter restocking the shelves. Crouched slightly, Washington darted past the front of the store and moved around the side of the building and into the dark rear alley. Hugging the wall, he came to the rear door. He grabbed the handle and twisted it slowly. The door opened. A sinister smile crossed his lips. Quietly, he slipped back to the corner and looked up and down the side street. Like Santa Barbara, Brighton Avenue was deserted.

In seconds, he was reunited with his three companions.

"We'll leave through the back," Washington told the group.

Unfortunately, Willie Gunn failed to hear this additional piece of information.

Reaching deep into their coat pockets, the four retrieved their ski masks and slid them over their heads. Then, with guns in hand, they entered the store with Washington leading and Gunn at the rear.

With many of the patrol units parked at the station awaiting change of watch, 3Tom65, a University traffic unit decided to travel up Santa Barbara to see if they couldn't get one last moving violation before asking for their forty-five minute dinner break.

Slowly, they drove through the night, drawing closer and closer to a lone figure, who had stepped off the sidewalk and was now walking in the middle of the street. Having identified them as police, the man began to frantically wave his arms.

"Is that a drunk in the middle of the street?" asked Dement, who was driving.

"Maybe," responded Tyree. "Let's see what he wants, and then we'll request Code Seven."

Dement brought the black and white to a stop next to the man who had moved out of the street and onto the sidewalk.

"What can we do for you, old timer?" Tyree asked through a small portion of the window that he'd rolled only half way down.

"Officers," shouted the man nervously into the window. "Four men with guns be robbin' the liquor store down on the corner, and one has hisself a rifle."

"Are you sure about that?" asked Dement skeptically as he leaned across from the driver's seat.

"I is sure," said the old man, shaking from the cold. "I is real sure."

Tyree grabbed the mike and requested backup. The radio crackled with the reply. As he placed the mike into its holder, the night was shattered by three beeps. The Cavalry was on its way.

The small bell above the door of B&O Liquors tinkled as the late night customers pushed their way in through the glass door.

Yung turned with his customary smile.

It was too late when he realized that his customers wore ski masks. Frightened, he wanted to reach the silent alarm beneath the counter, but before he could move, a huge man stepped in front of him and pointed a large revolver at his forehead.

Quickly, the small Chinaman looked around.

One masked man shuffled to the back door and one stayed at the front, while the fourth stepped behind the counter and pulled out an old rifle.

Gunn stepped forward and lifted the barrel of the carbine closer to the frightened man. Yung could see the weapon shake.

"How may I help you, s-s-sir?"

"You alone?" Washington snarled from across the counter.

Bowing politely, Yung said, "Yes, I work alone tonight."

"We want two bottles of Ripple," Gunn said, his head on a swivel while his eyes darted back and forth and the carbine continued to jump in his hands.

Yung reached behind him, grabbed two wine bottles off the shelf, placed them in a brown paper bag and handed them to Gunn.

"Open the cash register," Washington ordered.

The minute the old cash register drawer chimed and opened, Gunn pushed the carbine closer to Yung's head.

"Put the money in another bag and don't forget the big bills under the drawer," Washington said.

Yung began to bob up and down in acquiescence. With trembling hands, he snatched up the bills lying in the top of the drawer. Gunn placed the barrel flush to the side of Yung's head and pushed. With hands that now shook almost uncontrollably, Yung lifted the money drawer and grabbed up all the larger bills. He stuffed them into the bag and handed it to Washington.

Suddenly, Potts began to yell.

"Bubba! It do be the po-lice!"

Washington glanced at the front window and saw the reflections of the high-beam headlights. In mere moments, Washington knew that they would be surrounded. Time was critical.

Dement slipped out of his car and crept beneath the front window. Looking in, he saw four masked men. Scurrying back to his car, he waited.

One by one the responding black and whites screeched up and positioned themselves around the storefront. Then, it grew eerily quiet. Unfortunately, in the rush to secure positions of advantage at the front, no one had taken up a position to cover the back door.

Gunn grabbed Yung by the collar and jammed the carbine harder against the terrified little man's right temple.

"Let's go," he shouted as he jerked the store owner around the corner of the counter and pushed him toward the front door.

"I wouldn't go out there," Washington said softly.

Gunn ignored the admonition. He had slipped into a world of his own making.

Gripping his hostage, Gunn made his way towards the front of the store. Looking into the blinding brightness of the police high beams and brilliant red lights, he froze.

"*Open the wine,*" he shouted to the diminutive store owner.

Yung, quivering violently, reached into the bag and removed the bottle. He struggled to find a grip on the metal cap.

"*Open it!*" Gunn screamed.

Again, the store owner gripped the top, squeezed, and turned. The bottle top cracked open and a whiff of cheap wine filled Gunn's nostrils. Sliding the carbine under his armpit, he grabbed the bottle and downed the contents.

While focusing on the spectacle that lay before him, Willie Gunn never heard the others slip silently out the back door. Clenched tightly in Washington's left hand was the brown paper bag that contained the money.

Once into the darkened alley, the bandits crouched behind a large trash dumpster and glanced back to see if they were being followed.

"It looks like Willie ain't comin'" Potts whispered, staring into the deserted alley.

"Stupid, nigga," Washington snarled.

Quietly, three figures slipped along the edge of the buildings. Within seconds, the alley was vacant.

"Is you ready, Bubba?" Gunn shouted. "I got us a hostage."

There was only silence.

"Bubba?" Where is you?" All was quiet except the sniffling of his hostage.

Dement looked at the police cars that sat idling, and then turned his attention back to the store.

"You standing at the door, put the rifle down, release the hostage, and send him out first. The rest of you drop your guns, put your hands straight over your heads, and come out single file."

"*Please, don't kill me,*" Yung pleaded. "*Please!*"

Gunn twisted the store owner's shirt collar and jerked him closer to the front door. "We is goin' for a walk, Chinaman."

"I no go," Yung whimpered, as his small heels tried to dig into the smooth linoleum floor. "They kill me, too!"

Yung's pleading fell on deaf ears.

Again, the command by Dement.

"Drop the guns! Send the hostage out first, then, put your hands high in the air and walk out the front door single file."

Dement waited. There was no response.

Looking around, he saw that everyone was in position. The scene reminded him of a band of Indians encircling a wagon train in a western movie. On his right were Hutton and Hestily. Then officers Matt Cunningham and Mike Rice, Bob Allen and Bob Nava, and on the far end, Patterson and a probationer named Hodges.

Gunn yanked at Yung's shirt collar, pushing the little man flush against the front door. He pushed the barrel of the carbine harder against the back of his head.

"We're commin' out, Mister Po-liceman," he shouted. Gunn pushed the door open with his foot, and using Yung as a shield, pushed him out the front. All he heard was the tinkling of the small bell above the door, the sniveling of his hostage and the muffled idling of five cars.

Gunn followed his hostage onto the sidewalk keeping his back to the right corner of the building. Death was stalking the street. Gunn felt it; Patterson knew it, and Yung Lee the Chinaman prayed that it would not be his night to die.

Gunn's eyes darted from side to side as his hand holding the barrel of the carbine to Yung Lee's head shook.

William Jefferson Gunn was a little man, who would be mourned by few and missed by even fewer.

Blinded by the high beams, his mind reeled off the events that would rather see him dead than return to prison.

September 1967. San Quentin Prison.

At the farthest end of the yard four men in prison blues hustled around one another shooting hoops, while a fifth pumped heavy iron. Stretched across the weight bench lay a huge, hard-bodied black man. Meet Cornelius Lightner, known to the other inmates as "Moose."

Moose was a lifer. Standing six foot three, he tipped the scales at a tightly coiled 270 pounds. He was big, he was mean, and he was feared. What Moose wanted, Moose got. No questions asked.

Two years earlier, Willie Gunn had been sent to the big house with a two-year sentence for robbery and auto theft. This was when Willie met Moose and Benjamin "Bubba" Washington.

On his second night in the joint, "Little Willie"—or "Sweetness" as he became known in the tiers—was moved into a cell with Moose. For the next two years, Willie was Moose's "Bitch"—his boy toy.

Out in the yard, Moose strained to finish his last reps. He was very much aware that at the far end of the yard Washington and Gunn were talking. Every few seconds, between lifts, he glanced suspiciously toward them.

Willie saw the picnic-style table where he and Bubba talked. He remembered that Bubba had been sent to Quentin for killing a cop three years earlier during a liquor store robbery in Los Angeles. He got life without parole, but the conviction was overturned. So Benjamin "Bubba" Washington, cop killer, would hit the streets tomorrow, September 29th, the same day as Gunn.

No one quite understood why, but Washington and Gunn had become friends. Maybe it was because both came out of the same ghetto of South Central Los Angeles, or maybe it was because both were set to leave the hated prison the same day.

"Bubba," Willie whispered. "I don't want to be done again by Moose."

"I got a plan, little man."

"What kind a plan?"

Washington bent his head close to Gunn's ear.

"*Just before lunch, Whitey, who's working in the license plate shop, is gonna slip a real thin piece a metal between the sole of his shoe. At lunch, he'll slip it to "Albino" Dixon, one of the cooks. Then, Albino is gonna slip the shank on my tray and then slop potatoes on top of it.*"

Washington stopped and shot a quick look up the yard. Moose hadn't moved.

"*Albino is also gonna get some powdered rat poison from the storeroom off the kitchen. Just before Moose gets his meal, Albino gonna salt that poison into Moose's 'tatos and gravy.*"

Washington watched Gunn as the color drained from the little man's face.

"*You with me, little man?*"

"*Ya,*" *Gunn answered softly.* "*I is with ya.*"

"*After lunch the poison'll start making him feel sick. He'll head for the crapper. When he does, I slip you the shank.*"

"*But he's bigger'n me,*" *he whined.*

Washington shot him a look. "*Do you remember the story of David and Goliath in the Bible?*"

"*Yeah.*"

"*Well, you do be David.*"

Gunn nodded his head up and down.

It was still raining outside after lunch, so Moose and his companions went to the inside basketball court to pick up the game while other inmates lined the walls.

Just as planned, Washington and Gunn stood against the wall near the middle of the court. Washington savored the sharpness of the steel pressing into his forearm. The plan was in motion.

Suddenly, Moose doubled over, moaned and stumbled his way to the head. Washington slipped Gunn the metal. With the shank slipped up his sleeve, Gunn waited, then, with a slight shove from Washington, he headed for the bathroom.

When Gunn entered, Moose was at the far urinal, his back to the door, retching violently, gagging and shaking with the effects of the poison.

Gunn suddenly knew he could do the job.

"*Moose,*" *Gunn called out.*

Moose's head turned. His expression was contorted and agony was etched deep into his sweat-streaked face. Turning slowly, he pulled himself upright, arms dangling heavily over both steel urinal dividers. Struggling to breathe, his tongue tried to wipe the spittle and vomit that clung to his lips.

"What do you want?" Moose coughed.

Willie stood silent.

Moose looked confused.

Willie stepped forward.

Moose retched onto the tile floor.

Gunn slid cautiously in front of the man who had made his last two years a hell on earth.

Sensing something was not right, Moose tried to stand erect. As he struggled, Gunn lunged and threw all of his 150 pounds at the big man's chest. With adrenaline pumping and fear motivating, he drove the sharpened steel as deep into Moose's belly as it would go.

"Aah," Moose bellowed as the wind left his lungs and the stall dividers sank deep into his armpits.

His eyes suddenly went wide as the smirk dropped off his lips. Gunn slammed the palm of his hand against the small incision in Moose's gut, and then he jumped back, dancing nervously.

Moose's eyes bulged, he began to shake, his mouth opened and shut, gulping for air. There were no words uttered as foam formed on his lips.

Sliding his right arm forward, Moose let go of the side rail and frantically clawed at the razor thin wound, visible just below his sternum. Unable to feel the shank, he let go of the other stall divider, as both hands clawed at the fire in his belly.

"You faggot mother f....." Moose never finished the sentence. Swaying from side to side, his eyes froze, the muscles in his face tightened, his mouth remained open, but there were no words, only gargling coming deep from within the throat. Slowly, he staggered toward Gunn with outstretched arms. After taking two steps, he fell forward, his head cracking against the cold tiles. He lay there-unmoving, eyes staring across the cold tile floor.

Gunn let out the breath it seemed he had been holding ever since he rushed Moose. He walked over to the door, but couldn't help turning back to look one last time at the hulk crumpled on the tiles, a thin stream of blood seeping from beneath his torso, eyes looking right at Gunn, glazed and unseeing. Moose lay dead. Washington was right. Moose would never rape Sweetness ever again.

With a grin spreading across his lips, Gunn scurried out of the head. Leaning against the wall next to Washington, he continued to watch the basketball game. Gunn cheered with new enthusiasm.

"It do be done," Gunn said, a look of relief crossing his face.

Shortly thereafter another inmate entered the bathroom. Seconds later he ran out of the head, yelling frantically at the top of his lungs, "Moose is dead!" Pointing back to the door, he yelled again, "He's been offed!"

Washington whispered sidewise to Gunn.

"Let's get on back to our cells."

In the chaos of the moment, no one noticed as the duo slipped out the side door.

It didn't take long for the prison grapevine to telegraph the news that Moose was dead. No one had any idea who did it, but most were grateful it had been done. Now the gossip in the tiers was who would take his place.

For Bubba Washington and Willie Gunn, it didn't matter.

"Drop the rifle and release the hostage," Dement yelled.

Gunn was back on the sidewalk. He shoved the barrel harder into Yung's neck.

Just around the brick corner of the building, two plainclothes University Division Special Operations Squad cops had pulled onto Brighton Avenue and parked in the shadows. McGrath, a tall lanky cop, opened the driver's door and made a crouched run to the corner of the building. Stallcup, his partner followed.

Reaching the corner, McGrath stopped and peered around the building. Not less than four feet from him was Gunn and the hostage—both with their backs to the corner. McGrath cautiously held his badge out into the blazing lights to identify himself as a cop. Stallcup crouched under McGrath and rested his gun on his right thigh and waited.

Gunn continued to stand defiantly with his hostage. For "Sweetness," everything in his life had suddenly turned sour.

He could see the breaths of the officers. As each cop exhaled, a small cloud floated in front of their faces. Slowly, the gunman and the Chinaman shifted to their right, closer and closer to McGrath and Stallcup.

Stallcup peered around the corner. Beads of sweat had popped out on his forehead. If all did not go perfectly, they might lose might lose the hostage, and even worse, a cop.

Dement realized that there was going to be a blood bath, but it was too late to stop it. Again, from behind the driver's door he called out to Gunn.

"Release the hostage and drop the rifle!"

Gunn stood defiant.

"This old man is my insurance policy, Mr. Po-liceman," Gunn screamed to everyone, yet to no one. "Where I goes, he goes!"

As the verbal exchange took place, Gunn was slowly edging himself to within Stallcup's reach.

With his .38 in his right hand, Stallcup leaned around the corner. Swiftly, he reached out with his left hand, grabbed Yung by the arm and whipped him around the corner to safety. As Yung flew around the corner, Stallcup jammed his revolver into Gunn's right side and fired two quick rounds. Gunn felt his hostage ripped from his grip, but before he could react, he felt two sharp pains in his side, and then he heard the shots.

Yung screamed.

"Please don't kill me! Please don't hurt Yung!"

"We're the po-lice," McGrath shouted into the ear of the frightened man. It failed to sink in. Repeatedly, Yung pleaded for his life.

Mortally wounded, Gunn spun and faced the semi-circle of cops. "I ain't goin' back to jail," the frenzied little man screamed. "I ain't goin' back!"

Struggling, he lifted the carbine toward the bank of black and whites and aiming at Patterson, he pulled the trigger.

Click! A misfire.

His wish of not going back to the joint was about to be granted.

Pushing his back against the brick building, he planted his feet and tried to eject the misfire and chamber a fresh round. Before he could do this, every weapon in the semicircle belched flame and spewed lead.

The first two shotgun rounds to find the ten-ring came from Patterson's twelve-gauge. Each slammed itself into Gunn's chest, pinning him against the building. Patterson slammed the third round into the chamber and stood momentarily, watching his own breath plume whitely from his lips. Then he fired.

Glass from the front window exploded inward and shards knifed their way down like the blade of a guillotine.

After the barrage of shotgun blasts ended, the sound of service revolvers erupted.

Gunn flopped and danced like a rag doll, but he remained on his feet.

Billows of acrid, white smoke rose slowly into the cold winter night and hovered eerily over the scene.

The brick storefront was pockmarked from shotgun pellets and covered in Gunn's blood, but still he didn't fall!

Suddenly, all was quiet.

Gunn stood, pinned firmly against the bullet-riddled brick building. Everyone watched as he slowly lowered the carbine and let it tilt toward the sidewalk.

Then, the man all knew was dead, tried to raise the rifle. As if from a macabre movie, it slipped from his hands and clattered to the ground. Patterson tossed the empty shotgun onto the back seat, drew his .38 and leaned across the hood of the black and white to his immediate left.

He waited.

No one moved. All watched as Gunn took one step forward.

"The dude's dead," Hodges muttered. "But he's still walking!"

Patterson ignored the comment.

Gunn just stood there, his eyes frozen in a deathly stare.

Suddenly, the warm air from his lungs began to escape, slowly at first, then more rapidly. As if on cue, it formed an eerie, wispy cloud around the dead man's head.

The cloud grew, forming what appeared to be a large iridescent halo. Then, a small gust of wind blew the vapor off and down the street.

William Jefferson Gunn, thief, ex-con, and heroin addict fell face first in a crumpled mass on the sidewalk. His wish had been granted. He was not going back to the joint.

Hidden in the darkness, three bandits ditched their black masks and headed in different directions.

Patterson glanced back to the open passenger door where Hodges had taken cover. The kid was trembling.

"Did you get off any rounds?" he asked in a tone of voice that indicated he already knew the answer.

"No," Hodges sheepishly mumbled as he watched a search team carefully form-up to the right of what was once the front plate glass window.

Patterson didn't say another word. As cops began a cautious search of the liquor store, Patterson caught Hodges' attention.

"Get in the car," he said as he reached down on the ground and retrieved all of his spent shotgun shells, and then slipped them into the pocket of his black leather jacket.

"Why keep the casings?" Hodges asked as he climbed into the front seat.

"The French took scalps and in Vietnam, some of the guys took ears. Here, we cut off the brass end of the shell and make tie-tacs."

While gun-smoke hung heavily over the street and red lights pierced the night, 3Adam76 quietly backed from the scene and disappeared.

Patterson drove a few blocks without lights, but once the liquor store was out of sight, he turned them on and drove north. Crossing Exposition Boulevard, he pulled onto a dark street, coasted into an alley and turned off the car. Getting out, he popped the trunk and grabbed his black helmet bag.

"Grab me the shotgun," he said as he opened the bag and pulled out a gun cleaning kit.

Hodges reached to the back seat and retrieved the empty weapon. He handed it to his partner and watched as the seasoned cop broke it down and cleaned it. Next, he removed four shotgun shells from his helmet bag and loaded the Ithaca.

"Put it back in the rack and lock it up."

Then he poured some solvent on a rag and thoroughly cleaned his hands, removing any gunpowder residue.

At end of watch, Patterson drove Hodges to the Los Angeles County Morgue to watch the autopsy of William Jefferson Gunn.

SEVEN

At the end of the two-week Christmas assignment, McLean's class gratefully returned to the Academy. Within the next fourteen days, each recruit had completed two additional week-end patrol assignments. While some had meaningful experiences, McLean felt it a waste of time.

Sitting at lunch in the cafeteria, he overheard others talking about their experiences.

"I went to the Valley," said Dvorak. "Van Nuys Division sucks. I worked with some old dude who just wanted to write tickets and book drunk drivers."

McLean, who also had been assigned to Van Nuys, remained silent. He also felt it sucked. Gibbons, who was sitting in an adjacent booth, spoke up.

"I went to Hollywood. It was bitchin'—we were busy Friday and Saturday nights. Nothin' but hot calls. I even got to meet the Captain when we rolled on an officer involved shooting. His name is McLean. Captain McLean." Turning in his seat, he saw Nick sitting quietly finishing his lunch.

"Hey McLean! The Captain in Hollywood has your name. Any relation?"

"Could be. I'll have to check it out."

McLean had been told earlier that morning that permanent divisional assignments would be made at the end of the week. He also recalled that his class would be sent either to direct traffic or serve in a jail for their first six months.

I'll quit before I direct traffic again, he thought, a tinge of anger edging his thoughts. As he finished lunch, a plan had formed.

After lunch, he stopped by the Captain's office to ask his secretary the name of the commanding officer of Personnel Division.

"That would be Captain Robert Preminger," the secretary answered smiling.

Armed with that bit of critical information, McLean walked directly to the telephone booth near the flagpole on the first level of the quad. Stepping in, he closed the bi-fold door, dropped a dime in the slot and dialed Personnel Division. Three rings and the phone was answered.

"Los Angeles Police Department, Personnel Division, Kathy speaking. May I help you?"

McLean took a deep breath and shoved his back against the glass door.

"Kathy, this is McLean up at the Academy. Is the Captain in?"

"One moment, Captain," the sweet voice on the other end of the phone answered. "Let me see."

Mclean cupped the receiver with his left hand and cleared his throat. After a brief pause, another receiver was lifted and a jovial male voice spoke.

"Hey Mac, Preminger here, how are you doing?"

"Great, Bob, and yourself?"

"Couldn't be better. What can I do for you? You want out of Hollywood?"

"Not yet, but I could use a favor."

"Name it."

McLean felt his heart rate increase. His palm holding the old black telephone receiver was damp. He knew that if he got caught trying to pull off this ruse, it would end his career before it started. With an air of confidence, he continued.

"We have a recruit in the Academy named McLean. He's due to graduate in a couple of weeks and rather than send him to direct traffic or book drunks in a jail, I'd like to see him assigned to patrol in a south-end division. Think we can pull that off?"

"McLean, huh? A little nepotism, Mac?" Preminger said, once again laughing. "Hey, that's an easy one! Consider it done. Anything else I can do for you?"

"That'll do it," McLean answered, his eyes erupting in boyhood glee. "And, thanks."

A week later permanent assignments were posted on the bulletin board just outside the Captain's office. McLean stood in the hallway and scanned slowly down the assignment sheet looking for his name. There it was.

Nicholas Hunter McLean
Serial Number, 12600
Wilshire Division, Patrol

His face broke into a wide grin. It had worked. He was going to a south-end division.

～

Three days before graduation the class of seventy-two recruits entered the upper classroom and took their assigned seats. When all were seated, Peoples, dressed in his blue shorts and yellow T-shirt, began his final lesson on Officer Survival. McLean was listening so intently that when the rear classroom door opened, he didn't notice, not until he heard words that froze him in his seat.

"McLean!" Officer McCourt bellowed. "Get your hat and books and follow me!"

It was not a request. It was an order.

McLean's mind raced to identify why he would be called out. He was stumped. Anxiously, he followed McCourt down the worn front steps. Neither spoke. He could hear the hollow tattoo of his own leather soled dress shoes against the well worn cement. The sound seemed to reverberate in the thick silence between the men.

Entering through a door on the lower level into the corridor containing the staff offices, McCourt vigorously rapped on one of the wooden office doors, opened it, and with his head, motioned McLean to enter.

Removing his hat, McLean placed it under his left arm, adjusted his books, straightened his black clip-on tie and stepped into the room with as much composure and dignity as he could muster.

He was surprised at the starkness of the surroundings and the smallness of the room. Sitting behind a well used, dark wooden desk in the middle of the room were three men whose faces appeared to be chiseled in unforgiving stone. Without flinching, and hoping for a hint as to why he was summoned, he looked into the eyes of each man. Their blank stares revealed nothing.

Looking around, he saw that the chair designated for him had been dumped in a corner, upside down. He watched as the board silently waited to see what he would do. Trying not to appear nervous, he continued carefully to note everything he could.

Each man was dressed in the regulation Department blue wool uniform and all had sleeves crammed with five year service-stripes, or hash marks as they were fondly referred to on the L.A.P.D. He became very uncomfortable when he looked at the man seated in the middle and saw Captain's bars on the shirt collar.

"Have a seat," ordered the hulk of a man to the right of the Captain.

McLean looked directly at the robust man who wore Sergeant's chevrons on his upper sleeves. He quickly counted eight, five-year hash marks and realized that this man had more than forty years on the job. To the left of the Captain sat a white haired, deeply tanned Lieutenant, identified by the single silver bars affixed to his collar.

"Gentlemen, Recruit Officer McLean requests permission to place a chair in front of the board."

"Permission granted," Captain Stringer responded, a slight smile crossing behind his eyes.

McLean walked over to the corner of the room, righted the wooden chair and set it upright in front of the board. Standing at attention, he waited for permission to be seated.

"Have a seat, McLean," the Lieutenant ordered in a raspy voice.

Remembering protocol, McLean sat using only the first three inches of the chair and immediately pondered his situation. Then it occurred to him that maybe Captain Preminger had spoken to the Academy brass about the phone call he had received. His stomach knotted tighter when thinking of the possibilities that lay ahead if a call was made.

"We understand, McLean," growled the crusty old sergeant, "that while you were assigned to Van Nuys Division over the Christmas holidays, you ran into some problems."

"Major problems," interjected the Lieutenant.

"What the hell happened, boy?" the overweight man with the Sergeant chevrons asked as he lifted his large body from the chair and leaned closer.

"No problems, sir," McLean calmly responded. "Just challenging experiences."

"Challenging experiences my ass!" bellowed the sergeant as he slammed a beefy fist onto the table causing it to jump as the room echoed with the angry sound. Through punctuated words which gained momentum in intensity, he continued.

"First, you leave your intersection, walk into a bathroom and trip over two queers. Then, if that wasn't enough, you walked to the rear of a shopping mall where you would have gotten your ass kicked if one of the dicks working Hollywood hadn't come to your rescue. If it weren't for Robinson, McLean, you wouldn't be here today!"

He was fairly shouting and his face showed tinges of red from his growing irritation. McLean slightly winced but refrained from wiping the spray of spittle that escaped the angry sergeant's thick lips landing on his left cheek.

He sat in front of the board in monumental silence.

A red flush of anger erupted on his pale cheek. The emotion cooled, then sobered to the issue at hand. Then he spoke.

"Yes sir, you're right," he said, attempting to stay calm and composed.

"I'm not called 'sir,' Recruit Officer McLean," the red-faced sergeant yelled. "I'm Sergeant Handwerker. See those stripes? That means I'm a Sergeant of Police! The other men in this room are called 'sir'!"

"I understand, Sergeant Handwerker, but if Sergeant Robinson hadn't been there, two assholes would have joined me in the hospital."

"You're one cocky son-of-a-bitch," Handwerker bellowed.

McLean looked into the eyes of each board member.

"Not cocky, gentlemen. Just confident."

"Enough of this," said the Lieutenant, his voice barely above a whisper. "Let's get rid of him now."

McLean's body stiffened.

Stringer's eyes fixed on McLean's. "Are you trying to con us?" he asked.

"No sir. But Sergeant Handwerker is right," he said, looking the enormous man directly in the eyes.

"After I stood in that intersection for over three hours, I needed to use the bathroom. So I secured my post and walked over to a gas station where I located the restroom. When I walked in, I found two males on the floor engaged in what appeared to be a homosexual act."

McLean glanced at the other board members, their expressions had not softened.

"Seeing me, they stumbled out the open door and disappeared into the night," McLean continued. "I used the restroom, but since I was still angry about a carload of gang members who tried to rip off my tie, I decided to take a walk and cool down."

"And that's when you went to the rear of the Mall?"

"Yes, sir."

"Go on," said Stringer.

"You're also right about the help I received from Sergeant Robinson. I've been taught that there isn't a blue ribbon for second place in a street fight. You either win or you lose. Those two wanted to kick my ass and that wasn't going to happen."

"Did you say that you needed to take a walk to cool down?" asked the Lieutenant.

McLean realized that he was in trouble.

"Yes sir."

"Does that mean that you're a hothead and unable to control your emotions, Recruit Officer McLean?"

"No sir. I am able to control my emotions and that has been demonstrated during my time at the Academy. It was a poor choice of words, sir."

"A poor choice of words; now that would indicate that you have a problem in the decision making process, wouldn't it, Officer McLean?"

"No sir. It would *indicate* that it was a poor choice of words."

"Do I sense a belligerent attitude, McLean?" asked Handwerker as he again rose from his chair, placed the palms of both hands securely on the table top and leaned forward.

"No, I was just trying to clarify a point."

"I want to know why you felt it necessary in the first place to leave your post?" asked Handwerker as he leaned further across the table. "And forget about that bullshit of having to use the bathroom."

"But it's..."

Stringer sensed the tension.

"Officer McLean, why don't you sit back, take a deep breath, and using the correct words, explain to us what you meant."

McLean sat quietly on the edge of the chair, thinking. It was now or never. Stringer was giving him one more chance. His explanation would either mean a career on the Los Angeles Police Department or the shattering of a dream. He uttered a silent prayer, continued to occupy the first three inches of the hard wooden chair and continued.

Inhaling slowly, McLean began.

"While I was standing in the intersection, a car-load of gang members made a number of passes at me, trying to see how close they could come. On each occasion, I was able to dodge their car. On their final pass, the driver aimed right at me while a passenger in the rear seat leaned out the window and tried to grab my tie. Granted, it's a break-away tie, but he was also trying to grab my throat." McLean straightened his back, and continued to look each board member directly in the eyes as he glanced, one to the other.

"On the last pass, I was able again to jump out of the way way, but when the car made a u-turn, I felt it best to remove myself from the situation rather than suffer great bodily harm, or, become involved in a police action; so to answer the question, no gentlemen, I don't feel that I am a hothead and unable to control my emotions. Considering the admonition we were given by the Academy staff not to become involved in any police work, I feel that I handled the situation to the best of my ability."

The board was quiet. McLean sat silent as heads turned and eyes locked.

"One last question," said Stringer, his tone much friendlier than Handwerker's. "How badly do you want to be a Los Angeles Policeman?"

His throat constricted and his breath came hard. The air was stale.

"It's been my goal since I was fourteen, Captain."

"Why?" asked the Lieutenant coolly.

McLean shifted uneasily in the chair.

"I'm not quite sure, Lieutenant. It was just something I *knew* that I wanted to be. There was never any doubt in my mind, nor did I think about pursuing another career path. Was it because I wanted to provide some type of service? Possibly. Did I want action? At fourteen that is probably closer to the truth. But as the time approached to test for the Department, I realized that I wanted not just a job, but a career."

"How old are you, McLean?" Stringer asked.

"Twenty-one, sir."

"Married?"

"Yes sir."

"Children?"

"One. A little girl."

The room was as silent as a tomb. McLean looked into the eyes of his interrogators and ignored the flickering of the lights.

"Thank you, Recruit Officer McLean."

McLean's heart seemed to stop beating as the board members glanced at each other.

"Take your hat and books and get back to class," said Stringer in a voice laced with approval.

"Thank you, gentlemen."

It was over.

McLean read the look of each man and registered the words and was momentarily speechless. Then it sank in.

He stood, came to attention and saluted. Then he placed his right foot exactly behind his left, his toe pointing down, barely touching his heel. Turning with precision, he stepped to the door, opened it slowly and entered the hallway. The men watched as he closed the door.

Grins crossed each face. "The kid's got balls," Stringer said, laughing.

"I think that he'll do fine on the street, but we're going to have to submit Handwerker's performance for an Academy Award. Bruce, your interrogation techniques kept John and me on our toes, especially when you slammed that fist of yours on the table and lunged at the kid."

Laughter again filled the room.

McLean walked back up the concrete steps to the classroom, grateful that the telephone call to Preminger hadn't been discovered.

EIGHT

McLean sat in the dimly lit apartment and waited. He stared intensely at his uniform and Sam Browne gun belt, his deep blue eyes reflecting a trace of restlessness. A deep furrow cut through his brow in a series of grooves and hung there in the pale skin. It wasn't that he was angry. That wasn't the case. He was frustrated in that he felt that the time should pass more quickly. Glancing again at his wrist watch, he saw that it was only nine P.M.

Darlene had fallen asleep in the large armchair while nursing the baby. Quietly, he shuffled across the worn carpet, reached down to the floor and pulled his Smith and Wesson .38 from its holster.

Reverently, he turned the gun in his hands. Throwing open the cylinder, he dropped the bullets into his cupped right hand, then he extended the empty weapon and looked down the top of the ribbed barrel to the front sight. Snapping the cylinder shut, he aimed, squeezed the trigger back slowly and listened for the first click. When he heard it, he squeezed further knowing that just past the second click the hammer would fall, and it did.

After reloading his gun, he unsnapped each leather ammunition pouch. Dropping the live rounds into a palm, he counted them. Exactly twenty-four, twelve in each case. He struggled to slide the rounds high enough into each pouch to allow it to be snapped. Then he checked his baton, handcuffs and keys.

He was as ready as he ever would be for his first night as a Los Angeles Policeman. Grabbing his uniform, he threw the gun belt over his shoulder and snatched up the small workout bag that contained his dress shoes, helmet bag and books. His tennis shoes glided softly across the carpet as he stepped to the door, stopped, and looked back at Darlene and the baby. Confident that all was well, he quietly opened the door and stepped out on the small stoop. He took a deep breath of the cold night air. Lowering his head against the brisk breeze, he descended the steps.

Walking to the rear carport, he quietly climbed into his V. W. Bug, and closed the door. He cranked over the old engine and was grateful when he heard it sputter, cough, and start. After a few minutes, he slipped the gearshift into reverse and slowly backed from the parking space. In first gear, the car inched its way down the driveway and into a new chapter in his life.

The streets were mildly congested; not as bad as he had imagined. Approaching the Oxnard Street on-ramp to the Hollywood Freeway southbound, he downshifted to second, and then pushed the small black accelerator pedal to the floor.

Spitting and coughing, the car made its way up the ramp and onto the freeway. In minutes, he saw the Highland Avenue off-ramp that would take him through Hollywood Division.

Exiting the off-ramp, he drove past the Hollywood Bowl and approached Hollywood Boulevard. It was a street that had once felt the footsteps of the rich and powerful, and its buildings had housed the famous and infamous. Now, the sidewalks were stained with tears, and blood flowed in its gutters.

He shook his head as he slowed for the red light.

Yep, he thought, *Tinsel Town is dead*.

The expensive Rolls Royces had been replaced by rusty shopping carts powered by society's castaways. Many of the old storefronts had been replaced by cardboard hovels and urine stained sleeping bags. Cheap wine bottles had replaced expensive magnums of Champagne. The effervescence of life was replaced by the moroseness of death.

Sitting at the light, he glanced out of the passenger window and watched two black working girls strut their stuff. He ignored the girls, his fingers softly tapping the steering wheel. Staring out of the front window, he soon became lost in his thoughts.

He wondered about his first partner. What will he be like? Will I fit into the watch?

Suddenly, he was drawn back to the two girls who were darting in and out of the stopped cars. Fascinated by the show, he laughed as their long blond wigs bounced rudely on their heads and their large butts wiggled as they jumped from car to car.

Suddenly, they started towards the Volkswagen, but before they could get to his window, the light changed. McLean popped the clutch and the car lurched forward, sending the two street-walkers jumping back in surprise. Blond hair twirled heavenward in the cold winter air. Mini skirts were hiked up above the thighs as they turned. The girls twisted this way and that, all in an attempt to make it back to the sidewalk.

He glanced into the rear view mirror and watched as the traffic started through the green light. Whether the two hookers scored, he never knew. However, that would not be his last encounter with women who made their living turning tricks.

In minutes, the squalor of Hollywood was a memory.

Driving down Highland Avenue, he crossed Beverly Boulevard and entered the north-end of Wilshire Division. He was impressed by the majestic homes that lined the street and was struck by the fact that in life everything had its opposites. Good and evil, light and dark, whores and princesses, but nowhere were the opposites more discernable than in Wilshire.

The Volkswagen glided into the left hand turn lane and proceeded on the green light east on Pico Boulevard. The squalor had returned. Driving through the darkness, he noticed that small businesses lined the north side of the wide avenue and on the south, a faded sign identified a weather-beaten building as Sears & Roebuck.

The wide street ascended, and he drove slowly past the police station that rose in the night like a ghost at midnight. Further up the street he found the employee's parking lot. He pulled into the driveway and found a space on the back wall. Climbing out of the car, he reached into the back seat and grabbed his uniform, Sam Browne and workout bag. Unsnapping the holster flap, he removed his service revolver and shoved it into his waistband.

Fighting the wind, he walked down the hill to the station. As the gusts increased, he dropped his head and walked with an increased determination.

Reaching the front of the station, he teetered awkwardly and then regained his balance. With a reverent awe, he looked at the old edifice like an artist would peruse a blank canvas struggling for inspiration. He was lost in its dreariness yet captivated by its sense of mystery. In the cold winter night, the station looked old beyond her years.

With only the cold winter wind as a companion, he looked up and read the words: "Wilshire Division-Los Angeles Police Department—1925."

Resolutely, he climbed the worn concrete steps to the landing, reached out and grabbed one of the large, tarnished, brass door handles. He struggled to break open the door. Inching it back, he slipped into the lobby where he set his bag on the distressed wooden floor and stared at the front desk.

Standing in the foyer, he could hear a strange muffled noise. Stepping closer, he peered behind the counter and smiled at a solitary figure seated in the back corner, obviously asleep.

Scuffed black shoes were propped up on the desktop, and enormous hands were clasped snuggly behind a large head that was bowed, while laborious breathing produced the muffled sounds of a stifled snore. Gazing at the lone figure, he wondered if he ever would get to the point where he would be that out of shape, his uniform that disheveled and because of age, relegated to the front desk.

Before the front door completed its unhurried effort to close, a sudden gust of cold air blasted into the lobby and forced the old timer's spindly gray hair to dance in myriad directions, finally coming to rest over his eyes. Startled, he grumbled softly at the interruption, then looked up and saw McLean. Meticulously, he brushed back his few strands of hair and then slid his hands again behind his head. He smiled, but never said a word.

Trying not to appear nervous, McLean looked beyond the weathered old cop to the rear wall where he saw a picture of the Department's Chief, William H. Parker.

Surrounding the Chief's picture were those of men from Wilshire Division who had been killed in the line of duty. The earliest was 1925. The most recent was 1964.

Nervously, he stood on the scarred floor and waited for the large figure to speak. When the silent mastodon failed to utter a word, McLean, threw his shoulders back and stepped closer to the desk.

As he neared, he saw that the man's body had long ago stopped fitting comfortably into the timeworn, ill-fitting blue uniform. A uniform that featured numerous shiny worn spots and a tie that proudly bore the remnants of many dinners. On the left side of his barrel chest rested a tarnished green badge that appeared to have never seen polish or a soft cloth, and down the front of the shirt were buttons pulled so taught that they seemed ready to pop off. His enormous stomach hung unceremoniously over his waist, and his sergeant's chevrons that were once white, had become a drab gray. On his left sleeeve just above the cuff, he wore six hash marks.

After looking deeply into McLean's eyes, he finally spoke. "Need some help, son?"

McLean relaxed. "Yeah, Sarge. Where's the locker room?"

"Through the door to the right, then up the stairs, and watch your step," he added. "It's dark in there." As the final words rolled off his tongue, he erupted into a hearty laugh. Being a fat man, the layers of flesh under his shirt rippled.

"Thanks," McLean said as he threw his uniform over his shoulder, picked up his gear and struggled to open the side door. Standing on the small landing, he looked up the wooden stairs.

Hanging over the stairwell was a bare light bulb that was suspended by a single black cord. Both swayed softly back and forth, moved by the cold gusts of wind that crept into the lobby area and worked their way under the side door and into the shadowy hallway.

The stairs were wooden and marred by deep indentations that attested to the many years of foot traffic. They went up for twelve steps, and then stopped at a small, poorly lit landing. There were two doors. One labeled *LOCKERS*, and the other, *DETECTIVES*.

McLean stepped onto the stairs and stopped as they creaked and moaned under his weight. His concentration was broken when a low, gravely voice from behind the front desk spoke. "If you need any help son, let me know. I'm Sergeant Bloom. Sol Bloom."

McLean bounded up the stairs and stopped on the small landing. He entered the door marked, *LOCKERS* and found himself in a large room partially lit by flickering overhead fluorescent lights suspended from the ceiling and surrounded by rows of exposed water pipes. On the floor, a quarter-of-an-inch wide crack ran the entire distance of the room.

The room contained rows of full-length metal lockers; all painted a drab, metallic gray. In the center of each row was a narrow wooden bench that once had been highly lacquered and brightly polished, but now showed the signs of many years of hard wear. On each side of the bench was a space of three feet. The air in the locker room was cold and stale, and reminded him of a mausoleum.

After walking around the lockers and tugging on a number of handles, he found one unlocked. Opening the bent metal door, he placed his equipment in the narrow confines of the steel cabinet and watched as others slowly entered the room. As the group grew in size, the muffled conversations increased. Some lit cigarettes, and after a few strong drags, placed them on the scarred wooden bench. Suddenly, a man with a locker just down from McLean's, broke the silence.

"Hey Buck," yelled a man with black hair and a pure white streak racing down its middle from front to back.

"Looks like we've got a boot with us. If they put him with Wallace, he won't last a week."

Laughter erupted from the other side of the lockers.

"Go to hell, Marzullo," a soft voice from the end of the bench responded.

"Hey, Brad," Buck Wright yelled from the opposite row of lockers. "We didn't know you were sensitive."

"I'm not. But you can still go to hell."

McLean looked past Marzullo and saw the cop called Wallace. He was a large man with muscular shoulders and short cropped brown hair. He stood alone next to the narrow bench. He glanced briefly at McLean, and then continued to dress.

McLean continued to stare, unable to break his gaze. Suddenly, he felt a presence standing next to him. He turned and found himself looking into the eyes of Bloom.

"How's everything going, son?" the obese man asked, sporting a friendly grin while he straddled the wooden bench and filled the entire area between the lockers.

"Fine, Sarge," McLean answered, trying not to let on that he was nervous.

"Had a chance to look over the watch?" Bloom asked as his eyes darted down the row of lockers.

"A little," McLean answered as he shot a look at Wallace. "They're quite an interesting group."

"That would be an understatement," replied Bloom. "Now to a new guy on the watch, they might look like some unfriendly sons-of-bitches. But they're not. They'll warm up to you when they trust you. So my advice to you, son, is just keep your eyes and ears open and your mouth shut. If you do that, you'll do just fine."

As Bloom turned to walk away, McLean lightly touched his arm.

"Hey, Sarge," he whispered, "Who's the big guy at the end of the bench?"

"That's Wallace, Bradley Wallace. He's one of the best street cops on the Department. He keeps to himself, doesn't talk much, and is one tough hombre."

Smiling, Bloom winked and slid his large body sideways between the lockers and slipped through the narrow door into the dark stairwell.

McLean finished dressing and then followed the others into the roll call room. He dropped his gear on the floor and then sat down in the middle on one of the long wooden benches. Studiously, he looked around.

The desks were scarred, no different than the long benches in the locker room. Cigarette burns marred the tabletops, and occasionally he saw a dark blackened blotch burned into the wood by a forgotten cigar. In the front was a wooden podium that stood a foot off the floor.

On the podium sat a scratched wooden table with a stained Formica top and three hard-latticed backed wooden chairs. Hanging on the wall behind the desk was a vintage 1925 light green chalkboard, scarred, ignored and apparently seldom used. Large yellowing maps of the division lined the walls. Hanging beneath the maps, on two-ringed clipboards, were the already fading mimeographed sheets of daily arrest and crime reports that were run off on a rotating drum the night before.

It was Friday night approaching midnight and the moon was full. Each guaranteed that the shit would hit the fan.

McLean waited for his first roll call to begin. He could hear mumbled conversations behind him but didn't turn around. His introduction to the world of these hardened street cops would come soon enough.

Suddenly the side door opened, and three men entered. Lieutenant Daniel Watson, Sergeant Terrance Ridgley, and a familiar face, Sol Bloom.

"Gentlemen," Lieutenant Watson said, "it's a Friday night, so we won't have a formal inspection. But before we begin, I'd like to welcome Officer Nicholas McLean to Wilshire Division."

"Shit, all we need is another probationer," yelled a booming deep voice from the back of the room.

"They're a pain in the ass, Lieutenant!" the same voice added.

"All right, Strong," Bloom bellowed, "It wasn't that long ago that you didn't have enough time on the job to sew on your first hash mark."

"Yeah, Sarge, but I..."

"No butts, Bill," Bloom interjected.

Watson watched for a few more moments as though he were refereeing a tennis match, then he spoke. "Let's get back to the business at hand," he said softly.

McLean began to analyze the three men on the podium. Bloom, he liked. Ridgley was a slim man with dark hair parted and combed to one side. He had high cheekbones, was pale with hollows at his temples. He had a narrow face and a mouth that curled at the side. His black eyes were set close to the center of his head, reminding McLean of a bird. His uniform was immaculate and contained only one hash mark. He sat stiff in the hard wooden chair.

Next, he examined Watson whom he thought didn't look at all like a cop, but more like a banker. His appearance was somber and his complexion exhibited the 'Morning Watch pallor,' a condition caused by too many nights and not enough time in the sun.

Stress lines cut deeply between his eyes and dark furrows crossed his forehead like rows in an Iowa cornfield. His speech was soft and McLean wondered how a man with his demeanor could handle one of the toughest watches in the city.

Following the reading of the teletypes and vacation checks, Ridgley turned his attention to making car assignments.

"7Adam99, Strong and Englander."

McLean turned in his seat and saw that Strong was a robust man with short sandy hair, a barrel chest and biceps that stretched the top of his long sleeve shirt. He threw McLean an icy stare with eyes as cold as a snow patch in the Artic. Englander was just the opposite. He was a lanky, thin cop who wore a uniform that looked two sizes too large. Unlike Strong, he sported a large smile.

"Here," both men responded while continuing to sip their coffee.

"7Adam76, Oakes and Dumas."

McLean's eyes quickly darted to the back row.

"Here," Oakes responded.

"Dumas here," answered the man seated next to Oakes.

Sherman Oakes was an impressive man. He was athletically built and had a heavy crop of thick red hair that he combed straight back. He looked more like a movie star than a street cop. His complexion was fair, and he had a mischievous smile on his lips that lit up his entire face. His eyes were emerald green and well positioned in his head. Overall, he appeared to be a man who loved his job, enjoyed life, and had a good time no matter what the circumstance.

Dumas was just the opposite. He was a slender man with sallow cheeks and bitter eyes. He was dark and swarthy and reminded McLean of a snake-oil-salesman with oily slicked-back, black hair and a protruding Roman nose. He had thin lips with a small mouth that was formed into a sneer. His uniform was tailored, and his badge was shined to a bright luster, as were his four brass buttons. On his left sleeve, he wore a single hash mark. McLean instantly formed a dislike for the man.

"7Adam65, Marzullo and Wright."

"Here," responded the man who had the silver streak in his hair.

"Wright?"

"Here."

Buck Wright sat next to Marzullo. He was quiet, but his eyes told that he missed little.

His stature was the same as Marzullo's, medium height, robust in stature and though he appeared subdued, McLean saw a twinkle in his eye's that testified that he, like his partner, liked a good joke. McLean liked them both.

"7Adam52, Simpson and Petrunik."

"Present," Simpson, answered.

McLean's eyes darted across the aisle into the center section of the desks. His glance fell on the man who answered as Simpson. McLean could see that even seated, he was small in stature. Everything about him shouted perfectionism. His badge was highly polished and his leather sparkled. His books were placed in the middle of the desk; each set perfectly one on top of the other. His hat sat on top of the pile, perfectly centered. A small Officer's Notebook sat open on the desk. Where others in the room sat comfortably, he sat as though he had a corncob up his ass. McLean immediately formed the opinion that Simpson couldn't be trusted.

Then his attention was drawn to Petrunik. He was a little older than McLean and sat quietly. He was of average height; average looks and what McLean would later learn, average intelligence. Nothing about him stood out.

Ridgley held the car assignment board steady on the desk and turned it slightly to see the last car assignment.

"7Adam42, Wallace and McLean."

The room erupted in catcalls, led by Strong. Wallace sat quietly ignoring the banter. McLean didn't need to look back to identify his partner.

"All right gentlemen, we'll have some brief training by Sergeant Bloom, then, hit the field."

"Bloom doesn't know the meaning of brief," whispered Marzullo to Wright, while sipping gently on the steaming cup of coffee.

Bloom sat up straight. The lines around his eyes smiled as he pushed the wooden chair away from the desk. When he looked at Ridgley, his eyes danced and he broke into a large grin.

"We're in trouble now," Englander commented loud enough for all to hear. Then Strong farted with gusto. The back row cleared, but it didn't phase Bloom. He'd traveled back in time.

"The old man's a has-been," Dumas said with a brutal overtone of indignation.

"Let him be, Dumas," Wallace said contemptuously.

Dumas broke the moment with a laugh, one void of humor, and one that betrayed his fear.

Alexander Xavier Dumas not only hated, but also feared Wallace. After his remark, Dumas sneered and shot him a look with eyes that exuded a deep loathing. Dumas held tight the vendetta formed after his first encounter with the hardened street cop.

New on the watch, Dumas reminded everyone of a pompous French aristocrat, and his attempt to secure himself a top spot in the pecking order almost proved a disaster for the little man with a large ego. Sitting on the hard bench, Dumas remembered why he hated Wallace.

It was early on a Saturday morning and Wallace was working with Jimmy Hardin, the second man assigned to 7Adam42. Oakes and Dumas were working 7Adam76. The radio had been quiet until the lull was broken when the voice of the dispatcher crackled over the airwaves.

"7Adam42, ambulance cutting, man down, 1800 South Kingsley Avenue. 7Adam42, handle the call Code Two."

Irritated, Hardin slipped the mike from its clip, pushed the side button and responded.

"Why the hell do we get these chicken-shit calls?" he asked Wallace in his deep Southern drawl.

"Maybe it's because they know how much you enjoy public relations, Hardin," Wallace commented as he broke into a rare smile.

"I like these calls as much as you like correcting your crime reports after Ridgley has marked them up."

"Ridgley and I aren't on the same page," Wallace responded. "We're not even in the same book."

"I wouldn't trust the guy as far as I could throw him," Hardin said as he slipped the mike into its holder.

"7Adam42, be advised that 7Adam76 is Code Six, out for investigation at 1800 South Kingsley Avenue."

"A little out of their area, aren't they?" Hardin asked. Wallace mumbled something inaudible and turned the corner onto South Kingsley Avenue. As he rolled up to the call, he cut off the headlights.

Getting out of the car, both he and Hardin stopped, looked around, and then walked toward the front of the house where they saw a man sprawled on the front path bleeding from a severe neck wound. Oakes hovered over the man, just staring. Dumas was on the porch with a female, who was ranting and shouting obscenities.

"What do we have, Sherm?" Wallace asked.

"The guy's old lady cut him," Oakes answered coldly. "But it looks like she missed the carotid."

"That's too bad," mumbled Wallace.

"That black bastard cheated on me," the incensed woman screamed. "He deserved what he got. I cut him real good!"

Wallace left Hardin with Oakes and stepped onto the dimly lit porch. He didn't speak, but watched as Dumas reached into his handcuff case and pulled out a pair of gold plated bracelets.

"A little pretentious," he said to Dumas. Ignoring the comment, Dumas snapped the handcuffs on the struggling woman.

"Settle down, bitch," Dumas yelled as he struggled to snap the second cuff. "I'm doing you a favor. Not everyone can say they've been arrested by Alexander Xavier Dumas and taken to jail wearing gold plated handcuffs!"

The muscles in Wallace's face tightened. His expression turned mean. With a piercing stare marked with disgust, he glared into the beady black eyes of the swarthy little cop who had jumped his call.

On the pathway, both Oakes and Hardin stood watching. Neither spoke, but each knew that Dumas had made a mistake.

"Take your damn cuffs off the woman," Wallace said between clenched teeth as he hovered over the smaller man.

Dumas spun and faced the larger cop.

"Who in the hell do you think you are giving me orders," he said as he stepped into Wallace's face.

Without warning, Wallace's left hand shot off his hip and grabbed Dumas by the collar. As Dumas choked and his eyes bulged, he was lifted off the ground and slammed into the rear wall of the small porch. Struggling violently, he tried with his right hand to grab his Colt Python from its holster.

Without breaking his hateful stare, Wallace's right hand shot across and incapacitated Dumas' right hand. A sudden snap of the wrist sent the arrogant little cop writhing in pain. Oakes jumped onto the porch and grabbed Wallace's shoulder.

"Don't kill him, Brad," Oakes shouted.

Slowly, Wallace let the frightened man down. Dumas was shaking, but soon regained his bravado.

"You faggot son-of-a-bitch," he screamed uncontrollably. "I'll kill you! Nobody touches me. Nobody!"

"You shouldn't have said that," Oakes said flatly.

Wallace had stepped back and was about to step off the porch until the final affront.

"You arrogant little asshole," he bellowed as he spun and snatched at Dumas. Adroitly, Oakes flew between the two men.

"It's okay, Brad," Oakes said as he tried to restrain the giant. "I'll handle it."

Wallace was incensed. "He's all yours, Sherm," he said, his words cascading forth like thunder rolling across a canyon. "Just keep the little prick out of my way."

"Next time it'll end differently," Dumas yelled while he readjusted his black clip on tie, buttoned up the front of his shirt and combed back his black hair using a small black plastic comb he kept in his shirt pocket.

"Shut the hell up!" shouted Oakes as he shook his head.

Wallace stepped off the porch and onto the front path.

"The call is all yours, Sherm," Wallace said as he walked toward his black and white.

Oakes stepped off the porch, stopped and glanced down at the forgotten victim on the walkway. He looked deep into the bleeding man's eyes.

"You want to sign a crime report and put your old lady in jail?" he asked.

"No, ossifer, just call me an ambulance."

Oakes leaned closer to the bleeding man while Hardin stood on the sidewalk with a grin on his face.

"I'll ask you one more time, friend," Oakes shouted above the wailing of the woman on the porch.

"Do you want to sign a crime report and put the bitch in jail?"

"No, ossifer, I don't want to sign no crime report. All I want is for you to call me an ambulance."

"All you want is for me to call you an ambulance?" Oakes asked.

"Yes sir, just call me an ambulance," the man coughed, spitting blood and spittle across the toes of Oakes' polished black shoes.

Calmly, Oakes leaned down and looked directly into the man's pleading eyes.

"Okay, friend, listen to me carefully," he said. "I just need to verify that all you want is for me to call you an ambulance?"

"Yes, ossifer. Just call me an ambulance."

"YOU'RE AN AMBULANCE!" belted out Oakes.

Shocked, the man turned his head and watched as the red haired white devil with the piercing green eyes stepped over his prone body and walked away.

NINE

Bloom pushed the uncomfortable chair away from the desk to make more room for his large belly. Pushing his fat legs straight out in front, he stretched, crossed his ankles, put his hands behind his head, and leaned back slightly, interlocking his fingers behind his spindly gray hair. In mere moments, visions of the past had surfaced.

"I was working alone and decided to check out the old 'If Club' up at Eighth and Vermont," he said as he cocked his head back and looked upward.

"When I walked into the joint, I told everyone to put their hands on the bar and keep them in plain sight. Everyone did it, except one big black son-of-a-bitch. Like a snake uncoiling, he shot off the stool and stepped directly in front of me."

"Now what have we got here," he grunted. "Looks to me like a fat-ass bull."

"The guy was doing fine until he called me a fat-ass."

Bloom chuckled as he slid his butt to the end of the seat and combed his fingers slowly across his balding head.

"That's when I reached out, grabbed his left elbow and began to turn him around. Before I could slam him against the bar, he reached into his waist and pulled out a small Iver and Johnson, .22.

"Well, I gave him a shove, then cleared leather ..." Bloom took a long, deep breath and with a yellowed cotton handkerchief, mopped the perspiration from his face. *"And before he knew it, my nine-inch barrel was aimed square between his eyes. Then I snapped the trigger. The sorry son-of-a-bitch was dead before he hit the ground."*

Bloom wiggled his large butt from side to side, trying to get more comfortable.

"*Well, when my commendation was written up, not even Inspector Buddy Nardone could get me my Medal of Valor. But I showed 'em. I went home and told my wife about me getting screwed out of my medal, and she went to work and made me one. It was beautiful. Red, white, and blue ribbon, with a big, gold, city seal. It even had a real jewel in it that I got from a jeweler on Fifth and Grand. He owed me a favor so he popped for the stone. That medal didn't cost me a dime.*"

"You haven't paid for anything since the day you came on the job," yelled Marzullo.

"Neither have we," mumbled Wright.

Bloom stretched, lifted his body from the chair and continued.

"*Well, boys, we had a formal inspection one day, and old Bill Parker showed up. That's right, the Chief himself. There we stood all spit and polish. The Chief started down the front row where I was standing. When he came to me, he stopped, looked hard at the Medal, then into my eyes. I could have crapped.*"

Bloom walked over to the edge of the table and leaned against the corner.

"*Then he put out his hand, shook mine, and with a serious George Patton look on his face, broke into one of his rare smiles. Well done officer,*" he said. "*Keep up the good work.*"

The room erupted in hoots and hollers.

"*When old Bill Parker gave my Medal the Papal blessing, that made it official. So it didn't matter who made it. I earned it ...I got it ...and he accepted it.*"

Bloom slid off the desk, shoved his hands into his pockets and thrust his massive chest forward.

"So boys, tomorrow night we're having a formal inspection, and Sergeant Solomon Bloom is wearing his Medal. And if any of you sorry sons-of-bitches says a word, you'll be working the front desk for the next thirty days."

Turning to Watson, he asked, "Is that all right with you, Lieutenant?"

"It's fine with me, Sergeant," Watson said smiling.

Roll call ended on Bloom's remarks.

Quietly, each man grabbed his gear and left the room. McLean followed their lead, but hesitated to see what direction Wallace might give. When none came, he silently walked out.

The worn stairs creaked loudly as the watch descended to the main floor. Wallace walked into a small cramped room that held the shotguns, ammunition, and car keys. Not waiting for the station officer, he grabbed the keys, his shotgun and shoved five shells into the pocket of his black leather jacket.

McLean stood with his back against a wall, waiting. Everything his partner did seemed to be done in a methodical way. No emotion, no conversation, just a silence that exuded a coldness that made McLean more apprehensive.

Finally, McLean spoke.

"I'm McLean," he said. "Looks like we're partners."

"Looks like it," Wallace commented dryly.

"Here are your keys," Wallace said, tossing them casually in the air.

"I'll drive. You handle the radio, take the reports and keep the log. Think you can handle all that?"

"I think so," McLean said, a tinge of sarcasm in his voice.

Then Wallace tossed McLean the Ithaca. Reaching into his coat pocket, he pulled out the five shotgun shells and tossed them one at a time to McLean.

"You might need these. Do you remember the five-point safety check?"

"Yeah," McLean said, as he looked at Wallace and wondered about the fifth round.

"When we get to the car, conduct the check, load the shotgun and place the fifth round in the chamber with the safety on."

"Why the fifth round?" McLean asked puzzled. "I thought that we were only authorized four?"

Wallace cast him an icy look.

"Just do it, and when you're finished, slide the gun into the rack and lock it up."

As McLean stepped out the side station door and onto the driveway, he was approached by Marzullo.

"McLean, I'm John Marzullo," he said extending a hand.

"Welcome to Wilshire Mornings." McLean extended his hand, grateful for the friendly introduction.

"Bloom tell you anything about your new partner?"

"Only that he doesn't like probationers."

"It's not that bad. As long as you back him up, you two will get along fine."

"Sounds like he ran into some problems in the past," McLean commented, fishing for more information.

"Only one," Marzullo said as he chuckled.

"Okay, I assume there's more I should know," McLean said, ignoring the cold and wanting to know more about the man who appeared to be an enigma.

"It was last month," Marzullo said as he stepped under one of the brick arches and away from the wind. "He was working with a probationer named Lussier when they saw two suspects standing in front of a closed liquor store.

"Something didn't look right so Wallace made a u-turn and pulled up about ten feet behind them. When he got out of the car, Lussier also got out, but planted himself behind the open passenger door. After that, everything went downhill."

"Interesting," McLean said as he shoved both hands under his armpits for warmth.

"Wallace walked up and told the suspects to turn around. Seeing his partner planted next to the car, they jumped him."

"What did Lussier do?"

"Nothing. He just stood watching."

"He didn't jump in?"

"Nope."

Marzullo shifted his feet slightly, and then continued.

"When it was over, Wallace had beaten the shit out of the two suspects, and also Lussier."

"All three of them?"

"Yep. Then he cuffed the three together, locked them to a gate and left."

"What happened next?"

"Wright and I booked the suspects for Battery on a Police Officer, and Lussier was fired the next day. So, McLean, that's your training officer's background. You're his second probationer in less than a month. Good luck."

As Marzullo finished, the side station doors flew open and Wallace walked out.

The night continued cold. The wind blew from the north, whipped through the station archways and into the small, dimly lit parking area where Night Watch units were waiting to be relieved.

McLean followed Wallace over to a black and white. He felt like a puppy following its mother. As they approached, two officers exited the warm car. McLean stood at the passenger door and conducted the five-point safety check as Wallace talked to the two cops.

After slipping the barrel back onto the sliding mechanism and tightening the top nut, he slid the four magnum rounds into the magazine. Then he slammed a round into the chamber. Once in place, he slid the fifth round into the magazine and pushed the safety button to an 'on' position.

Leaning into the front seat, he slid the gun into the shotgun rack that was located across the bottom of the seat. Once secured, he threw the locking mechanism down and snapped it shut.

"Is that your new partner?" Carlson asked as he removed his gear from the trunk.

"Yeah."

"A boot?"

"Yeah."

"Lucky you," Carlson said smiling. "You'd think that you would be the last person in the world they'd give another probationer."

"You'd think so."

"You shared with the kid what happened to your last probationer?"

"No."

"You intend to?" Carlson asked as he turned toward the station doors.

"No."

Wallace threw his riot gear into the trunk and left it open. McLean tossed his into the darkness and shut the lid. Then he and Wallace checked under the back seat. Working together, they pulled it out and checked the floorboard. Confident the car was clean, they replaced the seat and threw their hats into the darkness.

McLean stood next to his door and watched his partner walk around the car and inspect the two red lights he had switched on. Finding them illuminating the parking lot in a brilliant red hue, he walked to the rear of the car to check the two rear circular amber lights to guarantee that they were on and flashing in an alternating sequence. Satisfied, he leaned into the car, reached under the dash, and switched off the reds.

He then slid into the front seat and removed a Marlboro from a fresh pack he kept in his sock. Throwing one into his mouth, he shoved in the dash lighter and waited.

McLean shoved his long wooden baton into the rubber grommet attached to the inside of the door panel, and then slid into the car and jammed his three cell chrome flashlight into the front seat crack. Pulling the tan mimeographed single page Hot Sheet from his notebook, he slid the paper into the metal holder attached to the dash. He flipped on the small light to see if the Hot Sheet was illuminated from the rear. It was.

Smoke billowed from exhausts as the warm air of the engines mixed with the cold night air. Heaters were cranked on and windows rolled up.

When McLean started to roll up his side window, he was stopped abruptly.

"Leave the window down," Wallace ordered. "It's down in the winter and down in the summer. Out here, your ears can be as valuable as your eyes."

So, come rain, shine, sleet or even if it snowed in South Central Los Angeles, the two front windows of 7Adam42 were always down, and would be, as long as Wallace and McLean were partners.

TEN

Within three months, Wallace and McLean's relationship had developed into one based on trust and respect. McLean learned from his aggressive partner that to stay alive, he had to anticipate what his opponent was going to do. He understood that his life depended on his being able to think like a criminal, then react like a cop.

He also took on the appearance of Wallace: the black leather jacket, the low slung Alfonso holster, the black leather gloves and the cocky, self-assured attitude. McLean learned that on the street, appearances were critical, and he knew that he must assume the stature of the street cop he was to become.

He learned never to fill his gun hand with anything other than his service revolver and when using his flashlight, to keep it out and away from his body so as not to provide a target. He watched and listened as Wallace handled radio calls, and put up with little to no bullshit from either the street clientele or cops he didn't trust.

McLean began to develop a sixth sense, which included the feelings and premonitions about danger that only a rare breed of street cops have, a sense that warned him to take action when there was no outward signs that something was amiss. He also learned to play his hunches and do so without questioning why.

"Learn to anticipate and think about the worst that can happen," Wallace told him one night as they sat at Winchell's. "Think about what the bad guy is going to do. Create scenarios around this and play them out in your mind."

Then Wallace stopped. McLean knew that the conversation had ended, but he hoped for more.

"Is that it?" McLean asked, anxious for the lesson to continue.

Wallace hesitated, and then broke into a wry smile.

"No, there's one more thing," he said as he leaned back. "Remember ...when it comes to flying off the handle, don't do as I do, do as I say!"

Wallace chuckled, and then mentally left the car.

As each man sat, lost in his thoughts, McLean remembered an incident that happened just last week, an incident that bore mute testimony that he was developing the ability to act not out of anger, but rather cold defiance.

Wallace hated traffic accident radio calls, a dislike that went so deep that on that rare occasion when a call was assigned, he would immediately pull the black and white onto a dark side-street, park, and then jump from the driver's door screaming, "We're in foot pursuit, McLean. Advise Communications that we're in foot pursuit!"

McLean would then take two or three deep breaths, pant heavily, and while feigning being winded, advise Communications Division that 7Adam42 was in foot pursuit. When the dispatcher requested further information, there would be no response. After the radio call was reassigned, 7Adam42 would clear.

This ruse generally worked, but last week they were forced to accept a traffic accident call on Pico just west of Western. As McLean acknowledged the call, Wallace turned and with a peculiar smile said, "Well, they got us. There's nowhere to run to and not a damned place to hide."

Exasperated, Wallace pulled the black and white behind the two damaged cars that were sitting in the middle of the street.

"I'll talk to the idiots, while you set out a flare pattern."

McLean popped the trunk and pulled out an armful of red flares. After determining that there was no gasoline spill, he methodically went about laying a pattern down the middle of Pico Boulevard that blocked off the center lane. As he snapped the cap off and ignited the second to the last flare, he heard loud music approaching from his rear. Turning, he watched as a drop-top Cadillac with two male occupants swerved from lane to lane down the middle of the street, rolling methodically over each flare.

"Look out, Brad," he screamed as the Cadillac bounced over the closest flare sending it catapulting through the air amid a multicolored fan of phosphorus flame. Seeing McLean, the driver veered in his direction.

Mclean jumped to the side and watched as the car with its two laughing occupants swerved slowly past.

Emotionless, he twisted the cap off his final flare and snapped it across the abrasive top. Red, orange and yellow flame exploded into the night like a Roman candle on the Fourth of July.

His dark blue eyes had never taken themselves off the slowly meandering car. Cocking his head to the side and drawing a bead, he drew his arm back just like he was playing catcher again in the North Hollywood Little League.

He bent his elbow and with a snap of the wrist, threw the flaming projectile. With uncanny precision the flare twirled through the night air, hit the rear of the front seat and toppled softly onto the back seat. Within seconds, smoke began to billow from the rear. A thin spiral at first, then a large billowing cloud that was marked by orange and red flames.

Suddenly, the passenger jumped up from his seat, tore off his black leather jacket and made a futile attempt to extinguish the growing fire. It didn't help. As the flames increased, he decided to sprinkle the contents of his quart sized bottle of beer on the inferno. As pockets of flames shot skyward, Wallace and McLean watched the "pimp-mobile" jump the curb, fly across the sidewalk and crash into a bus bench.

"Nice throw," Wallace said as he reached into the car, grabbed the mike and requested a tow truck.

McLean nodded and acknowledged the compliment with a simple, "Thanks."

McLean also learned that for all his toughness, Brad Wallace had a chivalrous side that few saw.

It was just after two in the morning, mid-week and the streets were deserted. Wallace had decided to set-up in the darkness to watch the businesses on Wilshire Boulevard that had been recently plagued by burglars, who would toss fifty-gallon drums through the plate glass windows and then snatch and grab the merchandise. After an hour, he grew restless and was about to drive off when the radio crackled.

"7 Adam 42, see the woman, possible kidnapping in progress at the northeast corner of Wilshire and Crenshaw. Female victim is pinned in a telephone booth by the suspect's vehicle and is on the phone to Control. 7 Adam 42, handle the call Code Two."

In less than five minutes Wallace had pulled into the service station and located the telephone booth. The suspect's vehicle had vanished, leaving behind a hysterical young lady holding the telephone receiver.

Before McLean could open the door, Wallace was assisting the young woman from the booth. Sitting her in the back seat, the story unfolded.

"I was at an office party and my date got very drunk. I couldn't find a ride home so I walked over to the telephone booth and tried to call my parents. While I was on the phone a car pulled up and pushed the front-end against the door and pinned me in. Then two black men got out. That's when I called the police and you arrived."

"Do you want us to call you a cab," Wallace asked as he looked into the tear filled eyes of the beautiful young woman.

"I would like that, but I don't have enough money for the fare."

Wallace reached for his wallet and pulled out some money. "Here," he said, "use this."

"But I ..."

"Consider it a loan."

"My name is Mary Angel, Officer. . ." she stopped to look at his name tag..."Wallace. And I promise that you will get your money back."

In minutes a taxi had arrived. Wallace walked over to the driver's side of the cab, placed both hands on the open window ledge and leaned in.

"The young lady wants to go to the west-side," Wallace said, his tone soft, yet authoritative. "I gave her some money, but it might not be enough for the whole fare. I want you to take her home where she'll get you the rest. Do you understand?"

"Si Señor, but..."

"What's your name, and cab number?"

"Juan Alvarez. 3019."

"Well, Juan, I'm Officer Wallace, Wilshire Division, and I'm holding you personally responsible for this young lady's safety. If she doesn't arrive at her destination in a timely manner, I'll come looking for you. And you don't want that to happen, do you?" Wallace had lowered his voice to just above a whisper. His tone had changed. It was now hard, cold and threatening.

"No Señor."

"Good. If there is any problem with the payment of the fare, I'll make it good. Any questions?"

Alvarez was silent.

Wallace then walked to the passenger side of the car and looked down at the beauty, who was dabbing at her eyes with a small folded Kleenex.

He leaned forward. His expression was soft and his words kind. "The driver knows exactly what to do, Miss Angel. He'll see to it that you get home safely. I told him that once home, you would make good on any additional fare not covered by the money you have."

"Thank you so very much, Officer Wallace."

"My pleasure."

Wallace tapped the roof of the cab with his hand. In seconds only taillights could be seen driving westbound down Wilshire Boulevard.

"Think you'll ever see the money?" McLean asked.

"Yeah. I have a feeling that I will," Wallace answered as he slid his hefty frame back into the front seat.

A week later Wallace and McLean walked into roll call to a throng of whistles and cat calls.

"Hey Bradley dear," called out Marzullo from across the room. "Bloom has something for you from a secret admirer. And boy does it smell of perfume."

Wallace looked to the front podium where a grinning Bloom was waving an envelope through the air while sniffing at it and rolling his bulbous eyes.

"You want me to open it, Bradley dear?" he asked.

"I think that I can handle it," Wallace said as he walked to the podium and snatched the small envelope from Bloom's grasp.

"Read it out loud," yelled Wright. *"I'm sure we'd all be interested."*
"Go to hell," Wallace responded.

Wallace sat down and opened the envelope. It contained a handwritten note and a ten dollar bill. It was signed, Mary Angel.

ELEVEN

In McLean's fourth month in Wilshire Division, something new was added to the police arsenal: tear gas.

Two nights after being issued their individual canisters, the Morning Watch walked from the station steps and into the parking lot, where they were met by the most horrendous howling that came from inside the jail.

"Hey, McLean," Marzullo shouted. "Come here, I need your help."

McLean turned and saw Marzullo standing adjacent to the side of the station, ten feet below a small jail window.

"Give me a lift," Marzullo said as he snapped the cap off his canister.

McLean bent down and after Marzullo was standing firm on his shoulders, he lifted him up so he had access to the window. Then there was the distinct sound of aerosol spray. In no time, the howling stopped.

"Let me down," Marzullo said. "That should take care of that asshole."

Not two minutes passed when suddenly the station doors were thrown open and cops coughing and gagging flooded the parking lot. The first to bolt out were the jail personnel followed by Lieutenant Watson, then Ridgley, Bloom and the desk crew.

"We're under attack," yelled Ridgley as tears streamed down his cheeks.

"The station has been hit by a tear gas attack," yelled one of the jailers.

"Set up a command post, then call the Chief," shouted Watson.

McLean and Marzullo stood next to a black and white and silently watched.

"Somehow they got it into the damn air conditioning," bellowed Bloom between coughs.

"It musta been black militants," coughed another jailer.

As the station emptied, the Morning Watch stood silently and watched. Then the laughter began, beginning with Marzullo. Realizing that it was best to leave, each unit wasted no time in driving from the station and clearing in hopes of snagging a radio call.

"That went well," Wallace said as he sucked on a Marlboro. "Until you get caught."

"Who'd snitch us off?"

"Simpson."

McLean fidgeted, and before he could start the nightly log, the radio came to life.

"7Adam42, return to the station."

"Like I said, until you get caught."

Wallace swung the car in the direction of the station. After parking, he pulled a Marlboro from the pack hidden in his sock and slipped the cigarette into his mouth. Then he shot McLean a confident look.

"Don't cop out to anything," he said as he drew hard on the cigarette and then blew the smoke through the open window. "If Simpson snitched you off, it's your word against his."

"What about the rest of the guys?"

"They're on your side."

McLean walked through the station doors and saw Marzullo sitting in a hard wooden chair just outside the Watch Commander's office.

"You're first, Mac," Marzullo said grinning.

As McLean opened the door, his gaze was met by the stern countenance of a very unhappy lieutenant.

"Sit down, McLean and close the door."

McLean glanced around the office. In the middle sat an old wooden desk. His seat was one of the hard, straight-backed wooden chairs, vintage 1925.

McLean sat down in the chair that faced Watson. The silence was deafening. Not a word, nothing.

"I could hear my heart beat," he later told Marzullo.

"McLean, somebody sprayed tear gas through an outside jail window and into a cell in a feeble attempt to silence one of our boisterous drunks. But the drunk passed out before the gas could have any effect on him."

McLean's stomach muscles tightened and his heartbeat increased.

"And unfortunately, the fumes ended up entering the air conditioning ducts and the gas permeated the station. I was told that you might have an idea who did it?"

McLean hiked his shoulders, cocked his head, raised his eyebrows and threw his arms out in a what-gives gesture.

"Lieutenant, I'd love to help, but I didn't *see* anyone spray tear gas into the jail."

"Are you sure?"

"Yes, sir, positive."

Watson's tone became more threatening.

"Don't bullshit me, McLean. I know you were involved and when I prove it, it'll get you a twenty-one day suspension."

McLean knew that Watson was fishing.

"Lieutenant, I'm sorry that I can't be of greater assistance, but again, I didn't spray any tear gas into the station, nor did I *see* it being sprayed."

Watson leaned forward, and looked over the top of his glasses. "McLean, your reputation in the division is that of a tough street cop and I don't want to see you corrupted by the antics of some rowdies."

McLean sat quietly and listened. His shoulders were tipped slightly to the right, his head cocked and his open hands placed lightly on each knee. As he sat in the hard chair with a tight knot in his stomach, he remembered Wallace's parting words: *"Don't cop out to anything."*

"Like I said before, Lieutenant, I didn't spray tear gas into the jail, nor did I *see* it sprayed."

McLean sat waiting, staring into the cold eyes of his interrogator.

"Go back to work, McLean, but just remember that I'll do my best to get you those twenty-one days if I find out you were involved."

"Yes, sir."

McLean stood, opened the door and walked out. As he passed Marzullo, he smiled and gave him a wink.

"Marzullo, you're next," commanded the gruff voice from within the office.

Marzullo walked in and sat down. A few moments of silence passed, and then Watson spoke.

"John, McLean copped out on you. He spilled his guts and I'm recommending that he get a twenty-one day suspension. You come clean and your time will be less. You've got a career to think about, as well as a family and future promotions."

"Come clean about what?" asked Marzullo innocently.

"Don't play games with me John! One of you two cowboys sprayed a full can of tear gas into the station, and I want to know who it was!"

Marzullo settled back in his chair, a deep look of concern on his face.

"Gee, Lieutenant, I'd love to help you out, but I just can't. And about McLean copping out on me. Well, he'd have to be lying if he said he *saw* me do anything that stupid."

Watson pushed himself away from the desk and stood. His face again erupted in crimson, as his open hand smashed itself onto the top of the desk.

A little out of character, Marzullo thought.

"Marzullo, it's my responsibility to find out who did this, and I aim to do just that. So if you and McLean were involved, I'll see to it that you *both* get twenty-one day's without pay."

"Yes, sir," Marzullo said calmly.

"Go back to work," Watson said as he lowered himself back into his chair and snatched at the mound of paperwork that sat in his In-Box.

As Marzullo walked into the parking lot, he smiled at McLean and gave him a thumbs up.

John Marzullo knew that in time, he and McLean would be identified as the perpetrators of the great tear gas fiasco and the incident would then pass into the world of cop folklore, and he liked the thought.

TWELVE

It started as a quiet week night, but that didn't last long. As Wallace and McLean were driving down Pico, the radio crackled with an "officer needs help" call. It seemed that 7Adam99 had stumbled onto a gas station robbery at Venice and San Vicente. After a few shots were fired at the police, three suspects bolted up San Vicente and into the darkness.

In minutes, two of the three gunmen were in custody. The third had disappeared. When 7Adam42 rolled up, McLean saw that Sergeant Adolph Heindricks was standing at the rear of a black and white with one suspect.

"You'll enjoy this," Wallace said as he stepped from the car. "I'm not even this talented."

McLean walked to the rear of the parked police car and watched as Heindricks, in his thick German accent, asked the suspect where his partner was hiding.

"I ain't gots no partner," shouted the man defiantly.

"Are you sure about that?"

"I is sure. What you be roustin' me for. I ain't done nothin'."

"Very vell," Heindricks said as he removed a small pen knife from his trouser pocket and opened the blade. "I vill ask you vone more time. Ver is your partner?"

"What is you, stupid? I tolds you, I ain't gots no partner. I was walkin' down the street and the po-lice jumped me and started to beat on me."

Heindricks stepped closer to the handcuffed man, slipped his left arm between the suspect's right arm and his torso, and extended the man's right hand to the side. Without a word, he slipped the knife blade under the nail of the thumb and pushed. A piercing scream shattered the early morning.

"Now, I vill ask you again. Ver is your partner?"

"I ain't gots no partner," the man shouted belligerently, "and you can't be treating me like this."

"Very vell," Heindricks said, his face reddening as he shoved the blade firmly under the index finger.

"Ahhh..." the man screeched. "You can't do this, it's against the law."

"If you haven't noticed," Heindricks whispered into the man's ear, "I am the law."

"But I ain't got..." the words were interrupted by another shrill scream as the small blade pierced the flesh beneath the nail of the middle finger.

"And vhere is his place of abode?"

"He don't live in no adobe, man, he do live in an apartment!"

"An vere vould that apartment be located?"

"On the corner."

"Vhat is the apartment number?"

"I don't..."

Heindricks moved the small blade to the fourth finger and began to place it under the nail.

"Two-C."

"And the veapon?"

"Say what?" the terrified bandit asked.

"The gun," Heindricks said patiently. "Veapon is another vord for gun."

"He has it with him in the pad."

Heindricks directed three units to the apartment building on the corner. In five minutes, they had the suspect...and the gun.

Sitting in the car, Wallace slipped the key into the ignition.

"Well, whaddya think?" he asked.

"That was intense," McLean answered as he threw his back into the corner between the seat and the door. "Right out of the Third Reich handbook on interrogation."

"Was it ethical?" Wallace asked.

"No."

"Was it legal?"

"No."

"Was it successful?"

"Yes."

"Then the means justify the end," Wallace coolly remarked as he started the car and drove away.

McLean sat silently and stared out the window. The world of music he'd known prior to the Department was quickly becoming a memory, replaced by the brutal reality of life on the street.

McLean suited up and walked into roll call. Silently, he sat on the back row, waiting for the black coffee to kick in.

"Simpson and McLean, 7Adam56," Ridgley announced.

McLean glanced across the room. Simpson sat stiffly directly behind his books, daydreaming.

Ridgley glanced at the row where Simpson was the only occupant. Checking him off, he moved on.

"McLean here," he said, a tone of resentment in his voice. "It looks like I'm working a one-man car."

"That's more truth than fiction," Marzullo called out.

Simpson sat stone-faced, lost to the discussion that was taking place around him.

"McLean's become as arrogant as Wallace," Dumas whispered to Oakes.

"Wallace and Hardin, 7Adam42."

McLean shot a look at Wallace. Wallace smiled and lifted an eyebrow and shrugged. When roll call ended, Wallace brushed up alongside McLean.

"Watch your back," he said softly.

"I plan on it," McLean said as he descended the worn wooden steps leading to the rear hallway.

Since Simpson was the senior man, he drove. Once in the car it was apparent he hadn't heard McLean's roll call comment for he immediately began to talk.

"I'm not one of the elephant hunters on this watch," he said as he threw a cigarette into his mouth and pushed in the dash lighter.

"I go after Deuces. My parents were both killed by drunk drivers, so that's what I do. I book all those assholes I can find."

"So you don't like to stop cars or shake people down on the street?"

"That's right. If we aren't booking a drunk driver, then we're writing tickets. That keeps Ridgley off my back, gives me some court time, pads the old bank account and gives me time to study for the Sergeant's exam."

Just then, a black Thunderbird blew a red light.

"He's mine!" Simpson yelled, elation jacketing his words.

On went the reds, and over pulled the T-Bird.

As Simpson approached from the driver's side, McLean walked to a position just behind the passenger window, and out of sight of the driver. Standing in the blind-spot, he removed his .38 and placed it behind his right thigh.

"Good evening, sir," Simpson said politely. "In a hurry to get somewhere?"

"Not really," came the cold response.

"Well, sir, I'm stopping you because you failed to stop for the red light before making your right hand turn. May I see your driver's license and registration?"

"This is nothin' but a roust," exclaimed the man. "You're only stopping me because I'm black."

Simpson continued to smile as he leaned closer toward the window.

"I'm sorry that you feel that way, sir, but again I must ask to see your driver's license and registration."

McLean slid his gun next to the doorjamb and rested the dark six-inch barrel on the open window ledge with the muzzle pointed directly at the side of the driver's head.

"The mayor is a friend of mine," the man bellowed, "and he's going to hear about this."

"I commend you on your choice of friends," McLean said barely above a whisper. "Maybe he'll pay your ticket."

Simpson shot McLean a look of disgust. "Really, sir, I must see your license and registration."

"They're in the glove box."

"I'd like you to get them for me."

McLean stiffened and the soft flesh of his right index finger softly fell on the trigger. Experience had taught him to play his hunches. So he did.

Suddenly, the man dove across the seat for the glove compartment.

The hairs on McLean's neck stood on end. Something was wrong. Just as the driver reached for the compartment button, McLean shinned his flashlight onto the glove box and jammed his revolver into the right side of the man's head.

Then he cocked the hammer.

"Don't open the glove box," he said. The man's fingers stiffened and the hand stopped inches away from the unlocking mechanism. He hesitated.

"Move that hand and I'll kill your black ass," McLean said calmly.

With the cold steel of the revolver sticking into his ear, the driver dropped his arm.

"Now ease back into the driver's seat and grab the steering wheel with both hands," commanded McLean.

"What the hell are you doing?" Simpson shouted. "It's only a ticket!"

McLean ignored the question and the additional outburst. He shoved his flashlight into his left armpit, reached across with his left hand and popped open the lock. As the door flew open, a small chrome revolver slipped out and landed on the open lid. McLean grabbed the gun and snapped open the cylinder.

It was fully loaded. Simpson stood silently puffing heavily on a cigarette. His face had lost all color.

The drive to the station was without conversation.

After McLean booked the suspect, he and Simpson were approached by Sol Bloom.

"That was a great piece of police work," Bloom told Simpson. "Fine way to teach one of our younger officers the nuances of the street."

McLean sat at the squad table and completed the arrest report. He remained silent, only casting Simpson an occasional hard look.

"I knew that the guy was dirty when we stopped him," Simpson said. "Just a gut feeling. You know Sarge, just something that comes after years working the streets."

"Mighty fine job," Bloom said again as he walked out the door.

"You're an asshole, Simpson," McLean said as he stood, grabbed up his paperwork and walked toward the Watch Commander's office.

"And you're too salty for your own good," Simpson responded, dragging hard and puffing heavily on his smoke.

In less than two hours, 7Adam56 was back on the street. This time, there was no conversation.

As the black and white slipped silently through the dark night, the radio crackled. "7Adam56, unknown trouble, Corner of Lucerne and Ninth Street."

McLean acknowledged the call. Simpson stared straight ahead and drove.

A mass of humanity met the police car as it pulled onto Lucerne. Slowly, Simpson pulled the car to the edge of the large, raucous group and parked next to the curb. It only took seconds before the car was surrounded by drunk partygoers.

"You had to drive right up to them?" McLean asked.

"Get screwed," said Simpson.

"You're one stupid son-of-a-bitch," McLean said as he pushed open the car door, threw the radio mike out the window and began to talk to some of the revelers. He estimated the size of the group at about three-hundred, and growing.

Surrounded, McLean talked fast and tried to diffuse the situation, but the hostility of the crowd increased and it became apparent that they needed some backup. Looking around and not seeing Simpson, he opened the car door and stepped up onto the door frame. Again he looked for his partner. Simpson had vanished. Then the crowd began to chant, "Off the pigs."

"7Adam56, officers need help, Lucerne and Ninth Street," McLean shouted into the mike, trying to be heard above the rhythmic chanting of the crowd.

In moments, sirens could be heard cutting through the night.

McLean again looked for his partner. He was still nowhere to be seen.

As the responding units approached and the crowd began to disperse, McLean's eyes were drawn to a cigarette ember that flashed behind a distant telephone pole. He had an idea who it was.

As the mob thinned, the solitary figure stepped out from behind the pole and began to walk back to McLean. It was Simpson.

McLean watched as his partner slowly walked, taking heavy hits off his cigarette. Returning to the driver's side of the car, he glanced at the dispersing crowd, then at the approaching sergeant's car.

"You chicken-shit son-of-a-bitch," Mclean muttered across the roof of the car.

Simpson shrugged his shoulders, adjusted his Sam Browne and put one foot on the bottom of the door ledge.

Ridgley pulled up and got out.

Walking over to Simpson, he extended his hand.

"I talked to Bloom earlier and he told me about the robbery arrest. Now you're handling of this sensitive situation. I'll be writing you a commendation on both."

Ridgley started to leave then stopped.

"Let's hope that McLean learns from you some of the finer points of police work that it appears Wallace has missed."

Simpson stood grinning.

"You couldn't make a pimple on Wallace's ass," McLean said after Ridgley had driven away.

Simpson threw McLean a shit-eating grin, cocked his head ever so slightly, raised one eyebrow and climbed into the driver's seat. Neither spoke the remainder of the watch.

The following day, McLean shared with Wallace the events of the past evening. Wallace, infuriated, went straight in to talk to Watson. It must have done some good; for never again was McLean partnered with the man the watch nicknamed "Chicken-Shit" Simpson.

THIRTEEN

Wallace was famous for his ability to throw a bar-arm-chokehold on a suspect and have him unconsciousness before his ass hit the ground. He had perfected this over the years, and it was something he wanted to have McLean refine.

So each night, Wallace would instigate a fight and just before the guy threw his first punch, Wallace would take one step back. This was McLean's cue.

Standing next to the suspect's right elbow, McLean's left hand would snap the intended victim's right arm forward, turning the suspect. Then he would slip behind the man, slam his right forearm across the throat, snap his left arm across the shoulder and curl it behind the head forming a modified half-nelson. This took less than two seconds.

McLean then would drop straight to his knees while snapping the suspects head forward, cutting off all air traveling through the esophagus. In less than three seconds, the victim was incapacitated and unconscious.

This hold was practiced nightly until McLean was able to match Wallace's quickness and effectiveness.

It took less than a year for McLean to become a hardened cynic. A transformation that he hadn't consciously cultivated, but one that occurred naturally, given the nightly clientele and his training officer.

So as McLean learned, he was becoming.

One summer night, however, he experienced some reassurance that the bad guys didn't always win.

For the past six months, two black, residential bandits had brutally victimized the senior citizens living in the area of 3rd

Street and Doheny Drive. The area was predominately white, Jewish, and wealthy.

The night was hot, and the radio was quiet. That is until 7Adam42 received its first radio call.

"7Adam42, see the woman, shots fired, man down. 7Adam42, handle the call, Code Two. Be advised that the reporting party is at 8704 West Third Street and an ambulance is on the way."

"I know Wallace, you hate handling calls out of your area," McLean said after he rogered the call.

"So now you're a mind reader," Wallace said as he turned off Western and onto Beverly.

"Sure, why not? If Carson can pull it off, so can I. Now let me see," he said as he tore a piece of paper from his notebook, folded it in half and raised it to the right side of his head emulating Johnny Carson's 'Carnac the Magnificent'.

"The answer is? ...I see it; it's coming ...who'd the old lady shoot?"

"What old lady?" Wallace asked. "No one said anything about any old lady."

"I did, well, the spirits did. Anyway, I saw an old lady, a smoking gun. A warm summer night and noise."

"All right Carnac, knock off the bullshit and log the call," Wallace said, a grin on his face.

"But 'McLean the Magnificent' has more for the doubting Officer Wallace," he said as he again put the paper to his head, closed his eyes and feigned deep concentration.

Suddenly, McLean broke into hearty laughter.

"Had you going, huh?"

"You're crazy, McLean."

"I'm in good company."

Wallace shot McLean a quick look and then shook his head.

As they entered the darkened residential neighborhood located just south of Beverly Boulevard, they watched as an old ambulance unit and a single black and white preceded them by two blocks and pulled up to the south curb.

Wallace parked behind both units.

Being one of the older and more affluent areas in the division, it was encompassed by large single story homes that sat majestically on oversized lots, while enormous trees lined both sides of the street.

As Wallace and McLean stepped from their car, they could see a male Negro lying face up on the sidewalk. A pool of blood had formed around his head, and when McLean stepped forward, he saw two bullet holes in the man's face, one just below the right eye and another in his forehead.

The deceased was dressed in a long tan raincoat and held in his right hand a small, sawed-off, single-shot .22 caliber rifle. He died with his trigger finger still twitching in the awful reflexes of muscles commanded by a mind now gone. On the ground next to his head was a small stingy brim hat.

"I'll call for the dicks," Wallace said as he turned to walk back to the black and white. "Why don't you interview the old lady and find out what happened."

Wallace stopped short, and then turned.

"How did you know it was an old lady with a gun?"

McLean grinned. "It's the area. All old, wealthy Jews. The gun, we were told that when given the call."

"You never cease to amaze me, McLean."

McLean had been so intent on examining the dead body that he had failed to see an older woman standing in the shadows speaking to one of the other patrol officers.

She appeared to be about sixty-five, was wearing an old house coat, and was trembling. Seated at her side was a very large, agitated dog, restrained by a leather leash. As McLean approached the woman, the uniform officer showed him a small, blue steel six shot .38 revolver. McLean glanced at the open cylinder and saw three dented primers.

"I'm impressed," McLean said.

"So is the asshole on the sidewalk," the cop said as he turned and walked back to his black and white.

McLean unloaded the gun, closed the cylinder, shoved it into his waistband and asked the distraught woman to have a seat in their car. After securing the dog's leash to the door,

Wallace took a seat in the front and listened carefully as McLean patiently asked the woman to describe what happened. Shaking, she began.

"I live alone in my home that is just down the block. I've lived here for over forty years and watched as each year the neighborhood gets worse and worse."

"So why don't you move?"

"Because I don't have anywhere else to go. My husband died ten years ago and my children are all on the East coast, and I don't like the snow. I'm comfortable here, that is, I *was* comfortable until about three weeks ago."

"What happened three weeks ago?"

"Well, every night for years I've taken my dog for a walk before I go to bed. Three weeks ago, I did the same thing and returned home. I wasn't in the house ten minutes when there was a knock at the front door. Without thinking, I opened the door and standing on the porch were two Colored men. One was wearing a long tan raincoat and had a funny looking hat on his head. I thought the raincoat was odd since it was summer, but as I started to say something, he pulled a small rifle from under his coat and then he and his friend forced me back into my house."

"Where was the dog?" Wallace asked from the front seat.

"He was in the bedroom, and although he was very upset at the sight of those two hooligans, he didn't do anything since they were inside."

"What happened next?" McLean asked.

"Well, they tied me up and robbed me. They took my money, all my jewelry and every piece of sterling silver. Everything sentimental. Then they left."

"How did you get free?" McLean asked.

"Fortunately, I was able to untie myself and then I called the police. I made a report, and nothing happened again until tonight."

"Exactly what happened tonight?" Wallace asked as he turned his body and leaned over the seat.

"Well, like I said, I was in the habit of taking my dog for a walk every night and I wasn't about to let two hoodlums stop me from doing that. So each night after the robbery, when I went out with the dog, I put a small gun in my house coat. That's the gun you have. I've owned it for years. It belonged to my late husband.

"Well, tonight I put on my housecoat and put the gun in the right front pocket. I wasn't going to walk far, just let Ollie out for a couple of minutes. I put him on his leash and off we went. We weren't out ten minutes when I looked down the sidewalk and there, coming in my direction, were the same two hoodlums who had robbed me. And they were wearing the exact same clothing, including the tan raincoat and stupid little hat. I couldn't believe that anyone would be that dumb."

"It appears that they were," said McLean.

"What happened next?" Wallace asked.

"Well, I didn't really have time to do anything. They walked up to me very fast and the man in the raincoat didn't say a word. He just started to bring out that damned little rifle from under the coat, just like he did on my porch. But this time it was different."

"How so?" McLean asked.

"Ollie remembered him. So as he started to raise the rifle, Ollie lunged. And as he lunged, I already had my hand on my gun and was bringing it out of my pocket. Then everything went very fast. When Ollie lunged, it knocked me off my feet. I was in the air when the hoodlum with the rifle pulled the trigger. I heard a shot as I started to pull the trigger on my gun. I didn't aim at anything. I just pulled the trigger. I shot three times while I was in the air and before I hit the ground."

Wallace shot Mclean a look. Behind his eyes was a grin.

"When I landed, the sidewalk knocked the wind out of me. I didn't really know what happened to the two men, but as soon as I regained my breath, I lifted my head and looked around. The man with the gun was on the ground, he wasn't moving. The other man was running down the street. Ollie was barking and I still had hold of his leash in my left hand and the gun was still gripped tightly in my right. That's when the neighbors ran out and they called you."

Wallace and McLean exchanged glances as the ambulance driver walked past.

"How many hits did he take?" Wallace asked.

"Two. Both head shots."

"That renews my faith in the common man," Wallace said.

Wallace and McLean were later told that the little old lady was cleared of any criminal actions, given back her gun and the Los Angeles City Council presented her with a citation.

❦

The summer months were eventful. The McLean family added a second daughter to their growing family and moved into a small two bedroom home in North Hollywood. On the job, McLean had handled riots, anti-war demonstrations, anarchy attributed to black militants, and hippie love-ins. In less than eighteen months, he'd been transformed from a raw police recruit to a street hardened veteran, a transformation that normally required five years. Under Wallace's tutelage, he learned to fight hard and drink daily.

While life continued to improve for McLean, it only worsened for Wallace. Two weeks earlier, he had run into problems with four Deputy Sheriffs who responded to his Agoura home after his wife called complaining of spousal abuse. Upon their arrival, the deputies asked if they could come in. A very drunk Wallace told them to go to hell and attempted to slam the door. The deputies forced their way in and the fight was on. When it was over, Wallace had kicked the hell out of the first four, and it took three more to finally subdue the drunken giant. In handcuffs, he was transported to a sub-station where he was stripped, thrown into a padded cell and beaten. The Deputy Sheriff's would later call it 'an attitude adjustment.'

When Deputy Chief John Cleary was called, he sent a team from Internal Affairs to the jail where a still drunk Wallace was immediately suspended pending a Board of Rights inquiry. So for the past two weeks, McLean had been assigned to work with Scott Knapp, a new officer on the watch.

It was mid-week, darkness hadn't brought any relief from the blistering heat, and the streets were strangely quiet. 7Adam42 was driven by Knapp, while McLean rode shotgun. McLean and Knapp were as different as night from day. Where McLean was abrupt and no-nonsense, Knapp was friendly and more geared to public relations.

At two A.M. the radio awoke.

"7Adam42, family dispute, 1804 South Bronson."

In disgust, McLean acknowledged the call.

"I know, you don't like family dispute calls, or any radio calls for that matter," Knapp said as he made a left onto Pico Boulevard, "but just remember, it says on the side of the car that we are here not only to 'Protect', but also to 'Serve.'"

"That's where we differ, Knapp. You want to solve the unsolvable. I'm not out here to stroke the assholes. I'm here to put bad guys in jail, and I don't give a shit if the natives kill each other, or not. If they do, it saves court costs. If they don't, they're mine."

"You're cold, McLean," Knapp said as he pulled to the front of a small single family residence that was built at the turn of the century. "Looks like I'm doin' the talking."

"Looks that way," McLean said as he opened the car door and started up the narrow concrete path.

From the sidewalk, they could hear violent screams coupled with profanities and the breaking of glass.

McLean threw Knapp a look as he stopped on the pathway that led to the front porch.

"You ever performed a marriage?" McLean asked smiling.

"Have I ever performed a what?" Knapp asked incredulously.

"A marriage. You know, 'Do you Leroy take Beulah,' etc."

"You're crazy, McLean."

"Okay, I'm crazy, but if they don't want to get married and just want to fight, I'll conduct one of my famous silent drawer opening searches. That always quiets them down."

"Now what the hell is a silent drawer opening..." his words were cut off by more glass breaking and furniture being thrown against the walls.

"You're on, partner," McLean said as he stepped onto the porch, took a position to the side and knocked on the door.

"Who's there?" a shrill female voice screamed.

"Po-lice," yelled Knapp as he turned the knob and threw open the door.

"We ain't called no po-lice," shouted a black woman with fire in her eyes and a beer bottle in her right hand.

"Who called you?" barked a large black man, who had a large welt forming on his forehead.

"A concerned citizen," Knapp said as he moved deeper into the house.

"We ain't got no concerned citizens livin' here," the woman yelled. "And besides, you ain't got no right commin' in here."

"Only want to help," McLean said somberly. "You two married or just playin' house?" he asked.

"Why?" the woman snapped.

"Just asking."

"We ain't like legal married," answered the woman as her focus shifted from her companion to McLean. "But we do be livin' as husband and wife."

"Would you like to get legal married?" asked McLean, now grinning at a confused Knapp.

The shouting and fighting had stopped. The beer bottle had been tossed onto a three legged sofa. With a dead pan serious look on her face, the woman answered. "Of course, don't everyone. But we ain't got the money for no paper and a preacher."

"Well, this is your lucky day, Ma'am," McLean said. "For I can provide you both the paper and the preacher."

"You? How can you do that?" asked the woman, a spark of interest in her voice.

"Why it's quite simple" McLean said as he removed the top card from his pack of Officer's Field Interview Cards.

"You see my badge? It says Policeman, City of Los Angeles. See the City Hall in the middle of the badge?"

"Yeah," they both answered.

"That's the city seal, and since I'm an honest-to- goodness city official, I can conduct marriages and grant divorces."

"Is that right, ossifer?" asked the man as he rubbed the welt softly and leaned in closer to get a better look at McLean's badge.

McLean glanced at Knapp, who was shaking his head.

"Let's go McLean," Knapp said as he walked to the front door.

"Now wait a minute partner," McLean responded. "I believe that this wonderful couple can use our services."

"That's right officer," answered the woman. "We wants to get married."

McLean smiled at Knapp and turned his attention back to the couple.

"Now my partner, here, since he has the same authority, he can act as the witness. So I need your names."

"He's James and I'm Henrietta."

So, James and Henrietta would you like to become husband and wife?"

The faces of the once battling couple shone brightly.

"We'd like that," Henrietta said, her white teeth sparkling brilliantly.

"Wonderful," McLean said. "Now each of you place your left hand on my badge and lift your right hand in the air. Good, now repeat after me. I, give your own name..."

"James," said the man nervously as he swayed from side-to-side.

"Henrietta," said the woman still smiling.

"Do take, say the other persons name, as my husband or wife. James you say wife, Henrietta you say husband."

"Wife."

"Husband."

"Excellent. By the authority invested in me as an official for the wonderful City of Los Angeles, I pronounce you man and wife. James, you may kiss the bride."

James hesitated. "Give me a damned kiss," Henrietta said as she jerked her man closer. James gave his new bride a peck on the cheek.

"Is we really married?" Henrietta asked, beaming.

"More so now than before," McLean answered.

McLean then turned the Field Interview Card over, filled in the newlyweds names, and signed it Officers Dwight David Eisenhower and Richard Millhouse Nixon.

Without another word, he gave James the 'license,' winked at his astonished partner, and with a mischievous sparkle in his blue eyes, walked out the door.

"You can't do that," an angry Knapp snapped as they opened the car doors.

"Can't do what?" McLean asked, a tone of astonishment in his voice. "You said that you wanted me to be more receptive to the feelings of the citizen's, so I took your request to heart."

"You're cold, McLean," Knapp growled as the two got back into the car. "Just plain cold."

As Knapp cranked over the black and white and threw it into gear, a strained silence settled on the interior.

Slowly, 7Adam42 drove eastbound on Pico Boulevard. When Knapp came to 4th Avenue, he made a sharp right hand turn, then a quick left into the alley that paralleled Pico. As he turned into the dark alley he shut off the engine and leaned his head out the open window. It was silent as a tomb.

The black and white crept noiselessly down the alley, its tires moving gently from pothole to pothole. Halfway through the darkness, they came to the rear of an old service station which sat on the left.

Not a word had been spoken by either man since leaving the marriage ceremony. Knapp was still angry, and McLean, still wearing a shit-eating-grin, could care less.

For some unknown reason, Knapp stopped the car just behind the rear of the two arched service bays. Looking through the darkness and into the station, both men saw the small manager's office that was located on the middle island and sat halfway between the street and the alley.

Staring at the office, they saw a tall male standing in the doorway.

"Do you see what I see?" Knapp whispered.

"Yeah, the dude has a gun."

Then they saw the attendant standing just inside the door. Looking into the peripheral darkness, they spotted the lookout who, not seeing the black and white, stepped out of the darkness holding a gun in his hand.

"Unlock the shotgun," McLean whispered.

"Put out a help call," Knapp whispered back, his voice barely audible.

A bolt of adrenaline surged through McLean's body.

Shaking slightly, he slipped the mike from the holder and activated the key.

"7Adam42," he whispered, "we have a 211 in progress, Fourth Avenue and Pico. Requesting assistance at that location."

He completed the transmission, snapped off the radio and slipped the shotgun from the rack. His mouth was suddenly dry, while his eyes remained focused on the lookout.

Knapp switched off the dome light as each slowly pushed softly down on the door handles releasing the locking mechanisms. Both men then inched the doors open and stepped softly into a darkness that had fortunately completely engulfed the black and white. Knapp went to the left toward the office, while McLean went to the right to confront the lookout. Slowly, both men crept forward.

McLean, gripping the shotgun in both hands, moved closer to the unsuspecting lookout.

As they approached their intended targets, the bandit standing in the office doorway struck the gas station attendant a vicious blow that sent him reeling back into the small office. With the attendant huddled in a corner, the bandit proceeded to beat him brutally using the gun as a club. The sound of the gun striking the helpless man was similar to the sound made when a person slaps a ripe watermelon with a cupped hand.

As Knapp moved toward the open office door, McLean stepped closer toward the lookout. When he was twenty-five feet away, he slammed the wooden slide of the Ithaca .12 gauge back and then threw it forward, sending a magnum round into the chamber. The sound was electrifying. The lookout froze, then, like a cat on a hot tin roof, he spun with gun in hand. As McLean stepped forward and into the man's line of sight, the bandit bolted to his left and ran toward the intersection of 4th Avenue and Pico. As he darted across the darkened station lot, so did McLean.

"*Freeze,*" McLean shouted.

The bandit kept running.

With adrenaline flowing, and his knees jarred with each bounding step, McLean jerked the trigger.

"*Boom!*"

The shotgun barrel jumped violently skyward while flame belched from its barrel sending nine deadly pellets into the night.

A miss!

McLean's pellets perforated three gasoline pumps sending their volatile contents streaming across the asphalt.

Still running, he jerked the trigger and fired again.

"*Boom!*"

Another miss!

The pellets flew past the station pumps and blew out store windows and shattered the windshield of a car parked across Pico.

His right hand slammed the receiver back, then forward, ramming his third round into the heated chamber.

Still running, he fired.

"*Boom!*"

Another miss!

The lookout was nearing the far sidewalk when a sudden calmness engulfed McLean. Abruptly, he stopped at the edge of the driveway, chambered his last round and aimed at the small of the fleeing bandit's back. He and his prey were only thirty feet apart. Three more strides and the bandit would round the corner and be gone. To his rear, he faintly heard Knapp's muffled shots, but he paid them little attention.

McLean leaned forward and squeezed the trigger. The shotgun butt slammed solidly against his right shoulder and the barrel jerked upward. He watched as the pellets struck true, hitting the fleeing bandit in the lower back, lifting him skyward and tossing him like a rag doll into the gutter.

McLean now held an empty shotgun.

When McLean began his approach on the lookout, Knapp inched his way toward the station office. At the piercing sound of McLean chambering his first round, the suspect inside the office spun, faced Knapp, and then jumped from the elevated office.

Knapp fired.

"Pop! Pop! Pop!"

Three misses. His .38 sounded like a cap gun compared to McLean's first shotgun blast. As the bandit bolted toward Pico, Knapp capped off three more rounds. Again, three misses. In seconds the escaping gunman ran onto Pico Boulevard and darted down the middle of the street.

Out of ammunition and struggling to keep up with the fleet footed suspect, Knapp drew his small backup gun and was ready to start firing when the suspect ran directly past McLean and into his line of fire.

McLean threw the empty shotgun into his left hand, drew his service revolver and began to chase the armed suspect down the middle of the street. When they were about fifteen feet apart, McLean fired his first round. The fleeing bandit jerked at the hit, and then turned slightly, extended his weapon and fired. Flame plumed from the barrel and McLean heard the bullet whistle past his head.

McLean was now in a full run, his feet slamming the pavement while his upper body bounced from the impact.

Again and again he snapped the trigger, watching as the suspect jerked from each hit, but he didn't fall.

"Fall, damn you, fall!" he muttered while sucking in deep gulps of air. But his assailant didn't fall, nor did he stop shooting. Two more bullets flew past McLean's head before the bandit reached the corner of 3rd Avenue and bolted into the darkness.

McLean, out of ammunition, stopped behind a telephone pole, dropped the shotgun and threw his gun into his left hand. He then ejected his six spent casings and with a trembling right hand, unsnapped one of his two ammunition pouches. As the snap flew open, he slid his cupped hand under the falling rounds, only to see half tumble to the ground. With his cylinder open, he tried to hand feed six live rounds into the small cylindrical holes. His shaking made the task far more difficult than it had been when shooting at paper targets on the Academy range. His breathing continued rapidly, only accelerated by the powerful surge of adrenaline that was pumping through his body.

Snapping the cylinder shut, he walked slowly around the corner and into the darkness. It was pitch black, the hazy streetlights failing to shed any light onto the narrow side street. Thirty feet down the street, he stopped at the mouth to an alley. Without a flashlight, he was going no further.

As he stood in the darkness and tried to catch his breath, he could hear the wail of sirens coming from all areas of the city in response to the help call. Frustrated that the suspect escaped, but grateful he was alive, he turned and walked back onto Pico Boulevard and down to 4[Th] Avenue where he was met by Marzullo.

"Here Nick," Marzullo said as he dropped six brass shell casings into his cupped hands. "I thought you might want these. Especially if your ammo wasn't authorized."

"Thanks, John," McLean said, as the severity of the past few minutes began to sink in.

Knapp and McLean each received a major Class A commendation for the shooting, but this was soured by some other news McLean received two days later.

"Sit down, Nick," Captain Drake said, a look of concern crossing his face. "I've got some bad news for you."

McLean sat in one of the two hard wooden chairs that faced the desk.

"Wallace was visited again by Internal Affairs, and this time he resigned."

"You're kidding?" McLean said, a tone of disbelief in his voice.

"I wish I were, Nick. Internal Affairs caught him at home, drunk again. They told him that if he resigned, the Sheriffs Department wouldn't pursue the four counts of Battery on a Police Officer they were thinking about filing."

"That's bullshit," McLean exclaimed angrily. "Those bastards were gunning for him, and they knew that if they caught him drunk, they could get a resignation."

"Sadly, it wasn't the Sheriff's Department that pushed for the resignation, but one of our own, Deputy Chief Cleary. But you never heard that from me."

"Cleary's an asshole," McLean said softly.

"You're probably right," Drake said. "But what is done is done, and we can't change it."

McLean got up to leave. "Oh, I've one more piece of news for you."

"I hope it gets better."

"It does. You're aware that you're eighteen months in Wilshire are up and you're due for a transfer?"

"Yes, sir."

"It appears that others are also aware of it, because I received a personal note from Captain Preminger in Personnel Division and was advised that in two weeks you'll be transferred to University Division, Morning Watch. You know Preminger?"

"One might say so," McLean said slyly.

The two weeks passed quickly, while the pain of Wallace's resignation continued to fester.

FOURTEEN

McLean's last day in Wilshire Division found him hunched over the long oak bar in Steve's Tavern, staring vacantly into a shot of whiskey. His mind clawed at the events of the past few weeks. Thoughts and memories shot past his unblinking eyes and disappeared into the still brown liquid which threatened to dull the edges of reason as well as pain and fury.

Why was there always a price tag?

Swirling the whiskey slowly in the glass, two prevailing thoughts refused to fade away: the memory of the suspect he killed with his fourth shotgun blast and the feeling of resentment he harbored because of Wallace's resignation.

McLean remembered the conversation with Captain Drake. After Drake had finished, he stood and again told McLean how sorry he was for the loss of a good street cop. McLean shook the captain's hand, not out of necessity, but respect, mumbled his goodbye and as if in a hypnotic state, walked from the office.

He could not remember walking upstairs to his locker, changing to street clothes, or driving east on Pico to Steve's. Even now, he didn't hear Steve as he stood behind the bar, cleaning glasses and carrying on a one-sided conversation.

It ate at him that there was something wrong in the way Wallace had been treated. Suddenly, anger shot through his mind, but it was soon clouded from the inner recess of his brain by the booze. As quickly as the anger rose, it fell back into the void from which it surfaced.

Out of the corner of his eye, he saw the front door crack and admit Marzullo, who made his way over, slid onto one of the red vinyl covered bar stools and lean on the bar beside him.

"Steve, two more shots and a couple more beers," Marzullo said.

"Don't know if I should, John," McLean said as he threw back his first shot and wrapped both hands around the cold beer.

"From the looks of it, Nick, you could use it."

Without a word, Marzullo threw back his whiskey and then downed the beer chaser.

"Any eggs, Steve?" Marzullo asked the old Hungarian bartender, who had a fondness in his heart for Wilshire cops.

"Sorry, Johnny. I didn't get to the store yesterday, but I'll have some for you boys tomorrow."

"We're going to miss you, Nick," Marzullo said as he tapped the bar and motioned to Steve for another round.

"It'll be nice to be missed," McLean grunted as he continued to stare into the empty shot glass. "But I'd rather stay."

"You'll do fine. Just remember all that we taught you."

McLean broke into a smile. "You nearly got me twenty-one days, Marzullo," he said as he began to chuckle.

"Yeah, but it was me, not you they made mop down the jail."

"You're kidding?"

"Nope. You and Wallace hit the street and I was called back into the station, handed a mop and metal bucket and told to get rid of as much tear gas residue as I could."

"Then they knew?

"They knew."

"Simpson?"

"That would be my guess," Marzullo answered.

"Asshole."

McLean took more of his beer.

"Do me a favor, John."

"Name it."

"If you talk to Wallace, tell him to call me."

"I'll do it," Marzullo said as he threw back his drinks and slid off the stool.

"Good luck, Mac."

"Same to you, John. And ...thanks."

McLean shook Marzullo's outstretched hand and watched as the cop with the silver streak walked out the front door.

McLean sat alone at the long, scarred bar. He still hadn't touched his second set of drinks. After Marzullo left, he felt a deepening loneliness, despite Steve's constant chatter and the occasional opening and closing of the front door. McLean had the urge to get very drunk.

He wanted to forget the shooting, the nightmares and the anger he felt because of Wallace's resignation. He wanted to concentrate on more important matters, such as his reporting to University Division in less than seventy-two hours.

With both elbows planted solidly on the bar, he threw back the second shot, downed the beer, and then glanced at the clock that sat above the large mirror: nine-thirty A.M. For most, the day was young, but for McLean, his time at Steve's was cutting into his sleep. Actually, that wasn't all that bad since when he was awake he didn't dream about bullets whizzing past his head and a black bandit trying to kill him in the middle of Pico Boulevard.

He was just about ready to leave when the front door flew open. Stepping into the dim light was a flamboyantly dressed figure. Although McLean didn't want to be bothered, he was mesmerized by the persona that stood before him.

Atop the head was a shag wig that sported the colors of red, pink and yellow. The eyebrows had been covered with thick white makeup, with dark black eyebrows painted above. The eyes were accentuated by heavy silver eye makeup and long black eyelashes extended from the upper eyelid. Red lipstick adorned the robust lips and a thin black line had been drawn around the mouth.

Laboriously, McLeans eyes continued to work their way down. The figure wore a short, bright red satin dress with a pink boa thrown around the neck. Black, mesh nylon stockings were fitted into silver high-heeled boots that sported small red leather hearts that sat below each knobby knee. And in her hand, she clutched a sequined black purse.

As he sat speechless, the Western Avenue drag queen floated across the floor and plopped herself on the stool to his right.

Dumb ass must be new to the area, he thought. *Only someone new or a fruit with a death wish would sashay into a cop's watering hole.*

"Helloooo, handsome," the queen said, her words formed between puckered large red lips. "Are you alone?" she continued softly in a high pitched squeak as she shook her narrow shoulders and tossed her head from side-to-side.

"Yeah, darling, I'm alone, and I'd recommend that you take your pink boa and black handbag and swish your way back to the street."

"Oh, be nice, handsome. What kind of work do you do?" she asked as she slid her stool closer.

"I work for the city as a sanitation engineer," McLean answered as he threw back another shot, and then rolled the empty glass between the fingers of both hands.

"The Sanitation Department? A good lookin' man like you collects trash?"

"That's right, sweetheart. I collect and dispose of trash."

"I've always wanted to meet a real engineer," she said as she shook her shoulders and crossed her skinny legs. "They can run the engine while I play in the caboose."

"Get lost sweetheart, I'm busy."

"You don't look busy."

"Hey you flamin' faggot," Steve shouted in words wrapped in a heavy European accent. "Get your sorry black ass outta my bar. This is a respectable place."

"Now, now, let's not get nasty, honey," she said as she moved closer to McLean. "I was only looking for this handsome young man to buy me a drink."

"I'm not in the buying mood," McLean said, trying to ignore the interruption.

McLean suddenly felt a bony hand moving back and forth on his right thigh, inching its way up his groin. Spinning to his right, he thrust his left hand between his seducer's legs and grabbed him by the balls while his right hand tightly encircled the throat. In one fluid motion, he jumped off the stool, lifted the queen into the air, while squeezing with his left hand and clamping tight with his right. The air was filled with choked screams as McLean, with a violent thrust, pushed the terrified queen toward the front door, her feet dangling just above the floor.

Releasing more fury, McLean kicked open the door and threw the screaming transvestite into a traffic lane where she flew ass-over-tea-kettle with arms and legs thrashing violently in the air. Morning traffic screeched to a stop as the frightened queen clawed at the pavement to get out of harm's way. Managing to jump to her feet, she flipped McLean the finger and half hobbled, half ran across the street, and to safety.

Mclean reentered the bar, returned to his seat and sat down.

"Thank you, Officer McLean," Steve said grinning.

"My pleasure, Steve."

"Another drink?"

"I'd better not," McLean said as he opened his billfold, threw a couple dollars on the bar and looked down at the picture of his family he carried in his wallet. McLean loved his wife and two children, but he shook his head sadly in resignation as he realized he had grown to love the job more.

PART TWO

FIFTEEN

Bobby Hutton walked out the back door of University station only to find Tommy Hestily asleep in the front passenger seat of their black and white. Quietly, he inched open the door and slid into the driver's seat, reached down to the siren toggle switch and flipped it on. He then slammed his left foot against the chrome siren button on the floorboard. An ear piercing wail erupted through the parking lot to the accompaniment of Hutton's hearty laughter as he watched his partner bolt upright in his seat, slam his head against the headliner and drive both knees into the thinly padded dash.

"You're an asshole, Hutton," Hestily bellowed as he rubbed the top of his head and slid his knees off the dash.

"You want a cup of coffee before we hit the street?" Hutton asked as he slipped the key in the ignition.

"Wouldn't help," Hestily said, trying to stifle a yawn.

"What I need is a good night's sleep."

"Problems at home?"

"Not really. What's killing me is having to spend every day in court. I haven't slept in three days."

"Why wasn't I subpoenaed?" Hutton asked as he started the car.

"Probably because it's an old homicide case where I took the dying declaration and you were on a day off."

"Good reason."

"I've got a favor, Bobby," Hestily said wearily as he slipped the mike from its holder. His voice was hoarse and his words slurred betraying his exhaustion.

"What is it?"

"Let's not get into any shit tonight. I need to get some sleep," he said yawning, "and this is the only time I can do it."

Hutton didn't like the idea of not working, but knew that Hestily was right.

"Fine with me," he said as he backed the car from its parking space and pulled out onto Santa Barbara Avenue.

"3Adam58 clear," Hestily sleepily muttered into the radio. In less than two minutes, he was again reclining in the passenger seat, snoring softly.

Fortunately, the radio airwaves were quiet, so Hutton had little difficulty letting his exhausted partner sleep.

As he drove westbound on Santa Barbara and approached Crenshaw Boulevard, he spotted a See's Candy truck speeding. Hutton pulled behind the truck and clocked it at 45 miles per hour in a 35 mile per hour zone.

"That'll work," he muttered softly.

Reaching down, he switched on the reds and watched as the truck pulled to the curb and stopped.

Cracking the door, Hutton slipped out and approached the driver's side of the big, white truck.

"Good morning, officer," the driver said nervously. "What'd I do?"

"Well, sir," Hutton said seriously as he looped both thumbs through his belt and rocked back on his heels. "I clocked you doing ten pounds over the speed limit."

"You what?"

"I clocked you doing *ten pounds* over the speed limit."

"But I was only going ..."

"Ten pounds over the speed limit," Hutton quickly interjected.

"Oh ...oh, *now* I understand. You clocked me traveling *ten* pounds over the speed limit."

"Yes, sir, that's it exactly. Ten pounds over."

Chuckling, the driver walked to the back of his truck, threw open the doors and removed two, five pound boxes of chocolates.

"I think that this should do it," he said smiling. "Ten pounds over the limit. That take care of it?"

"Yes, sir, it's perfect," Hutton said as he threw the boxes under his arm. "Have a nice day," he said as he strolled back to the car.

"Ah, you too, officer," the driver said as he shook his head and watched Hutton place the boxes in the rear seat of the police car and drive off.

Hutton glanced over at Hestily, who hadn't moved since they left the station. He made a left turn onto Crenshaw and had traveled about two miles when he saw a Webber's Bread truck double-parked in the street making its early morning deliveries. "I know the kids could use some fresh bread," he said softly to the still sleeping Hestily as he pulled in behind the truck and switched on the reds.

"Good morning, officer," yelled the delivery man as he rolled his cart from the rear of the market. "What can I do for you?"

"Well, sir, we have a small problem."

"What kind of a problem?"

"It appears that you're parked four loaves away from the curb, which is two loaves beyond the double-parking limit."

A look of astonishment crossed the driver's face.

"Four loaves away from the curb and two loaves over the double parking limit? I ...I ...I don't understand," he said as he rolled up the rear door and threw his cart into the back.

"Well, sir, if you'd join me at the curb, maybe I can make it clear."

Hutton walked over to the curb and stared at the distance between the gutter and the parked truck. Then he began to pace off the distance. "It's like I said, you're parked four loaves away from the curb."

A deep look of consternation shot across the driver's face as he studied the distance. Then, as if a light went on, he smiled. Walking to the side of the truck, he threw open the large rolling door, reached in and pulled out four loaves of freshly baked white bread.

"Are you sure that this will take care of the problem?" he asked still grinning.

"I'm sure," Hutton replied.

"Well, just to make sure, here are four more. I'd hate to see L.A.'s finest go hungry."

Hutton smiled and stuck out both arms. After the eight loaves were stacked, he turned and walked back to the car, a bounce in his step. Quietly, he eased open the rear door and gently placed the bread on the seat next to the candy boxes. Sliding into the car, he looked at Hestily whose snoring had grown progressively louder as he sank deeper into sleep.

"Too bad you're missing all of the fun, Tommy," Hutton chuckled to himself as he slowly drove away, wishing there was such a thing as a delivery truck for freshly brewed coffee.

❦

Bubba Washington and Ta-Ta Lastice stood in the darkness hidden from the rear door by a large trash dumpster. The End-Zone Bar, a joint frequented by USC football fans, off-duty cops and students from the University of Southern California, was ready to close. USC had beaten UCLA that afternoon, and the cash register was full.

Washington pulled a wool ski mask from his jacket pocket and slid it over his large head. Lastice followed suit.

"Let's go," Washington said as he stood, pulled a revolver from his waist and walked to the door.

Lastice snaked the sawed-off shotgun out from under his black leather jacket, adjusted his mask and followed.

The bar was quiet. The juke-box had been shut off, Julie the bartender was wiping down the bar, and the three remaining diehard drunk USC fans were slouched on their bar stools throwing back their last drops of beer. No one saw the two bandits slip through the rear door and step into the shadows just behind the pool table.

"Just one more round, Julie," shouted an obese man who was seated on an end stool. "We've got to savor every win over the Bruins," he slurred.

Julie glanced up at the clock. Two-o-five.

"Bars closed, Walt," she said as she threw a soiled rag over her shoulder and walked to the cash register. "You wouldn't want me to get shut down would you?"

"Nah, I guess not," the man mumbled as he stumbled from the stool and headed for the restroom that was located just beyond the pool table.

Julie hit the ivory button on the old brass cash register. As the bell chimed, the money drawer snapped open.

Washington stepped from the darkness as the obese drunk stumbled behind the pool table.

"Who the hell are you?" the drunk slurred.

A violent blow from the butt of Washington's gun sent the swaying drunk to the floor. As bar stools clattered, Julie turned, only to find herself staring directly down the barrel of a sawed-off shotgun. Quickly, she slammed the cash drawer shut. As she turned to face her assailant, she slipped her hand under the counter and gently pushed the silent alarm.

"Bitch!" Lastice cried as he pulled the shotgun back to strike the diminutive owner in the head with the wooden stock.

"Leave her be!" Washington shouted to his incensed partner. "We need her to get into the safe."

Lastice pulled back and leveled the shotgun at the two customers who sat on their bar stool's, paralyzed by fear.

"Put your wallets and watches on the bar," Washington commanded as he stepped behind the bar and walked up to Julie. "You, open the register," he ordered as he pushed the barrel of the revolver to the side of her head.

Angrily, she snapped down on the register's open button. Washington reached into the drawer and removed the bills from both the top and bottom drawers and stuffed the cash into his pockets while Lastice reached across the bar and scooped up the wallets and watches.

"Now, the safe," Washington ordered.

Julie bent down below the register and opened two small wooden doors exposing the safe. Slowly, she reached forward and nervously fumbled with the dial.

"*Open it, bitch!*" Washington whispered through tightly clenched teeth.

❧

As Hutton drove away from the Webber's Bread truck, the silence of the radio was broken by three, distinct beeps. Before the final tone had stopped resonating through the car, Hestily was awake.

"All units in the vicinity, and 3Adam58. 211 silent at the End-Zone Bar, 3911 South Figueroa. 3Adam58, handle the call Code Three."

While Hestily acknowledged the call, Hutton jumped on the accelerator. The big-bore Plymouth lurched forward and shot up Crenshaw.

"Think it's any good?" Hestily shouted, trying to be heard above the high-pitched wail of the siren.

"Might be," Hutton shouted back. "Saturday night. Big football game, a lot of money, and the bar just closed."

As the black and white shot down Santa Barbara and approached South Figueroa, Julie spun the dial, pushed down on the handle and opened the safe.

"Give me a bag, bitch," Washington commanded as he reached into the safe and scooped out the cash.

Julie stood, walked to the end of the bar and grabbed a paper bag from above the trash can. Silently, she walked back and handed it to the still kneeling bandit.

"You're both assholes," shouted the man at the bar as he swung his legs off the stool and reached his feet toward the floor. "I know the Chief, and both of your asses will be in..." His words were cut short when Lastice lunged across the bar and struck him in the head with the pistol grip of the shotgun sending him sprawling onto the floor. The second man didn't move or speak.

Hutton cut the siren three blocks from the bar and let the car glide onto a side street.

"You take the rear, and I'll hit the front," he said as he stopped the car to let his partner off in the alley.

Hestily slid from the car, slipped his gun from the holster, and approached the rear door. Hutton parked on the side street just east of Figueroa.

Washington stuffed the cash into the bag. Then he turned and faced Julie. Grabbing her by the back of the head, he pulled her close.

"Blood, we needs to get outta here," yelled Lastice.

Washington looked down into the dark brown eyes of the terrified woman. "Next time, I'll show you what a real man has to offer," he said gruffly as he threw her against the sink.

Suddenly, the front door opened and Hutton stepped in, gun in hand. Washington, spun, and fired. Hutton dropped into a combat stance, threw his left arm over center mass and cranked off six rounds into the smoke filled room.

The lone patron at the bar flew off the stool, dropped to the floor and rolled into a fetal position with his hands clutched tightly around his head while Julie dove for cover underneath the bar. Lastice, shotgun extended, ran to the end of the bar and in his excitement fired an errant round into the ceiling, blowing out three fluorescent lights.

Hutton, with his gun empty, backed out the door. Both bandits, seeing their chance for escape, bolted to the rear and barged through the door, knocking Hestily to the ground where he hit his head and was knocked unconscious.

In less than thirty seconds, a red Cadillac burst onto Figueroa from the rear alley and disappeared.

SIXTEEN

McLean sat in the coffee room and watched as the uniformed cops dropped their dimes in the old coffee machine, grabbed the full paper cup, and silently headed for the stairs. He wasn't impressed, and the thought passed through his mind that there wasn't a University Division Morning Watch cop that could make a pimple on the ass of a Wilshire cop.

Trying to shake the cobwebs because of too little sleep and too many boilermakers, he sipped gingerly on his coffee as he trudged up the stairs and walked in the rear door of the roll call room. After tossing his gear on the floor, he took a seat on the back row.

He sipped gently on the steaming brew and listened as the End-Zone Bar robbery was discussed by members of the watch and conjecture made as to the identity of the suspects and the tactics used by Hutton and Hestily.

"You sure you didn't hit one of them?" asked Tony Sabatello.

"Shit, Sabatello," Hutton said, a deep tinge of frustration in his voice. "I was lucky to get out of there alive!"

"And Hestily couldn't add anything," added Ernie Federico, a squatty dark-haired Italian, who figured himself a comedian, "'cause he was out for the count!" Only Federico laughed.

Hutton threw a disgusted look at the house comic and then shot a glance at his partner. The always amiable Hestily sat quietly, softly massaging a large welt that had erupted in the middle of his forehead. Hutton knew that his partner was nursing more than a welt.

"What about a description?" asked Al Martucci, another Italian who was short and squatty, and who could have stepped into the role of Doctor Frankenstein's helper in a B horror movie. His cadaverous face was pale with hollows at his temples. His uniform was a size too small and he rarely smiled, always watching through pale blue eyes. His arms were abnormally short and his hands wide, accentuated by short, stubby fingers.

"Both wore ski masks. One was a big dude and the other was much smaller," Hutton answered.

"What kind of guns did they have?" yelled Sabatello from across the room.

"The big guy had a revolver and the runt was carrying a sawed-off shotgun."

McLean sat silently and scanned the room. It was a real mix. Some young cops, a few seasoned street veterans and one old-timer that appeared to have been on the Department longer than McLean had been alive. McLean's eyes locked on a large man sitting quietly alone. He reminded McLean of Wallace, except he was larger, his hair was blond and he had a large, deep scar running down his right cheek.

"How do you think it went down?" Federico asked Patterson, fishing for a comment from the silent, blond haired giant.

Patterson turned his head and looked straight at Federico. "I wasn't there," he said as he hunched over the table top. "And since I wasn't there, I don't have an opinion."

"Well, neither was I but..."

"Then we both should keep our mouth's shut," Patterson commented, never lookin up.

"Work's for me," McLean whispered into his cup.

Suddenly the side door opened and Lieutenant Jack Mahon and Sergeants Rod Bock and Al Evans entered the room and took their customary places in the front. When McLean was introduced by Mahon, not a head turned, nor was a word spoken. His reputation had preceded him.

Sipping his coffee, he awaited his first assignment. He didn't have long to wait.

"3Adam81, Cunningham and McLean," Evans said as he held the deployment board on top of the table.

McLean looked at the man who responded as Cunningham. He had eight, hash marks running up his left sleeve and his hair was pure white. McLean was right; he'd been on the job longer than McLean had been alive.

Cunningham and McLean were as different as night and day, a difference that surfaced when they answered their third radio call of the night.

"3Adam81, see the woman, victim of an assault, 30th and Vermont at the bus stop. 3Adam81, your call is Code Two."

McLean slipped the mike from the holder and acknowledged the call. Cunningham hadn't spoken since they left their last radio call where McLean told an obnoxious burglary victim that complained about their response time that "he'd give them a dime so they could phone someone who cared."

The insult offended Cunningham, who had grown up in the area and thought of all residents as his friends and neighbors.

Cunningham drove slowly to the radio call, an act that not only made McLean nervous, but also angry. Deliberately, he headed the black and white from the farthest end of the division to the northeast section. The streets were deserted and the Plymouth was fast, but that didn't matter. Cunningham had his own routine, and McLean had enough common sense than to further provoke his partner.

After nearly twenty minutes, they arrived at the intersection of Vermont and 30th Street. All was dark and the reporting party couldn't be found. Then, McLean spotted the bus stop in the distance.

"Make a left," he said. "The bus stop is about one hundred feet on the right."

"You've got good eyes," Cunningham said softly.

Cunningham made a left hand turn that took them into the darkness of 30th Street. Just as McLean had said, the bus stop, concealed in the darkness, was located mid-block on the right hand side. As the black and white slowed to a stop, McLean saw a large black woman standing next to the stop sign. She was wearing a white Licensed Vocational Nurse's uniform that was soaked in blood and had a large purse slung over a shoulder.

"Are you all right?" McLean asked as he approached the large woman.

"Damn sure I'm all right," was the sarcastic response, "but that sucker that tried to rob me, he ain't all right. I got him good."

"Then, that's not your blood?"

"Of course it ain't my blood, honey," the woman said as she leaned her back against the pole and adjusted her purse. "It belongs to the sucker who tried to rob me!"

"Do you need us to call you and ambulance?" McLean asked.

"Hell no, I don't need no ambulance. But that sucker that wanted to take my money, now I'm sure he'll need one if'n he ain't already dead."

A smile crossed McLean's thin lips. "My kind of woman," he whispered as he walked the woman back to the police car, sat her in the back-seat and continued his interview. Cunningham hadn't moved from behind the steering wheel.

"I'd like you to tell us what happened," McLean said.

"Well," she said as she sat back and straightened her uniform. "I work every day. I'm a Licensed Vocational Nurse. I got six children and no sucker who ain't workin' is gonna take my hard earned money."

"I understand that," McLean said patiently, "but what happened tonight?"

"Well, Officer…" she stopped and looked at McLean's name tag, "McLean. I was standing at this here bus stop like I do every night. And out of the darkness steps this skinny ass black man. He comes up to me and wants all my money."

"I ain't givin' you no money, fool," I said. "And then he made his big mistake. The sucker grabbed my purse. Well, the fool didn't know what I carried for protection."

"Protection?"

The woman reached into her purse and came out with a twelve inch flathead screwdriver.

McLean was astonished at the size of the weapon.

"You used that on the guy?"

"You is damn sure right I used it. As we fought for my purse, I started to stab the little sucker. I done stabbed him in the head and then in the neck, and then in his ugly face a bunch of times. I just worked my way on down. Lordy, I stabbed that puny little sucker all over."

"Why didn't he run?" McLean asked quizzically.

"Well, he tried, that he did. He squirmed and wiggled all over the place. But he wasn't gonna go no where 'cause his damn puny hands were caught in my purse straps and he couldn't get away. And anyways, I was bigger than him."

Now, it all made sense. So did the large amount of fresh blood on her white uniform and the trail of blood that led down the sidewalk and away from the scene.

McLean looked in the front seat. Cunningham hadn't taken his eyes off the rearview mirror.

"I'm going to follow the blood trail," McLean said as he stepped from the car and switched on his flashlight. Cunningham remained silent.

McLean shone his light on the first drop that was the size of a half dollar. It was like following a road map. Drop after drop had hit the ground at regular intervals. He could see that at the scene of the assault the distance between drops was longer because the suspect was running.

Then, apparently exhausted from the fight and weakened by the loss of blood, the distance decreased, as did the size of the drops. *He's bleeding out*, McLean thought. As McLean's flashlight beam illuminated each successive drop, he knew that the man was dying.

Coming to the intersection of 30th and Vermont, he crossed the street and continued east on the sidewalk into the darkness. On and on the small drops went, until the trail went to the left and headed up a small concrete sidewalk that led to the backyard of an old home.

Walking up the path, he came to a gate. Removing his revolver, he pushed the gate open and stepped into the darkness of the backyard. Holding the flashlight in his left hand and away from his body, he continued on until he came to an old screen door that led to a dilapidated enclosed patio. Looking down, he saw that the blood drops stopped in front of the door which had been forced open.

Cautiously, he pushed open the door and stepped into the patio area. The only light in the room came from his flashlight.

Just inside the door, the droplets began again. With the light fixed on the floor and his ears listening for any movement, he walked slowly forward. It was quiet, too quiet, and it was dark, too damned dark.

The blood drops were now very small, more pin spots than drops. Slowly, he moved his light along the floor until he came to a far corner, where he found an old mattress shoved against the wall. Folding the mattress back, he found the suspect curled in a fetal position. Leaning forward, he placed the barrel of his revolver in the man's ear and nudged him with his foot.

"Hey friend, it's the po-lice, get up."

There was no movement, no sound, only silence. McLean shone the light across the body. Blood covered the man from head to foot. Again, this time a little harder, he nudged the body with his foot. Still there was no response. He shoved the flashlight under his left arm and put his service revolver in his left hand. Using his right hand, he found the carotid artery and checked for a pulse. He found one, but it was very weak. The man was close to death.

Rolling the suspect over, McLean frisked him for weapons. Finding none, he handcuffed him and went to look for his partner. As he walked to the sidewalk, Cunningham pulled up in the police car with the victim still seated in the back.

"Did you find him?" Cunningham asked.

"Yeah. He's lying on a dirty mattress on the back patio, dying. So we've got a couple of options."

"Options?" Cunningham asked skeptically. "What do you mean, options?"

"Yeah, options. We can leave for five minutes, let him die and come back when it's over. That would save us time and the city court costs. Or you can call him an ambulance. My vote ...let him die."

Cunningham shook his head slowly as his face erupted in a bright scarlet. "For one so young, you're a cold son-of-a-bitch, McLean, too cold. I'm going to call the guy an ambulance."

It was apparent Cunningham didn't like McLean's style. Not many did.

At end-of-watch, McLean watched as Cunningham walked directly toward the Watch Commander's office. As he walked past McLean, he threw him a gruff look, mumbled a few words and stomped down the hallway. McLean never again worked with Matt Cunningham.

SEVENTEEN

Patterson sat in the shadows, his right hand methodically moving back and forth on his right thigh while his eyes penetrated the darkness and watched customers approach the front window of the Jack-in-the-Box.

Occasionally, he would hunch his large frame forward toward the steering wheel to stretch his back, but other than that one movement, he remained stealthily still and all but ignored Kirkland, who sat silent in the passenger seat.

"I really don't like sittin' on these here damned stakeouts," Kirkland drawled in his strong Southern accent.

"What would you rather be doing?" Patterson asked, speaking into the windshield.

"Me, I'd rather be a stoppin' some niggas in a car, findin' a gun and bookin' 'em for robbery. This here a waitin' for some knuckleheaded bandit to pull a robbery just seems like a waste a time."

Patterson shot his partner a quick look, and then refocused on the front of the restaurant.

"KMA 367, zero-two-hundred hours," the link broadcast.

"Shit, Patterson, we've been staked on this place for over two hours, and we ain't seen nothin'," Kirkland drawled. "Besides, I need another cup of coffee."

"We'll give it another thirty minutes, then head up to Winchell's at Adams and Fig.," Patterson mumbled as he slid forward in his seat and continued to stare out the windshield of the black and white that was parked deep within the shadows of a long driveway.

"Hell-a-dee-wops, partner, I thought that your snitch was reliable," Kirkland said as he slouched down and threw his knees firmly against the dash.

"She is."

"Now how can you be so damn sure? I'd bet my next paycheck she's some down and out street 'ho that'd lie just to get a few bucks."

"Not a bad guess, but like I said, she's reliable."

"3Adam43, meet 3Adam58 on Tactical Frequency two."

Kirkland reached down and dialed the red knob on the radio to the requested frequency.

"Great white hunters to fifty-eight, ya'll go ahead, boys," he said.

"Anything interesting?" Hestily asked.

"Nope," Kirkland replied. "Not a damn thing."

"Ask them how long they are going to keep the Code Five on the location," Hutton said.

"Great white hunters, the illustrious Officer Hutton wants to know how much longer you're planning to sit on the location."

Kirkland glanced at this watch. It read two-fifteen.

"According to my partner, who is the chief of this safari, we've got fifteen minutes more."

"Then what?" Hestily asked.

"Then this Southern boy is gonna take a piss and get some more rock-gut coffee up at Adams and Fig."

"We'll stick around until then," Hestily said.

"And so will we," McLean interjected from 3Adam9.

"Hot damn, the cavalry is here," Kirkland drawled, excitement in his voice.

"Good Lord, if some nigga decides to go robbin' this fine establishment, he won't stand a snowball's chance in hell to make it alive across the street."

Rastus Snow, 'Tree Tall' Jackson and Blackie Jones stood hidden in the darkness across the street from the Jack-in-the-Box and watched as the last person in line was served.

As the final customer turned and walked into the parking lot, Snow reached down into his waistband and nervously repositioned a small chrome revolver. Stepping into the light, he stopped and looked up and down Slauson. The street was deserted. With his head, he motioned to the others to follow, and then shoved his hands deep into the pockets of his black leather jacket. In unison, the trio stepped off the curb and walked toward the fast food restaurant.

"Well, I'll be damned," said Kirkland as he watched the trio walk across the street. "If'n I didn't know any better, partner, I'd think that we just might have three bandits comin' into view."

Patterson had seen the men step from the shadows but remained silent. He too felt that this might be their suspects, but he wanted to see more than three male Negroes wearing black leather jackets headed for the order window. He wanted to see a gun.

After crossing the street, Snow stopped at the corner and again looked up and down Slauson. The street was still deserted.

The three men slowly sashayed up to the order window, stopped, and again looked around.

"We got three heads twirling faster than a windmill in a dust storm," Kirkland said, trying to contain his excitement.

Seeing they were still alone, Snow reached into his waist, slid out the gun and shoved it through the window.

"We've a two-eleven in progress," Patterson said before his partner could react. "Get us some backup."

As Kirkland requested assistance, Patterson slid his key into the shotgun locking mechanism and snapped open the lock.

"It's all yours," he said as he slipped out the driver's door.

Larry Kirkland reached down and slid the Ithaca out of the rack. It felt familiar in his hands.

"This here'll be like shootin' coon's up a tree," he whispered to Patterson.

Stepping from the car, he glanced to his left and saw that Patterson was already moving through the shadows toward the lighted restaurant.

Three distinct beeps shattered all the radio frequencies. "All units in the vicinity and 3Adam9. 3Adam43 is requesting assistance at the Jack-in-the-Box, Slauson and Second Avenue. Possible two-eleven in progress. 3Adam9, handle the call Code Three."

McLean snapped the mike from the holder and rogered the call while Rico Conti thrust the steering wheel to the left and slammed the gas pedal to the floor. The Plymouth's rear tires spun wildly as they tried to grab the asphalt.

In seconds, the black and white was racing down Figueroa toward Slauson.

"3Adam58 to Control," shouted Hestily into the mike. "Show this unit responding Code Two to Second Avenue and Slauson."

Snow thrust his upper body through the window, grabbed the clerk by the shirt front and pushed the cocked gun into his mouth.

"Open the register and put the money in a bag, nigga."

The young clerk was shaking violently.

"Now!" shouted Snow, who had pulled the gun from the clerk's mouth and began to wave it wildly in the air. "Do it or I'll kill you nigga!"

The money was hurriedly stuffed into a bag and handed to the nervous bandit.

"We is still good," Jones said as his head swiveled from side-to-side.

"I don't see no pigs," Jackson said as he stepped away from the window and hurried into the parking lot.

Snow extracted himself from the window and bounded behind his partners into the empty lot.

Six blocks from Second Avenue and Slauson, Conti cut the reds and siren while McLean pulled the shotgun from its holder.

Patterson, staying in the shadows, went to the left, while Kirkland paralleled to the right. When they saw the trio of bandits step into the parking lot, they stepped from the shadows.

"Freeze, niggas," screamed Kirkland as he leveled the shotgun at the trio.

Snow spun and fired. His shot missed and slammed into a garage across the street.

Then he bolted toward Slauson Avenue with the barrel of the Kirkland's Ithaca aimed at his back.

"A coon up a tree!" Kirkland muttered as he planted his feet, leaned forward and squeezed the trigger. The night was shattered by an explosion. The pellets caught Snow in the back of the head. He was dead before he hit the ground.

Jackson darted to the right and directly into Patterson's line of fire. Three of six shots struck the fleeing lookout in the back. He stumbled, spun and lurched face first onto the pavement.

Jones had bolted to the left and before Kirkland could spin in his direction, the final member of the trio disappeared into the darkness of 3rd Avenue.

Patterson watched Jones disappear. Running back to his black and white, he grabbed the mike.

"3Adam43, we have two, two-eleven suspects down and a third running southbound on 3rd Avenue. Requesting that any responding units proceed northbound on 3rd Avenue."

Patterson threw the mike back onto the front seat of the car, and walked over to his downed suspect, bent down and saw that he was still breathing.

"Is he still alive?" shouted Kirkland who was standing over Snow.

"Yeah," Patterson said in an icy tone.

"This here nigga is dead," Kirkland shouted back.

Then something incredulous happened.

As Patterson watched, Kirkland placed his left foot on the dead man's chest and cradled the shotgun in his arms. Striking a picture perfect pose as a big game hunter, he began to bellow in a loud voice.

"I need ya'll to listen to me, partner," he proclaimed as he looked into the open eyes of the dead bandit.

"Ya'll have the right to remain silent. Ya'll understand? Good. If you give up the right..."

Patterson had thought he'd seen everything. Standing in the middle of Slauson Avenue, he watched as his partner advised a dead man of his Constitutional Rights. Before Kirkland had finished the Miranda admonition, Patterson heard sirens responding from around the city.

A few blocks away another drama was about to unfold as Buford Hayes and his elderly wife, Bessie, were finishing dinner. As was Buford's nightly habit after his evening meal, he grabbed his hat and coat and told Bessie he was going for his walk. Stepping onto the porch of their small home located mid-block on 3rd Avenue between Slauson and 60th Street, he paid little attention to the sirens he heard in the distance.

Walking northbound on the sidewalk, he noticed bright headlights traveling slowly in his direction. Dressed in his black leather jacket and wearing a small stingy brim hat, he continued to walk in the direction of the lights. Suddenly, they angled in his direction and stopped. Then both doors to a police car were thrown open. Conti stepped from the driver's door, while McLean exited the passenger side.

"Freeze, asshole," shouted McLean as he leveled the Ithaca at Mr. Hayes. "And don't take your hands out of your pockets."

Buford panicked and yanked both hands from his pockets and began to wildly thrash them above his head. "Don't kill me! Don't kill me," he screamed. "I is just an old man and I ain't done nothin' wrong!"

When Hayes' hands cleared his pockets, McLean slammed the receiver back and forth, sending a live round into the chamber.

Leveling the shotgun at his intended victim, he hesitated. "He's too old," shouted McLean. "It's not our guy."

But it was too late.

Conti, who wore a cross-draw holster attached to his left hip, thrust his right hand across his chest, grabbed the rubber grips of his .38 and snapped the gun from the holster. As he thrust the gun toward Mr. Hayes, the momentum sent the gun flying through the air where it landed at Hayes' feet. Startled, Hayes stared down at the gun, his eyes open in widened astonishment.

McLean looked over at Conti whose right arm was now extended, his index finger pointing at the lone figure and his thumb sticking straight up, simulating a gun.

"Don't touch that gun," Conti screamed as he shook his extended index finger and pointed the simulated handgun at the man.

"Don't touch it!"

"I ain't gonna touch no gun," Hayes screamed. "It's a set up; I know it's a set up. No, I ain't touchin' no Po-liceman's gun!"

McLean began to laugh as he watched Conti hurry over to the frightened man and pick up the gun. The next day, Rico Conti bought a new, low slung, Western style holster and from that night forward, he had a new nickname: 'Fingers' Conti.

EIGHTEEN

Over the next few months, members of the University Division Morning Watch warmed to McLean, as he did to them; not because he was warm and friendly, but because he was one hell of a street cop and they knew he would always be watching their backs.

After working at one time or another with everyone on the watch, including a night with Patterson, he and Conti were made regular partners and assigned 3Adam9. Conti was tall, thin with coal black hair, and dark circles under his eyes that gave him a sullen look.

McLean enjoyed the stoic Italian who had a dry sense of humor and would chide him about being a "bad ass." This assessment was one accepted by all on the watch and was solidified one night when they stopped a 1967 Mercury Cougar with four occupants.

It was about three in the morning, the radio was quiet and the streets were empty. Conti pulled into the darkness of a closed gas station located on the northeast corner of Adams and Hoover, shut off the engine, leaned back in the seat and stretched. As they sat in the darkness, McLean switched on the small light located on the right side of the Hot Sheet holder and began to update the nightly log.

As he wrote, a yellow '67 Cougar drove slowly past their location. McLean looked up, caught a quick glimpse of the license and then checked the paper Hot Sheet. There it was. The Cougar was stolen.

"The Cougar is on the Hot Sheet, Rico. Let's go."

"You're kidding, McLean."

"Conti, it's stolen. Go!"

Conti pulled out onto Adams Blvd. Giving the Plymouth the gas, they were soon directly behind the Cougar. Pulling close, they saw that the car had four occupants: two in the front and two in the rear. McLean grabbed the mike and ran the license for confirmation.

"3Adam9, your vehicle is a Wilshire stolen, armed and dangerous. The vehicle and occupants are wanted for armed robbery and auto theft. Hold for Wilshire Detectives."

"3Adam9, show us Code 6 at Adams and Magnolia."

Conti reached below the dash, snapped the toggle switch and activated the red lights. Instead of pulling to the right, the driver hit the brakes and stopped in the middle of the street.

"Asshole," McLean muttered.

"The dumb ass couldn't find another parking place?" Conti said as he looked around the deserted street.

McLean slid the Ithaca from the rack. As he stepped from the car, he placed his left hand on the slide and wrapped his right hand firmly around the wooden stock just below the dark metal receiver.

Conti slid from the black and white and stood behind the driver's door, while McLean took a position behind the passenger door and began issuing commands to the Cougar's occupants.

"Put your hands out the open windows, arms extended, and fingers apart." When all had complied, he continued.

"Passenger," he shouted. "Open the door from the outside, step from your vehicle with your hands over your head, and then lay flat on the pavement with your arms extended."

Slowly, the passenger slipped his right hand to the exterior handle and opened the door. As he stepped from the car, McLean leveled the barrel of the .12 gauge at the uncoiling bandit and slid his finger to the trigger. After stepping from the car, instead of taking a prone position in the middle of the street, the suspect turned and began to walk away.

McLean stepped forward.

"Get on the ground!" he shouted as he stepped within feet of the man's back.

The bandit took an additional step, then spun, lunged at McLean and with both hands grabbed for the shotgun barrel.

Death lingered behind McLean's eyes as he dropped the gun's stock toward the ground, buckled his right knee and thrust the solid wooden stock upward in a vertical butt stroke directed toward the bottom of the suspect's nose.

The blow struck the bandit just under the nose and above the teeth. As McLean drove the shotgun butt through the face, he felt the bones disintegrate. As he finished his upward thrust, he realized that the shotgun had shattered. Standing over the body, McLean held in his left hand the sliding mechanism and receiver, while in his right hand he held the shattered, bloody stock.

The suspect didn't move, nor did it appear he was breathing. McLean turned toward the Cougar, dropped both pieces of the Ithaca onto the street and drew his revolver.

Conti still stood to the left rear fender of the car, his weapon extended. McLean glanced back at the body on the ground. A large pool of blood had formed on the asphalt and surrounded the gunman's head.

McLean felt nothing.

The trio in the car remained silent and watched with their hands fully extended. It appeared that no one wanted to put McLean to another test.

McLean stood in the middle of the street and covered Conti while he ordered the others from the car and onto the ground. Their compliance was immediate. After they were searched and handcuffed, McLean walked over to the police car and requested an ambulance and a supervisor. He looked over to the suspect on the ground. There was no sound and he still hadn't moved.

After the three suspects were placed in the rear seat of the black and white, Conti climbed into the front, while McLean leaned against the car and waited for the ambulance.

He watched as a police car drove toward them. Sergeant Jack Elkins parked and walked over to the prone body.

"Is this your doing, McLean?" he asked.

"Yeah Sarge. It's *my* doing."

"I might have known it. Is he dead?"

"I don't know. I'm not a doctor."

"Well, if you're involved, I don't want anything to do with it."

With that, Elkins shook his head, walked back to his car, climbed in and drove away.

When the G-Wagon finally arrived, the still unconscious suspect was placed in the ambulance and transported to Central Receiving Hospital.

As Conti and McLean pulled into the station parking lot, they were met by Hutton and Hestily who were walking out the rear doors. Seeing the shotgun pieces held by McLean, Hutton asked, "What the hell happened to the shotgun, McLean?"

"I broke it over some asshole's face," came the cold response.

When Mclean left, Hutton turned to Hestily.

"That guy is one tough son-of-a-bitch, Tommy. I'm glad he's on our side."

Two weeks passed before McLean heard anything else about the suspects condition.

"Got a minute, Mac?" asked Jenkins, who was working the Robbery table.

"Sure, what can I do for you?"

"I just talked to Wilshire dicks. The guy you nailed with the shotgun butt didn't make it."

"What a loss," McLean said flatly as he stared into Jenkins' eyes.

"That doesn't bother you?"

"No, why?"

"Just asking."

"What about the others?"

"DeLeon made them on four additionally robberies and they all copped. It seems that you put the fear of God into them."

"Someone had to; it wasn't coming from the courts."

"What about the Coroner's Inquest?"

"It's on hold."

"I won't hold my breath," McLean said.

McLean turned, and then hesitated.

"I've got a question."

"Shoot."

"Was he an ex-con?"

"Yep. He'd just been released from Quentin for armed robbery. Looks like he was going to kill you and Conti before having to go back."

"That wasn't going to happen."

"Appears not," Jenkins said as he turned and walked back down the corridor to the Detective squad room.

Following the shotgun incident, it was determined that McLean and Conti should be separated, for it was felt that together, they stirred within the other man the most "primal of instincts."

When McLean returned to work following three days off, he had a new partner.

NINETEEN

Captain Charlie Reese sat in his black executive chair, leaned back, clasped his hands behind his balding head and lingered in his thoughts. After some time, he spoke.

"Well, what do you think we should do with McLean?" he asked Mahon and Bock, who were seated against the far wall.

"The kid is one hell-of-a-street cop, especially for one with so little time on the job. But he goes through partners like sand through an hourglass," Mahon answered.

"I heard that he had a shooting in Wilshire before his transfer down here," Bock said.

"That he did," Reese answered.

"Was it a good one?" asked Bock.

"It was," Reese replied.

"The kid has balls," Mahon said.

"Maybe a little too much testosterone," Bock added. "The kid reminds me of the proverbial 'rebel without a cause.'"

"You could be right. He did make short work of that guy who tried to take his shotgun," Mahon said.

"It was a necessary reaction to a tough situation," Reese said, "but the bottom-line is it was his second kill in less than six months."

"So who should we put him with?" Mahon asked.

"I've got an idea," Bock. "Let's put him with Patterson."

"*Patterson?*" Reese asked incredulously.

"Shit. He's meaner than McLean and just might be able to keep him on a short leash," Bock said.

Reese propped his feet up on the corner of the desk. "Are you sure about that recommendation?"

"I've got a gut feeling that they just might compliment each other," Bock answered.

"I think he might be right," Mahon added. "They're both good street cops, have a sixth sense that can't be taught and they're respected by the others."

"A match made in heaven," Reese said chuckling.

"I wouldn't go that far, skipper," Bock said. "But I think it could work."

"O.K., let's make the change," Reese said. "Jack, make it effective tonight."

"Consider it done."

"One other thing before you both leave."

Mahon and Bock settled back into their chairs.

"Jack, I'm having to make a change in the supervisor running the Special Operations Squad, and I want to replace Stanley with Rod. What do you think?"

"I hate to lose him. He's the best supervisor I've got."

Bock sat straighter in his chair.

"That's why I'm making the assignment. It'll begin next deployment period."

"Will you accept the assignment, Rod?" Reese asked.

"Of course, but where is Stanley going?"

"To Metro. It's also effective next deployment period," said Mahon.

"After the shuffle, you can make any personnel changes you deem necessary," Reese added.

"Can I start now, and make a future request?"

"Hell, skipper. I knew he wouldn't wait stripping men from mornings," Mahon said grinning.

"What's the request?"

"Once I've settled in, and after Patterson and McLean have been together a month, I'd like them transferred to the squad."

"I see no problem with that, but I want to see if they can stay out of trouble before I make a concrete commitment."

"That's fine. And thanks for the vote of confidence," Bock said as he lifted his large frame from the uncomfortable chair and shook Reese's hand.

❧

Patterson walked into Reese's office, closed the door and stood, waiting.

"Have a seat, Chris," Reese said as he stood, walked to the end of his large desk and straddled the corner.

Patterson slid into one of the less comfortable hard-backed wooden chairs, wiggled his muscular frame back and forth trying to find a comfortable position, and then waited for Reese to speak. His first thought was that he'd screwed up.

"What do you know about McLean?" Reese asked.

"He's tough and seems to be a good street cop."

"He is, but he's rough on partners. Think you can work with him?"

"Do I have a choice?"

"Of course."

"I can work with him."

"Good."

"What car will we be workin'?"

"That's up to Lieutenant Mahon," Reese answered as he slid off the desk and walked over to Patterson.

"Thanks," he said as he extended his hand.

"That's it?"

"That's it. Should there be more?"

"Not as far as I'm concerned," Patterson said as he held out his hand.

The next night, Patterson and McLean began their working relationship, and it didn't take long for the tough Englishman and the aggressive Scotsman to determine that they had a good thing going.

❧

It was early, three-ten A.M. to be exact. The airwaves had been quiet all night and 3Adam9 sat nestled in the darkness of Winchell's at Adams and Figueroa.

Patterson sat behind the steering wheel and stared into the lighted intersection. He pondered a moment, and then reached over and poked the figure in the passenger seat, who it appeared was lost in his own thoughts.

"You still with me, McLean?" He spoke in a softer tone than usual, only because it was McLean, and not another cop in the seat.

"Yeah."

"You need some coffee."

In less than a minute, Patterson was walking back to the car carrying two paper cups containing coffee that could strip paint from a wall. After handing the cups to McLean, he slid his large frame into the seat, slouched down and resumed staring into the night.

"Don't you get any sleep at home?" Patterson asked.

"A little. The kids have been sick, and I've tried to help out during the day."

"You're a better man than I am," Patterson said as he continued to stare at the large church that sat on the northwest corner of the street.

McLean lifted the scalding liquid to his lips and sipped gently. He looked over at his pensive partner.

"Okay, what's on your mind?" he asked.

"I got the divorce papers yesterday. The old lady wants half my pension, the house and custody of the boys."

McLean continued to stare at Patterson, who had linked his arms around the steering wheel and was leaning forward again staring blankly into the night. "That hurts," McLean said.

"Yeah. I don't give a shit about her, but I'll miss my kids. But I guess that I should have thought about that before."

"Any chance you two will get back together?"

"None," Patterson said as he leaned away from the steering wheel, clasped his hands behind his head and stretched, and then grabbed the coffee cup that was sitting on the dash.

"What about the girlfriend?" McLean asked.

"What about her?"

"I was just wondering about her and the baby."

"Internal Affairs paid her a visit and wanted to talk about our relationship, but she refused to talk to them. They got pushy and she told them to go to hell and then slammed the door in their faces. They weren't real happy."

"I don't imagine they were. So what's next?"

"Don't know. I guess that I'll just wait it out."

Suddenly, the conversation was interrupted.

"All units in the vicinity and 3Adam9. Four-five-nine silent, 3026 South Vermont. 3Adam9, handle the call Code Two."

Patterson swung the car from the driveway and onto Adams Boulevard. When they reached Vermont, he made a quick left and slammed the accelerator pedal to the floor. The Plymouth lurched forward, its throaty growl reverberating off the adjacent buildings. Approaching 30th Street, he rolled toward the gas station that sat on the left hand side of the street. After swinging a quick U-Turn, he coasted into the service station driveway where he angled the high beams toward the small office.

McLean's narrow blue eyes focused on the office. The glass door was shattered and shards littered the front stoop. Suddenly, long, brown hair began to bob up and down in front of what appeared to be the safe. As the head lights illuminated the office, a solitary figure sprung into a standing position and shot a look at the black and white.

"We've got one," shouted McLean.

Patterson was already out of the car and nearing the front end.

McLean threw open his door and bolted toward the office as the suspect jumped through the hole in the door.

"It's a dude," screamed McLean as he paralleled Patterson's pursuit.

Patterson had taken three steps and then he stopped. When he pulled up, so did McLean. Both had their weapons extended and pointed at the fleeing burglar. McLean knew what was next.

Bobby White, transvestite and burglar, pulled his red dress up to his waist and began to sprint in front of the accordion gates that secured the service bays. As his stiletto heels clicked lightly on the pavement, Patterson, with his gun extended, leaned forward. When White came to the end of the metal grating and was about ready to flee into the darkness, Patterson fired.

White never heard the shot. The .38 slug struck the right rear of his head, flipping his torso through the air and sending his legs sprawling. After the lifeless body completed a full revolution in the air, the feet were thrust through the grating where they became entangled. As his body dangled against the grating and blood began to flow down the concrete into the street, his head bobbed suspended a foot above the asphalt and was surrounded by the red dress that billowed softly around his shoulders.

Neither Patterson nor McLean spoke.

While Patterson examined the body, McLean walked back to the police car. In minutes, Sergeant Elkins parked and walked directly over to the body.

"You involved in this, McLean?" he asked as he pulled up the red dress and looked into the distant eyes of the dead man.

"Yeah," McLean answered.

"I might have known it."

Without another word, Elkins jumped into the supervisor's station wagon and drove off.

"Dé jà vu," McLean muttered as he watched the station wagon disappear around the corner.

Reese sat behind his desk, leaned back, and stared at the ceiling. Bock sat in the chair directly across the desk.

"In your opinion, Rod, was it a good shooting?"

"In my opinion, Captain, it was," Bock said as he crossed his legs and tried to get comfortable. "He was a fleeing felon, Captain. Besides, the Coroner's Inquest found it within policy, so that should put the matter to rest."

"I heard that there was some excitement after Patterson testified?"

Bock leaned back in the hard chair and thrust his long legs forward, crossing the ankles. "More than a little. After Patterson testified, he walked into the hallway where White's family was gathered. When they saw him, they went nuts."

"Upset about the shooting?"

"No. They wanted to know who was going to get the car and his personal property. After Patterson slipped out, the Marshalls had to break up a major family dispute."

"Why didn't McLean shoot?" Reese asked, changing the subject.

"He said that when he saw Patterson stop, he knew what was next. So he pulled up and waited."

"He's that confident in his partner's appraisal of a use of force situation?"

"That confident," Bock confirmed.

"What about you, Rod? Are you that confident in them that you still want them working the Special Operations Squad?"

"The timing's right and I'm still that confident in their ability. And since we're losing two to Metro, now would be the perfect time."

"Consider it done," Reese said. "Why don't you tell them both that beginning tomorrow night, they'll be assigned to you. I'll let Jack know so he can adjust his deployment."

TWENTY

Patterson drove the unmarked police car slowly down Adams
Boulevard. The night was bleak-shrouded in fog, and both he
and McLean were bored.

"3Zebra9 requesting a time check," McLean said into the
tan Motorola radio mike.

"3Zebra9," the sweet voice of the dispatcher on the other
end of the radio answered, "the time is zero-four-ten."

Patterson leaned his large body forward toward the
steering wheel and meticulously adjusted his skin-tight black
leather gloves.

"It's only ten minutes later than the last time you checked,"
he grumbled as he stared into the soupy night.

A cotton fog hung heavy over the Adams District, the
streets were damp and above the mist, a full moon struggled to
shed its light on the city.

The street was deserted, all except for a black '57 Ford that
pulled slowly to the curb and parked in the darkness on the
southeast corner of Adams and Hoover.

As the car came to rest, a high-pitched hissing sound
whistled from under the dented hood while a thin, small spiral
of steam rose rapidly through the front grill and into the night
air. Slowly, and in unison, four dark figures slid deeper into their
seats, their heads barely visible.

Motown filtered softly from the window cracks as four sets
of eyes peered above the seats. The occupants in the weathered
Ford were looking for prey, not those they could rob, but
those they could kill. Not those in a pimped-up ride, but those

driving an unmarked police car. They were waiting for Officers Christian K. Patterson and Nicholas H. McLean.

The windows inside the Ford had fogged from alcohol-laced breath and the smoke from four tightly pinched joints. Washington slouched behind the steering wheel. He wore his customary black three-quarter length leather jacket and had a black silk dew-rag pulled tightly around his head. Between his legs was pushed the Colt, four-inch, blue steel .38.

His ebony complexion was marred by narrow eyes sandwiched between large protruding cheekbones and a wide forehead creating a menacing, brutish look.

Beneath the outer corner of his right eye were tattooed two perfectly sculptured black teardrops. "Death Drops" as they were called by the in-house prison artisan, who placed them perfectly on the ugly face.

He sported a large nose that had been brutally shattered by a guard's baton during a prison riot, leaving it wider than was natural, which added to his ferocious look.

In the front passenger seat sat Lastice. He also wore a long black leather coat, as did those in the back seat, and a small, black suede fedora pulled down snuggly on his head with its brim stopping just above his eyebrows. He carried his trademark sawed-off shotgun that was slung under his left arm and secured by a long, brown weathered shoelace.

"Hey, Bubba," Lastice said as he reached forward, adjusted the rear view mirror and preened himself in the cracked glass. "Where'd ya snake the ride?"

Washington turned and looked at Lastice who was flashing a toothy grin into the mirror. "From Adams and Central," Washington answered as he reached over and adjusted the mirror with the barrel of the Colt so as to have a clear view of the street through the back window.

Slouching lower in the left rear seat, Eddie Woods put his left hand over the end of his cigarette to block the glow and took two, long drags on the joint. Leaning forward, he coughed and exhaled all the dope-filled smoke.

"This weather's hell," he said, coughing a second time and sending spittle across the back of Washington's jacket.

"How do ya know Patterson'll be comin' this way?" Lastice asked Washington.

Washington took a long, deep drag on his joint and continued staring into the haze.

"'Cause I gotta friend workin' at the University po-lice station," he said, his pin-pointed eyes dancing in the darkness.

"So what," Lastice said haughtily. "I got friends a workin' all over the city, and that don't mean shit."

"Can your friends tell you where the po-lice do be workin every night?"

Lastice sat silent.

"No, I guess not," Washington said with a slight slur, never taking his eyes off the intersection to his left.

"Well, mine can. And she done told me this was Patterson's area. Besides, in about five minutes, Rosie'll be puttin' out a pretend call that'll get the pig's a drivin' right by us."

"I wish Gunn was here," said Terrance Potts.

"He ain't," Washington said abruptly as he reached over and grabbed a half-full bottle of Ripple from Lastice. He took a healthy drink and refocused on the street. Staring into the fog, he remembered Willie and was bound to make good on his promise to kill the pig that offed his little friend.

"How do you know it was Patterson that offed Willie?" asked Lastice.

"'Cause the bitch at the po-lice station told me she heard Patterson talking to another pig named McLean." Washington took two more gulps of the cheap wine.

"He done said that he put the most holes in Willie and before anyone knew he was even there, he was gone."

Washington cracked the mist-laden window, stuck his head out and looked up and down the street. Seeing no movement, he shoved the .38 into his waistband, pushed open the door, and slipped into the fog. Cautiously, he shuffled to the rear of the car and stopped at the left rear fin. Again, he looked up and down the street. Nothing moved.

"Ta-Ta," he called, "you hear me, Blood?"

"Yeah, I hear ya."

"Reach over and push on the brakes."

A sudden flash of red light illuminated the rear of the car, and then all went dark. Reaching into his waistband, he pulled out the Colt. Placing his left hand over the top of the left fin, he grabbed it snuggly and using the wooden grips of the gun as a hammer, struck the plastic lense. A muffled crack seeped into the night air as chunks of shattered red plastic scattered onto the slippery black asphalt.

"Hit the pedal again."

A brilliant white light shot through the remnants of the lense.

"That'll do jus' fine," he said as he sat down behind the steering wheel.

Potts took a deep drag on his reefer, held his breath until his face flushed and lungs stung, and then exhaled slowly blowing a billowing cloud of smoke toward the shredded headliner. Leaning on the rear of the front seat, he squinted through the driver's window.

"Blood," he slurred as spittle drooled unchecked from the side of his mouth. "Is you sure your snitch wasn't just bullshittin' you all? I mean Bubba, there ain't nothin' movin' out there but some sorry ass street dogs."

Washington ignored the comment. His mind remained focused on one thing: the killing of Patterson. Rolling down the driver's window, he stuck his head out, allowing a large cloud of marijuana smoke to seep into the darkness. Pulling his head inside, he wiped the moisture from his face, adjusted his dew-rag, and glanced at the dashboard clock. Four-fifteen, only five more minutes and Rosie would make the call.

Washington's legs were cramped, but he knew better than to stretch and chance hitting the brake pedal. Instead, he reached into his waistband and pulled out the Colt. He placed it between his legs and then snuggly wrapped both of his massive hands around the wooden grips. Rolling the gun from side to side, he became lost to its sensual feel.

In his hands, the gun felt better than any woman had ever felt. He smiled a sick, contorted smile and continued to stare into the darkness.

"How much longer is we gonna wait?" Lastice asked, gently stroking the sawed-off shotgun he cradled in his lap.

"Be patient, nigga," Washington snapped.

Washington slipped the revolver back in his waistband and wiped the small beads of perspiration from each side of his nose. It was becoming hot in the old Ford.

Four blocks away the radio in Patterson's police car crackled.

"3Zebra9, see the woman, victim of an assault. Reporting party is standing at the southeast corner of Adams and Portland."

"I hate those calls," Patterson commented as he leaned closer to the steering wheel and continued to drive slowly down Adams, passing Menlo Avenue.

"Some whore didn't get paid, so she wants to complain."

McLean reached for the mike. "3Zebra9, roger," Suddenly, he felt the need for another cup of coffee.

"It's eerie out here tonight," McLean commented. "I've got a strange feeling that something is going to happen."

Patterson threw McLean a quizzical look.

"So now you're telling the future, huh McLean? Another talent I'm just learning about?"

"Nah, just a feeling, that's all."

"Here they come!" Washington shouted, bolting upright in the seat. "Now, we do play it cool and do just what the pigs say. When they got us all outta the car, I'll drop my joint. Then we all spin. Understand?"

Three muffled acknowledgements were slurred through the smoky darkness.

An uneven rumble signaled the turning over of the Ford's engine.

Just as Patterson and McLean entered the intersection from the west, Washington punched the accelerator sending the rear tires into a spin and squealing on the wet asphalt. As the backend lost traction, the Ford fishtailed around the corner.

"*Chris!*" McLean yelled grabbing the dash with both hands as his partner slammed on the brakes.

"*Hit'em with the red!*" Patterson shouted.

McLean reached into the middle of the seat and grabbed the large, black spot-light that was plugged into the cigarette lighter. He slipped a red plastic lens over the front, and then pushed the large rubber light between the windshield and the dashboard. Once secure, he snapped the "on" switch. The back window of the Ford erupted in bright red. As if anticipating the light, the Ford hit the brakes sending a brilliant white light from the left rear taillight.

As the Ford pulled to the right and stopped in the curb lane, 3Zebra9, pulled behind in a felony stop position that found it parked about ten feet to the rear of the Ford with its left front fender offset about four feet into the street. As Patterson angrily slammed the select lever into Park, McLean slipped the mike from its holder.

"3Zebra9 requesting wants and warrants on Sam-Henry-Adam 187."

Patterson stepped out into the street. McLean stepped from the passenger side and took a position on the sidewalk just to the right rear of the Ford's rear fender.

"You in the front seat, put your hands out the windows with fingers spread," Patterson commanded, his revolver hidden just behind his right thigh.

"The rest of you put your hands straight forward where we can see them," he shouted as two flashlights beamed brightly into the Ford's interior. In unison, four sets of hands became visible.

They're too anxious to please, McLean thought, slipping his revolver from behind his leg to the front.

While Patterson stood issuing commands, the radio inside the black and white came alive.

"3Zebra9, Sam-Henry-Adam 187 is a Newton stolen, considered armed and dangerous."

The transmission went unheard by 3Zebra9.

McLean stood on the sidewalk in the shadows just to the right rear of the Ford. He held his service revolver in his right hand with his elbow pushed snuggly into his side and the forearm extended. In his left hand, he held his flashlight.

"Be watchin' me," Washington, grunted.

"Driver," Patterson commanded, "open the door from the outside, step out slowly, place your hands on your head, and walk to the curb side of your car and place your hands on the hood."

Washington pushed his hands out the open window, opened the door, slipped sideways from the car and sauntered to a position between the curb and right front fender. After placing his hands lightly on the hood, he glanced around to see where both Patterson and McLean were standing.

"You in the right front passenger seat," barked Patterson, his low voice cutting through the night like sharpened scissors shredding strips of paper. "Open the door from the outside, slide out of the car, keep your hands where my partner can see them, and take a position next to your friend."

Lastice reached out his rolled down window and opened the car door from the outside. With the sawed-off shotgun tucked snuggly under his left arm and hidden by the long jacket, he stepped from the car and took a position to the left of Washington, his hands placed gently on the roof.

Patterson then ordered Potts and Woods from the rear seat. Before sliding out, each adjusted the pistols that were stuffed into their waistbands. After sliding out the rear passenger door, each stepped toward the back of the Ford, with Woods putting his hands on the trunk and Potts grabbing the rear section of the roof.

Suddenly, a slight breeze blew from the east sending the poignant aroma of cannabis sativa whiffing into the night and filling Patterson's nostrils with the sweet smell of marijuana.

"They've got some dope in the car," Patterson shouted to McLean, who had holstered his revolver and stepped to the right of Washington. Washington turned his head to the left. The eyes of the others were riveted in his direction.

Washington took a long, hard drag on the joint. Holding his breath, he savored its effects. The muscles in his face tightened, while the black teardrops were moistened with dew. As the six men stood in the thick fog, tension built, and feet shuffled back and forth.

"Stand still," McLean, barked.

McLean dropped his flashlight into its trouser pocket and grabbed Washington by the nape of the neck with his left hand and began to wind his right leg around the giant's right leg. Suddenly, the killer's mouth opened and a small hand-rolled cigarette dropped to the asphalt. As the joint hit the wet pavement, its embers shot into the air as it twirled skyward.

As it bounced, Washington bolted upright, the mass of his body throwing the smaller McLean backwards onto the sidewalk. As McLean hit, he heard a throaty low growl shout, "*Patterson!*"

In one fluid motion, as though it had been rehearsed a hundred times, Washington pulled the Colt from his waistband. Then, the others spun, weapons in hand.

Patterson crouched into a combat stance.

He fired.

The bullet flew just past Washington's head and into the darkness. Suddenly, the tranquil night erupted in a cacophony of explosions.

Washington's first round caught Patterson in the right leg, shattering the thigh. As the bullet ripped through flesh and bone, Patterson fired again; his round slamming into the Ford's front-end just between Washington and Lastice.

Lastice snaked the shotgun out from under his armpit and leveled it at Patterson. Patterson saw the shotgun and suddenly it was too late as it exploded into sound. As flame belched from the barrel, the gun jumped in the wet hands of its owner.

Patterson whirled from the blast as his right leg buckled. He could hear the whistling pellets as they screamed past, sending nine-death dealing slugs inches from his head as he fell to the wet sidewalk. Rolling to the right, he fired again. His round struck Woods in the forehead, spinning him around and pinning him against the rear trunk lid.

McLean raised himself to a seated position and fired at Potts. His shot caught the would-be killer in the face, snapping his head back and throwing his gun across the trunk and into the middle of the street.

He fired again.

His second shot struck Potts in the right side of the throat, spinning him violently into the side of the Ford and dropping him at Washington's feet.

Washington took aim at Patterson; however, he was distracted when another shot from the still seated McLean struck the Ford.

Washington spun and fired at McLean who, upon seeing the larger gunman spin, rolled toward the grass. Just as he spun off the concrete, Washington's bullet struck the sidewalk and ripped out small pieces of concrete sending the bullet ricocheting through the window of a dimly lit house.

Because of the gunfire, no one heard the glass shatter or the muffled cry that came from within the residence.

Leanne Andrews was startled by the squeal of tires just outside her window. When she and her roommate peered out, they saw an old black car stopped in the street with a brown car parked just to its rear. Suddenly gunfire erupted, but she never heard the glass in the picture window crack and form small irregular circles. After uttering a hushed cry, Leanne Andrews crumpled to the floor.

After firing, Lastice broke open the shotgun, yanked out the spent cartridge and tossed it into the grass. Reaching into a jacket pocket, he pulled out his last round. Before he was able to reload, a shot flew past his head. Frightened, he dropped the round on the ground and watched as it quickly rolled into the darkness. Seeing Potts fall and Woods pinned against the trunk, Lastice forgot about looking for the lost shell.

His mouth was suddenly dry and his hands were shaking. Spinning, he jumped onto the hood of the Ford, slid to the street side, and bolted across Adams Boulevard disappearing into the fog and thick shrubbery.

Lying on his back, not knowing if Woods was dead, Patterson fired two additional shots into the still standing bandit that sent him flying spread-eagle over the trunk and sprawling into the street. He then turned his attention to the enormous darkly clad assailant that stood at the front of the Ford.

Washington turned and McLean fired twice. Both rounds missed and smashed into the Ford, shattering its side windows. As the second slug whistled by his head, Washington fired at the seated McLean, striking him in the large buckle of his gun belt. The impact threw McLean's upper torso backwards and smashed him against a small concrete retaining wall. There was an overpowering smell of gunpowder that burst into his nostrils. Then all went black.

Hutton and Hestily sat in their black and white sipping coffee at Winchells when suddenly their radio awoke from its deep slumber. "Beep ...Beep ...Beep." Simultaneously, both men tossed their half-filled cups out the window and waited.

"All University Division units and 3Adam58, a citizen reports officers need help, shots fired, Adams and Hoover. 3Adam58, handle the call Code Three. Any other University unit available identify to Control and handle the call Code Two."

In seconds, the big bore Plymouth was fishtailing diagonally across the parking lot and shooting through the deserted intersection of Adams and Figueroa.

As Washington took aim to finish Patterson, his attention was diverted to the east where a siren was screaming down in his direction. Facing Patterson, he was met by another round that was low to his left and slammed into the passenger door. As flames belched from the end of the barrel, Patterson slipped into unconsciousness.

Like a dog gone mad, Washington charged the prone body. Reaching down, he ripped the badge from its leather belt holder, and frantically searched for his gun. Distracted, by the wail of the siren, he glanced down the street and saw the bright red lights of a police car. Forgetting about the gun, he bolted into the thick fog darting into the mist covering South Hoover Avenue.

As 3 Adam 58 locked its brakes and its high beams illuminated the scene, Hutton saw four bodies on the ground.

Two were cops.

"Call an ambulance," he shouted to Hestily as he slammed his left foot down onto the parking brake. Jumping out, he heard the wail of other sirens.

❧

By the time Bock arrived, four plainclothes Zebra units along with six black and whites were at the scene. The neighborhood had been secured by patrol officers and Air-3, the division's helicopter, was flying tight circles above the scene while shining its halogen spotlight into lightless backyards and down the dark alleys.

Jack Mahon was shouting orders.

"It's Patterson and McLean," he yelled to Bock, his ruddy Irish complexion erupting in a hue of scarlet.

"Patterson's hit in the leg and McLean is laying unconscious next to that small retaining wall."

Bock ran over to Patterson and knelt down.

"Chris, can you hear me?" he asked, raising his voice to be heard above the incoming sirens. There was no response.

"We need to stop this bleeding," Bock shouted.

"Inglis, find a pressure point and slow down this bleeding."

Inglis gently extending Patterson's leg, cut open the top of the trousers with his small Swiss Army pocketknife and then searched the inside of the white leg until a throbbing artery was located. Placing three fingers on the pulsating point, he pressed firmly, using the index and first and second fingers of his right hand.

Patterson moaned, but remained unconscious.

Inglis watched as the dark red fluid spurted from the open leg wound, then gradually lessened to a slow dribble over the protruding bone.

Standing on the grass, Bock heard muted sobs coming from an apartment to his rear. Turning, he saw a small hole surrounded by concentric rings in the middle of a large glass picture window.

"Shit," he muttered as he ran to the front of the building, located the apartment and knocked on the door. There was no answer, but the sobbing was louder. Snapping the knob, he threw the unlocked door open and stormed into the room like a terrorist carrying a satchel of plastic explosives.

Carol Young sat on the floor of the small student apartment cradling the head of her roommate in her hands while her lifeblood ebbed slowly into the carpet.

"*Don't die, Leanne,*" the distraught girl sobbed.

"*Please ...please don't die.*"

Bock ran to the wounded girl and placed two fingers on the side of her neck. He found a slight pulse.

"Call another ambulance," he shouted to Sabatello, who had just entered the room. Sabatello disappeared, and in moments was again standing in the doorway breathing heavily.

"It's on its way, Sarge."

"Help me get this other young lady into another room," Bock said as he reached down and gently lifted the sobbing Carol Young to her feet.

"Sabatello, stay in here until the ambulance arrives," he added while peering out the small hole in the window.

Walking outside, Bock heard a siren in the distance that was a different pitch than that of a police car. He walked to the corner and waited. The city ambulance screeched to a stop in front of the idling Ford. Two ambulance attendants jumped out, the passenger carrying a small black satchel. They stopped and looked at the two darkly clad bodies.

"What the hell are you looking at?" Bock yelled, his face red and the veins in his neck distended.

"Forget those two, assholes," he screamed. "Get working on my men, and start with the big cop on the sidewalk."

Inglis stepped back, allowing an attendant to kneel and take up a position to maintain pressure on the artery. The second attendant rushed over to the dazed McLean, who was propped against the retaining wall.

"Did we get'em all" McLean asked, his voice barely above a whisper. "There were four of them."

"Sarge!" the attendant yelled to Bock. "You need to hear this."

Bock hurried to McLean and knelt down in the moist grass.

"You still with us, Nick?"

"Yeah, Sarge. There were four of them. How many did we get?"

"Two."

"But there were four of them," McLean again muttered.

"It looks like the other two escaped. But we'll get them."

"Shit," McLean mumbled as he pulled his knees to his chest.

"How's Chris?"

"He took a round to the leg. We'll get you both to the hospital. Just take it easy."

McLean's head slowly fell forward as he slipped back into a deep labyrinth of darkness.

"Get my men into the ambulance," Bock shouted. "And cover up the two assholes."

"Rod," Mahon called. "Can some of your men help with the search until we get some more patrol units out here?"

"Brown, you and Stemples stay with the cars. LeFrois, Brooks, Johnson, Stallcup and McGrath, help with the search. Inglis, you ride with Patterson and McLean."

Inglis climbed into the rear of the ambulance and took a seat on the hard wooden bench that was attached to a side panel. In minutes, ambulance unit G-3 was screaming towards Central Receiving Hospital with its precious cargo.

"All right, I want you to conduct house-to-house searches and see if anyone saw or heard something," Bock said as he pulled a folded white handkerchief from his left rear pocket and wiped the small drops of moisture from his forehead and around his nose.

"Be careful, gentlemen" Mahon yelled as he climbed into his car.

"Oh, one other thing, Rod," said Mahon. "Evans is making the notifications, and I'm confident that when the dicks get here they'll start to sort this thing out."

"Let's hope so," Bock said as he ran his large hands through his jet-black hair.

TWENTY-ONE

Charlie Reese caught the phone on the fourth ring and wearily picked up the receiver.

"Reese."

"Captain, it's Al Evans."

"What can I do for you at this ungodly hour, Al?"

"Sorry for the lateness of the call, Captain, but there's been a shooting. We've got one officer shot, another hurt, and a USC coed struck by a stray bullet."

Reese bolted upright in bed. The sleep was beginning to leave his voice.

"Who are the officers?"

"Patterson and McLean."

"How bad is it?"

"Patterson was hit in the right leg. McLean took a round in his gunbelt that threw him against a wall and knocked him unconscious."

"Where are they now?"

"On their way to Central Receiving."

"And the suspects?"

"Two dead and it appears that two escaped."

"And a USC coed? How the hell did that happen?" Reese asked, struggling to pull on his trousers while trying to balance the telephone receiver between his thick neck and left shoulder.

"It looks like a round smashed through her window and hit her in the face while she stood watching the gun battle go down."

"Is she dead?"

"She was hanging on by a thread when she left the scene."

"I'm on my way, Al," Reese said as he quickly put the receiver back in the cradle rest, finished dressing and gave his wife, Flo, a kiss on the forehead.

In less than ten minutes, he was on the Pasadena Freeway heading towards Central Receiving. Reese shot a look at the speedometer. Ninety...One hundred...One hundred- ten. He pushed harder on the gas pedal trying to squeeze out any additional horsepower. Like a professional race car driver, the stocky ex-fighter from Oklahoma cajoled the big engine until the Plymouth was tearing down the freeway in excess of one hundred-twenty miles an hour.

His hands tightly gripped the steering wheel and his mind raced. Other than himself, he was certain there was no one out.

He was wrong.

Looking into the rear view-mirror, he saw a solid red light gaining on him quickly.

"Highway Patrol," he muttered.

Tapping the brakes lightly, he brought the Plymouth to a stop on the shoulder of the freeway. The red light in his rearview mirror did the same. As Reese got out, rather than seeing a California Highway Patrol officer, he watched as an off-duty rent-a-cop wearing a drab gray uniform and holding a flashlight approached.

Reese went nuts.

In two strides, he stood facing the wanna-be-cop. Throwing open his wallet, he removed his badge and pushed it into the man's face.

"Read it, asshole!" he screamed, his voice quivering. "It says, 'Captain, Los Angeles Police Department'!"

The rent-a-cop went white and started to speak, but Reese cut him off mid-sentence.

"You stupid son-of-a-bitch!" he screamed. "I have two officers shot and you have the balls to pull me over!"

"But, but, I..."

Reese stepped closer to the man.

"And so you never forget tonight..."

With one swift blow, Reese caught the man in the middle of the forehead with his badge, knocking him to the ground, unconscious. As the wanna-be-cop lay prone on the asphalt, Reese looked down and saw implanted solidly on the man's forehead the words: "Captain, Los Angeles Police Department."

꿏

Al Evans sat sequestered in the Watch Commander's office, monitoring Tactical Frequency two. Suddenly, the phone rang. Irritated by the interruption, he snapped down the volume on the radio squawk box and picked up the phone.

"Sergeant Evans."

"Sarge, this is Inglis up at Central Receiving."

"How are Patterson and McLean doing?" Evans asked.

"Patterson's still in surgery."

"What about McLean?"

"He'll be fine. He suffered a mild concussion. He's one lucky son-of-a-bitch cuz' the bullet that would have sent him end-of-watch was low and slammed into his gun belt. But we have a problem."

"What's that?" Evans asked in anticipation.

"Patterson's badge is missing."

"Any chance it's lost and not stolen?" Evans asked, a deep concern in his voice.

"The guys checked the scene and I searched the ambulance. Nothing."

"Okay, I'll let the Lieutenant know. Keep looking around the hospital, John. Maybe someone removed it when Patterson was rolled into surgery."

"Doesn't appear to be the case, but we'll keep looking."

Evans cradled the receiver and then turned up the volume on the squawk box and grabbed the mike. Before he could broadcast, he heard Bock's voice cutting across the airwaves.

"3Zebra20 to 3Lincoln90 come in."

"3Lincoln90, go ahead."

"Al, anything else on Patterson's badge," Bock asked.

"Nothing yet, but we'll keep looking."

"Al, one other thing. Don't bother trying to notify Patterson's wife. It appears that she wouldn't give a damn if he lived or died."

"I'll scratch it from my to-do list."

Evans hung up and immediately vacated the watch commander's chair as Mahon walked through the door.

"It's all yours, Lieutenant," Evans said smiling.

"It suits you better than it does me."

"Thanks, Al. You did fine," Mahon said as he sat down in the aluminum armchair and rolled it closer to the scratched gray metal desk.

Mahon was tired. Not because of the hours spent in the field after the shooting, but because of the stress he felt when one of his men was hurt. With two down, the drain increased dramatically.

"Did you start the Incident Log," Mahon asked as he removed his glasses and with the palms of both hands rubbed his eyes.

"Only some hen scratches," Evans replied. "I was just starting to piece it all together."

"I'll do it," Mahon said as he pulled out a yellow legal pad and began to decipher Evans' notes and outline the calls made along with their times.

Watch Commander's Log

1/3/1968 Wednesday 05:45

Notifications

Division Commander/Captain Reese-04:45

Robbery-Homicide/Sgt. Del Rio -04:50

University Division Detectives/Steele, Van Drew-04:55

S.I.D. Prints & Photo's/Wiggins-05:00

Communications/Lt. Holmes-05:05

Officer's Families/Patterson-None/McLean, made by officer.

Mahon stopped writing and stared at the list, but before he could again put pen to paper, the phone rang.

"Lieutenant," Officer Purington called out from the front desk. "Inglis is on line twenty-two."

"Thanks, Tom."

Mahon pushed down the flashing button and picked up the receiver.

"This is Mahon, John. Patterson's conditioned worsened?" he asked, anxiously waiting for the answer.

"No, but the second ambulance they sent to Adams and Hoover just brought in the young female that Bock found shot in her apartment. She's hanging on by a thread."

"Shit."

Silence.

"Keep me posted," Mahon said as he retrieved his yellow pad and picked up a pencil.

"There's more," Inglis added, hesitatingly. "Her name is Leanne Andrews. Her father is Congressman Andrews from the Twentieth Congressional District in the San Fernando Valley."

"You're kidding," Mahon muttered.

"Nope."

"How the hell did that piece of information slip through the cracks?"

"I don't know, Lieutenant, But when she got here one of the nurses who knows the family recognized her."

"Did anyone notify her parents?"

"That I don't know. One other thing. We've got reporters climbing over each other to get the story. What do you suggest?"

"Just tell them that Captain Reese is on his way, and he'll address their questions when he arrives."

Mahon hung up the phone and sat thinking.

"Lieutenant, line forty-four," Boyd yelled again from the front desk."

"Lieutenant Mahon, may..."

"Jack, it's Rod. We've got a problem."

"So I've heard."

"You talked to Inglis?"

"Just hung-up."

"I thought it best to warn him about what might happen at the hospital. You were my next call."

"That's fine. What can you tell me?"

"The roommate called the parents when Sabatello stepped into the hallway to have a smoke."

"Shit."

"On that we agree."

"I'll let the Captain know. He's on his way to the hospital as we talk. Anything further from the scene?"

"The guys are still trying to hunt down witnesses. Do we have an ETA on the dicks?

"They're on their way. Just hang tight."

"Thanks," Bock said as he stepped back from the telephone and again looked at the small hole in the window.

"What a mess," Mahon said as he hung up the telephone.

Elkins stood outside the supervisor's station wagon holding the radio mike. McGrath stood next to him holding a small, white, rectangular card.

"Let me have the Field Interview Card," he said as he activated the talk key.

"3Lincoln90, go ahead 3Lincoln40," Mahon said.

"Lieutenant, no sign of Patterson's badge, but McGrath found an old lady who was walking her dog when the shooting started. She hid in the bushes on the opposite side of Adams and watched everything go down."

"She didn't try to get out of there?"

"No. It appears that she was too frightened to run and too curious to move."

"What did McGrath get out of her?"

"She told him that after the shooting stopped, she saw a big man who looked like King Kong walk over to a man who was down on the sidewalk and rip something off his waist."

"That solves the case of the missing badge. Can she come up with a better description?"

"Only that he was a large male Negro, wore a long black jacket and had a black bandanna tied around his head. She also saw another man run into the fog while the man she called 'King Kong' was still shooting."

"Any description on the other shooter?"

"Just that he was small, appeared to be male Negro, and was holding some type of a rifle in his hands."

"Thanks, Jack. Be sure you get that out over the air, and I'll update the boss."

❧

Standing on the corner of Adams and Hoover, Bock watched his breath waft into the air. Reaching into the Plymouth, he grabbed the mike.

"3Zebra20 to Control, show this unit to Central Receiving Hospital."

Stepping onto the sidewalk, he watched as his men returned from their search.

"Anything new?" he asked.

"Nothing other than what McGrath found," replied Eddie Brown.

"So we don't know anything more about the two assholes who escaped than we did," Brooks said, a touch of frustration in his voice.

"That's it. Two males, one who looks like King Kong and the other much smaller. Both were wearing long black three-quarter length leather jackets, and the smaller man had what we have now determined to be a shotgun."

"Who are the dicks handling?" Johnson asked.

"Steele and Van Drew."

"If they don't solve it, no one will," added Stemples.

Bock began to walk to his car, and then stopped.

"They'll be handling the investigation and we've been asked to provide tactical support, so whatever you're working on, put it on hold."

"Do they think that a stray bullet from Patterson's gun hit the coed?" asked Stallcup.

"No one knows. That's one of many unanswered questions," Bock said as he pulled a small black comb from his shirt pocket and while stopping to think, combed back his hair.

"I want you guys to secure the scene until Steele and Van Drew arrive, and then meet back at the station. I'll meet you there after I check on Patterson and McLean."

❦

Reese pulled into the parking lot at Central Receiving and parked in a space reserved for LAPD. The lot was crowded with two ambulances, four black and whites, and two civilian cars that had press passes hanging from the rear view mirrors.

As he stepped from the car, he was cornered by Sal Weinstein, a seasoned police-beat reporter from the *Times*, and Mike Teich from the *Examiner*.

"Caught the action on the scanner, Captain. What do we have?" Weinstein asked as he aggressively pushed his short, squatty body closer to Reese, who was fighting his way through shoving bodies.

"Don't know yet," Reese said, "but as soon as something substantial surfaces, Press Relations will let you know...along with all the other newspapers."

"Off the record, Captain," Teich shouted above the clamor of the crowd. "Was a Congressman's daughter shot by a stray police bullet?"

Reese ignored the question and continued walking.

"Come on, Captain," Weinstein yelled as he pushed his way up the long ramp that led into the hospital. "Just a yes or no."

Reese threw open the glass and aluminum hospital doors. "Dammit," he muttered under his breath, "all we need is the press leaking that fallacious story."

He walked into the crowded, white-tiled hallway, and looked for one of his supervisors. As he passed the crowded nurse's station, he saw Jerry Bova walking out of one of the rooms accompanied by Inglis.

"How's Patterson?" he asked.

"He's still in surgery, Captain," Bova said as he gently took Reese by the elbow and led him into a quiet corner just beyond the nurses' station.

"Keep the wolves at bay, John," Reese said softly to Inglis as he stepped into the alcove with Bova.

"Will do, Captain," Inglis responded. "We've never been on a first name basis."

"I was told by a nurse that he lost a quantity of blood that required a transfusion, four units to be exact, but overall, he should live," Bova said, stepping deeper into the shadows.

"The bullet was through-and-through. It shattered his right femur, causing a compound fracture. No one knows when he'll be back to work, or if he will."

"And McLean?"

"He took a bullet in the buckle of his gunbelt. The impact threw him backwards and slammed him into a retaining wall where he was knocked unconscious. He's complaining about having one hell of a headache."

"What about his family? Have they been notified?"

"He called his wife and told her what happened. He's in Room 5 if you want to talk to him."

"I do, but first tell me about the girl?"

Bova winced.

"When they brought her in, there was a slight pulse. She died on the operating table."

"Did she ever regain consciousness?"

"No. All we have is the statement made by her roommate, Carol Young. She told Bock's men that she and Miss Andrews had just returned from a fraternity party on 28th Street when they heard cars idling and voices talking outside their window. When they looked out, they saw two cars parked in the street.

"They watched as two white men ordered four male Negroes from a black car. When all four men were standing next to their car, they spun and the shooting began."

"Did the witness see who shot her roommate?"

"No, but she did say that they saw a large colored man turn and shoot at another man on the grass. She said it looked like he was pointing toward the ground, but suddenly, her roommate fell and she saw blood on her face."

"Thanks, Jerry," Reese said as he turned and stepped into the brightness of the hospital lights. Walking down the hall, he ignored the shouts from Weinstein and Teich that came from near the front doors.

He stopped at Room 5 and pushed open the heavy white steel door. McLean was sitting up in bed with his back resting on two fluffed pillows. When he'd first regained consciousness, he thought he was dead. All was silent and stark white. If he were dead, as he assumed for a moment that he was, it was vexing to feel the pain in the back of his head-the same pain he would have felt if he were alive. On the other hand, if he was in heaven, it was a disappointment because he hurt like hell.

McLean saw a form through the white haze—a stocky form. As his vision cleared, he saw that the stocky form was Reese.

"Glad to see you're alive, Mac."

"Thanks."

Reese stood silently and waited.

McLean broke the brief silence.

"How's Patterson?"

"He's going to live, but he might limp." Reese saw McLean's almost imperceptible nod as if he was acknowledging the report.

"Now tell me all you can about what happened out there."

McLean pushed his elbows deep into the pillows, slid his back firmly against the bed frame and settled back.

"We stopped four male Negroes, got them out of the car and lined them up to search. Just as I began to shake the first one down, he dropped a cigarette," McLean said as he moved around in the bed trying to find a comfortable position.

"Then all hell broke loose. They fired and we fired. I don't remember much after I took the shot in the belt," McLean said softly.

"Nothing else?"

McLean hesitated and tried to clear his head.

"Yeah, there is something else. Right before the shooting started, the big guy who dropped the cigarette spun, and called Patterson by name."

After Reese left the room and closed the heavy door, McLean's mind somersaulted into the past when he experienced his first realities of what to expect from the Los Angeles Police Department. As he reeled off the events, he wondered if he had made the right decision.

TWENTY-TWO

Steele and Van Drew stood on the southeast corner of Adams and Hoover taking in the scene.

"One miserable night," Steele said as he and Van Drew turned and walked into the apartment of Leanne Andrews.

The apartment was empty. At Bock's direction, Carol Young had been driven to University station to be met by her parents.

Steele stood and stared at the small hole in the plate glass window. It was round, but the irregular concentric rings led him to believe that it was not a straight shot.

"Get a sketch of the room, Van, I'm headed outside."

Walking through the thinning fog, Steele stopped next to the front-end of the Ford. He peered down at the concrete, then looked up and focused on the small hole in the window.

"Put your penlight against the hole and aim it down at the angle of entry," he shouted to Van Drew who was standing next to the window. When Steele saw the small bead of light, he aligned himself with the hole. Once he had a straight line, he bent down and ran his hand across the sidewalk.

Steele dropped into a catcher's squat and waddling like a duck, he approached the thin bead of light while running his hand gently back and forth on the ground.

Suddenly, his fingers felt a chip that lined up directly with the angle of the light. Reaching into his trouser pocket, he pulled out a shinny dime and placed it over the indentation. He then reentered the apartment.

Inside, he walked across the living room, his shoes whispering through the thick rug. Stepping over to the plate glass window, he reached into his tweed suit pocket and pulled out a large safety pin and a small wooden spool that contained white kite string. Pushing the end of the string through the window, he unwound a length of string, snapped it off the spool and tied the end to the safety pin. Then he stepped closer to the window and again examined the angle of entry.

"Hold the safety pin close to the hole and feed me the string once I'm outside."

"I thought that the Firearms Unit at S.I.D. handled the trajectory problems," Van Drew said as Steele walked out the door.

"They do," Steele yelled back, "but they're not here, and we are."

Stepping through the waist-high shrubbery, he located the tail of the string dangling just outside the hole. Grabbing the end, he backed up and slowly pulled it toward the dime.

"Now I have that line," he muttered to himself. "All I need is one more."

"Put the safety pin flush to the window and make sure the string is tied tight."

With the pin flush with the glass, Steele pulled it snuggly, then tied the string around the head of his flashlight and placed the flashlight facedown directly over the dime.

Removing more string from his pocket, he wrapped a second thin line around the handle of the flashlight. Stepping backwards, he slowly released the string until his back stopped at the Ford's right front fender. Stepping to the left, he aligned the second piece of string with the string coming from the hole in the window.

Perfect, he thought as he gently pulled the string taught and placed it on the ground, held in place by his notebook.

He walked to the rear of the Ford where he found a quantity of blood on the sidewalk. Removing a piece of white chalk from his coat pocket, he circled the blood and chalked out the word, "Patterson."

He then stepped back to the front of the Ford. Glancing across the lawn, he found the area that had been smashed down by McLean's body. Stepping closer, he found a small blotch of blood on the retaining wall. Using the chalk, he circled the blood and wrote above it, "McLean."

"The bullet that killed the Andrews girl came from a suspect, not from Patterson or McLean," he said under his breath as he leaned back on his haunches.

Flipping to a blank page in the small notebook he kept in his pocket, he made some notations and a quick sketch. Distracted by the noise of a car approaching, he turned his head and saw Reese's car cut through the haze, stop, and park.

"So who shot her?" Reese asked as he walked up to the still squatting Steele. "And please don't tell me it was one of us," he added.

"It wasn't," Steele said as he stood and pushed his hands through his curly gray hair.

"Good. Then what happened?"

"After you had left the hospital," Steele said as he threw a cigarette between his lips, "I walked across the street and called Central Receiving. McLean had just regained consciousness and I was lucky enough to catch him awake. He told me what he told you about someone calling out Patterson's name."

"Go on," Reese said as he shoved his hands into his trouser pockets and shuddered slightly.

"When I walked back down Hoover, I found pieces of red plastic taillight lense scattered on the ground. Between that and the fact that one suspect called Patterson by name, it has all the appearances of a set-up. Someone wanted Patterson dead."

"So we have an ambush."

"Exactly," Steele commented as he unwrapped the string from his flashlight and wound it back onto the spool.

"And McLean adds credibility to that theory."

"So we know it was Patterson they wanted," Reese said as he stepped back to his car and leaned on the warm hood.

"Yep," Steele said as he picked up the dime and dropped the spool of string into a suit pocket.

Steel continued. "During the gun battle one of the shooters

fired low and the round struck the concrete. This round appears to have ricocheted through the window and struck the Andrews girl."

"Your two pieces of white string and a dime told you all of that?"

"Two pieces of white string, a dime and twenty years working homicide," Steele answered with boyish glee.

"After that shot, according to the witness that McGrath found hiding across the street, Kong walked over to Patterson and ripped something from his waist. We believe it was his badge since it's missing. Then Kong and another shooter disappeared into the fog. So we have two bad guys end-of-watch and one USC coed injured."

"Dead," Reese interjected. "She died on the table."

"That's too bad."

"Tell me about the witness?"

"She's an old lady who was walking her dog. McGrath pressed her for information, but she can't give us anything more than Kong was big, black, and wore dark clothing, and the smaller man appeared to be carrying a small rifle. Not a hell of a lot to go on."

"What's your next move?"

"Well, we've got two bad guys on the run. They can either steal another car and hole up at one of their partner's pads, or they can hoof it back to their own place if they live in the area."

"What do you think they'll do?"

"No idea."

"And the Ford?"

"It's a Newton stolen, taken last night in a street robbery. I'll check with Newton Detectives to see if they'll re-interview the elderly victim. I'd like to try and get a better description on the suspects."

"Any likelihood of prints?"

"Possible. These guys sat for sometime before the shooting. Their prints should be in the car, especially on the back of the rearview mirror ...unless they wore gloves, which is unlikely if they were hell-bent on a shootout."

"What about the dead suspects?"

"Neither appear to have gotten off a shot. Bock assigned two of his men to go down to the morgue with the bodies. After they're printed, they'll hand carry the print cards to Wiggins at Latent Prints to see if they can get a positive I.D."

"Thanks, Jimmy," Reese said.

Steele wasn't finished.

"With positive ID's, we'll have their packages hand searched and see if we can't identify some common partners. These assholes need to have associates."

"Did we find all the guns?"

"Yep. We found Patterson's underneath the Ford—must have slid there when he hit the sidewalk. We also picked up the guns from the dead suspects. We're running them through NCIC to see if they're stolen, and if so, when and from where."

"It sounds like you've covered all the bases," Reese said. "Now get me the two shooters who escaped."

Steele and Van Drew watched as Reese got into his car, and then drove off.

"He's going to have his hands full with this one," Van Drew said.

"And so will we."

As Steele stood on the sidewalk, a uniformed officer approached holding a spent shotgun round on the end of a pencil and a live round in the palm of his hand.

"Sarge, we found these in the grass near the sidewalk. Thought you might want them."

"Hell, yes," Steele said as he removed a small manila envelope from his outside coat pocket and dropped in the rounds. He licked and sealed the envelope and placed his initials and the date over the small flap.

"If these assholes caper again with that shotgun, the spent

round with its dented primer just might prove useful," Steele commented as both men walked back to their car.

"Where are we headed?" asked Van Drew.

"Central Receiving," Steele, said as he slipped the cigarette pack from his pocket and after tapping it softly, removed a smoke and slid it between his narrow lips.

TWENTY-THREE

After the ambush of Patterson and McLean, Lastice quickly moved down Adams Boulevard, darting in and out of the deep shadows. The night was soggy, the fog turned to a heavy mist and the streets were wet. It was cold, but thin beads of perspiration trailed from under his black fedora and trickled down his forehead, leaving a slight trail on his dark face.

When he could run no more, he stopped and stepped back onto the darkened front porch of a small house where he readjusted the empty shotgun that hung loosely under his left armpit. It wasn't until now that he wished he'd slipped more shotgun rounds into the deep pockets of his black leather jacket. When he saw the firepower his three partners toted, he felt that two rounds were sufficient. He was wrong.

Fearing the approach of any car, he froze as dim headlights cut a hazy swath in the distance. Once the danger passed, he resumed his search. Finally, he found a small Corvair parked deep in the driveway of an old home.

Stepping down the long driveway that was cloaked by thick trees and overgrown bushes, he stopped next to the car and reached into his right front trouser pocket where he removed a small, oblong piece of rubber shaped like a small cucumber. He unscrewed the two sections of the rubber container, opened it and after fingering through a host of miniature tools, removed a small screwdriver.

Looking around one final time and seeing he was alone, he quietly opened the car door and slipped into the driver's seat. Once seated, he hurriedly closed the door to extinguish the dome light. Feeling for the small chrome ignition located on the right side of the steering column, he found the entry for the key. Smoothly, he slipped the screwdriver in and snapped it back toward the dash. The ignition switch snapped off and tumbled silently to the rubber floor mat.

Pushing the screwdriver in farther, he snapped the switch to an "on" position starting the engine. Snapping the selector into Reverse, he idled down the long driveway and hesitated a brief moment to look up and down the street. Seeing no headlights, he backed the car into the street and then drove west on Adams toward Western.

⟋⟍

Bubba Washington fled the scene and was soon lost in the shadows and thick fog of South Hoover Boulevard. He headed south, scurried past Fraternity and Sorority Row on 28th Street, and then continued towards Jefferson Boulevard.

Approaching the V-shaped intersection of Hoover and Jefferson, he slowed and stopped. On the southeast corner, wedged into a small space, was a hippie hamburger stand called Alice's Restaurant. It sat wedged in the apex of the V, and served burgers, soft drinks, and drugs.

As Janis Joplin blasted out her scorching blues from blaring speakers inside the open-air business, he walked cautiously behind the crowded restaurant, staying deep in the shadows.

For his enormous size, Washington adroitly wove his way past the stand, through the shadows and shrubbery towards the campus of the University of Southern California. Standing in the cold early morning hours, he wondered about Lastice, but the shrill scream of Janis Joplin belting out a heartfelt *Down on Me*," snapped him back to the problem at hand.

He was cold, wet and he needed a fix. Trembling, he looked to the east where the dawn was soggy and the streets wet.

As the morning sun struggled to burn off the film of the night, the fog gradually thinned. Washington could see the large, gray buildings of the university. Though the fog and drizzle had been depressing, it had given him some protection. Now it was lifting and he felt exposed. He knew that he must get to the campus before the streets erupted in a cacophony of honking horns and more cops.

During the escape, he had thought of only one thing, his mistress—heroin. As the shaking increased, he knew that soon his body would be wracked by pain. Time was critical. He needed to get to the apartment, to his darkened corner of the room, to his needle, and to the white powder that was his only true friend.

He cautiously moved across the campus and soon came to Exposition Boulevard. Across the street, were Exposition Park and the Los Angeles Coliseum. Moving quickly, he passed the front of the Natural History Museum and then started west on 39th Street. He was nearly home, but the shaking had worsened, and he was perspiring heavily. Only two blocks more. He tried to hasten the pace, but his legs would not respond. Stumbling around the corner of Budlong and 39th Street, he saw the faded pink of his apartment building.

❧

Lastice drove cautiously up Western and across Wilshire. Slouched low in the driver's seat of the stolen Corvair, he was aware of the increased activity of the police, even in Wilshire Division where his apartment was located. After crossing Wilshire Boulevard, he made a left turn onto 4th Street.

Suddenly, a black and white pulled around the corner. Lastice tapped the brakes.

"The guy seem hinky to you," Paraboshi asked his partner.

"He was too eager to pull over and stop," Moen answered.

Pulling behind the faded red Corvair, the black and white activated its red lights. Lastice pulled slowly to the curb. Reaching under the front seat, he felt the barrel of the empty shotgun.

7Adam43 sat idling in the middle of the street. Paraboshi calmly reached down and slipped the mike from its holder.

"7Adam43 requesting wants and warrants on Robert-Henry-Zebra 918."

Moen and Paraboshi sat patiently waiting for a return on their request.

"7Adam43, no wants or warrants on Robert-Henry-Zebra 918."

"Let's see what the guy has to say," Moen said as he opened the driver's door.

Lastice watched through the rear view mirror. When he saw Moen and Paraboshi get out, he slid lower in the seat.

Lastice watched the two cops approach and decided to try and bluff his way free. He had no choice. Hunkered down low in the seat, he used the heels of his shoes to slip the shotgun onto the floor mat and within reach. Sliding his hand between his legs, his fingers encircled the pistol-grip stock. Slowly, he lifted the weapon, its barrel angled toward the driver's window.

As Moen and Paraboshi walked toward the small Corvair, their radio crackled.

"7Adam43, possible 459 there now, 2805 W. Pico Boulevard, House of Good Spirits: 7Adam43, handle the call Code Two."

"How good can a burglary call to a liquor store really be this early in the morning?" Paraboshi asked.

"I wonder if the ride is hot?" Moen said as he turned back towards the police car.

With eyes focused on the two cops, Lastice watched as they returned to their car and drove away.

In minutes, Lastice was sitting down the street from his apartment. He strained to look through the haze and determine what, if any, movement was taking place on the street. When convinced that he was alone, he slipped out the driver's side and darted up to the lower front apartment.

The door key grated in the old lock as the tumblers dropped open. Stepping inside, he closed the door and darted into the bedroom where he threw the mattress off the bed. Sitting on the box spring were two red balloons of heroin and one well-used syringe. Snatching both, he slipped them gently into his coat pocket.

Stepping over the trash, he watched as the floor became alive with hundreds of cockroaches. He jumped to the side and his effort was met by the scurrying of two large brown mice from under the bed. Dashing into the closet, he reached up and pulled the cord that turned on the naked light that dangled from the ceiling. On the top shelf sat a small box with the words: "Remington 12 Gauge OOB Shotgun Shells" printed on the front. Throwing the contents of the box into his pocket, he ran to the front door.

Stepping onto the front stoop, he hesitated and cautiously looked up and down the street. Still no movement. A quick sprint put him at the driver's door. Another look up and down the street. A large black rat scurried mid-block.

Lastice jumped into the car.

Seated in the Corvair, he reloaded the shotgun and drove south toward 3856 South Budlong Avenue.

TWENTY-FOUR

Congressman Morton J. Andrews stood at the front door of his luxurious home in the San Fernando Valley and gazed into the eyes of the young uniformed cop who stood on his doorstep.

"Congressman Andrews," the cop said nervously, "I'm Officer Roberge..."

Andrews glanced to the small white piece of paper held in the officers trembling hands. Printed on the paper were the words: "LEANNE ANDREWS-CONDITION-CRITICAL."

"Who is at the door," asked a sobbing Joanne Andrews as she stepped closer to her husband.

"A police officer."

"Mr. and Mrs. Andrews," whispered Roberge, "there's been an accident and I have been sent to direct you to Central Receiving Hospital."

Andrews talked over the officer's words.

"Officer," said a trembling Andrews, "I received a frantic telephone call from my daughter's roommate. She said Leanne was hurt."

"We want to see our daughter," shouted Joanne. "Where is she?"

Morton snapped the note from Roberge's hand.

Looking at the bottom of the paper, he read, "CENTRAL RECEIVING HOSPITAL-1401 West 6th Street."

"And when were you going to share this information with us!" he shouted.

Roberge stood silent.

"What happened to our little girl!" screamed Joanne.

"Is she still alive? Who would hurt her? Oh, my God, Morton, this can't be happening. Not Leanne! She's all I have!"

Controlled, Roberge spoke.

"Congressman and Mrs. Andrews, I'm sorry, but all I know is that there's been an accident and your daughter is at Central Receiving Hospital."

There was a momentary silence.

"Central Receiving Hospital? Is that what you said?" Joanne Andrews sobbed.

"Yes Ma'am. Do you know how to get there?" Roberge asked.

"It's on this piece of paper, Officer Roberge, and I'm confident that we can find it," the Congressman snapped as he grabbed Joanne by the arm and hurried her toward the car.

Morton J. Andrews was born and raised in Southern California. While attending Hollywood High School, he became interested in politics. When he was elected student body president, his future was sealed. He had been bitten by the political bug.

After high school, he attended the University of Southern California, and it was there he met his future wife. Joanne was a statuesque blond who loved parties and the excitement of an active social life. She also had a passion for politics and when she found out that Morton wanted to enter the political arena, she knew that she had found her soul mate.

Leanne was their only child. She was doted on and spoiled. When she was accepted into her father's alma mater, there was no thought of how dangerous the area was; only that she would be surrounded by the rich and famous.

Charlie Reese stood at the Nurse's station and watched as the distraught husband and wife approached. He never liked these notifications, especially when they involved people who spent their life in the public eye. He knew what he would say, or he thought he knew, but when he saw Mrs. Andrews trembling and heard her wailing uncontrollably, he knew that the press had somehow found out about their daughter's death and told them. Now he stood silently watching them approach, and he wondered what he could say.

As Morton Andrews approached, Reese knew that he was not only devastated, but angry.

"Congressman, Mrs. Andrews, my name is Charlie Reese. I am the commanding officer of University Division, Los Angeles Police Department. May I express..."

He was cut off mid-sentence.

"Who killed our daughter, Captain?" Andrews said, ignoring those crowding the corridor. "I understand that it was a police bullet!"

Andrews' face was bright red, his eyes bloodshot, his fists clenched tightly and his words spewed forth between firmly clenched teeth.

"If it *was* a police bullet ...I'll have your job!"

Quietly, and with a face that exuded great sympathy, Reese stepped closer.

"Your information is erroneous, Congressman. But I'd like to speak to you and your wife in private, not in the middle of the hallway," he said, as he looked behind the couple and saw Weinstein and Teich writing.

"I don't want to go somewhere and speak in private," Andrews shouted, "and I don't want any of your damn excuses. I want to know who killed my daughter!"

Weinstein and Teich stood with heads tilted toward the conversation, while writing furiously on small, light green steno pads. When the exchange of words ended, they raced for the bank of pay phones located on a far wall.

Joanne Andrews stood next to her husband with her arm laced through his. Suddenly, she silently crumpled to the floor.

Reese watched the color leave her face and anticipated the fall. Throwing out his left arm, he slid it under her neck before her body struck the hard linoleum.

"We need a doctor over here," he shouted as he held her head in the bend of his arm. As hospital staff scurried, Morton Andrews stood watching helplessly. He had panicked.

"Let me through," shouted a slightly built man in a white doctor's smock. Kneeling next to Mrs. Andrews, he removed a small vial from a coat pocket and cracked it open. The strong smell of ammonia wafted into the air.

Slowly, he gently swept the vial back and forth under her nose. Amid coughs and shudders, she awoke, startled at the number of people surrounding her. Her eyes were glazed and her breathing rapid. The sobbing had stopped.

"Are you all right, Mrs. Andrews?" asked Reese. The question went unanswered.

"Morton, I want see our little girl," she said from a sitting position.

"I'm sorry Mr. and Mrs. Andrews, but that won't be possible, at least not now," advised the doctor who had assisted with the ammonia vial.

"And why not?" said Andrews as he helped his wife to her feet. "It appears that you forget who you're dealing with. I'm ..."

"We know who you are, Mr. Congressman, but that doesn't change a thing. As we speak, your daughter is being transported to the Coroner's Office."

Joanne Andrews began again to sob.

"Permit me, doctor," Reese interrupted.

Reese looked hard into the eyes of the Congressman.

"Congressman, after the Coroner has conducted his preliminary examination and conferred with the investigating detectives, you will be able to see your daughter and make the necessary arrangements to have her transported to the mortuary of your choice. But to see her before that time is out of the question."

Joanne Andrews again began to shake.

"I don't want to stay here," Joanne sobbed.

"Leanne isn't here...she's gone. Please, please...let's go, Morton."

Turning, she pulled her husband away and led him through the uniformed officers and medical staff to the front doors.

Reese stood silently. *Those situations are never easy*, he thought.

❧

Patterson lay in Room 7. The white sheet and colorless walls cast a pale hue on his sleeping face. With sheets pulled taut under his chin, the aggressive street cop slept.

McLean quietly stepped into the room. Walking over to the bed, he placed his hands on the steel guardrails. His eyes narrowed as he studied his partner's face.

Patterson's eyes were gently closed and his mouth relaxed. His breathing was slow and rhythmic. His face exhibited a peaceful countenance, a state not known when awake and struggling with his inner demons.

The effects of the anesthesia were wearing off. His eyes suddenly fluttered, then struggled open.

"That you, Mac?" Patterson asked in a voice barely above a whisper.

"Yeah, it's me. You need anything?"

"Yeah. A drink," Patterson whispered hoarsely as his lips curled into a slight smile.

Suddenly, the door opened and in walked Reese, followed by Bock, Steele and Van Drew.

"I was just leaving," McLean said, walking for the door.

"I'd like you to stay," Steele said.

McLean turned and walked to the opposite side of Patterson's bed and sat in an aluminum chair located in the corner.

"You were in surgery when I was in earlier," Reese said to a still groggy Patterson. "Hell of a way to get some time off."

"It wasn't supposed to hurt this bad," Patterson whispered.

"You know Steele and Van Drew don't you?"

"Yeah."

"Patterson, we need you to try and remember everything that happened this morning," Steele said, anxious to get what information he could.

With as much detail as he could remember, Patterson revisited the night's events.

"Can you think of anything else?" Reese asked.

"Nothing," Patterson whispered.

"One more question?" Steele said.

"What?" whispered Patterson.

"Do you remember hearing one of the suspects call out your name before the shooting began?"

"Yeah."

"Which one?"

"The big dude on the end."

"That's it, we're through," Van Drew said.

Steele was already out the door. As Bock and Reese stepped towards the door, Reese turned back to Patterson.

"Anyone you want me to call?"

"No. Just let me to talk to McLean."

After the door closed, McLean walked over to the bed and leaned on the guardrails. Patterson's eyes were again closed.

After about five minutes, his eyes fluttered and then opened.

"Guess we did okay out there," he mumbled.

"We did fine," McLean assured him with a huge smile on his face. "It's two down, two to go," he added.

"We only got two?"

"Only two. But we got them good."

"A favor," Patterson said as he struggled to stay awake.

"Name it."

"Find and kill the asshole who shot me."

"I'm sure that you'll be able to do that in about six weeks."

"I don't think so. You know those feelings you get?"

"Yeah."

"Well, I've got one of those feelings."

"So now you're becoming a spiritualist?" McLean chided as he walked around to the other side of the bed.

"Yeah. Me and Jeane Dixon. No, I'm serious, Nick. If anything happens to me, I want you to find the asshole who shot me and kill him. Promise me."

McLean settled his forearms on the guardrail, leaned forward and clasped his hands.

"It's a promise. But like I said, in six weeks we'll both be looking for the guy."

Just then, a nurse entered. Without a word, she swabbed Patterson's inner right arm with a piece of cotton soaked in alcohol and injected a full syringe of liquid into a distended vein. Immediately, a red darkness swept over Patterson. Again, he was lost in a swirl of wild dreams, dreams of a black giant and erupting gunfire.

McLean walked from the room. He was now more worried than before.

TWENTY-FIVE

Charlie Reese sat in his office deep in thought. Picking up the telephone, he dialed Steele's extension.

"It's the Captain," Van Drew whispered as he cupped his hand over the mouthpiece.

"Steele here, Captain. What can I do for you?"

"I just wanted to stress that Bock and his men will be working with you on this case. So use them, Jimmy, but remember, they're Bock's men."

"Yes, sir."

Steele didn't need to be reminded. He knew Bock and his plainclothes teams. They had worked closely in the past solving a homicide that involved a USC student stabbed to death on 28th Street.

With the help of a witness, a composite drawing of the suspect had been circulated. Brooks and Inglis remembered stopping the guy two weeks prior and shaking him down as a possible robbery suspect. At the end of the stop, Inglis completed a Field Interview Card with the man's name, address and date-of-birth. Three days later, Inglis saw the composite and knew who it was. It was only hours later that he and Brooks found the suspect and he was arrested for the murder. A conviction followed.

❧

Bock sat in the Special Operations Squad room with eight of his ten-man unit. The room was small and contained a wooden desk, ten scratched and dented aluminum chairs, and a thread bare sofa that was brought from Inglis' home under cover of darkness. Although crowded, the room served the unit well, allowing them to meet nightly without interruption or interference.

On one wall was attached a large weathered map of the division. On the opposite wall was a small corkboard on which hung pictures of the "ten-most-wanted" by University detectives and downtown Robbery-Homicide Division. Below the photographs and hanging on screws drilled into the wall were two clipboards. The first held the most recent teletypes, while the other contained the license numbers of Southern Division stolen cars and vehicles wanted for their involvement in crimes. On a third wall was a whiteboard with a narrow lip that held a variety of colored pens.

"All right, let's talk about what we have," Bock said as the different teams tried to get comfortable.

"Jack, keep notes," he said to Johnson. With that, a recap of events began.

❧

The front lobby of University station was crowded not only with the normal clientele of pimps, prostitutes, parents, and bail bondsmen, but also with two newspaper reporters. Weinstein and Teich had left Central Receiving shortly after Reese and the two detectives. Now they were hoping for an opportunity to talk to the stern Captain, alone.

"Excuse me," Weinstein said to Officer Von Ahn who was busy taking telephone calls and fielding insults slung by angry citizens. "We're here to talk to Captain Reese. Is he in?"

"Now how in the hell would I know," the frazzled Von Ahn answered. Seeing the press passes hanging around their necks, he decided to refer them to Mahon. If they thought that Reese was stern, neither knew the toughness of the stocky Irishman sitting behind the desk in the Watch Commander's office.

"Lieutenant, I've got two reporters out here wanting to talk to you."

Mahon looked up from his paperwork. He wasn't happy. He didn't like interruptions, especially when they came from the press. Sliding his chair back, he stepped out from behind his desk and walked around the corner to the rear of the front counter.

"Lieutenant, I'm Sal Weinstein from the *Times*," Weinstein shouted as he extended his hand across the counter.

The hand was ignored.

"And I'm Teich with the *Examiner*."

"Fine, gentlemen, and I'm Jack Mahon from the Los Angeles Police Department. What can I do for you?"

"Can we talk in private?" asked Weinstein as he pushed himself onto his tip-toes and leaned across the counter.

"No," Mahon answered abruptly. "Just tell me what you want."

Weinstein was unnerved, for he was as tough a reporter as Mahon was a cop.

"What can you tell me about the death of Congressman Andrews daughter?"

"Nothing."

"But, Lieutenant..."

"We're through, gentlemen," Mahon said coolly.

Teich stepped forward to try his luck, but it was too late. Mahon had turned and walked back into his office, closing the door.

Just as he sat down, the phone rang. He tried to ignore it, but after six rings, he realized that Von Ahn was not going to pick it up.

"University Division, Lieutenant Mahon, may I help you?" he said as he gently held the receiver between his right shoulder and ear and continued to make notes.

"Jack, this is John Cleary. I heard we had some excitement this morning."

"Yes chief, we did," he said, trying not to let his agitation show in his voice.

"Jack, I'd like a quick update. How are our two officers? I believe I was told their names were Curtis Patrick and Donald McClelland?"

"Patterson, sir. Christian Patterson and Nicholas McLean. Patterson was hit in the leg. He'll mend. McLean took a bullet in the middle of his gunbelt; he's already up and around."

"What about the suspects?"

"We have two dead at the scene."

"Good," Cleary said, pretending to know what it took to survive a gun battle.

"Were you notified about the girl?"

"What girl, Jack?"

Mahon suddenly realized that in all the turmoil, a critical piece of information had slipped through the cracks.

"A bullet crashed through a window and killed a USC coed. Her name was Leanne Andrews. She was the daughter of Congressman Andrews of the Twenty-Eighth District in the San Fernando Valley."

The line went stone silent.

"Who the hell was going to give me that information?" Cleary said, anger hanging on every word.

"It appears to have been an oversight, chief. For that, I assume total responsibility and apologize."

After a long pause, Cleary spoke.

"I'll notify the Chief. Another question. Did one of *our* bullets kill the girl?"

"It doesn't appear so. From what the detectives said, the trajectory of the bullet shows that it came from one of the suspects' guns."

"Did we kill the shooter?"

"No. The killer and one accomplice escaped."

"Shit. What about the press?"

"Reporters from the *Times* and *Examiner* confronted Captain Reese at the hospital when he was talking to the Congressman and his wife. It appears that it was the press that leaked the fact to the Andrews that it was possibly a police bullet that killed their daughter."

"Judas priest, Jack, don't those vultures ever give up?" Cleary growled into the phone.

"Not as long as I've been on the job."

"Are you going to be in the office for a while?"

"I'll be here," Mahon said respectfully.

"Good. If you talk to Reese before I do, ask him to give me a call."

"Yes, sir," Mahon said as he studied the silent phone for a moment, shook his head, and hung up.

Steele and Van Drew sat in their straight back wooden chairs in the Detective squad room. Holding a paper cup of scalding black coffee, Steele sipped gingerly at the steaming brew, and then opened the file he had started on the Andrews murder. It was already over an inch thick.

He thought for a moment, then picked up the telephone and dialed Bock's extension.

"Rod, this is Jimmy Steele. When can we get together?"

"Anytime. Your place or mine?"

"We'll come to you, if you've got the room?"

"We'll make room."

In less than five minutes, Steele and Van Drew were sitting on the old sofa. Bock sat on the wooden desk with one leg thrown over a corner and the other dangling over the desk front.

"Wiggins called from S.I.D.," Steele said as he thumbed through his handwritten notes. "After Brown and Stemples hand carried the print cards from the two dead shooters to Latent Print's, his group began searching files. We got lucky and they identified the two dead suspects.

"Both locals?" Bock asked.

"Yep. One is Eddie Woods, the other, a Terrance Potts. Each has a healthy rap sheet, so we should be able to identify local addresses and associates."

"Anything back from NCIC on the suspect's guns?" Stallcup asked.

"We got two hits," Van Drew answered. "One was a Lennox stolen. It was taken during the riots from a gun store at 102nd and Avalon. The other is an Oakland P.D. stolen and was taken from a murdered motor cop."

"So one cop killing has been solved," added McGrath.

"Technically, they can clear the case, but it'll take more digging before we can actually know who pulled the trigger," Van Drew added.

"Unless we get someone alive and he cops to it," said LeFrois, grinning at the absurdity of the thought.

"We heard that the girl died," added Bock as he stood and stretched.

"You heard right," Steele said.

"One of our bullets?"

"No. That isn't official, but from what I've been able to gather, she was killed by a bullet from the suspect we call Kong."

"When are the autopsies?" asked Johnson.

"All three will be this morning," Steele said, "and Van and I plan on being there."

Steele and Van Drew parked in the rear of the Los Angeles County Morgue and walked to the large, austere building. Opening the obscure back door, Van Drew almost gagged when hit by the smell of decomposing flesh mixed with formaldehyde.

"Shit, Jimmy, I wasn't ready for that so early in the morning," he said as he held a white handkerchief over his mouth and nose.

"You going to be all right, Bobby?" Steele asked.

"Yeah," responded the much younger homicide detective, trying not to lose what little food remained in his stomach.

As the two men walked down the long corridor that led to the main autopsy room, Steele pulled out a long dark cigar from an inside coat pocket. Lighting it up, he offered one to his partner.

"I guess I'd better," Van Drew said. "They might not have any Mentholatum inside to dab under the nose."

After Van Drew lit up and took a long deep breath, both men opened the shinny stainless steel doors to the autopsy room. It was cold, and the smell of death permeated the air. They worked their way to the middle of the room where five identical stainless steel tables contained naked bodies, including Potts and Woods.

After scanning the room, Steele found Leanne Andrews stretched out naked on one of the tables. Her posting had not yet been conducted. Doctor Archibald Everett, one of the Coroner's was waiting for the arrival of the two detectives.

"Welcome, Jimmy," Everett called out. "Haven't seen ya in at least a week."

"Eight days to be exact, Doc."

Both men turned and saw Van Drew standing next to a bloated body that had turned green and was at least four times its normal size.

Steele glanced at the body, and then back at his young partner.

"You *sure* you're okay?"

"Yeah," Van Drew answered. "I've seen my share of dead bodies, but never one that looked that bad."

"The Jolly Green Giant is a drowning victim," Steele commented academically like a professor speaking to a freshman student.

"When the body starts to decompose, it begins in the stomach and gasses form. Without insects to make holes in the skin, the gasses have nowhere to go and the body bloats. Over time it rises to the surface."

"How do they get rid of the gasses?" asked Van Drew as he blew a cloud of thick, gray cigar smoke upward and then waved it away with his hand.

"Watch."

As both men watched, Everett walked over to the bloated body and removed a scalpel from a stainless steel instrument tray.

"Step back, gentlemen," Everett ordered. "This guy's gonna explode!"

Van Drew stood frozen, transfixed by the spectacle before him.

"You'd better get back here, Van," Steele shouted above the whirl of adjacent radial saws.

Van Drew stepped back to Steele, who was standing at least fifteen feet away from the cadaver.

With one forceful thrust, Everett drove the silver scalpel into the middle of the bloated stomach. A geyser of awful smelling fluid shot skyward, where it was stopped when it exploded against the acoustical ceiling tiles.

Both detectives watched as the fluid splattered, then slowly dripped down. Before it could reach the white floor tile, one of the attendants rolled a small steel table and collection pan under the emerald green liquid.

"Shit, that stuff stinks," Van Drew muttered.

"Hey Doc," Steele yelled, "Shows over. Can we get started on the Andrews posting?"

Wiping the green residue from the scalpel onto his smock, Everett walked over to a refrigerated stainless steel cadaver locker, opened it, and removed a brown paper lunch sack. He then stepped over to the corpse on the table, sat the lunch bag near the head, and reached into a pocket of his stained white smock and withdrew a pair of latex gloves.

"You never know when you'll get a lunch break around here," he said, grinning as he pulled the gloves tightly around his narrow wrists, "so it's best to be prepared."

Van Drew looked at Everett and then back to Leanne Andrews, a faint look of sorrow and pain knifing his eyes.

Standing to the right side of the cadaver, Everett made a deep incision from the top of the right ear to the top of the left ear. Putting the scalpel in a tray, he placed his fingers under the ear-to-ear incision, peeled the scalp forward, and down over the face. Roughly slipping the fingers of both hands under the rear flap, he jerked it once to free it from the scalp, and then pulled it over the back of the head. The top of the skull was now visible and the galea aponeurotica shone dull red. Picking up the Stryker cranial saw designed to cut through bone like a hot knife slicing butter, he made a circular cut completely around the skull.

Grabbing a ball-peen hammer and sturdy chisel, he wedged the chisel into the saw cut and gently levered the skull open. Removing the bowl-like skullcap, he placed it in a tray. Cutting the medulla oblongata, he removed the brain. After making an incision into the left frontal lobe, he shoved his fingers into a large hole and picked out a gray, mushroomed piece of lead.

"It looks like you might be in luck," Everett said, turning to Steele and Van Drew.

"The bullet entered the cranial cavity through the left eye and shot into the brain. Doesn't look too damaged, so it should still have its lands and grooves in tact," he said as he placed the bullet under water to rinse off the blood.

"If it had slammed into a thicker part of the skull, you'd have nothing."

"We'll need that slug when you're finished, Doc," Steele mentioned casually. "I want downtown to run it against all the weapons from Adams and Hoover; especially those of Patterson and McLean. *I know* it wasn't theirs that killed the girl, but I want some solid corroboration."

Everett reached into the pocket of his smock and removed a small plastic vial.

"It's all yours," he said, as he dropped the bullet into the bottle, then snapped on the cap and handed it to Steele who initialed the white evidence seal and wrapped it around the cap. "Now for the chest cavity," he said as he snatched up a clip board onto which was secured a piece of paper containing the diagram of a human body. Hurriedly, he jotted some notes and then grabbed the scalpel from the tray.

Van Drew stood silently watching. He was suddenly cold. Thrusting his hands deep into his trouser pockets, he stepped back and away from the table. A shudder coursed through his large frame. He knew that it was his responsibility to watch and learn, but it never got easier, especially when young women or children were involved.

His mind raced to the other night as he tucked his young son into bed. He remembered the angelic countenance on the face of his boy and the look of innocence. As he pulled the covers snuggly around Randy's chest, he leaned over and kissed his forehead. It was an act he had no doubt had been performed by both Congressman and Mrs. Andrews on many occasions when their daughter was young, but one that would never be repeated. A momentary sorrow stole across his heart. Then it disappeared as the sharp sound of a cranial saw kicking on shot him back to the present.

Both detectives stood silently as Everett cut a large oblique line from just above Leanne's left nipple, dipping slightly toward the center of the chest and stopping just below the sternum. He repeated the same cut on the right side, slicing deeply through the dead girl's flesh until the scalpel blade reached bone. This incision also dipped slightly toward the center of the chest and intersected the first incision slightly below the sternum. Where the two cuts intersected, he stuck the scalpel in again and thrust straight down making an incision that continued from the intersected cuts down the midline of the body to the level of the pubic bone. Deepening the initial incisions to ensure he struck bone, he then pulled back one side of the chest, exposing the rib cage.

He repeated the same action on the opposite side. Once the entire rib cage was exposed, he took a pair of industrial strength bolt cutters and snapped through each one of Leanne's ribs. Then he lifted the rib cage off, like the lid of a roasting pan, exposing the shiny, internal organs. After removing the rib cage, he weighed and then cut the individual organs for a sample. When this was completed, he tossed the organs into a bowl where they glistened under the harsh overhead lights.

When the posting was completed, the internal organs were unceremoniously dumped back into the chest cavity and the rib cage was placed back on the cadaver. Being the daughter of a Congressman made no difference when one was wheeled into the morgue. It was the same for everyone; they were dead and it did not matter what name they carried in life.

The brain was set in the cranial cavity and the top of the skull was replaced. The front and rear flaps of skin from the face and rear of the scalp were pulled tightly forward securing the brain inside the cavity and the scalp was sewn together.

After all the internal organs were thrown back into the abdominal cavity, Everett picked up a large stainless steel needle that was threaded through with heavy twined cotton cord and proceeded weaving the large stitching that would pull the skin from Leanne's chest back into position. When the task was finished, it was not pretty, but it did the job.

"So what's the official cause of death?" Steele asked.

"Acute trauma and internal bleeding to the left frontal lobe area of the brain caused from a single gunshot wound," Everett said blandly as he opened the wrinkled lunch sack and removed a tuna fish sandwich.

"The bullet entered the left orbital socket where it then lodged in the left frontal lobe."

Van Drew's face remained expressionless, except for a faint passing film of pain that covered his eyes for a moment and then darted away as quickly as a frightened gazelle.

"It's sad to see such a beautiful young woman stretched out naked on a cold, steel table," he muttered just above a whisper.

"It would have been even sadder if it were one of our own," Steele said flatly, as he turned and walked toward the rear doors.

ॐ

The two detectives walked into Parker Center, took the elevator to the eighth floor, and crossed their fingers hoping that a member of the Firearms Section would be able to start immediately on the ballistic check. One hurdle was cleared when the patrol officers transported the four weapons recovered at the crime scene to Parker Center. Now all 3William4 needed to do was drop off the slug taken out of the Andrews girl's brain and wait for the comparison to be completed.

After discussing with Dave Hatch the story behind the slug and the criticality of the comparison, they drove back to

University station. Walking through the rear door, they made a hard right and entered the squad room. Steele moved slowly over to his desk that was buried under piles of miscellaneous papers, telephone notes, and manila case folders. Sitting down, he leaned back, placed his hands behind his curly gray hair, and looked around the crowded room.

The room had its own look, sounds, smells and flavor. The Formica tables were yellowed and deeply scratched. The four chairs that sat at each table were scratched and marred. It seemed that the telephones rang incessantly, while the pungent smell of cigarettes mixed with cigar smoke hung heavily over the squad tables. During the winter, the air conditioner worked too well, and during the summer, the heaters kicked on without prompting.

"Sergeant Steele, line three," the sexy voice of Harlene Settles whispered softly over the intercom.

"Thanks," Steele shouted back as he picked up the receiver and snapped down the flashing button.

After a brief time, Steele ended the conversation.

"Thanks, Bill, we appreciate the work."

"What do we have?" Van Drew asked as he tilted his chair back on two legs and patted down his bushy moustache with the fingertips of both hands.

"That was Wiggins. They finished dusting the Ford. We have one good lift from the rear view mirror and four from the tail fin. All can be used in court if we can find out who they belong to," Steele said as he slid his chair away from the table, stood up, and stretched.

He shot a glance at the clock that sat just above the long row of steel gray metal lockers on the east wall. Two o'clock.

Two uniformed cops sat at the far back of the squad bay scratching out reports. Seated across from them were two black youths, both about sixteen years old. Each was handcuffed to a rung on their aluminum chair, and both had their heads on the table.

Sitting on the table was a long flat metal Slim Jim, a ring of keys similar to those carried by repossession men, and a chrome ignition switch.

Grand Theft Auto, Steele thought as he settled back in his chair and pulled out his pack of smokes. Tapping a single Pall Mall from the pack, he slid it under his moustache and between his pencil-thin lips.

"Steele, Van Drew, line four," Miss Settles again whispered.

Van Drew punched the button and pushed the receiver to his ear.

With the telephone resting precariously on his left shoulder, he grabbed a yellow legal pad and began to write.

"Got it," he said.

"Eliminated? That'll make the old man happy, and thanks."

Cradling the receiver, he turned to Steele who had stopped organizing his paperwork and sat waiting.

"That was Hatch. They ran ballistics on all four guns against the slug we dropped off. No hits."

"Well, that was the corroboration we needed," commented Steele matter-of-factly.

"So now that we've officially eliminated Patterson and McLean, all we need to do is identify Kong, the runt with the shotgun and find the weapon that killed Leanne Andrews."

"Be patient, Van, we will."

Steele took a long drag on the Pall Mall, and then shoved it into a small metal ashtray that hadn't been emptied in days. Leaning back, he was interrupted when a uniform officer walked up to his desk.

"Sergeant," the baby faced probationer said. "Captain Reese would like to talk to you. He's in his office."

"Thanks son," Steele said as he looked into the young face.

"How long have you been on the job?" he asked.

"A little over six months."

Was I ever that young and naïve? Steele wondered, shaking his head. If I was, I can't remember that far back.

"I'll be right back," he said to Van Drew as he got up and walked out of the squad room and into the long, narrow rear corridor.

The hall was deserted except for two uniform cops and a belligerent drunk they were trying to cuff to the long wooden bench in the holding tank that sat directly across from the Watch Commander's office.

Steele watched as the two burly cops danced around the cell trying to get the man seated on the bench and cuffed to one of the metal rings secured to the wood.

With his long hair matted, his face dirty, and his shirt torn down the front, the large drunk suddenly jerked free and pulled the handcuff attached to his wrist away from the struggling officers. Once free, he began to swing it furiously in the air. Repeatedly he swung the freed cuff while screaming and swearing, and over and over the two cops jumped and danced around the four by ten room.

Lieutenant Richter von Berliner sat at his desk in the Watch Commander's office and tried to ignore the disruption. Finally, the screaming and fist-a-cuffs in the small cell reached an unbearable level.

Von Berliner placed his smoking pipe in the ashtray, rose from his padded aluminum swivel chair, and walked across to the holding tank wearing an expression that could have frozen salt water. Silently, he opened the heavy steel door and stepped in.

Suddenly, one of the cops ducked the loose cuff and with his left hand shoved the belligerent man into von Berliner. Effortlessly, the stoic Lieutenant snapped his right arm around both sides of the drunk's neck, clamped tightly on the carotid arteries, then quickly threw his left arm across the man's left shoulder and snapped it behind his head. Lifting the body so that the man's toes danced inches above the floor, he squeezed the neck of his unwary victim as tightly as possible. In seconds, the man collapsed into unconsciousness.

Unfortunately, as von Berliner released pressure and turned the body to place him prone on the bench, the drunk vomited all over von Berliner's spit-shined shoes. Under his breath, von Berliner uttered an expression a hunter might give when his shot missed its mark.

Without a word to either officer, he shook the vomit off his shoes, and then used the remnants of the drunk's shirt as a rag. After throwing the soiled shirt onto the man's chest, he walked back into the Watch Commander's office, relit his pipe and resumed shuffling papers as though nothing had happened.

As Steele walked by the office, he stuck in his head.

"Nice touch, Richter," Steele said laughing.

"Thanks, Jimmy," von Berliner said, never lifting his eyes from the papers.

Steele chuckled to himself as he continued down the hall toward Reese's office.

"Come in," Reese called out when Steele knocked on the door.

"Have a seat," he said, pushing an unsigned stack of green overtime slips to the side.

Steele lowered himself into the only comfortable chair that sat directly in front of the desk, grateful for the softness that was not found in the squad room.

Reese reached down behind the desk and opened a bottom drawer from which he extracted a bottle of Jack Daniels and two shot glasses.

"It's been a long night, and longer morning. Can I interest you in a drink?"

"If you insist," Steele said as he pulled down his tie and unbuttoned the neck to his wrinkled white shirt.

Reese poured two stiff shots, then screwed on the bottle top and set the whiskey back in the open drawer. Without a word, both men threw back the whiskey, shuddered slightly and then settled in.

"I just got off the telephone with Deputy Chief Cleary and he wants daily updates on the Andrews case. Any problem with that?"

Steele's stomach knotted.

"I can't guarantee a dramatic report each day, so how about every other day?"

"Daily, Jimmy," Reese said, softening his voice as he raked his ace detective with his eyes.

"Yes, sir. Daily reports," Steele muttered through a forced smile and clenched teeth.

"Excellent and I also want to know how Bock's men are being used."

"Do you want Bock to report directly to you, or to me?"

"He'll report to you," Reese said as he reached back into the drawer.

"And you'll keep me in the loop."

"Of course."

"Another shot?" Reese asked as he poured two more drinks.

"Why not?" Steele said as he smiled a wry smile that didn't reach his eyes.

Steele threw back the second shot and felt the warm whiskey burn its way down his throat and drop into his empty stomach. Immediately, he felt the effects of the two shots.

"All right, Jimmy, what do we have?"

Steele recounted for Reese where the investigation stood. Reese nodded. Steele knew that it was time to leave.

"Thanks," Reese said as he abruptly stood and extended his hand.

Steele lifted himself from the soft chair and wobbled slightly.

As Steele stepped into the hall, he was met by Cleary who was followed by his Adjutant, Lieutenant Reginald Wade.

"Good morning Sergeant," Cleary said, an abrasive air of arrogance dripping from every word.

"Good morning, chief," Steele muttered, his words falling towards the floor.

"Any more information on the Andrews matter?"

"Some, but I think you'd better have that conversation with the Captain."

"Very prudent, Sergeant, very prudent," Cleary said, as he pushed past Steele and waited for Wade to open the door.

Steele shook his head and walked back into the detective bay. When he sat down, Van Drew took one look at him and knew that he was not happy.

"I see you ran into your old friend, Cleary."

"The dumb ass wanted me to brief him," Steele said as he slid back his chair and pulled open the drawer looking for matches. "And that wasn't going to happen."

Steele had just opened the Andrews folder when a shout came from across the room.

"Steele, line six."

"No rest for the weary," Steele muttered as he picked up the phone. "Sergeant Steele, may I help you?"

He listened and took notes for a couple of minutes, then replied:

"Thanks, LeFrois. I'd recommend that you and Johnson get back here right away."

"What's going on?" Van Drew asked quizzically.

"That was LeFrois. He and Johnson found a common name in the packages of the two dead suspects: Ta-Ta Lastice. The guy is a known shotgun bandit whose name showed up on more than one arrest report."

"Did they find an address?" Van Drew asked as he took small sips of the still hot coffee.

"310 South St. Andrews Place, apartment One."

"Any hard time served?"

"No hard time, but he did do a couple of stints at Wayside for aggravated assault and grand theft."

"If the guy is a shotgun bandit, why the hell hasn't he done hard time?" Van Drew asked perplexed.

"A note in his package says that he never went to trial for two robberies because the witnesses disappeared after the Preliminary Hearings."

"That figures."

"Let's find Bock," Steele said as he lifted himself from the chair. "I want to hit that apartment."

"It's Wilshire Division," Van Drew reminded his partner.

"I don't give a shit if it's on the moon," Steele said, agitated. "It's in the City of Los Angeles and our badges say, 'Los Angeles Police.'"

TWENTY-SIX

"*Wilshire and Saint Andrews Place, rear parking lot. We'll meet* you there," Bock said to Steele as the two men stood talking in the Detective bay.

"Another piece of good news," Steele said as he pulled out a crumpled note from the pocket of his wrinkled white shirt.

"When LeFrois and Johnson identified Lastice as an associate of Potts and Woods, I had Wiggins run him against the fingerprint that was found on the back of the rear view mirror. It's a match," Steele said grinning broadly.

"That puts him inside the car, and in the front seat. Since 'Kong' was driving and had a revolver, that leaves Lastice with the shotgun."

Pleased that another piece of the puzzle had fallen into place, Bock bounded up the stairs and entered the Special Operations room where four teams sat awaiting anxiously for their marching orders.

"More pieces to the puzzle," Bock said as he walked to the whiteboard and wrote Lastice's name in one of the two blank white squares, leaving the name of "Kong" unidentified. "He's a shotgun bandit who ran with Potts and Woods," he added.

"We've had a couple of liquor store robberies along Crenshaw where one of the suspects used a shotgun," McGrath said.

"Might be our guy," Bock answered.

Bock pushed himself deeper onto the desk, extended his legs, and then continued. "Steele and Van Drew want us to meet them and hit the apartment LeFrois and Johnson identified as occupied by Lastice. It's up in Wilshire Division. I told them that we'd meet them in twenty minutes at the rear parking lot of the Wilshire Café on the northeast corner of Wilshire and Saint Andrews Place."

Twenty minutes later, Steele and Van Drew pulled their car into the rear lot of the restaurant and parked toward the back.

"I hope we got here in time," Van Drew said as he leaned against the car and nervously patted down his bushy brown moustache.

Leaning back into the car, Steele grabbed his pack of Pall Malls from above the visor, tapped the back of the pack, and removed a cigarette. Searching in his shirt pocket, he found a small wooden match that he struck with his fingernail causing it to erupt in a brilliant flame. Lighting the cigarette that hung low beneath his well-groomed moustache, he took a long, deep drag and blew small smoke rings into the breeze.

"Where are Bock and his men?" Van Drew asked, his impatience apparent.

As the final word left Van Drew's lips, Bock pulled into the parking lot followed by four unmarked cars. Pulling to the rear, he parked and walked over to the two detectives.

"You guys are late," Van Drew said, agitation in his voice.

Bock glanced at his watch.

"By three minutes," he said, not offended by Van Drew's eagerness to get a cop killer off the street.

"Reason being, I just rolled past the apartment," said Bock. "I wanted to get an idea of the layout before I sent in the troops."

When all of Bock's units had pulled in and parked, he outlined the plan.

"Brooks, I want you and Inglis to go through the front door," he said as he sketched a rough schematic of the apartment building on the back of an old Hot Sheet.

"I know that we have a responsibility to adhere to the "knock and announce" statute, but I don't want to lose anyone because we announced ourselves and were then blown back out the door. So Jerry, consider this 'exigent circumstances.' Kick the damn door, then announce yourself."

"Brown and Stemples, you'll cover the rear. Stallcup will cover the windows on the north side and McGrath will cover the south side. LeFrois, you and Johnson stay on the front stoop and watch our backs."

Bock turned to the two detectives. "Anything else either of you can think of?" he asked.

"Nothing, except that we don't want another policeman hurt," Steele said. "So let's be careful."

With that last piece of advice, four Special Operations teams, a sergeant and one detective car moved out of the restaurant parking lot and drove northbound on St. Andrews Place toward the apartment of Ta-Ta Lastice.

One block south of the building, they pulled around the corner and parked.

"It's the weathered building, mid-block," Bock said. "Lastice's apartment is on the bottom left. Brooks and Inglis, give everyone thirty-seconds before you boot the door."

With Bock in the lead, eight shabbily dressed plainclothes cops moved silently toward their target. Steele and Van Drew followed. When Bock reached the south side of the building, he stopped and waited for his men. In seconds, Brooks and Inglis stood behind him. To their rear were three teams with their backs pushed hard against the rough stucco walls.

Bock motioned for Brooks and Inglis to take their position on either side of the front door. Like two cats, the large men jumped onto the concrete stoop. Once in place, the other teams silently deployed. Brooks looked down at his watch.

"Thirty seconds," he whispered to Inglis, who stood to the left of the thick, wooden door.

"Five, four, three, two, one!"

Then, in one fluid motion, the powerful right leg of the two hundred and thirty pound Brooks was raised and his foot slammed into the door just to the left of the old brass door handle. In an explosion of splintered wood, the massive wooden door flew off its hinges and flew across the front room.

"Police Officers!" bellowed Brooks in a voice that would have cracked granite.

In an instant, Brooks and Inglis charged into the room with revolvers extended. Right behind them rushed in Bock then Steele and Van Drew.

In tandem, Brooks and Inglis conducted room-to-room-searches. The apartment was empty.

"The place is empty," Brooks called out to Bock and the two detectives. "The mattress has been thrown off the bed and an indentation in the box springs appears to have been made by a hype kit. In the closet I found a shotgun round and an empty ammunition box. Looks like he took his dope and ammunition and split."

Bock stepped onto the stoop and called to the other units.

"We're too late," he said when the others had formed a tight circle.

"It's back to the drawing board," Van Drew said, disappointment registered on his face as well as in his voice.

"We'll get him, Bobby," Steele said. "It's just a matter of time."

⚓

Reese sat dozing in his large padded chair. His stocky athletic frame filled the seat. His muscular legs were outstretched and crossed with his small feet perched gently on the top of a large beveled piece of glass that covered the entire desktop. His massive hands with interlocked boxer's knuckles were place gently in his lap while soft snores filtered through his narrow lips.

Al Evans walked up to the door and tapped lightly. There was no answer. He didn't want to disturb the Captain, knowing the rough two nights he had experienced, but knew that he would want to see the morning newspaper.

Again, he knocked, harder this time.

Stirred, Reese woke with a start. Pulling his legs off the desk, he pushed his thin hair back, buttoned his collar and straightened his tie.

"Come in," he said, his voice gravely.

The door opened only half way.

"Sorry to bother you, boss," Evans said sheepishly, "but I've got something here I think you should see."

"Come on in, Al," Reese said as he coughed to clear his throat.

Evans walked over to the large desk and unfolded two newspapers.

"CONGRESSMAN'S DAUGHTER KILLED BY STRAY POLICE BULLET IN WILD WEST SHOOT-OUT."

"Those rotten sons-of-bitches!" Reese bellowed.

Throwing the newspapers open, he silently read each story.

"I had hoped that Weinstein and Teich would have held off until they had more information, but no, they had to take the snippets they scrounged at the hospital and fabricate a story. This is bullshit," he yelled.

Evans stood nervously, his thumbs locked over the buckle of his Sam Browne.

Propelled by a spasm of fury, Reese jumped from his chair, ripped the newspapers in half, then wadded them up and slammed them into the half-full waste paper basket.

"And that's exactly where that crap belongs."

During Reese's fit of anger, Evans had discretely inched his way back toward the door. When it hit a solid mass, he reached down and after fumbling around, located the door handle. Afraid to stay, but even more fearful to leave, he stood like a piece of stone hoping that he would not be the next object of the Captain's wrath.

"Damn them," Reese muttered as he shook his head from side to side. "Damn them."

Reese turned facing Evans who had not moved since he planted his feet in front of the only exit in the room.

"I'm sorry, Al...I know, don't kill the messenger."

"You need me for anything else, Captain?" Evans asked.

"No. And thanks."

With that, Evans slipped out of the office and walked hurriedly down the hall.

Reese leaned back in his chair. "Those bastards. And they wonder why we don't trust them."

Reaching down to the lower right drawer, he pulled it open and looked at the bottle of Jack Daniels. Grabbing the bottle and a shot glass, he placed both on the beveled glass desk top. Unscrewing the top, he wrapped his hand around the bottle, and then hesitated.

"Not now," he said as he screwed the cap on tighter than before and then slipped the glass and bottle back in the drawer. Closing the drawer with his foot, he began to contemplate his next move.

TWENTY-SEVEN

Deputy Chief John Cleary stood in the doorway of Chief of Police Thomas White's office on the sixth floor of Parker Center. Cleary had an idea why the Chief wanted to see him, and if he was right, he'd rather be somewhere else.

"Come in," White whispered, while continuing his conversation on the telephone. Motioning for Cleary to have a seat, White began writing on a small note pad located on the right side of the massive mahogany desk.

Cleary slid into a soft chair and folded his hands in his lap. Moving his head only slightly, his eyes took in the office. It was immaculate. Everything had a place, and nothing was where it shouldn't be. The visual of perfection only added to Cleary's discomfort.

"Thanks, Sam, we'll talk later," White said as he hung-up the telephone.

"That was the Mayor. He wanted a briefing on the Adams and Hoover shooting," White said as he lifted himself from the comfortable executive chair, clasped his hands behind his back and walked to the large picture window.

Staring out over the city, he spoke into the glass.

"And I'd like an update," his words were honed to knife the heart, "since I haven't received one in two days."

Cleary wiggled nervously in the chair. "I was waiting to get all the facts ..." His words were cut short.

"I didn't ask you for excuses, chief. I asked to be briefed so that I don't continue to look like an uninformed horse's ass when asked about the death of a Congressman's daughter!"

White didn't like Cleary, especially after the long-time married Deputy Chief had been photographed by Internal Affairs Division having a sexual liaison with his secretary in a sleazy downtown hotel.

White would have had Cleary by the balls except for the fact that Los Angeles was still in the throes of political upheaval and social unrest, and Cleary was his senior staff officer.

"Anytime, Chief," White said as he continued to stare out the window that allowed the City of Los Angeles to unfold in a hazy panorama.

"I assume that you probably know..."

"Assume I know nothing," White abruptly interrupted, his voice cold and businesslike.

"Yes, sir," said Cleary, speaking rapidly. After a brief synopsis, Cleary stopped.

White spun on his heels and faced Cleary. He was silent as he walked behind his desk and sat down. He leaned forward and placed his elbows on the desk top. Slowly, he placed the fingertips of both hands together forming a steeple.

Cleary swallowed hard. His mouth was bone dry.

"Please continue," White said through eyes that were momentarily ugly, then bland.

Cleary swallowed hard.

"That's all I have," Chief.

Cleary felt nauseous. He hated these inquisitions.

"Chief," White said gruffly, "Quit dancing with me. Dammit to hell, I want to know about the girl. What the hell happened out there? Who killed her? Was it a cop?"

"No, sir," Cleary replied, grateful to be able to answer a question with some assuredness.

"And how do we know that?"

"We've tested both officers' guns against the bullet removed from the Andrews girl. They don't match."

Whites voice softened. "That eliminates our men, but doesn't crack the case."

Clearly took a deep breath and waited. Suddenly, he felt perspiration mat his shirt to his back.

White stared deeply into Cleary's narrow eyes. "I want you to fill an assignment for me, chief."

"Yes, sir," Cleary anxiously said, willing to agree to anything just to be able to leave.

"I have a press conference scheduled for one o'clock today in the auditorium downstairs. I want you to handle it—any problem?"

"No problem," Cleary said.

Immediately, Cleary realized that he was not nervous at the thought of representing Chief White and the Department in front of the cameras; he was damn scared.

 ༙

The large auditorium on the first floor of Parker Center was full. A cacophony of voices reverberated across the room as members of the media jostled for seats and tried to place themselves in a position to be able to ask questions. On the front row were seated Weinstein and Teich.

Located in each side aisle were massive television cameras with a technician standing to the rear. Soon the room was choked by smoke as anxious reporters lit up one cigarette after the other and blew the ash gray smoke toward the yellowed, smoke stained, acoustical tiled ceiling.

Cleary stood behind the heavy blue curtains and peeked out at the hundreds who had found seats.

He now was beginning to understand why the Chief had given him the assignment and the deeper he thought, the more nervous he became.

"You think they'll give us anything besides the party line?" Teich asked Weinstein as he gently sipped his coffee.

"Not likely. Rumor has it that someone other than White is going to conduct this press conference."

"That might be to our advantage," Weinstein said.

"I doubt it," Weinstein said chuckling. "How many times have you been to a police briefing where anyone has talked too much?"

"Well, never, but this could be a first," Teich answered, a smile crossing his face.

"And if you believe that horseshit, Teich. . .then you're not cynical enough to be a reporter."

Weinstein took a deep drag on his unfiltered cigarette and blew the smoke up toward the ceiling.

As the curtains on the left parted, Cleary stepped out and walked briskly to the oak rostrum set center stage. He wore his dark blue staff officer's uniform with two stars on each epaulet of his coat. He stood stiffly behind the microphone and said nothing, waiting for the chatter to stop.

"Who's the clown with the corncob shoved up his ass," Teich whispered to Weinstein.

"Deputy Chief John Cleary," Weinstein responded, a grin on his face.

"You gotta love the guy, Teich," Weinstein said, leaning closer to his likeable competition.

"Rumor has it that he was caught in the sack screwing one of his secretaries, but it was whitewashed because of political in fighting."

"Where was I when that piece of news floated to the surface?" asked Teich.

"Probably following the Dodgers. How the hell would I know? But you didn't miss much. It was swept under the rug before it became a headline," Weinstein added as he settled back in the hard wooden auditorium seat and removed his reporter's notebook from an outside jacket pocket.

"Rumor also has it that the photographs are locked tight in White's safe. I guess they'll stay there until 'tricky dickey John' lets the blood run to the wrong head again."

Teich let out a muffled laugh, but caught himself.

Suddenly the lights dimmed on and off while a voice tried to override the clamor of the audience.

"Good afternoon, ladies and gentlemen. I am Deputy Chief John Cleary. Chief of Police Thomas White has requested that I conduct this press conference."

Cleary gripped the sides of the rostrum with his callous free hands and leaned his slender body slightly forward toward the tightly wrapped bundle of microphones. Ten small knuckles beamed white as he looked across the audience, his eyes involuntarily squinting as flash-bulbs erupted.

As the room settled into silence, Cleary began.

Weinstein and Teich listened intently, hoping to catch something that might help fill in the blanks. Reporters for small newspapers like the *Green Sheet* and *Sentinel* held large cassette tape recorders high in the air.

Cleary calmly recounted from the prepared script the details of the shooting, the solving of the murder of an Oakland Police Department motor officer and the fact that it was not a police bullet that killed Leanne Andrews.

When he had finished reading the very brief statement, he opened the forum for questions, an act he would rather not do, but one that he knew was required.

"Chief, what was the...?" yelled a woman seated to the right of Weinstein who was quickly over-ridden by a booming male voice behind her.

"Chief!" yelled the deep voice from the middle of the room.

"Anderson from The Green Sheet—what was the reason for the stop and...?"

Suddenly the room erupted with one question shouted over another, leaving Cleary standing nervously on the stage with his only protection the well-used wooden rostrum. Suddenly, he felt his throat begin to close and his chest tighten. He squeezed the podium and straightened his arms.

Sweat poured from under his white shirt and beads of perspiration formed across his forehead. A slight paralysis shot from his head to his feet and a feeling of panic engulfed his body. He froze and struggled to regain control. He had not experienced this feeling since he was a young traffic cop who had pulled over an abusive motorist who had threatened to kill him. John Cleary knew that he was having a panic attack.

No one knew of this condition, not his wife, not his staff, and certainly not Chief White. He had kept it a well-guarded secret and he knew that he must do everything in his power to keep it that way. But was that possible?

He paused, stared directly into the large spotlight that was thrown onto the stage, and knew he must continue. His fear had escalated. He was now terrified.

Thomas White stood unnoticed in the rear shadows. His arms were folded and his eyes glared in the direction of the rostrum. He stood and waited, wanting to see if Cleary would save himself or if his career would end in the auditorium of Parker Center.

Cleary began to speak. His tongue wiped his lips. Purposely, he took off his glasses, blotted the bridge of his nose, and then put the glasses on again. After taking another long, deep breath and exhaling slowly, he stiffened his back and looked down at someone he knew–Sal Weinstein.

He needed a familiar face, even one he didn't trust and Weinstein filled the bill.

"Sal, your question," Cleary said in a voice that tried to exuded confidence, yet caught the experienced *Times* reporter off guard.

"Thank you, chief," Weinstein said as he lifted his squatty body from the narrow seat and shoved his small reporter's notebook containing blank pages to arm's length in front of his small bifocals.

"First, what was the probable cause for the initial stop by Patterson and McLean, who, I have been told, are assigned to a plainclothes assignment which requires the use of an unmarked police car?"

Cleary glanced at his hands. His fingernails had imbedded themselves deeper into the hardwood. Without hesitation, and not allowing Cleary to answer, Weinstein continued.

"Secondly, if the police didn't kill the Andrews girl, who did?"

Cleary shifted nervously from side-to-side as he ran his hands up and down the side of the rostrum.

You're an asshole, thought Cleary who had focused his gaze from the blinding spotlight to the rotund form of the *Times* reporter.

"And while I have the floor, chief, one more question," Weinstein said, knowing it was a question that all in the room wanted answered.

"Do you have any leads on the identity of the two outstanding suspects?"

"Not bad for no notes," Teich said as Weinstein sat down.

"To answer the first question," Cleary said as he folded his sweaty hands on the top of the rostrum and leaned forward, "the suspect's vehicle was stopped for two traffic violations — and your sources are correct, the officers were in an unmarked police vehicle."

"And what per se would those alleged traffic violations be?" shouted a deep voice from the back.

"An exhibition of speed and a white taillight to the rear," Cleary blurted out angrily, not wanting to be bothered by such insignificant minutia.

He crossed his legs and leaned his body against the podium in an effort to relax. Then he continued.

"As I stated in my opening statement, we have eliminated both officers and the two dead suspects as being responsible for the death of Miss Andrews. We ran ballistic comparisons on all weapons found at the scene and then ran a comparison to the spent round removed from Miss Andrews."

He paused and sipped from a glass of water that sat on the shelf below the podium.

"There was no match."

Slowly, his body relaxed and his confidence began to return. "Please note that the death of Miss Andrews was an accident, an unfortunate accident, but an accident nevertheless, and was not precipitated by any illegal or negligent action by members of the Los Angeles Police Department."

"Okay, chief," blurted out the same deep voice from the rear of the auditorium. "But I'd like to know..."

"I'm sorry sir, but I haven't finished answering Mr. Weinstein's questions. Please have a seat," Cleary said in an icy tone as he leaned closer to the bundle of microphones to ensure the man heard his response.

"Finally, Sal, we don't know the identity of the two outstanding suspects, but we are confident that their identities will be known in the very near future."

"When you know, when will we know?" Teich blurted out before Cleary could change gears.

"Information will be disseminated to the press when we can guarantee that its release will not jeopardize either the investigation or the future prosecution of suspects."

"Congressman Andrews has stated that he wants to bring the FBI into the mix. What's your take on that?" asked Weinstein from his seat.

Cleary was now beyond being irritated at Weinstein, he was now angry.

"There is nothing, and I repeat, *NOTHING* that the Federal authorities can offer to this investigation." Cleary pulled a neatly pressed white handkerchief from an inside jacket pocket, and then removed his glasses. Gently, he mopped the sweat from his forehead, and then replaced the glasses on top of his aquiline shaped nose. On the glass of the left lens was a large thumbprint, but he decided to ignore the distraction rather than remove the glasses and clean them again.

From the middle of the auditorium, a man jumped to his feet waving his right arm.

"Yes, Mr. Anderson."

"Thanks, chief. Again, I'm Anderson from the *Green Sheet*..."

"I remember who you are. Please ask your question."

"Since Patterson and McLean were in an unmarked car and not in uniform, could the four occupants of the Ford have thought them to be street thugs and not the police?" Anderson asked, a tone of contempt lacing his voice.

"The guy's an idiot," Weinstein whispered as he turned his head and looked to the middle of the room.

"And he can't write worth shit," Teich added.

"Mr. Anderson," Cleary said, trying to control his disdain for a man who had a greater reputation for ignoring fact and writing fiction than either Weinstein of Teich.

"Yes, it was an unmarked police vehicle, and yes, both officers were in plainclothes or what we call soft clothes. They used a bright red spotlight that is placed on the dash of the police car to make the stop. I can guarantee you that those who see the car identify it immediately as a police vehicle and when they see the bright red light, because of prior experiences, they have no doubt who it is that wants to talk to them."

"But couldn't..."

"May I finish answering the question, Mr. Anderson? Thank you."

"When Patterson and McLean exited their vehicle, they identified themselves as police officers, and they also had their badges attached to their belts in plain sight. So to answer your question, no, the suspects did not identify them as anything but Los Angeles Police Officers." Cleary removed his glasses and gesturing with them, pointed to a young black reporter that was standing to the left of Anderson.

"Yes sir," Cleary said.

"Chief, what was the race of the officers and the suspects?"

"Is that relevant, sir? I'm sorry, I don't know your name," Cleary said, controlling his agitation at a question he felt was unnecessary.

"Jerome Caiden, chief. I represent the *Sentinel*," said the deep voice.

"Thank you, Mr. Caiden. Although I don't see the relevancy of the question, I will answer it. Patterson and McLean are both Caucasian. The two dead suspects were Negro, as are the two outstanding suspects."

"You mean all four were Black, don't you, chief?"

"I mean exactly what I said, Mr. Caiden. All four were male Negroes. Miss Andrews was Caucasian, and the elderly victim from whom the vehicle was stolen was also Negro."

"And what about the witness that surfaced?" shouted a voice from the left seats.

"I don't recall mentioning a witness," Cleary said flatly.

"She was listed on the crime report, chief, in case you hadn't noticed."

A slight buzz filled the room.

"The witness was also Negro, but none of that really matters, does it, gentlemen?" barked Cleary.

Cleary knew that he was becoming snippy and that the press conference should soon end.

He stood silent, then continued. "I hope that answers your question, Mr. Caiden."

"Not really," Caiden said caustically. "But what's new."

John Cleary was tired. His head hurt and his eyes were strained from staring out into the spotlight. Without further explanation, he raised his hand to cut off another question from Teich.

"Thank you, ladies and gentlemen. That will conclude this press conference."

Folding over the top sheet of his notes, he closed the small dossier and disappeared behind the dark blue curtain held open by Lieutenant Wade. He never heard the barrage of questions shouted by angry reporters. Mentally, he was elsewhere.

Morton and Joanne Andrews sat silently in their living room. Both were physically numb and emotionally drained. Morton sat in a deep, overstuffed chair while his wife of twenty-five years lay on the velvet green sofa that had been custom-made and imported from Paris, France. After switching off the television, the Congressman reached over to the small, elegant Louis XIV side table and grabbed his glass of imported Scotch.

Throwing the contents down with a quick flick of the wrist, he replaced the glass and continued to stare at the blank television screen.

"That was a waste of time," he said as he put his head in his hands and rested his elbows on his knees.

Breathing deeply, he wiped the moisture from his bloodshot eyes, then got up and slowly walked over to the sofa where his wife still lay wrapped in her own grief. Kneeling at her side, he gently slipped his slim fingers into her long, beautiful golden hair and softly pulled them through the strands.

"We'll get through this, I promise," he said in a quivering voice.

"Oh, Morton, I already miss her so much," Joanne said between deep sobs while her bosom rolled like the tide from under her nose.

"So do I, sweetheart ...so do I."

⚓

McLean sat on the raggedy-ass sofa next to Inglis.

"Good to have you back, Nick," Bock said.

"Good to be back," McLean responded, his eyes penetrating and his words emotionless.

Bock walked over to the whiteboard that was mounted on one wall.

"Okay, let's review what we've got."

Meticulously, Bock noted each piece of information and added every activity as precisely as a fundamentalist pouring over the Book of Revelations. When he had finished, the whiteboard was full, and they still didn't have any idea where Ta-Ta Lastice had fled, nor did they have a clue as to the identity of Kong.

"How did the press conference go?" Inglis asked.

"That's a sore subject."

"Did the Chief conduct it?" Stemples asked.

"It was conducted by Deputy Chief Cleary," Bock said as he bit down on his lower lip.

"The guy is God's own idiot," McGrath muttered under his breath.

"Well, if he wasn't considered one before the press conference, he now has that dubious honor. Scuttlebutt has it that he choked."

"I take it he's not a close friend?" Inglis said.

"We're not going there, John. But to answer your initial question, the press conference was considered by most to be a debacle."

TWENTY-EIGHT

Patterson sat alone in his small, one bedroom apartment, nursed his drink, and wondered why his leg still hurt like hell. He'd been drunk every day for the past two weeks. His life throbbed in agony, and the booze only added severe headaches to the list, but he couldn't stop. He didn't want to stop. Booze was his mistress, his friend and his savior. But since the shooting another seductress had been introduced: Morphine.

Pulling the bottle of prescription painkillers from his shirt pocket, he opened the smoky dark brown plastic bottle and slid two white tablets into his mouth. Swirling the last remnants of whiskey in the glass unevenly from side to side, he threw it back, swallowed hard, shuddered a few times and then slid the empty glass onto the coffee table next to his off-duty .38.

Leaning forward, he used both hands to lift the heavy plaster leg cast onto the table while gently placing his bare foot over the edge. Sitting back, his eyes stared at the snub-nosed revolver that lay next to his wallet.

Slowly, he leaned forward, reached down and picked up the gun. It was cool to the touch and the over-sized black rubber grip sank softly into his large right hand while his right index finger curled snuggly around the dark blue-steel trigger.

With his left thumb, he slid the cylinder release lever forward, then pushed the five shot cylinder out using the second and third fingers of his left hand. Fitting snuggly into the smooth cylindrical chambers were five, 158 grain, copper jacketed bullets, each of which had been customized by Patterson into deadly hollow-points.

He slouched down and leaned deeper into the couch.

He pushed the ejector rod back and with a quivering hand pulled out one bullet. Staring at the sleek projectile through what seemed to be a thickening fog, he knew that one bullet would take away all the pain.

Deliberately, he rolled the shinny brass casing between his thumb and the ball of his right index finger. Only one, he repeated to himself as his head swayed gently back and forth and his fractured thoughts shot aimlessly through his mind like golf balls careening off the walls of a concrete room.

Fumbling, he returned the bullet to its chamber and snapped the cylinder shut. Turning the revolver around, he grasped the dark grips with both hands, slipped his right thumb against the trigger and pointed the barrel between his eyes.

Trembling, he drew the gun closer to his face, watching the front sight loom in front of his eyes like a skyscraper caught in an earthquake. Slowly, he placed the cold steel of the short barrel snuggly against the skin of his forehead. As he stared forward and beyond the blurred revolver, the fleshy part of his thumb firmed against the trigger.

With the gun pressed snuggly between his eyes, small beads of perspiration formed across his forehead. Slowly, the flesh of the thumb widened and the hammer began to inch back.

The effects of the drugs and alcohol swept over him like a tsunami covering a small island. Hesitating, he took a deep breath and exhaled it slowly. The pungent stench of alcohol hesitated in front of his face, then was whiffed quickly off as the slow rotating ceiling fan pushed it into another room.

His thumb pressed down harder on the trigger.

The hammer moved back passing the second click.

Suddenly, his thumb shot back and froze the hammer in place.

Eternity was now sitting in a cocked, single shot position.

Suddenly, he was cold, yet he could feel the sweat erupt from under his armpits and slide down the middle of his back. The small revolver held tightly to his head was blurred. He pushed both elbows tighter into his sides to stop his arms from quivering.

He closed his eyes.

His chest tightened and his head began to throb. For the first time in his life, he felt fear crawl into his head like a nest of spiders. He paused, and the gun wobbled. Only slightly at first, then, both hands were trembling uncontrollably.

Cautiously, he lowered the hammer down. Thoughts shot through his mind like errant arrows, but then magically, one clear idea surfaced.

"I need another drink," he slurred.

Opening his eyes, he placed the gun back onto the tabletop, leaned back and stared blankly across the room into the dark screen of the television.

He was alone, but he had been alone for most of his life.

He missed the daily drinking sessions at Exposition Park, the Special Operations Squad watering hole. He missed the camaraderie of the men and the violence of the street. He was a warrior and sitting alone in a small apartment with a shot-up leg was not the way he wanted to spend his time. Emotionally, he was lonely; psychologically, he was depressed and physically, he was exhausted. All of which played out in his actions of the morning.

Emotions that during the past two weeks he tried to suppress by throwing back shots of whiskey followed by beer chasers and pills, until he was shit-faced. But today had been different. He had actually crossed the line and stood for the first time, one squeeze away from eternity; an event that had not happened because his thirst for a drink was greater than his desire for peace.

He inhaled deeply of the stale air. It was hot, the room was spinning and the walls seemed to be closing in. The thoughts of what had happened during the last few minutes tried in vain to knife through the impenetrable walls raised by his addictions, but they quickly were washed away.

Fear knotted his stomach and rose slowly into his throat. His body constricted as it was swallowed up and engulfed in a terror the likes of which he never had experienced. What was he doing? A sickening reality washed over him, and what he had feared and dreaded most of his life now had become a reality. Christian K. Patterson, Army Ranger, and ferocious street cop was no different than the addicts he arrested.

Shaking, he pushed his massive hands through his matted blond hair that hadn't been washed in over two weeks. His body reeked of body odor, but he was beyond caring. He couldn't shower, so he did nothing.

Thirteen days of stubble exploded from his pale, pock marked face. Life sucked and all he wanted to do was get drunk and stay drunk.

Lifting himself slowly from the couch, he forced a crutch under his left arm and clumsily hobbled into the kitchen where he threw open a cupboard door. It was empty, totally reminiscent of his stomach and his life, his dreams and goals; all of it was hollow emptiness.

His stash of Jack Daniels was gone. Angered, he swiped at the trash-filled counter, sending empty whiskey bottles, papers and used aluminum TV dinner trays flying across the room. Jumping on one foot, he grabbed the refrigerator door and swung it open. A lone yellow can of Coors sat in the middle of the center shelf.

"This is bullshit," the enraged blond giant slurred as he swayed from side to side.

Slamming the refrigerator door, he hobbled back into the living room. Angrily, he reached into the front pocket of his Levis and pulled out a hundred dollar bill.

Retrieving the second crutch, he thrust it under his armpit and hobbled to the front door where he grabbed the doorknob and yanked it open.

The telephone rang.

He stopped, looked back into the room and wondered whether to answer the call.

"Go to hell," he muttered as he slammed the door and headed for the stairway. Maneuvering the fifteen steps to the bottom level was exhausting, but as he stepped off the final step, he was met by a brilliant blast of sun.

Standing in the sunlight, he thrust his pale face heavenward. The warmth radiated from the top of his head to the bottom of his feet. After a brief time, the urge for another drink became overpowering. He lifted his right foot off the ground and headed for Heraldo's Licorería.

∾

McLean let the phone ring repeatedly, hoping that Patterson was either in the bathroom or sleeping. He was worried about his partner, not just a superficial concern over his gunshot wound, for he knew that would heal, but a deep anxiety emanating from the fact that McLean knew how obsessive his partner could be and how he would turn to the bottle, or something worse, for solace.

After ten rings, he hung up.

"Hey, Sarge," he called out as Bock walked into the squad room. "I just tried to call Patterson and there was no answer. You mind if Sabatello and I take a ride over to his place to check on him?"

"Go ahead, and tell Patterson that the Captain and I plan on making a visit tomorrow morning. So ...let's see if he can't be sober."

∾

Patterson's footsteps were unsteady, and he swayed precariously as he stumbled into Heraldo's Licorería. After weaving between the display counters and knocking some food cans off a shelf, he rocked his way to the refrigeration unit where he slid open the large, frosted door and removed a six-pack of Coors. Holding it in his right hand, he hobbled over to the counter.

"*¿Cómo está, Señor Patterson?*" the heavy set old Mexican politely asked from behind the counter. "A little under the weather, amigo?" he added.

"No, I'm not under any damn weather," Patterson slurred. "I'm just not as drunk as I want to be."

"Be careful, *Señor*. Too much cerveza and licor firme could be dangerous, and..."

"Knock off the shit-ass sermon," Patterson snarled angrily, "and give me a bottle of whiskey."

"*Si, Señor*," Heraldo answered timidly.

The rotund little Mexican with the silver hair reached back and removed a fifth of Jack Daniels from the shelf. Wiping it off on his soiled apron, he placed it in a brown paper bag and twisted the top.

"You are drinking too much, my friend."

"Son-of-a-bitch, Heraldo, you let me worry about how much I drink and I'll let you worry about runnin' the damn store," Patterson said as he uneasily shifted his weight from side to side.

"And I want two cases of Coors and two more bottles of whiskey delivered to my house. *Comprende?*"

"*Si, Señor*, I understand."

Looking more like a 5th and Main bum than one of L.A.'s finest, Patterson squinted through bloodshot eyes, leaned against the counter to steady himself, and then roughly wiped the spittle from both sides of his mouth with the back of his left hand.

"I will fill the order, *Señor*," Heraldo said, an expression of deep concern crossing his face, "but please be careful."

Patterson struggled to maintain his balance. He adjusted the crutches under his arms, pushed the whiskey bottle into his waistband and threw the wadded up paper bag on the counter. Then he tightened his grip on the six-pack that was held by his right hand.

As the unsteady gringo stepped out of the store, he was followed by the storeowner who knew that the large man with the golden hair was in trouble. Swaying irregularly, Patterson looked down the street for traffic. Impatient to get back to the apartment, he decided not to use the traffic signal but to cross mid-block. As he glanced to his left, his vision blurred as he squinted into the morning sun.

Dropping his head, he lowered the left crutch into the street. Then he stumbled.

Standing in the doorway of his store, Heraldo looked down the street and saw a large red car moving towards Patterson at a high rate of speed.

As Patterson struggled to keep from falling, the speed of the Cadillac increased. The last thing the blond giant heard was the roar of an engine and someone from behind him scream, "No, *Señor*, no!" Then all went black.

❧

McLean drove the unmarked green Plymouth from Santa Barbara Avenue onto the Harbor Freeway onramp. It would take a little more than an hour to reach Patterson's apartment in Agoura, but McLean had one of those feelings. Sabatello sat in the passenger seat, the familiar cigarette dangling from his bottom lip.

"You ought to give up the smokes," McLean said to the lithe, dark-complexioned Sicilian. "They're going to kill you."

"If the smokes don't, some asshole with a gun might."

McLean turned and looked over the top of his Aviator style sunglasses. "Let's hope it's not the latter."

"Let's hope."

Driving into Patterson's neighborhood, McLean pulled around the corner and saw an ambulance loading a form into the rear. His stomach knotted. Without being told, he knew who it was that lay covered beneath the white sheet. He parked and walked over to a uniformed Los Angeles County Deputy Sheriff who stood talking to a small, silver haired Mexican man and a younger female.

"*Señor* Patterson stumbled into the street," the distraught man said. "Then a big red car hit him. They no try to stop. No brakes, no horn, *nada*."

"No, Heraldo, it wasn't red," the teenage girl interrupted. "It was an orange car, faded orange."

McLean stood momentarily silent, and then he spoke.

"Did you say Patterson?"

"*Si, Señor*," answered Heraldo as small warm tears formed in his saddened eyes. "*Señor* Patterson. He was also *la policía*."

"You know the deceased?" the deputy asked McLean.

McLean's body stiffened. "Yeah. He was my partner," he answered, throwing open his navy blue windbreaker exposing his gun and badge.

"I'm sorry," the deputy said as he continued to diagram the accident scene.

"So am I."

McLean blindly walked back to the car where Sabatello was seated.

"I'm sorry, Nick," said Sabatello as he snapped a fresh cigarette between his lips and punched in the dash lighter.

"All he ended up with after the separation from his wife was his job, the bottle, and me. Looks like the first two proved fatal."

Seated behind the wheel, he reached over and slipped the mike from the holder. He hesitated; his eyes were shut behind his sunglasses and his breathing slow.

"3Zebra9 to 3Zebra20, come in."

He didn't wait for a response.

"3Zebra20, we're on our way to the station. Requesting that you meet us there."

Sitting in his car, Bock heard McLean's transmission.

"Any problems with Patterson?" Bock asked, concern in his voice.

"Not any more," McLean said.

Tossing the mike onto the seat, he cranked over the Plymouth. Pulling the selector into Drive, the car idled slowly down the street.

"Lastice and Kong killed Chris," McLean muttered.

"Not much you can do about it now," Sabatello said as he opened the window, coughed and spit into the street.

"There you're wrong," McLean answered.

The glimmer of innocence that once sparkled in McLean's eyes was gone. His deep blue eyes had changed. His expression was dark. The boyish likeableness was replaced by a look of hardness. The stalking of two killers was his quest and when it was over, someone would live and someone would die.

"It sounds like you've made up your mind," Sabatello said, interrupting a hacking cough that jarred his skinny frame.

"I have."

"You worried?"

"About what?"

"They got Patterson, Nick. Don't you think that you're next?" Sabatello said as he drew deeply on the cigarette stub.

"Hadn't thought about it," McLean lied.

The truth was that it had been on his mind since he had watched the ambulance attendants load Patterson into the back of the ambulance. Not until then had he thought about a threat to his family. Suddenly, it was a reality.

"Don't you think you should?" Sabatello asked as he rolled down the window and tossed out the stub. "I know that Patterson smoked the clown at Santa Barbara and Brighton, but you also nailed one of the group at Adams and Hoover. You've now moved to the top of the list."

McLean knew his partner was right. He also knew that he must find the two killers before they found his family.

TWENTY-NINE

Morton and Joanne Andrews sat in the hard-backed wooden chairs that faced the casket containing their daughter's body. Although neither had wanted to move the day of the funeral back nearly two weeks, it became necessary to accommodate the travel plans of those flying in from the East Coast.

Morton Andrews fixed his gaze on nothingness. His emotions shifted from grief back to the callous politician.

The crowd at graveside at the Forest Lawn Hollywood Hills Cemetery swelled to over two-thousand by ten o'clock.

The crowd was quiet, each waiting for the service to begin. In Washington D.C., both the House and Senate paused for a respectful moment of silence.

In Los Angeles, Don Marshall, Chief of Staff for the Congressman, ensured that a press release was issued before the funeral that called for the removal of Chief Thomas White, Deputy Chief John Cleary and Captain Charlie Reese because of "police incompetence that begins at the top."

Hundreds of chairs were placed on the slightly pitched green hill. Centered ten feet from the foot of the casket was a slender portable wooden podium with an angled top. Attached to the front were a number of small black microphones while large black speaker boxes had been placed to each side and faced the audience. One television camera sat in the middle aisle while others lined the periphery.

Andrews looked into the somber faces of the crowd and recognized family, political friends from both sides of the aisle, and many of his Hollywood celebrity cronies.

Brightly colored flower bouquets sat atop the baby blue casket while others were strewn in a circular pattern on the ground and swallowed up the green lawn in a myriad of vibrant colors. Bundles of red, white and blue helium-filled balloons had been attached to the large green canopy that had been erected to shade the casket. With each fresh gust of nippy winter air, they swirled skyward and bounced to and fro beneath the slate gray sky as if they were spirits seeking release from the cares of mortality.

While the seated mourners consoled each other, over fifteen hundred others assumed standing positions. From the rear, two men wearing dark sunglasses, dark suits and well-worn brown fedoras pulled low on their heads pushed their way through the crowd in an effort to get closer to the podium.

"Didn't know you'd be here," Weinstein said as he whispered under his breath to the man at his left.

"Come on, Weinstein, where else would I be," chided Teich as he broke into a subdued grin and perused the crowd over the top of his glasses.

Suddenly, a hush rolled over the crowd.

Reverend Obadiah J. Overton stepped forward and stood solemnly at the small rostrum.

"On behalf of the Andrews family, I want to thank each of you for your attendance this morning as we remember a beautiful daughter and wonderful friend, Leanne."

Overton's massive black hands were firmly placed on the sides of the wooden podium. He stood as one who had authority and believed that he represented God.

Those were the last words heard by Morton Andrews until he heard his name announced as the concluding speaker. As he stood, Joanne softly squeezed his hand.

"You'll do fine, Morton," she said as he left his seat and walked carefully to the rostrum.

I know I'll do fine, he thought. *I always do.*

Andrews stood at the podium, his hands folded lightly on its top, his voice directed into the microphones, and his eyes staring directly into the television cameras. Hesitating, he looked out over the large crowd. He was pleased.

Then he spoke.

"My dearest friends and family members. I want to thank you for being with us this morning. Both Joanne and I feel your unconditional love and are strengthened by your support. That is a blessing at this tragic time.

"Leanne was a wonderful daughter who had the rest of her life before her, but it was tragically cut short in a hail of bullets.

"She never thought ill of any man ...and while I know that she would forgive the person who took her life in its prime, I cannot say that I am able to follow her Christ-like example, for I am deeply hurt and very, very angry."

Andrews scanned the crowd. They were listening intently. It was time to increase the fervor of his words.

"I can guarantee each of you that this senseless killing will not be swept under the table. I will not allow it to be classified as one of the many unsolved cases by the Los Angeles Police Department. As long as I live, that will not happen."

Weinstein threw Teich a look. "The gauntlet's been thrown," he whispered.

Andrews continued.

"I promise that I will fight with all the energy I have to see this case solved and the guilty parties arrested and prosecuted to the fullest extent of the law."

He paused, wiped nonexistent moisture from his eyes and then continued.

"I have also been asked by friends and family how I feel about the way the Los Angeles Police Department is handling the investigation. My response has been: what investigation?"

A gasp rolled across the audience like breakers hitting the shore at Zuma Beach.

The Congressman's voice had taken on an edge of anger. He was ignoring the audience and focusing on the television cameras.

"Additionally, neither Joanne nor I were satisfied with the police press conference held at Parker Center. I realize that ballistics has possibly eliminated the police as perpetrators in Leanne's death, *or so they say*, but it appears that once they were eliminated, the investigative intensity subsided.

"This cannot and will not be allowed to happen. As a father, a husband and a representative for the State of California, I will *demand* that the Los Angeles Police Department brings this case to a successful resolution ...and if they won't, I will go over Chief White's head and request that the Federal Bureau of Investigation assume investigative responsibility."

Morton Andrews looked at the reaction from the crowd. He and they appeared to be of one mind.

"I was personally offended that Chief White had a minion conduct the press conference, and I aim to take that up directly with the Chief."

A lone figure standing in the rear stiffened. His small lips pursed and the knuckles of his folded hands erupted white.

"I am also calling on each of you to assist Joanne and me to keep this matter in front of the press, and I would laud any efforts by our Federal authorities to step in and help get to the bottom of the killing of two black citizens at the scene of a routine traffic stop and the ruthless murder of my daughter. I am convinced that with their help, we can get to the bottom of this and uncover the truth."

Morton Andrews' fingers that tightly gripped the sides of the small podium had turned white. His ashen-colored face was now red and anger hung on each word.

"In conclusion, I want each of you again to know how grateful we are for your attendance here today," he said as his eyes scanned the audience. "Thank you."

Deputy Chief John Cleary stood in the rear unnoticed. His small mouth was quivering, his thin lips were twisting back and forth, and his jaw was clenched.

"That arrogant bastard," he muttered softly to himself as he turned and started back to his car. As he approached the driver's side, he stopped and looked back toward the dispersing crowd. He was grateful that he hadn't worn his dress uniform. If he had, things might have become damn right ugly.

PART THREE

THIRTY

"Sergeant Steele, line four," Harlene Settles called from the front desk of the detective squad room.

"Thank you Harlene," Steele shouted back.

Steele pushed his stack of paperwork back into the middle of the desk, took off his Ben Franklin reading glasses, rubbed his eyes with the palms of both hands and then pushed the flashing light on his cream-colored telephone.

"Sergeant Steele, University Detectives, may I help you?" he said while reaching into his shirt pocket in search of a cigarette.

"Steele, Wiggins, S.I.D. I've got some good news for you, partner."

"Great, I need some good news," Steele said as his fingers slipped a long, unfiltered cigarette from its pack.

"We finished our search of the four prints we lifted from the rear of the Ford and got a hit."

"Are they different than the print on the mirror?"

"They are."

"Wonderful. So what name do we put to Kong?"

"The prints came back to..."

"Wait a minute," Steele said as he cupped his hand over the mouthpiece and let the Pall Mall dangle from the right side of his mouth. "Bobby, I want you to hear this."

Van Drew put down his coffee and picked up the telephone.

"Okay, Bill, go ahead," Steele said as he took a long, hard drag on the smoldering cigarette. "I wanted my partner to hear this."

"That's fine. You both on the line?"

"Go ahead," Steele said.

"The prints belong to an ex-con named Benjamin Washington. I thumbed through his package, and it appears that he served time in San Quentin for killing a cop in Seventy-Seventh. The conviction was later overturned because of a problem with the Miranda warning. It seems that some of your counterparts in Seventy-Seventh used what the court referred to as 'unfair and illegal physical and emotional methods to secure the admission.'"

"When was he released?" asked Steele.

"September of last year and in his exit interview he said he would be heading back to L.A."

"Do we have an address?" Steele asked.

"Not that I could find, but one of my contacts in the Fugitive Unit is trying to identify his Parole Officer."

"You've made my day," Steele said as he dragged harder on the stump of the cigarette that was pinched between his nicotine-stained fingers of his left hand.

"I'm not finished," Wiggins said. "Washington has an a/k/a of 'Bubba.'"

"Do you have his vitals?" asked Van Drew.

"He's six-three and approximately two-hundred and ninety pounds. A big man."

"Fits Kong," Van Drew whispered.

"Anything that links him to a woman?" Steele asked while he sipped gently on his steaming coffee.

"I did find the name of one woman on two arrest reports. Her name is Rose Marie Jones, but she has also used the name of Rosie Washington, Annie Van Buren, and Anita Maxwell. Take your pick."

"The plot thickens," Van Drew said as he pulled gently at his bushy moustache.

Steele lifted himself out of the hard chair and rubbed his numb ass with both hands.

"Let's get this information to Bock," Steele commented dryly as he stuffed some notes into the pocket of his white shirt. "Maybe they can locate Washington and the female."

THIRTY-ONE

Under a darkening sky, four black and white police motorcycles idled slowly through the sculptured black wrought iron gates of the Forest Lawn Memorial Park Cemetery. Perfectly spaced one abreast the other, they inched their way around the circular fountain that contained seven large bronze herons, which spewed geysers of water heavenward.

They were followed by a black Cadillac hearse, six unmarked police vehicles and four black and whites. The shroud of grief that surrounded the scene was darkened by huge black thunderheads that floated like warships across a threatening sky.

Slowly, the procession wound its way to the bottom of a spacious hill that was filled with hundreds of stark white crosses. Majestic pine trees bordered the lush, green lawn like eternal stone sentinels guarding the ancient Egyptian Valley of the Kings and beautiful purple and white flowers added to the serenity and sacredness of the location.

With eyes staring blankly forward, McLean stared up the grassy hill toward a small green-canopied tent and a freshly dug grave.

"Where are all the people?" Sabatello asked rather puzzled.

"This is it. Patterson's mother wanted it small," McLean answered, his hands tightly squeezing the black plastic steering wheel.

After the procession had stopped, the rear doors of the hearse were opened and a highly polished mahogany casket was pulled out. Six somber pallbearers took their places. Each wore a pressed blue dress uniform with brass buttons and badges polished to a brilliant luster, black shoes spit-shined so one's face could be seen in the mirror of the toe and highly polished black leather Sam Browne's. Looking at each of the other five, McLean knew that Patterson would have been pleased.

On command, the casket was slipped out the rear of the hearse and balanced. Once secure, the six men reverently began the difficult walk up the hill to the small green canopy. Arriving at the tent, the casket was carefully slipped onto the holding stand. Then members of the Army Honor Guard placed a new flag on the casket with the stars over the left shoulder and the stripes running down past the feet.

The flag-draped casket sat beneath the canvas canopy, while flowers sent by members of the Los Angeles Police Department Protective League were placed directly in front.

McLean stood silently with the other members of the Special Operations Squad and a handful of others that included Lieutenants Jack Mahon and Richter von Berliner, and Sergeants Evans, Bova and Elkins. Seated on each side of Mrs. Edmund Patterson were Sergeant Rod Bock and Captain Charlie Reese.

McLean stood directly behind Mrs. Patterson, but he never heard the words spoken by Officer Duane Wilkins, the Department Chaplain. His mind was elsewhere. He could not help but re-live what had happened that night at Adams and Hoover. Why was he not hit and why was his more experienced partner struck by a bullet that would eventually result in his untimely death? Why didn't he get off a round that was straight and not one that flew errantly to the left of the giant black man? *There are so many whys,* he thought. But there was one given: He would find and kill both Bubba Washington and Ta-Ta Lastice.

McLean was drawn back to the moment as Wilkins finished speaking. The honor guard presented arms and the dismal day was shattered by the report of simultaneous rifle fire that resounded through the trees like sharp claps of thunder. Following the rifle salute, two uniformed Army officers folded the flag into a perfect triangle and handed it to Moira Patterson, who softly sobbed into a white lace handkerchief.

"He was too much like his father," she whimpered to herself, then softly pleaded, "Please dear Lord, take care of my boy."

Warm tears left her tired eyes and streamed down her weathered cheeks. The sorrow and agony of her forty-five hard years of life came crashing down and around her as if orchestrated by the distant violent claps of thunder from the dark angry sky. Moira Patterson was lost to the greatest grief she had ever experienced. It wasn't just the loss of her son, but the loss of her dignity, and her courage; the loss of so many empty years of her life.

McLean glanced at the darkening sky and felt the chill of its winter breeze. He was anxious to leave. Moira's muffled sobs irritated both McLean and Sabatello, but for different reasons.

McLean felt for the small woman who had lost all in her life that she deemed important. He felt the pain of her loss and only wished there were words he could speak to soften the pain. But there were none.

It was different with Sabatello. He came from a tough world governed by Sicilian males who saw emotion as a sign of weakness. Therefore, not unlike Patterson, Antonio Sabatello drove his feelings deep into the farthest recesses of his soul and kept everything inside.

"I hate these things," he whispered, his deep-set black eyes emotionless. "They're damn right depressing."

"Well, it's over," McLean said, feeling that it was now time to begin to make good on a promise. "We've got work to do. Let's go,"

As McLean turned to leave, a hasty rain broke over the city.

THIRTY-TWO

Washington stood in the small kitchen of his dirty two bedroom apartment and sifted his last grams of heroin from a red balloon into the cup of a bent kitchen spoon. Using an old baby pacifier with a small needle attached and held in place by rubber bands, he sucked up some water from a small glass and emptied it into the spoon. He then began to gently swirl the solution with the end of the needle until the heroin and water had thoroughly mixed. Slowly, he moved the spoon over the flame that danced skyward from the chipped white four-burner stove, and when the solution began to bubble, he continued to meticulously mix the chalky concoction with the point of the needle.

Once the solution had thinned into a creamy liquid, he slowly sucked the contents of the bent spoon into the pacifier and walked into the living room where he sat down on the old couch. After he placed the syringe on a threadbare couch cushion, he picked up a long, dark brown piece of surgical tubing and quickly tied it tightly around his muscular bicep. He cinched the tubing to the point of nearly snapping in half, and then made a fist. His attempts to find a usable vein were unsuccessful. Repeatedly, he squeezed his hand tight and thumped the inside of his left forearm, but all he saw were the protruding black remnants of veins that had long ago collapsed.

"Rosie," he yelled, in a voice mixed with frustration and anger. "I need your help, woman."

"I is feeding the children," Rosie weakly called out from the bedroom.

"I got a needle full a shit that's gonna cool and I can't find me a vein so get your black ass in here!" Washington bellowed.

Slowly, Rosie set the baby in a crib made from a wicker clothesbasket and shuffled into the living room. Washington sat on the couch with a look of deep hatred in his eyes.

"Don't look at me like that, Bubba," Rosie said. "I gets scared when you look like that."

"Shut up, woman, and find me a vein," Washington growled.

Sitting on the floor next to the couch, Rosie thumped the massive forearm of the man who had fathered her two children and a man she feared.

No matter how hard she slapped, she couldn't raise a healthy vein. Frustrated and now fearful of Bubba's wrath, she took his massive hands in her bony fingers and began to examine the tops and between the fingers for the slightest protrusion of a usable vein. All she found were scarred, black, tracks.

"You is taking too long," Washington yelled as he snatched back his hands, drew back his left arm and struck the diminutive little whore a vicious blow to the head that sent her sprawling across the hardwood floor.

Struggling to sit up, Rosie felt a warm liquid flow from the side of her mouth. Reaching up, she wiped the blood from her chin. Tears formed in her eyes as she began to whimper softly.

"You didn't need to do that, Bubba," she sobbed, still feeling the warm red blood run down her chin from the wide split in her lip.

"You is nothing but one worthless black whore," he screamed. "Get outta here."

Rosie knew it best that she leave. She feared not only for herself, but also the children. Lifting her slim frame off the floor, she wiped more blood from her mouth with the back of her hand and glanced into the corner of the room where a silent Lastice sat on the floor with a sadistic smile on his face. Lastice hated the slim street whore, but the feeling was mutual.

Rosie checked on the two sleeping children, then walked silently to the front door and deliberately threw each of the seven deadbolts open. Without looking back, she slipped out into the cold winter night.

Still hurting from Bubba's vicious blow, she wrapped her threadbare coat snuggly around her skinny frame and walked slowly towards an area where she knew she could turn some tricks and earn a little money. With money came heroin, and Rosie knew that smack would buy back Bubba's approval.

Standing at the intersection of Exposition and Vermont, Rosie shuffled quickly to the driver's door of the first car that had stopped waiting for the signal to turn green. Within minutes, she had turned her first trick and was twenty dollars richer. After three hours, she had earned one hundred dollars.

Lastice stood at the top of the cement stairs and watched as Rosie trudged up one-step at a time toward the upper apartment. His lips curled in an evil sneer as he watched her struggle. He had never liked Rosie, but said nothing because she was Bubba's woman, but now it was different. Rosie had fallen into disfavor and unbeknownst to her, life would soon change.

"You ain't wanted here, no more," Lastice shouted at the haggard streetwalker, who had finally reached the top of the landing.

"This is my home, nigga," she panted, "and I is goin' in. Besides, I has two little ones inside."

"This ain't no longer your home, and besides, the children ain't here."

Rosie let out an anguished cry that brought Washington jumping off the couch and racing to the door. Throwing it open, he faced the hysterical woman.

"Get your black ass back on the street where it belongs!" he screamed.

"I loves you, Bubba, and I loves my children. Please Bubba, don't do me this way," she sobbed.

"Get off my porch!" he shouted as he struck her across the face with a blow that sent her careening down the steep stairs. Sprawled at the bottom, Rosie looked up at the two darkly clad figures who said nothing, but just glared at her.

Crawling onto the front path, her long black wig askew and her tight mini-dress hiked up to her waist, Rosie spewed forth her hatred.

"I'll get your black ass, Mr. Bubba Washington. I is gonna get you."

"You ain't gonna get no one," Washington screamed back.

Angrily, her slender hands flattened themselves on the concrete, and she pushed herself into a standing position. Hurt and shaking, she knew that she must leave or die. She would worry about the children later.

⚜

Washington steered the red Cadillac slowly down Crenshaw Boulevard and across Florence Avenue. After crossing 75th Street, he pulled the car into an abandoned service station and parked deep in the darkness. He had shot his last few grams of smack, was feeling no pain, and was now going to score some money.

Lastice sat in the passenger seat with his shotgun resting across his lap. In his coat pocket, he had dropped four additional rounds. After the debacle at Adams and Hoover, he vowed never again to be without extra ammunition, but while he realized the need for greater firepower, the thought never occurred to him that perhaps his dilemma would be solved by trading the single-barreled shotgun for one with two barrels.

It was Saturday, nearing two in the morning. Welfare checks had been mailed two days earlier and the area liquor stores would soon be closing with full cash registers and empty shelves.

"Isn't we gonna use masks tonight?" Lastice asked as he sat in the darkness and strained his eyes staring up and down Crenshaw.

At first, there was only silence, then Washington, answered.

"We won't be needing no masks tonight," Washington coldly remarked, never taking his eyes off the front of the small liquor store that sat mid-block.

Slouched deep in the front seat, two killers watched the store.

Inside, an old black man shuffled slowly back and forth restocking shelves while an elderly woman stood behind the ancient cash register and counted down the day's receipts.

"I is parking the ride on a side street. Then I'll go in while you pull the grating across the front and lock it. You understand?"

"Yeah."

"Once we is inside, we is gonna take care of business and go out the back," Washington added.

At five minutes before two, Washington decided that it was time.

As he pulled slowly onto the street and drove past the liquor store, he could see two figures standing behind the counter. He pulled onto an adjacent side street and parked in the darkness. Leaving Lastice standing next to the car, he walked down the darkened alley where he located the rear door to the liquor store. He turned the door handle slowly and was delighted when it opened.

Leaving it slightly ajar, he walked back to the Cadillac. After reaching into his waistband and taking one final squeeze on the grips of the Colt, he turned and motioned for Lastice to follow. Together they walked towards Crenshaw Boulevard and the front of the store.

Inside, Edna Dixon had just finished counting the money. After tying the bills with a rubber band, she slid the cash into a brown paper bag and placed it in a pocket of her flowered apron.

Lawrence, her husband, placed the final bottle of Thunderbird wine on the shelf, untied his apron, and stuffed it under the counter.

"I'll lock the grating and front door," he said to Edna as she walked back behind the cash register.

Walking in a deliberate shuffle, he had just reached the front door when it exploded open and the elderly storeowner stood directly in front of an enormous black man with a gun in his right hand.

"Get back inside, and you, old lady, step away from the back of the counter and don't go pushin' no buttons," Washington barked in a voice that sounded like thunder.

Lawrence stepped toward the cash register while Edna, ignoring Washington's order, slowly reached down under the counter and pushed a small red button. She then walked haughtily to the side of her frightened husband.

Looking to the front, both watched as the steel grating slowly closed and a man dressed in dark clothing and wearing a dark black hat reached down and snapped the padlock from the inside, securing the iron fencing.

"Open the cash register and put all the money in a bag," Washington ordered as Lastice slipped quietly through the front door and walked to Washington's side.

"There ain't no money in the cash register," Edna barked. "It's all in the safe and that can't be opened until morning."

Lastice stepped forward and struck the woman in the face with back of his hand, ripping open the side of her mouth and splattering her cheek with blood. Sprawled on the floor, she moaned, and then struggled to regain her feet.

"Oh, no," Lawrence screamed. "Please don't hit her again; we'll give you all the money."

"Give them the money, dear," Lawrence pleaded to his wife who stood behind the counter trembling. Reaching into her coat pocket, Edna removed the brown paper bag that was stuffed full with currency and handed it to Washington.

"Is that all of it?" he growled.

"Yes," Edna said whimpering.

Suddenly, Lastice head cocked and his eyes narrowed.

"Bubba, do you hear that, Blood?" he shouted, his voice hinged with fear. Washington stopped and listened. In the far distance, the shrill wail of a siren could be heard. Looking into the eyes of his two victims, his countenance darkened. As his eyes tightened, he stepped forward.

"Get to the back," he commanded.

Edna wobbled around the counter and stood next to her husband. Simultaneously, they turned and grabbed each other's hand. Slowly, as if they knew what fate lay ahead, they each whispered, "I love you."

Reaching the rear of the store, Washington pushed the trembling pair into a rear storage room.

"I told you not to push no button, bitch," Washington said as he stepped back and Lastice stepped forward.

"Kneel down, fools," Lastice commanded, a deathly inflection in his voice.

"Hurry up, Ta-Ta," Washington said, his eyes as cold as a snakes.

"Please, please don't kill us," Lawrence pled as he knelt down next to his wife and squeezed her hand.

Edna continued to whimper.

The siren grew louder.

Lastice stepped back, aimed the shotgun at the back of Lawrence Dixon's head, and pulled the trigger.

Flame flashed from the shortened barrel.

The roar inside the small room was deafening.

As the left side of the old man's head disappeared, he was jerked forward and sprawled in front of his hysterical wife.

As Edna shook and screamed uncontrollably, Lastice calmly broke open the shotgun, pulled out the spent round, and threw it to the floor, sending it rolling across the room and out the open door.

He then reached into his coat pocket, pulled out another shell and reloaded. As the terrified old woman knelt on the floor screaming and writhing in anticipation, Lastice fired directly into the back of her head.

Suddenly, it was quiet. The small stockroom was filled with acrid smoke and two mangled bodies lay twisted on a blood-soaked floor. Washington walked through the carnage and removed the wallet from Lawrence Dixon's right rear pocket. Opening it up, he found five, brand new twenty-dollar bills.

"We got ourselves four more balloons of shit," he said.

Calmly walking to the rear door, he was followed by Lastice, who tripped the lights throwing the small store into darkness.

Washington turned the small thumb lock located in the doorknob, and after both he and Lastice had stepped into the darkened alley, he shut the door, locking it from the inside. In less than a minute, the faded red Cadillac with its lights out was traveling north on Victoria Avenue toward 67th Street. In the distance, a police siren drew within blocks.

When 3Adam81 arrived at the scene, Cunningham let Rice off in the front, and then drove the idling Plymouth to the rear alley where he checked the back door, which he found locked.

In the front, Rice slipped to the side of the grating and peeked around the corner. The store was dark and all was quiet. He could see no movement from inside. Walking over to the grating, he pulled on the padlock that secured the two sections of wrought iron together. It was securely locked.

Finding the rear secure, Cunningham drove to the front.

"Find anything?" he asked his partner.

"The place is locked up tight," Rice answered as he opened the car door and slid in.

"3Adam81," Cunningham said as he held the mike close to his mouth and stared into the darkened liquor store, "Show a Code Four on the 211 Silent at 7568 South Crenshaw. It appears to be a faulty alarm. Please notify the Wellington Alarm Company at 485-2213."

3Adam81 flipped a U-turn and drove north.

THIRTY-THREE

McLean was sleeping soundly when the phone rang. On the third ring, he shot a quick glance at the clock: six-thirty A.M. Sliding his legs to the floor, he rolled out of bed, picked up the receiver and whispered into the mouthpiece.

"McLean."

"South Crenshaw?" His throat constricted.

With one hand he held the phone hard against his ear.

His stomach knotted.

Struggling, he slid on a pair of Levis and grabbed his blue nylon windbreaker.

"I'm on my way."

Turning around, he saw Darlene sitting up in bed rubbing her eyes.

"You don't have to go back to work this early, do you?" she asked.

"Yeah," he answered as he stepped forward and kissed her on the cheek. "That was Bock. They found an elderly couple executed in a liquor store on South Crenshaw. It could be our suspects from Adams and Hoover."

While McLean stepped out the front door, Steele and Van Drew were stepping through the partially opened back door. The odor of death filled their nostrils as they approached Cunningham who was standing in the doorway that led to the side storage room.

"They're in here," Cunningham said as he stepped back from the door. "The lab boys and the Coroner are on their way."

Steele stopped at the doorway and looked into the small room. Both he and Van Drew stared at the carnage. Neither spoke, but each felt a small knot erupt in the pit of their stomach.

"We also found this," Cunningham said as he held out a spent shotgun shell dangling on the end of a pencil.

"Where was it?"

"Under a far shelving unit."

"Remington, double-ought-buck," Steele said as he took the pencil and looked at the indentation mark in the primer.

"Déjà vu," he said as he reached into a coat pocket and retrieved a small manila evidence envelope. Opening the end, he dropped the spent shell inside, sealed the envelope and placed his initials across the flap.

Steele turned back to the two bodies that lay entwined on the blood soaked floor.

He paused, then after a moment, turned again to Cunningham.

"Matt, do me a favor. When you're done here, run the casing down to S.I.D and after you book it in, see that it gets to Dave Hatch in the Firearms Section."

Cunningham dropped the envelope into his shirt pocket.

"While you're enroute, I'll give Hatch a call and ask him to compare the indentation in the primer against the shell we recovered at Adams and Hoover."

"Got it covered, Jimmy," Cunningham responded.

Van Drew, who had been standing silently watching the interchange between Steele and Cunningham, seeing that both were finished, stepped into the conversation. "Who found the bodies?"

"Their son," Cunningham answered. "When they didn't answer their phone early this morning, he got worried, so he drove in from West Los Angeles."

"Did he have a key or was the place open," Steele asked.

"The place was locked, so he used his key. Came through the back," said Rice who had stepped through the open backdoor.

"Where is he now?" Van Drew asked.

"He's sitting in our black and white."

"Thanks, guys. We'll take it from here," Steele said as he slipped a cigarette under his moustache and between his lips.

Silently, the two seasoned Homicide cops stared at the grossly contorted bodies and studied the room without moving from the doorway. As they stood making notes, an S.I.D photographer arrived followed by George Varney, a member of the Coroner's staff. At their arrival, both cops slipped into the hall.

"I'll let you snap some overall shots," Steele said. "Then I'll point out the specific shots I want."

Under Steele's direction, photographs were taken. When done, the photographer stepped back and Varney stepped in. Gently, he rolled each body over, lifted their clothing and slid a long surgical thermometer into each liver to determine temperature. Searching Lawrence Dixon's pockets, he failed to find a wallet.

"Can't say that he had a billfold on him," Varney said, "but the crease in the rear pants pocket indicates that he carried one. Now, it's gone."

As Steele knelt down closer to the bodies, Van Drew leaned in, looking over his partner's right shoulder.

"Well, what do you think, Jimmy?" Varney asked.

"I've got my opinion, "Steele replied, "but I'd like to hear yours first," he said as Varney stood.

"Well, I'm confident that we're on the same page. Each victim sustained a single shotgun wound to the rear of the head. I'd say the suspect or suspects used a magnum load of double-ought-buck."

"You're right on the mark," Van Drew said. "One of our patrol officers found a spent round outside the door, and we slipped it into an evidence envelope and asked that it be taken to ballistics. Sorry we didn't wait for your approval, but..."

"If it had been anyone but Jimmy Steele, I'd be raising holy hell," Varney said, "but we go back more than twenty years and I trust his instincts. So forget it."

Steele grinned and his face lit up.

"Can you give us a time, George?" Steele asked.

"Time of death ...that'll be tough. The liver temperature is just over 92 degrees. Rough estimate puts death around four hours ago, plus or minus a half-an-hour."

"Has rigor begun to set in?" Van Drew asked.

"Hard to say. As you both know, when it's cold and the body drops temperature quickly, it can be inhibited. Normally, it starts in the face, but in this case, we have none. Any other questions?"

"Can't think of any now, but I'm sure that we'll have some later," Steele said as his eyes searched the room.

"We'll be in touch. Let me finish up and the scene is yours."

"Thanks," Steele and Van Drew said simultaneously as they each flipped to a fresh page in their notebooks. While Steele began to made detailed notes, Van Drew began a rough sketch of the crime scene.

❧

Bock sat in the coffee room holding a brown cup that contained a brew that had more the texture of mud than it did coffee. He hated the station coffee dispensed from an old machine because it reminded him of Army coffee, circa South Korea, something he wanted to forget.

"We need to get a small coffee maker upstairs," he muttered as he twisted the cup of brew in his hands and stared blankly at the black liquid. "I don't know how much longer I can drink this crap," he added with a shudder.

As he methodically turned the cup in his hands and stared into the vortex of the swirling fluid, McLean walked into the room, dropped a dime in the machine, and watched as the thick black liquid was slowly dispensed.

"This stuff is evil," he said as he set the cup on the yellowing Formica tabletop and straddled an aluminum chair across from Bock.

"How are you doing?" Bock asked as he took his gaze from the black liquid and focused it on the hardened blue eyes of the young officer he had grown to respect.

"I'm fine," McLean said, unconvincingly.

"Your sure?"

"I'm sure."

As the coffee room began to fill with uniform cops and motor officers, Bock motioned to McLean that it was time to head upstairs.

As they stepped out the door and into the hallway, the rear station doors flew open and two patrol officers bolted into the corridor struggling with three suspects. As one cop threw the first man against the far wall, McLean saw that he was securely cuffed with his hands behind his back, yet that didn't stop his feet from flaying up and out in a vicious attempt to plant a foot in the groin of the nearest cop, who happened to be McLean.

The other two arrestees shared a set of handcuffs. With this freedom, they fought the officers as they tried to push them through the double doors.

Dodging the vicious kick, McLean flew behind the taller of the partially handcuffed arrestees and slammed his right forearm under the struggling man's throat. Then he thrust his left arm forward across the man's left shoulder, encircling the back of the head while the right arm was pulled violently against the man's esophagus forming a lethal chokehold. Before the thrashing man or his shocked companion could react, McLean snapped his arms back and dropped directly to the floor sending the combatant onto his ass with his head thrust forward. The man gasped, jerked, twitched, and then, in seconds, he was unconscious.

The quickness of the move dropped the second arrestee against the floor, where he was quickly pinned when Bock slammed his foot across the side of the man's head. In moments, it was over. McLean released his hold and watched as urine seeped from beneath the unconscious man's groin area and the smell of fresh feces filled the air.

"There," McLean said to the two cops as he got up from the floor and brushed himself off. "After you get their attention, you explain it to them."

The first arrestee sat sullenly against the wall. A look of fear crossed his face as he watched one partner gag and begin to vomit while the eyes of the other bulged from the pressure of Bock's boot.

Stunned silence filled the corridor. When McLean turned toward the stairwell to leave, he faced Charlie Reese.

"You through stinking up my station, McLean?" Reese asked, smiling.

"Yes sir," McLean answered. "Sorry about the mess Captain."

"You should be," Reese said as he turned and walked back toward his office.

"What have you got?" Bock asked the two arresting officers, "besides battery on a police officer."

"Robbery," the probationer said puffing out his skinny chest.

"They were seen by a citizen tying bandanas around their faces and pulling a rifle from a golf bag before walking into a small bakery at Vernon and Slauson," the senior officer added.

"And since none of them looked exactly like Arnold Palmer's caddy, the wit called the police. We got them just as they stepped back outside. Still had the bandanas on, but they had stashed the rifle back in the bag."

"What type of rifle did they have?" McLean asked, more interested now than before.

"It was a .22 that was carried by the guy you choked out. We drew down on them before they could reach back into the bag and pull it out," the senior officer said, a tone of disappointment in his voice.

"It might not have been a good shooting," added the probationer, "since they didn't have the gun out of the bag."

McLean spun on the young cop. "Anytime you dump an asshole reaching for a gun it's a good shooting," McLean said as his face flushed red.

McLean's mind raced back to Adams and Hoover. He saw Washington and Lastice.

A door down the hall slammed shut. Startled, he was drawn back to the three bandits sprawled on the floor.

"But, sometimes, it might be better that a shooting doesn't happen," he mumbled. "Much better."

Reaching under his collar he removed the silver chain that held the sterling silver Scottish medallion for eternity. Slowly he twisted the quarter size piece between his right thumb and forefinger.

Eternity's a long time, he thought. *Especially if you're not expecting it.*

"After you book these three," Bock said, addressing his remarks to the senior officer, "do me a favor and tell Helvin and Berry that we'd like to talk to their suspect's when they're finished."

☙

McLean and Inglis sat comfortably on the old sofa, while Sabatello and the others occupied the hard-backed aluminum chairs. Bock sat on the corner of the desk.

"The L.A. County Sheriff's Department found three more witnesses who saw Patterson killed and each gave a pretty good description of the suspect's vehicle," Bock said as he flipped through his notes.

"All three identify it as a large red Cadillac. One thought it was a 55 or 56, while another said that he saw two male Negro occupants in the car.

"Steele ran DMV on all the registered owners of 1955 through 57 Cadillacs in the city. He came up with six hits in the Valley, one in Santa Monica and one hit closer to home. The Caddie in the south-end is registered to a Solomon Bloom, who, by the way, is one of us and works at Wilshire Division as a

Day Watch sergeant." Bock folded the note and stuffed it back into his shirt pocket.

McLean, I want you and Sabatello to take a ride over to Wilshire and talk to Sergeant Bloom."

McLean drove the unmarked Plymouth into the Wilshire Division parking lot and pulled into the first open space. After dodging two incoming black and whites, he and Sabatello walked under the brick archway, up the weathered concrete steps and through the large wooden side doors.

"This brings back memories," he said.

"Good or bad?" asked Sabatello.

"Both."

"Nick McLean," shouted Bloom in a loud voice. "Now what the hell brings you back to Wilshire?" he asked as he rose like a whale breaking the surface, stood in front of his chair and extended a beefy hand.

"Came to see you, Sarge. But first, let me introduce my partner, Tony Sabatello."

"If you can put up with this guy, you're all right," Bloom said as he pressed Sabatello's hand firmly and broke into a grin.

"It's tough," Sabatello said, "but the guy always watches my back."

"You're in good hands," added Bloom as McLean and Sabatello pulled barrel-back slatted wooden chairs up to the front of the desk.

"So what can I do for you two?" Bloom asked, a puzzled look on his rotund face.

"You still own a '56 Cadillac?" McLean asked.

"Nope, I sold it."

"What color was it?" Sabatello asked.

"Red."

"Why all the questions about that old car?"

"We think that it's being driven by a cop killer," McLean said.

"You're kidding?"

"Do we look like we're kidding," interjected Sabatello.

Bloom bristled. His green eyes narrowed as he shot Sabatello a hard look over his bifocals.

"Who was killed?"

"My partner."

"No shit," Bloom exclaimed.

"Well, I sold it last summer to a black guy named Lastice. I remember that he used two first names, but don't remember what they were."

"Could it be, Ta-Ta?"

"Could be, Mac. I just can't remember. He paid cash and he promised me that he would re-register the car in his own name. It appears he didn't."

"Appears that way," muttered Sabatello.

Bloom leaned back in his chair, a look of deep concern etched across his forehead while his swollen hands whisked back the few strips of stringy gray hair hanging from his skull.

"Now what are you insinuating?"

"Nothing Sarge," McLean cut in. "We're just trying to find the guy."

Bloom placed his elbows on the desk, clasped his hands and leaned forward.

"Do you remember making out any paperwork?" McLean asked.

Bloom thought for a moment.

"Well, I think that I gave him a bill of sale."

You dumb shit, thought Sabatello.

"I'll search my records for last year and see what I can find."

"Thanks," McLean said as he and Sabatello pushed their chairs away from the desk.

"If you find the paperwork, would you give us a call? We're at University working the Special Operations Squad," McLean said.

"You can count on it," Bloom said as he walked out the door with McLean and Sabatello."

"And Mac, I'm sorry about your partner."

"So am I, Sarge. He was a good cop."

It was two in the morning when Hutton and Hestily drove up Budlong Avenue and spotted a red 1956 Cadillac parked at the curb just north of 39th Street.

"Looks promising," Hutton said as he circled the block, cut the lights and parked about fifty feet behind the Caddy.

Quietly, both officers slipped from the car and walked cautiously toward the Cadillac.

"Hey, Bobby," whispered Hestily who had slipped to the front of the car, knelt down and was examining something.

"Take a look."

Hutton crouched over, duck-waddled to the front of the car and bent down next to his partner. Holding the slightly spread fingers of his left hand over the face of the flashlight to cut the brightness, Hestily watched the flashlight illuminate the right front fender like a flitting soul behind a dead man's blank stare.

"Looks like traffic accident damage to me," Hutton said with a grin.

"No shit, Bobby! I think we might have found the car that Bock and the guy's have been looking for."

Slipping back to the rear trunk, Hestily jotted down the license number in his small notebook.

Climbing quietly into the police car, Hestily grabbed the mike.

"3Adam58 requesting wants, warrants and DMV on 944 William-Henry-Sam."

"You ever see one of those communication operators?" Hestily asked.

"Yeah," Hutton answered abruptly. "Don't let their voices fool you. They do a great job handling the airwaves, and watching our backs, but there's a reason they work mornings."

"And what would that be?" Hestily asked as he stared down the street at the parked Cadillac.

"Because most of them aren't real attractive, Tommy."

"That's not nice, Hutton."

"Might not be nice, Tommy, but it's true."

"3Adam58, no wants or warrants on 944 William-Henry-Sam. Registered owners are Solomon or Susan Bloom, 2324 Lincoln Road, La Mirada, California."

Hestily reached down to the small tactical radio and snapped the red dial over to Tactical Frequency two.

"3Adam58 to 3Lincoln90, come in."

"3Lincoln90 to 3Adam58, this is Mahon, what can I do for you two super sleuths?"

"Lieutenant, we've got a red Cadillac out here that we think is the one Bock is looking. It came back registered to a Solomon or Susan Bloom in La Mirada," Hestily said excitedly. "And it has traffic accident damage to the front end."

"Sit on it guys, and I'll get Bock at home," Mahon said as he picked up the telephone receiver.

When Hestily ended the transmission, he snapped the small red switch back to the regular frequency and broadcast a Code Five, putting unit 3Adam58 on a stakeout at 38th Street and Budlong Avenue.

Hutton sat slouched in the driver's seat, his head back, eyes open and a shit-eating grin on his always-jovial face.

❧

Bock was in the middle of a pleasant dream when the phone rang. Startled, he clawed in the dark at the nightstand until he found the receiver.

"Bock," his gravely voice whispered.

"Rod, Jack Mahon. It looks like Hutton and Hestily might have found your Cadillac."

"Where is it, Jack?" Bock asked as he tried to clear the cobwebs.

"On Budlong between 38th and 39th Street."

"How sure are we?"

"Pretty sure. DMV comes back to a Sol Bloom."

"Do me a favor, and have Evans call my men and get in as many in as he can. I'll be there in forty-five minutes."

"Consider it done."

When Bock walked into the coffee room, he found four of his five teams sitting and waiting anxiously while sipping steaming cups of black coffee.

"Okay," he said as he dropped a dime into the coffee machine. "The Cadillac is on Budlong, between 38th and 39th Street," he said as he opened the scratched plastic door, removed the coffee cup and pulled up an aluminum chair.

"Hutton and Hestily are sitting on it, and I want to get out there as soon as possible. Lieutenant Mahon has offered to let us have 3Adam58, and I agreed. If things go south, it'll be nice to have a black and white available."

Bock sipped gingerly at the steaming black brew, then twisted the cup gently in his hands for the warmth.

"The car is parked on the west side of the street, facing south, so I want McLean and Sabatello to take up a position north of 37th street so they have a clear view of the car and any foot traffic that might approach.

"Brooks and Inglis will set up on the northeast corner of 38th and Budlong while Stemples and Brown will relieve 3Adam58 at 37th and Budlong and have them deploy down the street. I'll set up at the southeast corner of 39th and Budlong. LeFrois, you and Johnson set up on the northwest side of Budlong just south of 39th Street."

"What about McGrath and Stallcup?" asked McLean.

"Evans couldn't raise either of them, and we can't wait," Bock said as he lifted himself from the uncomfortable chair.

"One last thing," Bock said as the eight men grabbed their gear and began to file out the door headed for the Detective bureau where they would check out their unmarked cars.

"We'll be on Tactical Frequency two."

As Bock walked out the back door and into the parking lot that housed the vehicles, he was met by Reese who was pulling in.

"Rod, wait a minute," Reese called from his unrolled driver's window. "I'd like to talk to you."

After parking his car, Reese walked over to Bock's driver's window, placed both hands on the window ledge and leaned in.

"You're up rather early, Captain," Bock said, stifling a yawn.

"Only by a few hours and a day," Reese answered smiling.

"Jack called and briefed me on what Hutton and Hestily found," Reese added.

"That was pretty good police work," he continued, "but I'm not telling you anything that you don't already know. But I have a request."

"Name it."

"The heat on the Department has increased since we don't have any suspects in custody for the Andrews' girl killing, and if this Cadillac was the one sold by Bloom to Lastice and was then used to kill Patterson, I'd like to get Lastice alive so he can shed some light on the whereabouts of his partner."

"We'll do our best, Captain," Bock said, a little miffed by the thought that Reese might think he and his men were a bunch of cowboys who shot first and asked questions later.

"Be careful out there," Reese commented as he stepped back. "And take good care of our boys."

"Always."

Within ten minutes, all teams except Zebra9 had set up on the Cadillac. 3Adam58 redeployed three blocks south of the Cadillacs position at Brighton and Budlong.

Sabatello drove slowly up Budlong in order to conduct a quick drive-by.

"You see it?" he asked.

"Yeah. It's the fourth car on the left," McLean answered.

Sabatello slipped a bag of sunflower seeds from his coat pocket and slid his pack of Kool cigarettes above the visor.

Sabatello, like McLean had an abundance of nervous energy. When they worked together in patrol, Sabatello was never without a cigarette. He said it calmed his nerves.

But now that they had been assigned as partners on the Special Operations Squad and were required to sit for hours on a stakeout, Sabatello substituted sunflower seeds for cigarettes so as not to jeopardize the surveillance because of a glowing ember.

While this worked well, it infuriated the detectives who had to clean out the floorboard of the rear seat where a pyramid of saliva saturated disposed of shells would lie cluttered after every operation.

"3Zebra20, to all University Zebra units, everyone in position?" Bock asked as he spoke softly into the cream-colored mike.

After an acknowledgement by all the teams, McLean cut in.

"3Zebra9, we're approaching the Cadillac," McLean said as he watched his partner split open a sunflower seed between his teeth, remove the nut and spit the empty shell backwards onto the rear floorboard.

"You know that you're the dick's favorite person," McLean said without taking his eyes off the Cadillac.

"Who gives a shit," Sabatello answered as he split open another shell and immediately spit it into the rear seat adding to the growing pile of debris.

"This car belongs to the City, not to the dicks. And the last time I looked, their badge was the same as mine."

McLean shook his head and grinned.

"3Zebra11, we're ready, and we sent 3Adam58 to their new location," Eddie Brown said in a quiet voice.

"3Zebra12, count us in," Inglis said as he slouched low in the front seat, put both feet on the blue ripped plastic dash and sipped on his cooling cup of coffee.

"3Zebra14, we're sitting down the street at the corner," Froggy LeFrois said as he stared into the darkness in hopes of being the first to see movement around the old Caddy.

It now became a waiting game.

THIRTY-FOUR

Washington stood next to the old sofa that was pushed against the front window. The tomb like silence of the night was suddenly broken as a car idled slowly up the street.

Curious, he parted the black sheet that served as a curtain. On the street below, he watched as a dark green Plymouth rolled by without lights.

"Ta-Ta, wake up, it's the po-lice," Washington whispered as he snapped the curtains closed and reached under a sofa cushion for his Colt. Lastice, curled up and asleep on the other end of the couch, didn't move.

"Get up, nigga!" Washington growled as he cupped his hand under Lastice's legs and threw them to the floor, sending the shotgun bandit sprawling.

"Say, Bubba, what'd ya do that for?" Lastice meekly asked as he rolled over and took a seated position on the cold, hardwood floor.

"We got the po-lice outside," Washington said.

Lastice slipped onto the couch and parted a small section of the black sheet. As both men watched, the green Plymouth stopped next to the Cadillac, hesitated, and then moved slowly up the street.

"We been made," Washington said, "Let's go."

"Maybe it's not the pigs," Lastice whispered, hoping that some phantom green car was not going to send him on the run into the cold winter night.

"It do be the pigs, my man, and we is outta here."

In one sweeping motion, Washington snatched up his leather jacket, his silk dew-rag and shoved the Colt into his waistband.

"Get your gun, we is leaving through the floor," Washington whispered.

Just beyond 38th street, Sabatello pulled into a driveway, turned the car around and parked at the curb with the Plymouth facing south. With the front windows rolled down, the wait began. Slowly, two heads slipped lower in their seats until only their eyes peered over the dash.

Sabatello pushed the package of sunflower seeds between his legs and threw a handful into his mouth.

"I could use a smoke," he said wistfully.

"That shit'll kill you."

"So can working with you."

"Working with me is far more exciting," McLean responded as his eyes continued to watch the Caddy.

"But you don't calm my nerves."

"Touché."

"When are you going to get married, Sabatello?"

"You want to start keeping my social calendar?"

"Maybe I should. You know you're not getting any younger."

"That's what my mom keeps telling me."

"You should listen."

"Haven't found the right one."

"You aren't looking."

"You happy?"

"With you?"

"No. At home."

"Yeah. I wasn't for the first couple of years. Even thought about leaving."

"What kept you?"

"Two little girls."

"Things better now?"

"Much," McLean answered softly.

❧

Washington stood next to the window and slipped on his black leather jacket.

"I want one more look."

As he parted the curtains, Lastice threw back the frayed throw rug that covered the trap door that led to an unoccupied downstairs apartment.

Looking into the darkness, Washington watched as a dark figure slipped out from between the apartment building just north of the Cadillac.

"3Zebra9, to all University Zebra units," McLean whispered into the mike as he stared over the dash. "We have a suspect on the sidewalk walking slowly towards the Caddy."

"3Zebra20, roger," Bock responded. "Everyone get that transmission?"

All of the Zebra units acknowledged in the affirmative.

"That dude's head is on a swivel," McLean said.

"Is it Washington?" Sabatello asked.

"Too small."

"Might be Lastice. He's the same size and the clothing fits," McLean added.

"If it is, he's mine," McLean said as he unlocked the shotgun.

The night returned to it's solitary silence. All that was now heard were the metallic clangs of the car's engine as it began to cool, a muted cough coming from one of the upper apartments and an occasional dog bark in the distance. McLean sat perfectly still, focused on the lone figure with his eyes as cold as steel marbles.

All eyes were still focused on the lone figure who was walking up to the Cadillac's passenger door, his head swinging from side-to-side as he looked up and down the street.

Thirty seconds passed.

"I need a cigarette," Sabatello said. "These damn sun flower seeds are beginning to taste like wet cardboard."

"And I could use a shot of Tequila," McLean said. "But until we're finished, we're both going to have to forego life's little pleasures."

Sabatello glanced at McLean and knew he was right.

"Ta-Ta," Washington said. "We got someone walking up to the Caddy, and it don't look like no po-lice."

"Is the suspect still in view?" Brooks whispered into the mike, anxious to get into some action. Sitting quietly was not Brooks' strong suit. He liked jumping right into the middle of things, while Inglis, a hunter and fisherman, was far more patient.

"Do we still have the suspect in sight?" Bock asked.

"He just disappeared," McLean answered, his eyes narrowing as he squinted and searched the darkness.

"Okay," Stemples cut in. "Who the hell was watching the store?"

"He's back," McLean said as the suspect walked around to the driver's door.

"Some nigga is gonna steal our ride," Washington grunted.

"Come on, Bubba," Lastice pleaded as he grabbed the giant's arm and tried to pull him away from the window.

Washington hesitated for only a moment before he turned and stepped to the dark hole in the floor.

"Do we have a description?" Bock asked.

"A partial," McLean answered. "He's male Negro, medium height, black stingy brim and it looks like he's wearing a black three-quarter length jacket. Might be Lastice, might not."

Suddenly a car turned the corner and started toward the Cadillac.

"All units, we have a vehicle coming northbound on Budlong from Leighton," McLean broadcast.

"Didn't anyone see them before they turned?" Bock asked, frustration in his voice.

The air was silent.

"It would have been Hutton and Hestily," Johnson said as he watched the car pass.

"Okay, where the hell is 3Adam58," Bock asked, gruffly.

"We relieved them," Inglis said. "Sent them to Budlong and Leighton."

"Did anyone advise them to switch over to Tactical Frequency two?" LeFrois asked.

The radio was quiet.

"My fault," Bock muttered, not liking to be wrong, but never hesitating to admit it when he was. "I'll take care of it now."

"The car just passed us," McLean said. "They're still northbound."

Lastice lifted the trapdoor, lit a long wooden match and threw it onto the floor below. It jumped and the flame danced, then a small area of the apartment floor lit up as the flame flickered brightly.

"I'll jump down and get you the ladder," Lastice said.

Carefully, Lastice lowered himself through the hole and jumped to the floor. Finding the ladder hidden behind a door on the back porch, he slid it directly under the opening.

Washington slowly lowered his massive frame down until his foot struck a rung. Guardedly, he stepped down each rung until he was able to safely find the floor. As he jumped from the last step to the floor, the breeze caused by his massive body extinguished the flame.

"I want one more look," Washington said as he walked to the right side of the front window, inched back a tattered drape and peered out.

The suspect was just opening the car door.

"3Zebra9, he's got the door open and he's inside," McLean said.

"Let's take him," Bock roared into the mike.

"3Zebra9, we've got another suspect opening the passenger door. We've got two inside, repeat, we have two suspects in the Cadillac," McLean anxiously broadcast.

Behind them, McLean and Sabatello heard the roar of a truck. Spinning in their seats, they watched as a huge white city trash truck barreled past and pulled up behind the Cadillac blocking their view.

"We've got a trash truck blocking our view," McLean shouted into the mike, his pasty gray complexion erupting into a fiery red.

"Everyone hold tight," Bock ordered. "Let's wait and see what happens."

"Okay, the truck is moving, but the Caddy's gone," McLean broadcast, desperation in his voice.

"We've got it," shouted LeFrois as the Cadillac moved slowly past his location. "They're headed south on Budlong."

"I see it," Bock said. "He's approaching Leighton. 3Adam58, he's coming up on you, do you see him?"

"We've got him," Hestily said excitedly.

"3Zebra20, should we take the lead?" Hestily asked.

"That's a roger, 3Adam58. Take the lead and we'll follow. Make the stop before he..."

"3Adam58 to 3Zebra20, he's turning right on Exposition."

"Stop him, guys, and don't let him get onto Exposition," Bock said as he struggled with one hand to untangle the radio cord and the other to control the steering wheel.

"I think they're spooked," Hestily yelled, his voice erupting in a wave of static over the air. With eyes pinned on the Cadillac, Hutton and Hestily watched as two heads spun and looked in their direction.

"They've made us," Hutton bellowed.

"They're going to rabbit," Hestily shouted back.

Reaching down to the radio, Hestily snapped the switch over to the primary frequency.

"3Adam58, we're in pursuit."

"All units, all frequencies stand by, 3Adam58 is in pursuit," the Hotshot Operator broadcast.

"3Adam58, your location?"

Hutton shot a look down at the speedometer. . Sixty-five, seventy, seventy-five, eighty.

"3Adam58, we're westbound on Exposition approaching Normandie," Hestily screamed into the open mike as Hutton kept the accelerator on the Plymouth floored.

"We've got a red, Bobby," Hestily yelled.

"So do they," Hutton screamed as he floored the Plymouth and flew through the intersection.

"3Zebra20 to Control, advise all responding units that there are five unmarked police vehicles in the pursuit."

"3Adam58, what is the vehicle wanted for?"

"3Adam58..."

"3Zebra20 the vehicle is wanted for 187, murder of police officer. Advise all units that the suspects are armed and dangerous."

"Clear right," Hestily screamed as Hutton tapped the brakes and then slammed the accelerator back to the floorboard. Pulling closer to the Cadillac, he swerved radically to miss a bread truck that entered the intersection from northbound Normandie.

"What the hell is that thumping," Hutton screamed, trying to be heard above the wail of the siren.

Shooting a look at his partner, he had his answer.

"It's your leg, Tommy," Hutton exclaimed as he quickly glanced over at Hestily and watched his right leg pound rapidly against the door.

"You've got a new name, Tommy...it's Thumper," Hutton screamed as he began to laugh. "Tommy 'The Thumper' Hestily!"

"This ain't funny, Hutton," Hestily shouted as the Cadillac slid around the corner onto Vernon Avenue and fishtailed west bound, narrowly missing a parked bus.

"It isn't, but you are," screamed Hutton.

Two car lengths back, Bock made the same turn onto Vernon and struggled to control the wildly lurching Plymouth. As he straightened out, he glanced in the rearview mirror and saw four unmarked police cars in his rearview mirror, trailed by a long line of black and whites.

Suddenly, the rear taillights of the Cadillac blasted bright red. Hutton locked the brakes and the car shuddered. As Hutton slid closer to the Caddy, its rear window exploded as a bullet broke above the sound of the siren and slammed through the radiator of the black and white.

Hutton pulled off the accelerator as Hestily screamed into the mike, "3Adam58, shots fired we've been hit!"

"All units all frequencies, 3Adam58 is under fire. 3Adam58, is anyone hurt?"

"Not yet!" Hestily screamed into the mike.

Leaning out the passenger window, Hestily extended his .38 and cranked off six rapid rounds. Three slammed into the trunk of the Caddy, one flew through the missing back window and shattered the windshield, and two flew wide left and disappeared into the night.

"Use the shotgun, Tommy!" Hutton shrieked as he slammed both feet on the brake pedal.

"Kill the sons-a-bitches, Tommy," he bellowed, his oval face contorted in anger while his right hand groped in the darkness for his holstered revolver.

Suddenly, the oil pressure in the black and white dropped to zero.

As Bock locked the brakes in an effort to avoid hitting the slowing 3Adam58, McLean and Sabatello blew past both units and approached the driver's side of the smoking Cadillac.

"Oh shit!" Bock exclaimed.

"They're ours," McLean screamed out the window as they pulled up parallel to the driver's side of the slowing Cadillac.

A distorted look of hatred shot from the fiery blue eyes of the light-complexioned Scotsman while his thick brown hair danced on the top of his head. Death was now center stage.

As Sabatello paralleled the Cadillac, McLean shoved the Ithaca out the window and screamed at the driver who had his window down and was brandishing a gun in his right hand.

As the driver turned and pointed his weapon at McLean, a fan of brilliant colored flame belched from the Ithaca. Instantly the left front side of the driver's head disappeared, sending the Cadillac into an uncontrollable slide. As the car slid, the passenger spun in his seat and fired three rounds at 3Adam9 striking the window jam next to McLean's head.

Infuriated, Sabatello popped the brakes. The rear tires slid sideways, sending smoke billowing skyward as rubber burned on the black asphalt. McLean, still leaning out the window to his waist, chambered another round.

McLean pointed the Ithaca at the interior of the Cadillac and squeezed the trigger. As the barrel jumped, nine pellets smashed into the car's interior and struck the passenger in the head and torso as he tried to scramble into the back seat.

The Cadillac careened to its right, struck the curb, and blew both tires on the passenger side that sent two chrome hubcaps spinning across a front lawn. Then the Caddy flipped wildly into the air, twirled and ejected the faceless driver onto the asphalt.

Spinning through the air, the whirling car landed top first on the sidewalk where it skidded across the front lawn of an old house and came to rest just short of the front porch.

Bock locked his brakes, slammed the selector into Park and watched as the Caddy's white headlights shot aimlessly into the night while the tires spun wildly. Black smoked billowed from the engine compartment and steam whistled from the cracked radiator.

Bolting from his car, he was followed by his three remaining teams.

He looked over the wreckage and glanced at the faceless body sprawled in the street. Then he remembered his indignant feeling when he felt that Reese thought his group of handpicked men were a bunch of cowboys.

"It appears Reese was right. We are a bunch of cowboys," Bock muttered under his breath as he walked to the far side of the wrecked Caddy.

As the wail of high-pitched sirens wound down and the ear piercing howling of the neighborhood dogs decreased, McLean stepped around the trunk of the car and peered into the interior where he saw the male passenger pinned between the top of the bloody front seat and the crushed headliner.

Blood flowed freely from dime sized holes in the center of his chest, from his mouth and from under his head. McLean stood emotionless and stared deep into a pair of dark brown eyes that stared blankly straight ahead. He'd seen the look many times before and knew that the owner of the distant eyes would no longer pose a threat to anyone, especially the police.

"It's not Lastice," McLean casually remarked to Bock.

"Neither is the dude in the street," Hutton added, wearing a wide grin. "But one thing is for sure …they won't be shooting at 3Adam58 again."

Bock stepped away from the Cadillac and marveled at how fast the neighbors flooded the scene.

It's just like they were attending an old-time revival meeting, he thought.

THIRTY-FIVE

Rosie bent far into the car and let her long, black wig fall gently onto the shoulder of the baby-faced white man. Her cheap perfume whiffed slowly through the window and filled the car's interior. Rosie, the street whore, was permanently back on the street.

"Say, good lookin', you lookin' for a date?"

University Division Vice cop Richard Dixon hesitated, and then pushed his badge deeper under his left thigh and felt for the small Chief's Special that was snugly attached to his leg in an ankle holster.

Rosie shook her head, fluffed her black wig and hiked her mini skirt up.

"Say, cutie," she said as she softly serpentined her right index finger down Dixon's cheek and around his mouth.

"You ain't the po-lice is you," she whispered into Dixon's ear.

"Now do I look like a cop?"

"No, but I need to be careful. Let me see your wallet."

Dixon reached into his rear trouser pocket and pulled out his dummy wallet. Opening it, he began to slip out his driver's license.

"Why don't you let me look inside," said Rosie, her narrow fingers already reaching for the wallet.

"Sure."

Rosie took the wallet in her right hand and then leaned further into the car. Quickly, her left hand shot between Dixon's legs while her long fingers inched themselves under each thigh.

"What the hell do you think you're doing," he yelled, as his left hand grabbed Rosie's wrist and his butt slammed itself deeper into the seat.

"Just makin' sure you is who you says you is," Rosie answered as she pulled her hand away.

"And?"

"I guess you is all right."

"So what do I get?" Dixon asked softly.

"Half-and-half," she said, a smile on her face. "And it'll only cost you fifty dollars."

"That's too much," Dixon said as he cocked his head and licked Rosie's finger with his tongue.

"Okay, twenty-five," Rosie purred.

"That's all I need beautiful," Dixon said softly as he stepped from the car and flashed his badge.

"University Vice, sweetheart. You're under arrest for prostitution."

"Oh, lordy, no!" Rosie exclaimed.

"Oh, lordy yes," Dixon mimicked.

"Oh, please ossifer, please, I can't do no jail," Rosie pled.

"No one can, my dear," Dixon said while slipping his handcuffs from a rear pocket.

"What's your name?" he asked as he double locked the cuffs on Rosie's frail wrists.

"Rosie and I got some real important information for you."

"Does it concern the vice squad?" Dixon asked.

"No, sir, but..."

"Then, I'm not interested," Dixon said as he slipped the frail whore into the back of a black and white he had called for transportation.

Rosie sat handcuffed in the back of the black and white and sobbed.

"Please ossifer Dixon. I is just trying to make a livin'. Please don't put me in jail," she pleaded. "Please."

"Relax Rosie, if that's your real name."

"It is, I swear it is," Rosie said as tears ran down her chocolate brown cheeks.

"Rosie's my real name. Rosie ...Rosie Washington."

"Just be cool, Rosie Washington, and after we get you booked at Sybil Brand you can make bail and you'll be back out on the street in no time."

Rosie leaned forward and stuck her head out the open window while her eyes pleaded to be heard.

"Is you sure you ain't interested in the information I has?"

"Like I told you before. If it doesn't involve vice, I'm not interested."

"But ..."

"Sit back and shut up, Rosie," Dixon barked.

After a short drive, the transporting black and white pulled into the station parking lot. After sliding Rosie out of the car, Dixon walked her into the station and sat her on the wooden bench in the small glass faced holding tank.

"Sit down and relax," he said as he clicked one cuff to the metal ring attached to the bench.

"Please, won't you listen? I know where someone is the police want," Rosie said as she sobbed and her frail body shook from the cold and the beginning stages of heroin withdrawals.

"Like I told you, I'm not interested. Now sit back and relax."

"But I..." Her words were lost in the slamming of the heavy metal door and the clicking of a cylindrical lock.

❧

Not finding either Washington or Lastice in the wrecked Caddy, an irritated Bock pulled into the station parking lot, followed by Brooks and Inglis.

"Well, that turned out to be a crock of shit," Brooks commented to his partner as they walked through the rear station doors.

"Yeah, but you must admit that McLean did one hell-of-a-job eliminating those two assholes in the Caddy," Inglis responded grinning.

"McLean better be careful."

"Why?" Inglis asked.

"Because others don't think like we do, especially those working downtown on the sixth floor of Parker Center."

"You're right," Inglis said as he thrust his beefy hands into his Levis pockets and continued to walk down the long corridor toward the coffee room. "Okay, so we're back to step one. So where do you want to start?"

"With a strong cup of coffee," Brooks answered.

Sitting handcuffed to the bench, Rosie sobbed deep guttural sobs, as hoarse as a dying cow's bellows.

"*I got information that I know somebody wants!*" she screamed amid sobs.

"*Please, don't no one want to know about Bubba Washington?*"

The name stopped Brooks and Inglis in their tracks.

"Did you hear that?" Inglis asked his partner as they stood frozen in the corridor in front of the holding tank.

"Yeah."

Brooks opened the door to the Watch Commander's office and stuck in his head to where Evans was sitting reading the newspaper.

"Hey, Sarge, who brought in the wailing female?"

"Dixon up in vice," Evans answered not looking up.

"Why?"

"Just curious."

As Brooks and Inglis stepped up to the holding tank door, they saw Dixon approach from the coffee room.

"Is this female yours?" Inglis asked as Dixon approached with his trademark smile.

"Yeah."

"What's she in for?"

"Solicitation," Dixon said as he opened the door and stepped toward the distraught prostitute.

"What name did she give when you popped her?"

"Rosie, Rosie Washington. Why?"

Brooks stepped forward smiling.

"We need a favor, partner," he said as Dixon pulled out his handcuff key and began to unlock the cuff.

"Whaddya need?"

"We'd like to talk to the young lady before you book her."

"Why?" Dixon asked, a puzzled look crossing his face.

Brooks pulled Dixon toward the open door and away from Rosie.

"Because she might have some information about the suspects who killed Congressman Andrews' daughter and also Patterson."

"You're kidding?" Dixon said. "This raggedy-ass street whore?"

"Yep," Brooks answered smiling. "That raggedy-ass street whore."

"It's fine with me," Dixon said as he stepped forward and removed the handcuff from Rosie's right wrist and pushed her in the direction of the two plainclothes cops, who now stood just outside the door.

"Let me know when you're done. I'll be upstairs."

Brooks stepped in front of Rosie, smiled and in a soft friendly voice, spoke.

"Rosie, I'm Officer Brooks and this is my partner, Officer Inglis. We'd like to talk to you if that's okay?"

"Please, Mr. Brooks, I has information the po-lice wants and I don't wanna go back to jail."

As the two seasoned street cops looked into Rosie's sad brown eyes, they realized that her look was a prayer.

Leaving her unhandcuffed, Brooks gently walked her into the Detective bureau where he found an empty interrogation room. As Rosie stepped forward, Inglis stepped in and slid a hot cup of coffee onto the small square table.

"Miss Washington, please have a seat," Brooks said as he pulled out an aluminum chair for the woman he hoped would have information on where to find their killer.

"You can call me, Rosie," she said as she adjusted the nylon wig and pushed the long black hair from her face and wrapped her skinny hands around the warm cup.

Both veteran cops knew that Rosie was scared. Nothing was easier to detect in a person than fear. It showed in the way the eyes darted back and forth and jumped at each curious sound, and it showed even in the way she fumbled with her cup while sipping the scalding black coffee. But it was normal that she would be afraid. She was a street whore, alone, under arrest and sitting in a police station.

On one hand, she still feared Bubba. But on the other hand, she now feared what the police might do to her. She had heard stories about cops driving uncooperative prostitutes deep into the Mojave Desert and then dumping them in the middle of nowhere. An act that not only ruined a night's work, but also required that they make their own way back. Some made it, while others were never seen again-and this was not a fate she wanted to suffer.

"We understand that you have information about a man named Benjamin 'Bubba' Washington?" Brooks asked softly.

"Yeah, but if I talk to you two ossifers, I need you to promise me that you'll ask Mr. Dixon not to take me to Sybil Brand," Rosie whimpered.

"If you have information that is helpful to our investigation, we'll do all we can to help," Inglis said, empathy showing in his voice.

"Do you know a Bubba Washington?" Brooks asked.

"Yeah, I know him. He's my old man, or he was."

Brooks looked down at her inner arms. Her last needle marks had started to scab.

Rosie wiped the snot from her nose with the back of her open hand. "And he has hisself a partner."

"What's his name?" Inglis asked patiently as he pushed a Kleenex box across the table to the sniffling whore whose snot was dripping onto the table.

"Ta-Ta. Ta-Ta Lastice."

"Do you know where they're at?"

"No. But we all was living at an apartment on South Budlong," Rosie said as she began to tremble.

"Do you remember the address?" Brooks asked.

"No, I never knowed it. I just knowed how to get there. It's near Explosion Boulevard."

"Do you mean Exposition Boulevard?" Brooks asked quizzically.

"Yeah, that's what I mean. Explosion Boulevard."

Brooks shot Inglis a look. Inglis was leaning back in his chair, a large grin across his face.

Brooks leaned forward.

"We need you to point out the apartment. Will you do that?"

"Yeah."

"What kind of a car do they use?" Inglis asked.

"An old, red, Cadillac."

"Did Bubba or Ta-Ta talk about when they were going to go robbin' again?" asked Inglis.

"Well," Rosie said as she scratched the scabs on her inner left arm causing them to bleed. "Before Bubba throwed me outta the apartment, he talked about robbin' another liquor store over on Crenshaw."

"Another?"

"Yeah. They like robbin' liquor stores on Crenshaw."

"Do you know when this robbery is going to happen?" Inglis asked.

"They'd been watchin' some store and said something about robbin' it this Sunday night so as to get the money from the week-end."

Inglis shot Brooks a hard look.

"That gives us a little over twenty-four hours," he said.

"Did you know Eddie Woods and Tyrone Potts?" Inglis asked.

"Yeah. They was partners of Bubba."

"Did Bubba say anything about a shooting at Adams and Hoover where they were killed?" Brooks asked.

"Yeah. He said that they didn't off some pig and would get him later."

"Did they mention why they wanted to kill the officer?" Inglis asked.

"Bubba done said that it was because the pig, I mean ossifer, offed his main man, Willie."

Rosie stopped to blow her nose, wipe her eyes and try to wipe up some of the snot that had collected on the table top.

"Did Bubba ever say anything about having a snitch inside the police department?" Inglis asked.

"Yeah. I heard him tell Ta-Ta that she was an old school friend."

"Do you have a name?" Brooks asked.

Rosie reached over to the Kleenex box and snatched a handful of tissues. After blowing her nose and wiping the snot from the bottom of her chin, she blotted the blood on her arm. Then she continued.

"No, but Bubba told Ta-Ta that she worked at this here police station in records."

Inglis and Brooks shot a concerned look at each other.

As the conversation moved on, Rosie began to lose her ability to concentrate and both cops noticed that her arms were covered with goose bumps.

"When did you shoot-up last?" Inglis asked.

"Two nights ago. At least I think it was two nights ago. I can't really remember. That's why I was out on the street a workin' 'cause I needed money to by some her-on."

Suddenly, Rosie placed her hands on the table top and dropped her head onto her palms.

"I don't feel good, Mr. Brooks and I need some of my medicine. Please, let me go," she pleaded. "I told you alls I know."

Brooks stood up and pulled out Rosie's chair.

"We're going to find Officer Dixon and ask him if he'll cut you loose after we have you point out the apartment on Budlong. But you need to be patient," Brooks said as he gently lifted the slender black woman from her chair.

"Thank you, Mr. Brooks," Rosie said as she dropped her head, "and you too, ossifer Inglis."

Walking from the room and down the long corridor, her footsteps were unsteady as she shuffled between the two plainclothes cops.

"You're welcome, Rosie. And ...thank you," Brooks said as he opened the rear station door and walked the trembling whore to an unmarked police car. Within fifteen minutes, they had the Budlong address.

Before sunrise, a shivering Rosie stepped from University station as a free woman and walked down Santa Barbara Avenue towards Normandie. After her interview with Brooks and Inglis, she spent a short time with the narcotics cops and when she left, she had in her possession a small red balloon.

THIRTY-SIX

Bock sat in the squad room and stared at the photographs of the players in the Adams and Hoover shooting. He was exhausted, as were his men. It had been some long days and longer nights.

Brooks and Inglis sat across the table, heads back, eyes closed with their heads reclining on the rear of the old sofa. Two other teams sat straddling their chairs with arms crossed and heavy heads resting on the top. McLean and Sabatello sat in Reese's office with him and Sergeant Delbert Del Rio.

Bock stared at the faces of Potts and Woods who adorned the board and had the words, "DECEASED" printed across their black and white mug shots. To their left was the photograph of Ta-Ta Lastice and in the space reserved for Kong was placed the photograph of Benjamin "Bubba" Washington. Written below each picture where printed the words: **COP KILLER**.

"What's going to happen to McLean?" Brown asked, concern in his voice.

"Don't know," answered Bock. "Normally he'd be on the front desk until the shooting board meets. But considering the gravity of the Andrews case and its political implications, the Captain just might be able to sway the powers to be, and he'll be allowed to get back to work."

"The Captain have that much pull?" LeFrois asked.

"That and more."

"Do you think that it was a good shooting?" Stemples asked Bock.

"Yes."

Bock pulled his comb from a front shirt pocket and drew it through his hair.

"Didn't you have a shot?" Brooks asked, not opening his eyes.

"No."

As Bock stared at the whiteboard, a knock at the door interrupted his concentration.

"Come in."

"Got a minute?" Steele asked grinning.

"Have a seat," Bock said as he waved Steele and Van Drew to come in.

"You're just in time" Bock said. "We were just getting ready to hit..." Steele cut him off mid sentence.

"Sorry to interrupt, Rod, but before you mobilize the troops, we have some information that might prove helpful."

Bock slid an aluminum chair over to Steele and then seated himself on the corner of the desk. Van Drew sat on the other end.

"We've an address for Washington and it's been verified."

"Great minds think in the same circles," Stemples called out.

"Meaning?" Steele asked.

Bock broke into a large smile.

"I hate to steal your thunder, guys, but Brooks and Inglis interviewed Washington's common-law an hour ago. She's a street prostitute named Rosie Washington. They also got the address on South Budlong."

"You're kidding me," Steele said, somewhat chagrined but very impressed.

"Not at all. Vice arrested her for prostitution and she wanted to talk."

Bock continued.

"So after an interview she went with the guys and pointed out the apartment."

"No shit!" Van Drew exclaimed.

"Only problem is that it was right across the street from where the red Cadillac was parked and stolen from while we were staked on it."

"Do you think they made you during the stake-out?" Steele asked.

"Odds are that both suspects were across the street watching us all the time."

"But you're not sure," Steele said.

"Correct."

Suddenly the door opened and in walked McLean and Sabatello. Both looked haggard, appearing to have just finished a marathon.

"No front desk?" Bock asked.

"No front desk," McLean answered. "The Captain made a call and was told to send us back to work pending the shooting board."

"Good, we've got work to do."

Bock turned to the detectives. "Brooks and Inglis picked up one other tidbit of information."

"And?"

"They're planning to rob another liquor store tomorrow night."

"Where?"

"South Crenshaw."

"Which one?" Van Drew asked.

"The snitch didn't know," Brooks interjected.

"So if we don't find Washington and Lastice in the apartment," Bock added, "we're going to set up tomorrow night on five liquor stores beginning at Adams and ending at Slauson."

"You're in for one long day," Steele said as he turned and walked to the door.

As Steele opened the door, he was met by McGrath and Stallcup who were holding coffee cups.

"You're just in time," Bock said to the two latecomers. "We were just on our way out."

☙

Morning dawned, gray as slate. With tactical precision, the teams pulled into position. Unit 3Zebra11, Eddie Brown and Bobby Stemples parked on South Walton one block east of the location. Bock and units 3Zebra9, McLean and Sabatello, 3Zebra14, Frogy LeFrois and Jack Johnson, 3Zebra12, Brooks and Inglis, and 3Zebra15, McGrath and Stallcup, all parked on the east side of Budlong south of the apartment building.

Bock knew that daylight wasn't the ideal time to conduct a raid, but he had no choice. Cops couldn't always wait for the ideal time.

"Listen up," he said as he and his ten men hid wedged between two apartment buildings south of Washington's address. "LeFrois and Johnson, you take the rear. McGrath and Stallcup, you take the south side between the apartments. Watch the windows, they're crazy enough to try and jump from the second floor. Brown and Stemples, I want you to secure the north side."

Bock eased himself to the building edge and peered out.

"I want Brooks and Inglis to hit the door with McLean and Sabatello right behind. As far as I'm concerned, this also qualifies for exigent circumstances. So, Jerry, just kick the damn door, then worrying about the introductions."

"Got it, boss," Brooks said, his round face beaming.

Bock stepped out from between the apartments and was followed by ten men. Silently they ran across two brown front lawns to the first floor stoop of Washington's building. Stopping briefly, they listened. All was quiet.

"Go," Bock ordered his three ground floor deployment teams.

In seconds, six men were deployed around the apartment building.

With Brooks and Inglis in the lead, five men noiselessly bounded up the concrete stairs and deployed on each side of the door to apartment Four.

Brooks turned to Bock.

"Exigent circumstances, boss?" he mouthed.

"Exigent circumstances, Jerry," Bock whispered.

Without another word, Brooks stepped in front of the door, leaned back and gave the door a powerful kick just to the left of the doorknob. Splinters exploded inward as the door ripped from its hinges, broke free of the locks and skidded across the living room floor. Weapons in hand, four plainclothes cops followed by Bock rushed the apartment, each scurrying into a different area as Brooks cried out, *"PO-LICE!"*

"The kitchen is clear," Inglis yelled.

"Clear in the right rear bedroom," McLean yelled.

"Left rear bedroom is clear," Brooks added.

"Bathroom is clear," Sabatello coughed as he exited holding his nose. "Shit, this place stinks," he exclaimed.

"There's crap and old dirty diapers all over the bathroom floor."

"That's why I didn't volunteer to search the head," McLean said laughing.

"All right, what did we find?" Bock asked as the teams formed a tight circle around him.

"Not much," Brooks answered.

"Why doesn't that surprise me," Bock commented, a tinge of frustration edging his words.

Bock stopped and looked back into the apartment. His gaze fell on the shattered door and the dangling dead-bolts.

"Sabatello, get Property Division to replace this door."

As Bock stepped onto the front stoop, Brooks stopped Sabatello. "Here, just slip this between the hinges."

Brooks handed Sabatello a business card that read:
Los Angeles County Sheriffs Department
Detective Ryan Whitcomb
Homicide
(213) 458-6066
On the back was scratched:
Sorry we missed you.

With Brooks watching, Sabatello, wearing a gleeful look, slid the card between the top hinge and the doorjamb.

Then, both men bounded down the stairs laughing.

THIRTY-SEVEN

A few minutes after two in the afternoon, Mayor Sam Gibson walked into the office of Thomas White and sat down in a comfortable overstuffed leather chair. His dark blue suit was custom fitted to his lean body and his eyes flickered with warmth at seeing his old friend.

"What in the hell are you doing here on a Sunday?" White asked.

"Same as you. I'm trying to stay ahead of the wolves nipping at my heels and keep the Feds from entering the mix and really screwing things up."

"I've been thinking about that," White said philosophically, "and I've come to a conclusion."

"And what would that be?"

"Dogs bark, but the caravan moves on."

Gibson erupted into laughter.

"Seriously," Gibson said as he settled into the chair.

"Anything new on the Andrews case?"

"Plenty," White said as he stepped around the polished desk and took a seat in one of the comfortable office chairs directly across from Gibson.

After a ten minute recap, Gibson stood, stretched, and walked to the picture window.

As each stared out the window, they were momentarily lost in their own thoughts. Suddenly, a woman's shrill screams on the street below brought them back to the present.

"What do we do about Morton Andrews?" Gibson asked as he walked back to the leather chair and sat down.

"He calls my office daily wanting an update, and he isn't happy about the press conference Cleary held. But neither was I. He thinks Cleary is an incompetent buffoon and he wants your head, Reese's, the detectives', and as of yesterday, mine."

"I think I can ease some of the pressure," White said.

"How's that?"

"I plan on scheduling a press conference to update everyone."

"Who will conduct it?"

"I will."

"Excellent."

Later that afternoon, following an ad hoc press conference at Parker Center, Chief of Police Thomas White received a telephone call from Don Marshall, Chief of Staff for Congressman Andrews. Marshall announced, to the surprise of White, that the Congressman and his wife had concluded that their daughter's death had not been caused by a police bullet.

When White asked if he could speak to the Congressman, he was told that Congressman Andrews had taken his wife on an extended vacation to an undisclosed location and would be gone for six weeks.

THIRTY-EIGHT

McLean sat on the hard round stool in the rear of O'Jay's Liquor and stared out the two-way mirror into the storefront. He sat in the darkness, alone with himself. To his left was the sales counter, cash register and sufficient room for a single employee.

Looking through the mirror, he had a clear view of the store, all except the floor area to the far left, directly behind the counter. Resting comfortably across his lap was an Ithaca and on the floor was a small, hand-held walkie-talkie.

The closet was cramped and hot, sticking his shirt to his flesh. Methodically he inhaled, and then slowly exhaled the stale air. Staring into the brightly lit store, his eyes began to tire, while small beads of perspiration erupted on his forehead and covered the palms of each hand.

Across the street and hidden in the darkness of a long driveway, Sabatello sat in the passenger seat of their car. At his side was also a small hand-held walkie-talkie.

As McLean sat in the closet and stared into the storefront, his mind raced down the corridors of time. Suddenly, the glimpses of the Adams and Hoover stepped from a darkened room and stood center stage. Then another door opened and he slipped into a memory of rolling on his first call where a cop had been shot.

❧

Wilshire Division, sixteen months earlier. The Morning Watch cops were walking into the parking lot to start their watch when the help call hit the air.

"That's only five-blocks away," screamed Sergeant Dick Sterling.

"Let's go!" he had hollered as he snatched a set of car keys from a stunned Night Watch cop. In seconds, Sterling was behind the wheel of a black and white with McLean in the passenger seat and two uniformed cops in the back.

Sterling flipped on the red's, punched the siren button and slammed the accelerator down sending the wildly careening black and white traveling erratically out of the station parking lot.

Once beyond the large brick arch, he snapped the steering wheel to the left, dodged some frightened pedestrians and fishtailed down the sidewalk.

After traveling two blocks on the sidewalk, everyone saw a black and white parked behind a new Ford Thunderbird. Sterling raced up to the scene, locked the brakes and before the car slid to a stop, three young cops were rushing toward the T-bird.

McLean would never forget what he saw next.

Lying in the street about six feet to the rear of the Thunderbird's driver's door was a cop. A small stream of blood was running from the middle of his mouth and down his cheek. Also on the ground was the driver of the Thunderbird, a small chrome automatic just beyond his reach. The passenger officer stood on the sidewalk with his service revolver in hand as he commanded the gunman and his passenger to remain on the ground.

Running to the downed suspect, Sterling slid the automatic out of his reach and then rolled him over and cuffed him. As he finished, a city ambulance rolled up to the scene. The downed officer, who had been shot in the mouth, was immediately placed in ambulance unit G-7 and rushed from the scene. After it left, a second ambulance, G-6 arrived from Hollywood Station. The shooter was loaded into this ambulance.

"McLean, ride with the suspect!" Sterling yelled.

The muscles in McLean's body tensed and his heart beat quickened as more adrenaline surged through his system. Slowly, he walked over to the suspect's stretcher. The suspect's eyes were coal black, hard, cold, and filled with hatred.

After the two attendants slipped the primitive wood and canvas stretcher onto the ambulance floor, McLean climbed into the back of *the box-like shell and sat on the long wooden bench that was attached to the sidewall.*

As the passenger attendant entered, he closed both rear doors. McLean noticed that their fit wasn't tight and allowed a small sliver of night to seep through the crack.

The ambulance pulled off slowly and unlike unit G-7, G-6 drove from the scene without red lights and siren. McLean stared into the face of the suspect and he felt a deep hatred welling up inside, a hatred observed not only by the suspect, but also the attendant.

"We can get rid of that black son-of-a-bitch," the seasoned attendant said, sliding closer to McLean.

"How?" McLean asked, his interest peaked.

"The doors on these old meat wagons don't close snuggly," the man whispered, "and they've been known to fly open when the old bus is rolling along at a high rate of speed and hits a bump."

McLean leaned in closer. He was now very interested.

"So when we hit the Santa Monica Freeway and are doing about ninety, these damn rear doors could fly wide open and this rickety old stretcher might fly out the back, especially if my partner pops the brakes and punches the gas when the doors are flapping."

McLean smiled. He liked the idea and felt it had merit, but then he thought of his family and career.

"I like the idea, and…thanks for the offer," he said to the attendant, who was just waiting for the okay. "But I think that it's best if the asshole makes it to the hospital …alive."

"Well, it's your call, officer," the attendant said as he slid back to his seat at the head of the stretcher.

"But just remember, kid …I offered."

McLean shook his head at the memory that had etched itself indelibly into his mind much the same way that everyone talks about what they were doing when President Kennedy was shot, or when the Watts riots erupted.

Forcing his mind back onto the task at hand, he shook his head to clear his thoughts, and then forced himself to return to the stifling confines of the small, darkened storage closet.

Washington drove down Adams toward Crenshaw, watching for anything that might indicate that this wasn't the right night to rob a liquor store.

In the passenger seat, Lastice sat and nervously stroked the sawed-off shotgun. The streets were quiet.

After passing Crenshaw, Washington turned left on Victoria Avenue and doubled back on 28th Street. His eyes darted back and forth staring into the darkness for any sign of the police. He saw no one.

After re-crossing Crenshaw, he made a u-turn and parked in the darkness on 28th Street, just southeast of O'Jay's Liquors.

"I'll be waitin' here," he said to his diminutive companion. "You remember what to do?"

"Yeah."

Lastice pushed down on the door handle and slipped into the darkness. He was wearing his usual outfit: a black three-quarter length leather jacket, black pants, black shirt, and a black felt fedora that sat snuggly on his head and covered his small Afro.

He walked deliberately up 28th Street staying hidden in the shadows. At the corner of 28th and Crenshaw, he stepped deeper into the darkness and checked his shotgun. Quietly, he snapped the chamber open, twirled the magnum round, and then snapped the barrel shut. He took a long, deep breath and rounded the corner. O'Jay's Liquors was only fifty feet away.

As he walked briskly toward the brightly lit store, he glanced around nervously and was comforted when he saw that the street was still deserted.

❧

McLean wiggled his butt in an effort to get comfortable. He rubbed his jaw, rolled his neck until it cracked and continued to stare out the two-way mirror into the lighted store.

So what happens if Brook's snitch was wrong and the robbery wasn't going to go down tonight? Even worse, what would he do if it went down and he and Sabatello were set up at the wrong location? The theory that Washington and Lastice would hit in the north-end was just that, a theory, and a weak one at that since it was based on the information supplied by an untested, confidential informant.

Suddenly a new thought came to him. What if Rosie was a plant and her story fabricated to get the entire unit to deploy at the wrong locations? And why had Rosie been so eager to snitch-off her old man? Was it a woman scorned or something more sinister?

He shook his head. His eyes began to sting from the perspiration that was cascading down his forehead. Stroking the Ithaca, he blinked rapidly, wiped his eyes with the fingers of his outstretched hands and refocused on the front door.

Across Crenshaw, Sabatello had left the confines of the car and was now sitting quietly on an overturned fifty gallon barrel that was buried deep in the shadows. Between his legs was a large bag of sunflower seeds. On the ground, scattered, soggy shells.

"What I need," he muttered as he split open a seed with his teeth and spit the shell into the growing piles, "is a damn cigarette."

As he stared at the deserted street, he heard a rustling sound that came from his rear. His right hand deliberately moved to his holster and withdrew his revolver. Leaning deeper into the darkness, he turned his head and squinted into the blackness. He saw nothing, but the sound was moving closer.

"3ZebraBoy to 3ZebraAdam," Sabatello said as he held the walkie-talkie close to his lips. "You there, McLean?"

"Now where in the hell would I go, Sabatello," McLean said softly into the small communications unit.

"Nowhere, I guess, but..." There was a brief pause.

"Nick, I got something sneaking up behind me."

"You've got what?"

"Something sneaking up behind me."

"Well, what is it?"

"I don't know, I can't see it, but it's getting closer." Sabatello's breathing grew rapid.

"What do you think I should do?"

"Don't move, Tony. Just stay out of sight. And knock off the conversation."

Sabatello pushed his skinny body flush against the brick building, took a deep breath and waited.

The rustling of papers and sound of old cans being strewn across the gravel grew louder. Then it appeared.

A giant rat!

"No shit!" Sabatello exclaimed. "I hate rats!"

"It's a rat, Nick, and it's as big as a dog!"

"Don't let it bite you, Tony," McLean said softly into the radio through a large smile. "Those damn things can carry rabies."

Sabatello watched as the moonlight illuminated the foraging beast. With both legs drawn up tightly to his chest and arms wrapped around both knees, he sat atop the barrel and watched as the rat circled the barrel, snaked its nose through the discarded sunflower seeds, and then scurried across the street. Sabatello followed it with his eyes. It was then that he saw a lone figure turning the corner of 28th Street and Crenshaw.

McLean sat in the dark solitude of the small closet. His mind began to wander. Suddenly, he was drawn back to the moment by Sabatello's voice.

"Nick, you've got a suspect walking toward you from 28th Street," Sabatello said as he tried to mask his excitement.

"You sure it isn't a giant rat?"

"It is, but this one's human. And it looks like Ta-Ta."

McLean leaned closer to the mirror.

"Is he alone?" he asked calmly while clammy hands stroked the shotgun.

"Yeah," Sabatello whispered. "He's alone."

"Okay, where is he now?"

"He's near the front door, and...Nick, he just pulled a shotgun out from under his jacket. He's coming in, watch your ass!" Sabatello's last words were not heard by McLean, for they were overshadowed by the buzzing of the front door alarm as the door cracked open.

"3Zebra20 to all University Zebra units, we have a two-eleven in progress at O'Jay's Liquors, Adams and Crenshaw. Officers need help," Bock broadcasted over Tactical Frequency two.

As soon as his broadcast was finished, he flipped the small red radio selector switch over to the normal frequency and repeated the information.

3Adam58 was leaving a report call when their radio crackled. In seconds, their red lights cut through the night while their siren echoed through the darkened streets.

"Hey, Bobby," screamed Hestily trying to be heard above the shrillness of the siren, "I'll bet it's McLean!"

Hutton didn't answer, but kept his foot pushed to the floorboard and proceeded to run the next three red lights.

ॐ

McLean slowly lifted himself off the stool and noiselessly pushed it aside with his left foot. Then he reached down and switched off the walkie-talkie. Forgotten were the heat of the closet and the staleness of the air. Robotically, he readied for confrontation.

As he placed the Ithaca across his chest, through the front door walked Lastice. McLean felt his heartbeat increase, his breathing become rapid.

Lastice sauntered up to the counter and leveled the shotgun at the clerk.

"Is you alone, nigga?" he asked.

McLean watched as the clerk began to tremble.

"Just say yes," McLean whispered.

"I'm, I'm ...alone," the man whimpered.

"Good. Give me all the money."

McLean watched as Lastice stepped around the counter and stood directly in front of the two-way mirror with the shotgun aimed under the chin of the clerk.

The clerk opened the cash register and after snatching up all the bills, he stuffed them in a soiled paper bag and handed them to Lastice.

"Get on your knees, nigga," Lastice snarled.

Slowly, the frightened man's knees buckled and he knelt down, his eyes pleading for mercy as they darted to the mirrored door.

"Don't blow it now, pal," McLean whispered. "I won't let you die."

"Don't be lookin' around," Lastice shouted. "Look at the floor."

The clerk lowered his head. "Please don't kill me, Brother," the man pleaded. "Take whatever you want, but just don't kill me."

With the shotgun now aimed at the top of the man's head, Lastice turned and looked directly into the mirror.

Then he grinned.

Less than twelve inches separated the killer and the cop.

Expressionless, McLean stood and stared through the mirror. Time seemed to slow down. McLean's mouth opened and he slowly ran his tongue across his parched lips.

Gently, his right thumb pushed the safety to its 'off' position while his left hand cupped the ribbed wooden slide that sat directly under the sleek blue-steel barrel. Unconsciously, the fingers of his right hand reached under his shirt and began to massage the medallion that hung around his neck.

Lastice continued to smile, then he cocked his head and preened himself like a thousand dollar a night call girl. With his left hand, he cocked the brim of his hat so it fit lower on his forehead giving him the look of a Chicago gangster.

He then looked directly into the mirror.

McLean, who hadn't taken his eyes off the shotgun-totting killer, stared back with eyes that were honed as sharp as a Mayan sacrificial dagger radiating the coldness of death.

Suddenly, Lastice looked away and refocused his attention on the quaking clerk. Looking down at the trembling man's head, he pushed the shotgun solidly against the top of his skull.

McLean slowly slid his right foot back, bent his left knee forward and raised the Ithaca to his shoulder, placing the barrel against the mirror and aiming it directly at the left side of Ta-Ta's head. Pushing snuggly against the wood stock, he took a quick, deep breath, exhaled slowly and squinted his eyes to protect them from the glass fragments. Slowly, the soft flesh of his right index finger flushed firmly against the trigger.

"Die you black mother...f..," the words disappeared in an explosion that jerked McLean's right shoulder back and sent small glass fragments splattering past his face. Standing in the small closet, he realized that it was filled with an excessive amount of gray smoke, and then an eerie silence fell on the store.

✥

After Lastice entered the store, Sabatello jumped from the top of the trash can and inched his way through the darkness, stopping at the corner of a building that faced the street. The moment he heard the explosion, he bolted for the liquor store. Reaching the front door, he knelt down and peered through the glass.

He could see that the back of the store was filled with smoke and the glass of the two-way mirror was shattered. There was no one in sight. Cautiously, and with gun in hand, he pushed the front door open and belly crawled across the dirty white linoleum floor.

From behind the counter, he heard muffled sobs. As the smoke cleared, his eyes were met by a pooling of blood on the floor and a twisted foot sticking out from behind the counter.

"Nick!" Sabatello screamed, "Don't shoot, it's me, Tony!"

McLean watched through the shattered mirror as his partner crawled toward the closet.

"Hey, Tony, I can't get out of here," McLean shouted. "And I can't see Lastice. Is he dead?" he asked as he struggled to push open the mirrored door that appeared to be blocked by something on the floor.

Cautiously, Sabatello pulled himself along the floor never taking his gaze off the twisted foot. Reaching the foot, he peered around the corner of the counter. Sprawled across the sobbing clerk was the headless body of Ta-Ta Lastice.

A quick examination of the torso indicated that after absorbing the shotgun blast, Lastice was twisted so violently that it snapped his right leg at the thigh and wrapped the contorted limb back around his neck.

"Hey, Sabatello, are you still there?"

"Yeah."

"Well, is he dead?"

"He's dead, Nick," Sabatello said as he stepped toward the closet door.

"Shit, is he dead!"

Sitting in the darkness, Washington heard the muffled shotgun blast and waited anxiously for Lastice to come running around the corner. When nothing happened, he stuck his head out the open window and listened. Closing quickly on his location, he heard the high-pitched wail of a siren.

Suddenly, the Chevy without headlights idled toward the intersection of 28th and Crenshaw. As he approached the intersection, the siren drew closer.

"You is on your own, my man," Washington muttered as he slammed down the accelerator and fishtailed around the corner just ahead of 3Adam58.

"Shit, Bobby, that looks like Washington!" Hestily screamed as he threw his arms forward and sunk his fingers deep into the dash when Hutton slammed on the brakes.

"He's ours," Hutton yelled as he accelerated and pulled behind the Chevrolet.

Standing in the liquor store, McLean and Sabatello ran to the front door when they heard the wail of a siren followed closely by the acceleration of two cars.

"It's Washington!" McLean screamed as he bolted out the door and across the street in the direction of their car.

"What about Lastice?" Sabatello yelled as both men threw open the car doors.

"He's not going anywhere," McLean shouted as he slid into the driver's seat.

In less than a minute, McLean and Sabatello had pulled behind 3Adam58 as it pursued the stolen Chevy eastbound on Adams Boulevard.

"3Adam58, we're in pursuit." Hestily cried into the keyed mike.

"3Adam58, we're eastbound on Adams," Hestily shouted, "approaching Arlington."

"All units, 3Adam58 is in pursuit eastbound on Adams approaching Arlington."

"3Adam58, what is the suspect wanted for?"

"3Adam58, 187 of a police officer."

"3Zebra9 to Control, show us in pursuit in an unmarked vehicle," Sabatello shouted into the mike.

"All units all frequencies use caution, we have unmarked police vehicles in the pursuit," the Hotshot broadcast.

"3Adam58, suspect is traveling in excess of one-hundred miles an hour, and we are now passing Western approaching Normandie."

As Hestily finished the broadcast, his right leg began to rapidly thump the car door.

As 3Adam58 pulled closer, it was met by two flashes from the driver's window of the Chevy.

"3Adam58, the son-of-a-bitch is shooting at us," Hestily bellowed, anger in his voice.

"This shit is getting old," he yelled to Hutton.

McLean pulled closer to the rear of 3Adam58. His hands gripped the steering wheel while his right foot remained firmly planted on the gas pedal. As they passed Western Avenue, he made no attempt to brake, but pushed the accelerator pedal harder, trying to get more from an engine that was giving its all.

When McLean shot a quick glance in the rearview mirror, he saw that Bock and two other unmarked police cars who were in the pursuit had fallen behind.

"Don't get us killed," Sabatello yelled as he held the mike in his left hand and dug his right hand deep into the dash.

McLean, with a discernable look of hatred on his face, remained focused on the Chevy.

As he approached Figueroa, Washington tapped the brakes. Swerving wide into the westbound lanes, he snapped the steering wheel. Before he began his slide around the corner, he shoved the Colt across his chest and out the window. As Hutton pulled closer, two more gunshots rocked the night.

"3Adam58, suspect has fired two more rounds at this unit," Hestily broadcast as his right leg continued to thump the side panel.

"3Adam58, we're now headed southbound on Figueroa approaching Exposition."

Suddenly, black smoke began to pour from under the hood of the Chevy. Washington, seeing the dash explode in an array of bright red lights, locked-up the brakes that pulled the car to the right and sent it careening over the railroad tracks at Exposition.

Hutton slammed both feet down onto the brake pedal and gripped the steering wheel tightly in an effort to control the Plymouth as it swerved and flew over the railroad tracks behind the Chevy.

McLean, seeing the two cars lock-up and slide to a stop at the far curb on the south side of Exposition, slammed on the brakes, and after flying over the railroad tracks, came to rest just to the right of the Chevy. As 3Zebra9 slid to a stop, Washington jumped out the driver's door. Suddenly there was a quick stab of flame and something burned past McLean's head.

"That's five," McLean yelled to Sabatello.

As Washington spun, McLean ducked behind the car door and reached in for the shotgun, but Sabatello already had it in his hands.

Hutton, seeing Washington run toward two small Duplexes, took up foot pursuit. Looking to his left, he saw McLean running next to him, stride for stride.

Sabatello, with mike in hand, broadcast their location.

Hestily finished his broadcast and with Sabatello ran toward the small housing units.

Washington, winded, stumbled into a small porched area between the two buildings. Suddenly, he realized there was no escape. Spinning, he faced Hutton and McLean. As he raised the Colt, Hutton fired a single round from the shotgun that caught Washington in the upper left shoulder, smashing the bone and slamming his enormous body flat against the rear wall.

Undaunted, and from a semi-crouched position, Washington struggled to raise the Colt.

"You," he said.

"Me," McLean responded.

Hutton let the barrel of the Ithaca fall forward. He then stepped back and watched.

As Washington began to slide slowly down the wall, his eyes remained locked on McLean. Slowly, the barrel of the Colt began to inch its way toward the ground.

"It's over, Mac," Hutton said.

But it wasn't playing out the way McLean had envisioned. He wanted Washington dead.

Hutton stood, watching and listening while sirens pierced the night like fingernails scrapping a chalkboard.

McLean watched as Washington's body slid slowly into a seated position.

McLean held his gun at his waist, pointed at the killers head. As his index finger pressed the trigger, suddenly, he stopped. He wanted to shoot, but knew that it would be an execution.

"Don't do it, Mac," Hutton warned.

McLean hesitated.

Suddenly, Washington's gun jerked upward and flame flashed from the barrel.

As McLean snapped the trigger, he felt Washington's bullet fly by his head.

The explosion's echoed through the buildings. McLean's shot hit Washington in the middle of the forehead. On impact, the Colt pitched out of Washington's hand and slid across the concrete.

As Washington's body slumped to the side, a single small trail of blood began to run down the middle of his forehead and between his still open eyes.

McLean stood silent, and then holstered his weapon.

Hutton looked on, a grin crossing his lips.

"We're even," McLean said as he slowly stepped forward and began to search the dead man's pockets. Pulling the jacket open, he reached into an inside pocket and removed a small scribbled note.

"I'd leave that for the Coroner, Mac," Hutton said.

McLean didn't say a word, but unfolded the paper.

It read: 5628 Bellingham Avenue, North Hollywood. It was McLean's home address.

His hands began to tremble.

He reached into Washington's other coat pocket and after finding what he was looking for he turned, only to be met by Bock, Sabatello and Hestily.

"It's over, Nick," Bock said as he stepped forward and picked up the Colt.

"Yea, Sarge, it's over," McLean said softly as he turned, and with Sabatello at his side, walked back to the idling Plymouth.

As Bock turned, he was met by Sal Weinstein.

"Heard the action over my scanner," Weinstein said as he followed Bock back to his car.

"Any chance for a quick interview?" he asked as he watched Teich pull up.

Bock ignored him. Opening the car door, he slid in behind the steering wheel, rolled up his window and slid down in the seat. Lifting the mike from its holder, he began to make the necessary notifications. When finished, he slid deeper into the seat, closed his eyes and quietly awaited the arrival of Charlie Reese and 3William4.

THIRTY-NINE

White sat in his large executive chair that was turned toward the picture window and watched as the noon-day sun attempted to break through the heavy cloud cover. Four hours earlier he had received a telephone call from Deputy Chief Cleary advising him of the night's events.

Walking to the large picture window, he clasped his hands behind his back and stared thoughtfully into the distance where a thin veil of rain diminished and then disappeared. Fascinated by the beauty, he watched as a shaft of sunlight broke through a hole in the clouds revealing thin patches of snow on the San Gabriel's.

After the call from Cleary, White had called Sam Gibson and requested a meeting. He turned when the door opened.

"Glad you could come," White said as he blew a cloud of smoke and waved it along with his long, slender hand while beckoning Gibson to have a seat.

"Must be good news," Gibson said as he sat down in the comfortable leather chair and crossed his legs.

"Why's that?"

"Cause you're smiling like a damn Cheshire cat."

"It appears that we can put both the Andrews and Patterson matters to bed," White said, a look of relief crossing his face.

"Be more specific."

Sitting with his pipe hanging gently from his lips, his mind reeled off the facts as he meticulously placed each in its proper place.

"That's all well and good, but there are still two more pieces of the puzzle that haven't been placed on the board," Gibson said as he uncrossed his legs, leaned forward and studied the tops of his highly polished shoes.

"And what would those be?" White asked quizzically.

"It's about the leak in the Department. Has it been identified?"

"It has. After the interview of Washington's common-law wife, Reese called in Internal Affairs. When they walked into the record bureau, the clerk panicked and bolted. They grabbed her, sat her down, and before they could say a word, she broke down and copped out to her involvement."

"A little fear does wonders," commented Gibson dryly.

"Appears so."

"What about the couple on South Crenshaw?"

"The Firearms Unit ran and linked the spent shotgun shell from the Adams and Hoover shooting and the spent round found at the Crenshaw murders to the shotgun recovered from Lastice. It was a positive match."

White sat down behind his desk and opened the right bottom drawer.

Pulling out a bottle of Dunphys Irish Whiskey and a couple of glasses, he poured two drinks and raised his glass in a toast.

"Here's to the City of the Angels."

Both men smiled, swirled the rich brown liquid around in its glass, and then took a sip.

As both men savored the smooth whiskey, Gibson glanced to the scripted truism framed on White's wall.

"Without courage, all other virtues lose their meaning."
Sir Winston Churchill

FORTY

McLean sat in Reese's office, the effects of the adrenaline wearing off. Reese sat behind his desk with Del Rio, Steele, Van Drew and Bock seated on his left.

McLean's answers to their questions came in short, staccato bursts. Vividly, he recalled every detail of the shooting inside the liquor store, then, without a trace of feeling, his mind reeled off the facts, and he diagramed the pursuit and the shooting of Washington.

He squirmed in the hard chair, and as he did, the demon of doubt momentarily seized him. But now was not the time to doubt. If he wavered now, he might loose his career, and he wasn't about to let that happen.

Yet, even knowing that what he did was justified, he felt empty. He felt no elation, only a deep heaviness. Should there be more? Had he really done all he could?

After eight long hours, he wearily shuffled into the coffee room. Was it really four-fifteen P.M.? The debriefing had been grueling, more like a criminal interrogation than a garnering of facts. But that was to be expected since he knew that he was being primed for the Coroner's Inquest.

He stood alone in the crowded room. He had lost the vigor in his looks and the fire in his eyes. He needed some sleep.

Grabbing a cup of coffee, he swished the brew around in the cup and stared blankly at the swirling liquid. Stepping to the rear, he set the cup down, sank into a chair, put his elbows on his knees and pressed the heels of his palms into his eyes.

He was as exhausted as he could ever remember being, the kind of exhaustion that saps one physically and emotionally, the kind that drains even the soul leaving one spent and depleted.

Without finishing the coffee, he walked into the rear parking lot and slid into his Volkswagen. In minutes he caught the Harbor Freeway northbound and was headed for home. As he drove, he asked himself how Patterson would have handled the situation with Washington and Lastice. About the same he finally concluded.

Downshifting into third, he thought of his upcoming three days off. All he could think about was sleep, the kind of sleep that numbs the mind and escapes the world, that delicious place of nothingness where bad guys aren't real and friends don't really die. Yes, he would sleep for three days and hopefully resurrect back into good form and an acceptable disposition. But first he had one final stop.

෴

McLean pulled off the Ventura Freeway and snaked his way around Barnum Boulevard and through the front of the cemetery. His eyes automatically squinted as he looked into the thin, knife like rays of the setting sun that had pierced the cloud cover. Downshifting, he idled slowly through the sculptured black wrought iron gates and onto the drive that circled the fountain containing the seven large bronze herons. The fountain had a calming effect on the living who passed through the gates desiring to find solace within the walls. He drove slowly up the hill and parked. His eyes scanned the area; he was alone. Slowly, he made his way up the hill to Patterson's grave.

The incline was wet. Earlier that morning winter storm clouds had rolled across the sky, dropping some heavy moisture on the foothills. As he stepped onto the moist grass and walked up the long hill, he checked his watch, noting the lateness of the hour. He knew that he had but a short time to give his report before darkness closed in on the cemetery and the final curtain would fall on this act of his life.

Trudging up the hill and nursing a stream of thoughts, he arrived at the plot where he stood momentarily before using his shoe to brush the moisture from a small patch of grass. It was still wet, but he sat anyway and stared mutely at the beautiful granite headstone. It was lovely as far as headstones go; on the top was carved a lamb and a lion both sitting facing each other. That had been the idea of Patterson's mother and as McLean stared at the unlikely pair, he wondered which truly depicted his partner. The answer depended on the circumstances; his friend was both, and now he was dead. McLean felt a gripping in his solar plexus, a deep gut wrenching feeling of grief.

His thoughts turned to his purpose for being here, and the night's events, but he struggled to make his voice work, or which words to say. It all seemed so complicated and pointless, yet he knew that it was necessary. He smiled at his oxymoron, pointless but necessary.

McLean absent mindedly pulled at the blades of grass that needed mowing. Reaching out, he tore off the taller stems that were closest to the headstone which the cemetery's lawn mower couldn't reach and the cheap labor wouldn't think to crawl down from their riding perch to hand cut. He placed a piece of grass between his lips, and then reached out to trace the letters that were deeply etched in the granite marker.

Christian Karlton Patterson
January 6, 1940- January 16, 1968
Loving Son
And
Valiant Soldier

With his index finger pressed softly into the groves, his mind wandered. The remembrance of the Adams and Hoover shooting still gnawed at him. He wondered if Patterson would still be alive if he had been able to kill Washington. Unfortunately, he would never know.

The sound of rolling thunder brought him out of his memories, memories laced with Patterson's presence. Pulling his knees up to his chest, he wrapped his arms around his legs and spoke aloud. "Well, I made good on the promise."

The sky grew dark and menacing, but the clouds seemed to hesitate on the tips of the surrounding hills. It appeared that they too were waiting. He felt a chill, but it wasn't from the weather and he wondered if he should leave. But he wasn't ready to go back yet, he hadn't finished.

The dampness of the grass began to make itself known.

"I need to hurry," he said softly as he stared at the inscription on the headstone and rocked back and forth. "Darlene will be worried."

He stopped rocking, leaned from side-to-side and wiped the moisture from his butt. He stared blankly, lonely within himself.

Suddenly he had that old sensation of a presence and it startled him. He thought he heard someone laugh. It was so real that he stopped and looked around.

The clouds began to make good their threat and it began to sprinkle.

He glanced at his watch.

"I have something to show you," he said as he reached into his pocket.

He flashed Patterson's badge at the headstone, then stood and walked back to the old Volkswagen. Suddenly, he knew that his accountability to Patterson was over and he felt lost and lonely, a treasured relationship eternally severed.

As he left the cemetery, the drizzle suddenly stopped and allowed the sun to again knife through the clouds. The weather warmed, inviting him to drive with both windows down. As if in a trance, he drove down the Ventura Freeway toward home. Leaving the freeway, he pulled onto Fulton Avenue and proceeded north. Home was now only two miles away.

He had a green light and slowly approached the intersection of Fulton and Oxnard streets. As he entered the intersection, out of the corner of his eye and to his left, he saw a white Cadillac barreling down the hill. In an instant, it registered. The Cadillac was going to run the red.

McLean's hands choked the steering wheel just before the impact. It felt as though the world had exploded as the Cadillac slammed full force into the rear quarter panel.

It all happened so quickly, as these things always seem to do. McLean was puzzled to find himself out of the car and rapidly traveling down a long, dark tunnel with a brilliant white light in the far distance. He seemed cradled in quiet peace, ever moving towards the Light that drew him closer like a magnet draws iron.

He was at peace, a kind of peace he never had known in his life, and there was no pain; there was only a comforting warmth which encircled his body. Instantly, nothing mattered to him except reaching his final destination: the Light.

The tunnel was dark and warm. Suddenly, as the warmth reached its pinnacle, he realized that he was standing next to a prone body. It, too, was traveling down the tunnel. The eyes were closed and it looked familiar. He recognized the form; it was his. Together, he and his body continued toward the Light.

Then he looked down. Stretching out his hands he saw them both, white, soft, somewhat iridescent in color. Glancing back to the prone form, he saw that it appeared to be sleeping, certainly at peace, a look one would not associate with death.

Although he didn't understand the experience, he was unafraid and found that as he stood accompanying his body, he was able to see and comprehend all that was happening around him. There was no front. No back. No right or left. It was like standing in a fish bowl, and he marveled at the view.

The brilliance of the Light increased as he neared the end of the tunnel. What lay beyond? Suddenly, pain accompanied by the wail of a siren shattered the peacefulness he had experienced.

"Cover him up," one voice commanded. "He's gone."

"Wait, wait!" McLean screamed, but the words were choked in his throat. He wasn't heard. "I'm not dead. Please ...Don't do anything we'll all regret!"

"How in the hell did he get from the point of impact to the middle of the sidewalk?" one attendant asked. "It's at least one-hundred and thirty feet."

"He flew out the passenger window before the car flipped and he just sailed down the street," commented a witness.

Slowly, McLean's shrouded body was slipped into the rear of the ambulance.

Suddenly his eyes snapped open. All was white. Struggling, he sat up on his elbows, causing the sheet to drop to the floor.

"Shit, he's still alive," cried the stunned attendant, who was riding in the rear.

"I'm still here," McLean whispered, his words barely audible. "I'm a police officer. Get me to a hospital."

"Jimmy, hit it, this guy is still alive," the attendant yelled to his partner, "and he's a cop!"

McLean took a deep breath and exhaled slowly. As his breath whispered through pursed lips, a wave of dizziness swept over him, and then a sickening nausea gripped his gut. His vision blurred and he tried to focus, to force himself to stay awake. But he couldn't.

"Hold on, partner," the attendant said as he balanced himself precariously in the rear of the lurching ambulance. "Just hold on!"

McLean knew he would hold on, he had no choice. Darlene and the girls were waiting.